A Miracle or Two for Christmas

Trish Titus

Also written by Trish Titus

DELILAH and Others Like Her

Stories written by pet owners whose pets have passed away. Stories shared by those who have had pets pass away. We share memories of unconditional love, photos, and lessons learned.

A Miracle or Two for Christmas

Write to the author at TrishTitus.dyd@gmail.com

Cover Design: Rhine River Waterfront, Basel, Switzerland

Editing: Truly Trendy PR

Proofreading: Pamela Garcia

Graphic Designer: Rebecca Shaw, BrockleyDesigns.com

Title Collaboration: Trish Titus and Amy Jenson

Library of Congress Control Number: 2019919130

ISBN (978-1-7323352-4-0) (Paperback)

ISBN (978-1-7323352-5-7) (Ebook-EPUB)

ISBN (978-1-7323352-6-4) (Ebook–Mobi)

Also written by Trish Titus

DELILAH and Others Like Her, published March 2019

Stories written by pet owners whose pets have passed away. They meant the world to us. We share memories of unconditional love, photos, and lessons learned. If you have a story to share, she would love to hear from you. Write her at tmtpetstories18@gmail.com.

Chapter 1

Talia woke up and looked out the small oval window she sat next to, seeing a beautiful horizon slowly appearing. The earth's round shape was brimming with the soft glow of the sun in shades of orange and deep blue. Seeing the earth below was an incredible sight, as it was her first time getting to witness a brand-new day from so high up. Little by little, as the plane continued heading eastward, the sun was rising and getting brighter. The sky was so blue off in the distance, and she watched in awe at how spectacular it all was. Her mind wandered as she continued looking out the window, and suddenly, she thought of him. Talia didn't know why or where it even came from. How corny and crazy was that? The first time they met was well over twenty years ago, but oh, he was cute. She'd gotten up once to use the bathroom. Talia hated bathrooms on planes. They were small and sometimes smelled. The stainless-steel sink, toilet and wall felt sterilized, but with the number of passengers that use them, she knew that wasn't the case. She returned to her seat, putting her seatbelt on, and then continued looking out the window.

Soon, she felt the plane move downward as the captain announced that they were starting their descent. They'd be landing in about twenty minutes. She watched as everything became larger; the fields and roads with cars on them, no longer little specks below. Other passengers were peering out their windows or adjusting themselves in their seats; it had been a long flight. They heard and felt the doors for the wheels open up beneath the aircraft, and then the wheels coming down, locking into place. Buildings were quickly whizzing by, and the ground came up fast. Talia felt the nose of the plane lift, and then the wheels contacting the tarmac, followed by the nose gear touching down.

After coming to a complete stop, the passengers saw that the plane was nowhere near the terminal. This meant that they'd get to walk down the aircraft passenger stairs instead of walking through the air bridge, or walkway that connected the plane to the passenger terminal. At least they wouldn't have to carry their luggage, as there were those cute little carts that drove the luggage to the terminal. Everyone was getting up out of their seats, collecting their things from the overhead bins before heading toward the front exit door the flight attendant had opened. It was time to follow the other passengers after waiting her turn.

As she started walking down the stairs, she just felt excited to be here again, smiling and saying out loud, "Happy Birthday, Talia Rose." A couple of passengers behind her asked, "Is it your birthday today?"

She half turned, looking up at them. She smiled and said, "Yes, it is."

"Well, happy birthday," they said, along with a few others who heard and chimed in. She thanked them.

Stepping off the staircase, Talia was once again touching Switzerland soil. She followed the other passengers as they walked across the tarmac. She saw the name of the airport, just as she remembered so long ago: *EuroAirport-Basel-Mulhouse-Freiburg.* Getting through customs control took a little longer, but she headed out to get a taxi once through. There were shuttles also taking passengers to their hotels instead of a taxi, which was expensive, so saving money was a plus.

It was 9:30 a.m. Sunday morning. She kept smiling to herself as she thought, *This will be a great day.* She was so excited to be back. It had been a long time, and here she was, on her own. No family was here deciding what they would do or where they would go, much less where they would eat. She got to decide, and she had a plan for the most part, which included some business. Being a fashion designer allowed her to do some traveling, although not usually outside the United States.

Her three hotel reservations were in Basel, Bern, and Villars. Talia had some ideas of what she wanted to do while in Switzerland. She could take her time and not feel rushed by family trying to cram so much in. She turned her cell phone back on and saw that she had ten text messages, more than likely from family and friends, wishing her a happy birthday. She would wait until she got to the hotel to reply to her text messages so she wouldn't miss seeing the sights on the way. Talia's first reservation at the *Basel Hotel Spalentor* was for three nights. The 40-room hotel was a five-story, grey-and-crème building. It used to be a student residence that sat across from the castle-like *Spalentor* gate.

Arriving at her hotel and checking in, she took the elevator to the fourth floor, her room being at the south end. The hallway window was large, and Talia could see a long way off. Her room was nicely-sized, with a large bed, wood floors, a nice-sized bathroom, and a robe and slippers the hotel provided for the guests to use. The view looking out her window looked down on the street named *Schönbeinstrasse*, the same view the hallway window had. Looking at the castle entrance across the street, she saw people walking through it and wondered where it led them. That would be the first thing to explore today. Several things would occupy her time in the next few days before her journey took her to Bern and then down to Villars.

As she stood looking out the window, her thoughts took her back to when she was young, around nine or so. She remembered that her family (mom, dad, and Brother Kurt) had met another family here in Basel. They didn't fly over together, but came across one another at the Basel Zoo, which was always one of Talia's favorite things to see. She wanted to go to as many zoos as she could. It turned out that both mothers were nurses, in two different hospitals, in the same town. She remembered them talking and realizing they had met one another at some medical conference. So, between them, they decided they'd all have this experience and adventure.

The families did the normal tourist things. Talia remembered her mom speaking French several times when they went to different places, and she would translate if English wasn't spoken. She still had a few older living relatives that lived across the border in France at that time. The other family consisted of a mom, dad and a son. Talia smiled because she thought he was cute, even at her age. He was older than her but looked about Kurt's age, being three years older. She remembered that he kept looking at her, making her stomach flutter. He and Kurt seemed to hit it off. The whole time here had seemed magical. It was a different world than what they were used to.

She was just glad to be here now and able to explore, but a part of her wished she had someone she could share it all with. Before heading out, Talia checked with the front desk and they gave her a *BaselCard*, provided to all guests, allowing free travel on the trams and buses, and other perks. She would take advantage of those. She also picked up a few other pamphlets encouraging sightseeing.

It was close to lunchtime, and she was getting hungry. Talia ventured out and headed toward the castle entrance to see what was on the other side; hopefully some food. They called it *The Spalentor (Gate of Spalen)*. It was one of three medieval city gates and dated back to the early 15th century. The history of it already fascinated her. Once she passed through the huge gate, it led her to an old historic district. There were bookstores, bakeries, curio shops, and scenic shops. Local restaurants were calling everyone to come and enjoy some good cuisine while sitting and relaxing outside. She knew her dad would have loved this, since he had been an architect. There was so much detail and beauty, Talia started to appreciate what he was always talking about. She also knew she'd be taking lots of photos to share and send back home. She didn't want to make anyone "too jealous," but she was already enjoying this.

Talia found a few little souvenirs as she wandered through the old cobblestone streets, and a small café called her name. She took several photos of the shops with the intricately-designed windows and architecture. Inside, she could see people browsing for their souvenirs. She thought, *It's easy to lose track of time here.* She'd only spent a short time wandering, but saw that it was more like four or five hours.

Her feet were hurting. Talia was getting tired because of so much walking and jet lag, so she walked back to her hotel. One of the desk clerks asked about her day; she told them it was so nice and that she was soaking in all kinds of wonderful things. They asked if there was anything they could help her with tomorrow; she said she had some business to attend to, but otherwise, she was looking forward to the Botanical Garden, the Walking Tour and maybe a Rhine River Day Cruise. She was open to whatever would come her way or any suggestions they had; after all, it was her birthday. And with that, she said goodnight.

Before turning in, she took a shower and then read through her text messages. Like she thought, most were wishing her a very happy birthday and to enjoy her vacation. Several tried not to sound jealous and wished they could have come with her. The text messages were from her mom and brother, friends, and two of her staff. The last number she didn't recognize, but it also wished her a happy birthday.

Chapter 2

It's early morning, but she slept well. She took a deep breath and contemplated lying in bed, savoring the moments, or get up and get started with the day. She did both. After all, it was her vacation. After getting dressed and making sure she had good walking shoes on, she went down for breakfast. She could smell the rolls and assorted pastries; fresh fruit, cereal, hard-boiled eggs, and toast, along with beverages to suit everyone. And the coffee smelled so good, it was calling her name.

Walking toward the hotel door, she was greeted by the desk clerk, Laurel, who asked if she was ready for some adventures in her thick French accent. Talia said yes, with a smile, and if she could point her in the right direction to catch a tram. Talia told her she was a fashion designer, and was going to several fabric stores she had ordered from in the past and now planned to visit. Laurel thought, how exciting that would be. Talia told her which stores she wanted to go to, and Laurel gave her a few pamphlets showing her some tram schedules and other places of interest. Getting on the tram, she also thought, *By the end of this day, a walk through the Botanischer Garten would be a nice way to relax.*

The tram used electrical power fed by a pantograph sliding on an overhead line. Talia remembered seeing this same type of tram in Seattle on a visit there. She also remembered how they squealed going around curves in the road. There was so much to look at; homes and businesses, little cars and scooters, lots of people walking. The tram stopped, and she saw the first fabric store. They sold designer and Italian fabrics. Walking through the door, she stood for a moment, looking from left to right, and figured just start on one side. It was different being in the actual store rather than shopping online. Here, she'd get to touch and feel all the fabrics, letting whatever creative design come to her.

In the States, the process was the same, but you took your cart with you, placing items in it, and then took them to the purchase counter to pay for it. A clerk came to her and asked if she was finding what she was looking for. Talia said she thought so, telling the clerk she ordered from them online, and her items were usually shipped. The clerk asked her name, which Talia told her, also mentioning that she was a designer from the States. The clerk was eager to help. After heading up and down the aisles, she found what she was looking for. The clerk tagged everything that would be purchased, preparing it for shipping. It was nice that she wouldn't have to carry them back to the hotel, thinking how silly she would look lugging those bolts in her arms; and besides, they were heavy. So, now she could move onto the next shops.

She walked to the next two stores, as they were not that far apart. *The Sempiano* was more of a high-end fabric store. She had purchased from them once and had items shipped; this would be another treat. She walked into the store, and the clerks asked if they could help her. She told them her name and that she was a designer from the States and had ordered from them online. They were happy to meet her, shaking her hand. There was a lot to look over and choose from. She could see various fabrics of tweed, silks, beautiful brocade, and some fine linen and cotton. She could get lost in many of these stores and spend hours just looking, feeling, and imagining what she would do with them, the way she had at home. There was so much more here than what they showed on their website. She felt special as a clerk was trying to help in any way she could. They probably have top designers come into their store, finding fabrics that suit today's fashion and seeing their fabric on models walking down the runway and in department stores. Talia smiled to herself.

After making her purchases, they were happy to ship them. Now it was off to the last store, which was *R. Carrington*. Entering the store, Talia could see more brilliant colors. There were all kinds of embroidered trims and colored ribbons and lots of beautiful antique trims. She must have been in there a good hour. She knew it was close to lunchtime, and they would close for lunch as soon as she left. She purchased the trims she wanted, and again, they would ship those for her. She thought, *Why carry those around if I don't have to!*

Before leaving this morning, Talia had checked with Laurel to ask what out-of-the-way cafés or restaurants she would recommend. She said there was a small café close to the Rhine by the name of *Café Vonkutch.* She had gone there many times with friends, and said it was great. The Rhine River was on the other side of the building. People enjoyed walking along the river, and there were benches to sit on, relax, and soak up the sun and the view.

Talia decided that's where she wanted to go, so she got out her map and started walking after making her purchases. If she was in a big hurry, it might take fifteen minutes or so to walk, but there was no hurry. She wanted to walk at a more leisurely pace and enjoy all that was around her. There were some newer buildings among the much older ones, but that didn't detract from the original styles and structure.

She all but passed one café, with a name she couldn't pronounce, and stopped in to see what they had. It had been a bank, but was turned into a café serving coffees and pastries. The pastries looked very inviting and fancy, but it was mostly coffee she wanted until she could get to the café. Once she had her pick-me-up, she continued. All the structures and architectures of the buildings were wonderful; there was so much history here, except for one building. Well, it has a history, just not in Europe. She laughed when she saw across the street an American icon: a McDonald's. Not what she was expecting, but then there are American fast-food restaurants everywhere. It just struck her as funny. It was the first American thing she had seen since being here, which hadn't been all that long.

She continued down the street called *Marktgasse,* looking at everything along the way to a street called *Blumenrain.* There was so much to take in. She could see the river and thought to herself that she'd take a walk by the river after lunch before heading back to the hotel. It was amazing to be here; the sights, sounds, colors, and smells came from so many different places. She found the café and headed inside. It was small, but most quaint.

She ordered lunch, which was great, just like Laurel said. She sat back and enjoyed watching people walk by. It was middle to late afternoon. After getting her second wind, she got up, headed back down the street, and went around the corner to look at the river. She thought it would be nice to take a short Rhine River Cruise and see sights from that view. While walking near the river, she stopped to watch a ferry and a few other boats. She saw steps leading down to the water with a skinny sidewalk, and then more steps leading directly into the Rhine. She hadn't seen people swim in the water, but heard they often did when temperatures were much warmer.

Seeing a beautiful long-haired kitty walk toward her, noticing the unusual color, she said, "Oh, look at you. You're so pretty. So, you're just wandering around too? I hope you don't live too far away or that you're lost." As Talia talked to the cat, she bent over and picked up the calico that had walked right up to her. It started purring, and she just held it and petted it, with its fur gliding through her fingers as she watched the people. After holding the kitty for a while, petting it and rubbing under its chin, it wanted down. "OK, I'll put you down. I'd love to take you home with me, but I'm sure your people would miss you."

There were benches along the waterfront where people were sitting, enjoying the scenery, sun, and chatting. As she turned to head back to the hotel, she took one last look at the river and all the people. On one of the benches, not too far from her, she saw two men and a woman. They were talking and laughing and seemed happy. One of the men had his arm around the woman's shoulder, so a good guess would be that they were together. There was space between them and the lone man who sat facing her direction. The longer she looked their way and trying not to look too conspicuous, there seemed to be something vaguely familiar about the man, or so she thought. She could see his right arm and shoulder on the back of the bench and most of his face. He had dark hair, but also wore sunglasses, but it was just a feeling.

She slowly started walking in the direction of her hotel, but continued looking with a side glance. The man now leaned back a little and looked in her direction, bringing his sunglasses down halfway from his eyes. She thought he looked right at her for a moment, and then felt like she got caught doing something wrong. She saw the three of them stand up, the man now blocked by the woman. The men gave a hug and shook hands, and then the lone man gave the woman a quick hug and a peck on each cheek. She didn't want them to turn around and see her staring at them, so she left.

She couldn't help but feel like she knew him from somewhere, but where, and how? It was weird, and a light flutter appeared in her stomach. The hotel was now across the street. Getting ready to cross, she stopped and slowly turned around to look back, to see if anyone had followed her, but there wasn't anyone there.

As she approached the hotel door, little flashes of memory appeared, and it finally dawned on her, *It can't be. Surely not here, clear across the ocean. It's been fourteen years. The last vacation was in Colorado Springs, when I got those same flutters.* There were many trips she remembered, before graduating high school, to Michigan, Wyoming, the Dakotas, and several other States. After graduating high school, Colorado Springs would be the last with the Porter family for many years.

She knew it was silly to think he could be in this same place now, even if by pure chance. If they did come across one another, she wasn't sure what she would say without sounding like a silly schoolgirl. She hated to admit it, but she had a huge crush on him; she liked him. He was probably married with a family. Maybe someday she'd find that special someone. It just hadn't happened yet.

It was a good shopping day. New ideas were already popping into her head for her new line. She opened her room door, and as she stepped further in, the fragrant scent of lilacs hit her. She closed her eyes and took a slow deep breath in. She loved the smell of lilacs. She turned toward the credenza to see the small vase with lilacs in it. It was a deep amethyst with thin white swirls throughout. There was a tiny white envelope sticking out. Then she thought, looking at the vase, *Why is this vase in my room? Who placed it here?* She figured it was probably a mistake, so she called down to the front desk. Sophia, another desk clerk, answered. Talia asked her whether the vase with the lilacs was placed in her room by mistake or a courtesy they provided. Sophia said she didn't know anything about them, but would check and get back to her. Sophia soon called her back and said, all she knew was that they were to be delivered and placed in her room, if possible.

Talia thought it was weird, *Why not wait until I got back to the hotel and then hand them to me, instead of putting them in my room? Well, I can't change it, so might as well see who they are from.* She opened the tiny envelope, and all it said was: "Happy Birthday." She then said out loud, "Oh, I'll bet it was Mom. She knows how I love lilacs."

Chapter 3

After a long day of shopping and walking, she took a shower, then got dressed in the long, flowy skirt and peasant top she designed, and put on her sandals. She texted her mom and thanked her for the beautiful lilacs placed in her room. They smelled wonderful, and then she told her she was heading to the botanical garden at the University of Basel. It was close by. She grabbed her bag and left. Passing the front desk, Sophia asked about the lilacs. Talia said she was sure her mother sent them for her birthday, knowing how she loves lilacs. Sophia had a big smile on her face, telling her how nice she looked and to enjoy her evening at the garden.

It was free to get inside this huge botanical garden. She could see the outside garden was large. She strolled around, checking out all the various flowers and plants, something her dad enjoyed doing. He loved being outdoors. She remembered a few of the camping trips and how much fun they had. Many of the small plaques were in German or French. She didn't know the names of any of them. Birds were flying inside, and you heard their birdsongs. She could hear and see the little waterfalls while walking around, until the path led her to the lily ponds; they were huge. You could lie down on them. She always imagined a bunch of frogs sitting on them, making their croaking sound. She wondered how many frogs she might have to kiss before one turned into her prince. Several people walked behind her and headed down another path.

છ૩

It was nice being here, peaceful, letting her thoughts go wherever they wanted. She closed her eyes, taking a deep breath, and for a few minutes, she could daydream. She could hear her name being called. "Talia." The voice was soft and gentle. She could feel a smile on her face at the sound of her name. It made her think of her dad and how close they were, the smile now fading, the sadness arising and missing him. Again, she heard her name. "Talia." She opened her eyes and turned toward the voice. She looked at him standing next to the rail. He looked back at her with those beautiful eyes, and her heart skipped a beat.

She tilted her head just a little, while still looking at him. She couldn't believe her eyes. He was standing here, in front of her. "Jason?" she said. A slight curl of his lip went up, and a nod of his head. Talia had this huge urge to walk over to him and hug him. She started to take a step and then stopped, *Wow, handsome as ever,* she thought, *How did he know I was here? Why is he here?*

"How are you, Talia," Jason asked. It was more of a statement than a question.

It took her a moment to reply. "I'm good. And yourself?" A confused look on her face.

"I'm okay," he replied.

She started looking around and asked with a raised eyebrow, "Are you by yourself? What are you doing here?"

With a grin, he said, "Well, I thought I would find a beautiful garden like this, and wander around, and what should I see, but a fair and lovely young woman with a flowy skirt and colorful print top, with funny looking sandals on, standing next to a lily pond. She's probably looking for a frog, wondering if she kissed one of them, would it turn into her handsome prince." He looked at her and saw a half smile on her face, her eyes rolling up. "I then decided I would strike up a conversation with her, thinking, here's a native who might be willing to show me around this fair city while I'm here," he said, looking at her.

Talia shook her head, which felt like it was swimming. She remembered his dry, corny sense of humor, and replied, "Really? You just happen to be in the neighborhood and decided to check out this particular garden here, in Basel, Switzerland. So, what, they don't have botanical gardens back in the States, some forty-five hundred miles over the ocean?" She said it with a smirky grin on her face. She took a step toward him, hugging him. He didn't resist, giving a hug right back. "Really, what are you doing here?" she asked.

He gestured with his hand toward the outside gardens. "Would you walk with me?" She turned toward the direction he was pointing and started walking beside him, looking up at him. The flutter continued.

Jason told her why he was here. "I'm here because of a work-related program, or actually, in Germany. So, I was in Germany, but now I'm here. I'm a paramedic/firefighter."

"Wait, you live and work here?" Talia asked, stopping and looking at him, holding her breath.

He smiled and said, "No. That's what I do back in the States. The fire department I work for was provided information a couple of years ago about an international work abroad program, where paramedics can work with other paramedics in different countries. We learn skills from each other and that country's protocol, and the services we provide that help people who need us at the worst moments. We eat, sleep and go out on calls with them." They continued walking.

With raised eyebrows, she said, "Wow. If you're doing this work program in Germany, what are you doing here in Basel? Is Switzerland one of the countries?"

"No. There are six countries—New Zealand, Singapore, Ireland, Australia, Germany, and the United Arab Emirates," he said.

"So, you could have chosen any of these countries to do your work abroad thingy in, and you chose Germany, now," she said with curiosity in her voice. "Why not one of the other countries?"

"Ya, I could have chosen one of the other ones, but spots fill up quickly. You're talking about paramedics across the United States, and there's a waiting list," he said, looking at her, wanting to tell her why he was here in Basel: *I came to find you.* He continued, "So many paramedics who learned about this program wanted the opportunity to be a part of it. It allows us to work for one or two weeks at a time with others in their country. Many paramedics are married and didn't want to spend more than a week being away from their families. I am not married," he looked at her, "so I chose to do the two weeks. We signed up two years ago for Germany, which, at that time, wasn't filled up."

"So, you finished up your two weeks, and now you're just hanging out here in Basel? Are you heading back to the States?" she asked.

"I've split my time. I worked last week until this past Sunday, and I'll do another week in about eight days. With our fire station, there are six of us paramedics. Two of the guys, Ted Ericson and Mike Hanson, were here last week and had to get back to the States. The other two, Paul Daily and Jim Peters, will fly over and I'll join them for that week. David Lorry preferred not to do the program this year; his wife is pregnant with their first child, and he didn't want to leave her. We're compensated for our time here with the program. If there is anything else that we would like to do, that is on our own. So that has given me a lot of free time."

"Wow. A paramedic/firefighter," was all Talia could say at the moment, as she looked at him, feeling very proud of him. The times she and her brother Kurt did talk, Jason's name sometimes came up, but Kurt never mentioned anything about the work Jason did, and he didn't tell her. Jason was in her thoughts many times over the years, and although they never kept in touch, she was glad Kurt did. The first time they met each other here in Basel, the two became friends; she just didn't know how good their friendship was.

"So, you said you're not married. Any girlfriends?" Talia asked, looking at him as they continued walking.

He was quiet for a moment and then replied, "There have been a few. What about you? I don't see a ring on your finger. So, no husband, any boyfriends?" which he truly hoped she didn't have.

She answered, looking back at him, "No, I'm not married either. My career has kept me busy. I've had a boyfriend here and there. I wasn't ready for anything yet, and I couldn't see them in my future."

"Well, maybe it's a good thing we got that established and out of the way. Both of us being unmarried, that is," he said.

Chapter 4

Just then, her phone buzzed. She said, looking at him, "I'm sorry, I texted my mom about some flowers that showed up in my hotel room today. I figured she sent them to me just to continue wishing me a happy birthday. She knows I love lilacs and the smell of them." Talia looked at the message. "It is my mom, um, she texted: *I didn't send you any flowers, someone else must have been thinking about you. I hope all is going well. Love you much.* I wonder who they came from. You know, it was strange too. After arriving here in Basel, I turned my cell phone back on. It wasn't until I was getting ready for bed that I read through all the birthday wishes; several people wishing they were here with me. I could hear the jealousy in their text messages," she said with a smile, "but it was the last one wishing me a happy birthday. I didn't recognize the number." Jason almost told her it was his number.

"Uh." She sighed as she kept looking at the text from her mom and then put her phone back in her bag. She looked up at Jason, and he had this look of guilt on his face.

"What?" she asked.

He thought maybe now would be a good time to tell her. "I have a little confession to make. A little birdie told me it was your birthday yesterday, so I sent you that text wishing you a happy birthday." She looked at him, thinking he was lying. He pulled out his phone and showed her; it was his cell phone number.

"It was you? How did... who told you?" Jason looked at her with a sheepish grin. "Oh, I think I know. It was Kurt, wasn't it?" As she continued talking, she looked out toward a grassy area. "Kurt and I talk, but not like we used to. We both have a lot going on, but when we have talked, sometimes our conversations turn to...," realizing she almost said his name, Jason, she looked at him, "we talk about... uh, stuff...." She made a funny little face and turned her head so he couldn't see her blushing. "It's getting a little warm out here."

Jason looked at her with a tilt of his head and a raised eyebrow. "You're blushing!" he said with a smile. "What were you going to say... that you and Kurt talk about me?"

She took a moment, "Um, maybe, a time or two or three..." Talia had her head down when she said it. When she looked up, Jason was smiling at her with a little shake of his head.

"Then, as long as we are being honest," he said, with a scrunch of his nose, "I didn't think either Laurel or Sophia would allow me to put the lilacs in your room, so I asked them if they would."

Talia looked at him, "You, you got me lilacs? How did you know they're my favorites?"

Jason held up his hand as if to say, hold on, "I had to show the girls some proof that I knew you." Jason reached into his back pocket and took out his wallet with a small photo of himself, Kurt, and Talia. It was a photo taken in Colorado Springs, and the lilac bushes were behind them; the last time they were all together. He showed Talia. She took the photo from him and looked at it, smiling. "I remember this. This is where we all walked through that huge flower garden, and at the far end, there were all those bushes of lilacs. I loved it; the smell was so powerful. I hated to leave." She looked at him, handing him back his photo, still smiling and remembering.

He looked at her and then said, "If I remember right, you almost cried because you didn't want to leave. I think those lilacs got the best of you. That's what I told these two after showing them this photo. I explained the vacations our families sometimes shared in our earlier years, and that we all met here in Basel. They would take the lilacs and put them in your room for me; I think still not trusting me."

She shook her head. "Thank you for the lilacs. You remembered from Colorado," Talia said, looking at him with a smile. "That was a long time ago."

"I remember a lot of things from Colorado, and before," he said, looking into her eyes. "What brings you overseas?" After Kurt had called him, he knew what had brought her, but wanted to hear it from her.

Talia looked at him with a tilt of her head. "You know I'm a designer, right? Especially if you and Kurt have kept in contact. I've been designing clothes for many years for other people, and not too long ago, I started my own line, and I love what I do. I've purchased fabric from several places back home, either by going to the fabric store or purchasing online. An opportunity showed up where I could experience purchasing them here, which I did today, and loved it. I could probably get lost in a fabric shop for several hours. You'd have to send in a search party to look for me," she said with a grin. He smiled at her, seeing her passion. "And, I needed some time for me. So, it was a birthday wish for me, and I also wished for...."

She stopped before saying what she had wished for while standing in her hotel room. She's thinking maybe her wish is coming true, and her voice became softer. "This is how I wanted to celebrate it," she said, looking out over the grassy area with various plants she knew nothing about. Talia had gotten quiet now as she stared off in the distance. Her voice almost in a whisper, "I was walking through the *Spalen Gate* down through the streets, and I started noticing the structure and architecture of the buildings, the history; something my father would point out to Kurt and me, hoping we would understand and appreciate them the way he did. But because we were young, we didn't appreciate any of it when he would explain the various details and such." She paused a moment, her eyes tearing up. "He knew I really liked fashion and the creativity of it, and that somehow seeing all the designs and architecture of buildings like these with the creativity to build them, that was what made us so similar: our passions. I think he hoped I would take more of an interest in the old, and I wish I could share that with him now, and I can't." Her voice faded as the tears and sadness came up.

Jason saw the tears and knew she was thinking of her dad, who passed away six months ago. In a gentle voice, he said, "Talia, I heard about your father. I'm so sorry." More tears came. She thought she might get through this trip without them and feeling that loss. She was still grieving him and missing him so much. Jason took a step, putting his arms around her as more tears flowed down her cheeks. He didn't want her to feel alone. Her arms went around him.

After a few minutes, she took a step back, wiping away the tears from her eyes and cheeks with the back of her hand and fingers. She didn't have Kleenex with her. Jason pulled out a handkerchief and handed it to her.

"I'm sorry. It hits me in waves without warning. I miss him," she said.

"You don't need to be sorry. I know you were close to your dad. Never apologize." Jason knew exactly how she was feeling, but now was not the time to speak about it.

They stood there, looking out over the garden. Soon, she heard it, and now she thinks he heard it; her stomach was growling. She looked up at him, and he had a little grin on his face. "Sounds like someone's stomach is talking."

"I guess I am a little hungry. I sometimes forget to eat and need to. I wasn't paying much attention to the time, just enjoying the company," she said as she looked up at him.

"Well, I think we need to do something about that. I do know there is a little café a few blocks from here that we could walk to and have a bite to eat, if you are up for a short jaunt, and it's close to your hotel." Jason was hoping she would agree.

"I'd like that," she said with a smile, feeling less lonely and grateful for the company of someone she knew and deeply cared about.

"OK, then. This way. We'll just follow the unmarked, yellow brick road up and around the other side of your hotel. I've had the opportunity to eat at this one, and it's nice." They walked down the path heading out of the garden, crossing the street toward the hotel, and then up a few blocks. It wasn't more than a five- or six-minute walk, and they had arrived.

As they were eating, Jason asked, more on purpose but had to make it sound nonchalant-like, "So, what are your plans while you're here? Do you still have business to take care of?"

"No more business. But there are other things I'd like to do. I don't have a set itinerary. Why do you ask?"

"Well, I'll be here for the next full week, and while I wait for my other comrades to join me, I was just thinking, maybe we could spend some time together. See what other tourists see or eat or ride on."

"Um." She looked at him with a raised eyebrow and a slight grin, "I might be up for that. There is a historical museum that I think my dad would have been proud of me going through, a walking tour, and who knows what else. So, would you have a problem doing these things?"

"That sounds like a plan I could easily work into my unscheduled time here," he said with a smile.

Chapter 5

Having finished up, they left the café and headed back to the hotel. Jason opened the door for her and she headed through. She stopped abruptly, turning smack into Jason's chest. Looking up at him and taking a step back, she said, "I'm sorry, I didn't think you were that close. I meant to ask you where you were staying."

The desk clerk, Sophia, saw this and tried to hide the grin on her face.

"I'm staying at your hotel," he said, looking at Talia and then at Sophia.

"Welcome back. Mr. Porter, your room is ready."

Talia looked at Sophia, who was grinning, and back to Jason. "You're staying here. When were you going to tell me that little snippet?" Secretly inside, she was glowing.

"Um, when we got here, and you wanted to know where I would stay, and as long as Sophia said, they would have a room for me," he said.

"Oh, very sneaky. Anything else I should know?" Talia asked, looking at him.

"Nope," Jason replied, not looking at her.

"Mr. Porter, I'll get you checked in now and give you your key," Sophia stated.

They both walked over to the desk so he could sign in. Talia just watched him. Sophia noticed how Talia looked at him and then asked Talia about her lilacs. "So, you knew they were from him and you said nothing this afternoon? I see how this is." Sophia got a big grin on her face. In her best

English, she said, "It was after he told us about your family vacation to the mountains of Colorado? He showed us the little picture of three of you and told us of the garden with the lilacs. It was so very sweet. I also like lilacs."

"So, where is your luggage? Surely you brought clothes with you," Talia asked.

"Well, they were kind enough to allow me to put my bag in a closet down the hall rather than carry it with me all over the place and feel, and look, stupid. I think they felt sorry for me. Right, Sophia?" She just smiled at him.

"Ya, you might have looked silly, seeing me at the gardens, and walking outside, and having to place your bag on the ground to give me that hug," Talia said.

"Mr. Porter, here is your room key. You are on the second floor, Room 27. You'll take a right at the top of the stairs and to the end of the hall. Your room will be on your right. Breakfast is served between 7:00 a.m. until 9:00 a.m. Is there anything else I can provide either of you?"

"Thank you, Sophia. I think we'll be all right," Jason said. Talia also thanked her and said goodnight.

After retrieving his luggage, they both headed up the stairs. As they were walking up, Jason asked, "So, what room are you in?"

"Oh, I'm in Room 47," Talia replied.

"OK, so just down the hallway then?"

"The same end of the hallway as you, on the fourth floor," she said with a grin.

He looked at her with a boyish grin, "Oh, would you mind if I walked you to your door, just to make sure you're safe?"

"I suppose that would work," Talia replied.

Arriving at her room, she took her room key out. She turned toward the big hallway window, looking at the view of the city with all the lights. "You'll be able to see this view from your window, the same as me." She felt him standing next to her. The only view he was looking at was her. He took her by the shoulders, turning her toward him. She looked up at him and started to say, "Thank you for—" Looking at her, he bent down and gave her a gentle kiss on the lips. And with that, he picked up his bag and left to go to his room on the second floor.

☙

Talia woke up to the soft light coming through her window, the start of a new day. Her birthday wish couldn't have been any better. She would share it with a man she's had a crush on since she was nine years old, but it was becoming more for her. She wondered if Jason remembered some of the longer vacations, ones like the trip to Wyoming, visiting Old Faithful, and the mud pots where he had picked her up and threatened to throw her into one of them, or walking around Devils Tower—she received her first sweet-sixteen kiss on that trail—and the beautiful scenery.

They had also spent time near the Porcupine Mountains in Michigan. So many things to do, lots of trails, biking, and seeing an amazing view of Lake Superior. She smiled, remembering the small cabin they all shared; two big beds, one large overstuffed chair. Thank goodness they had also brought sleeping bags; seven people in a not-so-big cabin. Besides Basel, the biggest trip was going to Colorado Springs the year after she graduated from high school. Their parents had pitched in to rent a huge van for traveling through Nebraska into Colorado, and heading down to Colorado Springs.

So many wonderful memories. She missed those times. The feelings she had for him grew over time, but she shoved them down inside. Maybe while the two of them are back here in Basel, they could add a few new memories. She was happy to spend this time with him now, however long that might be. In the back of her mind, for so long, she thought, *What if he could be a part of my future? Is there even a chance he might see me in his?*

After getting showered and dressed, she finished her makeup and hair, sticking other items back in her bag and zipping it closed. She was about to go out the door, then stopped and thought about calling his room to see if he was up and would want to go have breakfast. Then she thought out loud, "What if he isn't up yet? Maybe he's already up and headed down or... I'm thinking too much. Either be brave and go knock on his door or just head down and check out breakfast and wait for him."

Heading out her door, there he stood at the window, leaning against the window frame, looking out the window. "Good morning, Talia." His voice was soft and velvety, and then he turned toward her.

"Good morning, Jason," she said with a smile. "Did you sleep well?"

"Mostly," he replied, but was thinking something different. "Would you like to go down to breakfast, and we can figure out what it is you would like to do today?"

"OK, and if there is something that you would like to go do, we can do that, now that there are two of us." This thought had also crossed his mind.

"Talia, I don't want this to be awkward between us because of last night, my kissing you."

She took a moment before responding and looked at him. "It wasn't awkward. It was a lovely way to end the evening, and it was nice."

"OK. Why don't we head downstairs," Jason replied.

Turning the corner and seeing many other guests enjoying breakfast, they could hear several languages, including English, French, German, and a little Italian. There were a couple of tables open. They each picked out what they wanted, along with juice and coffee, and sat down at a table. Here, they could take their time and enjoy breakfast and maybe plan out their day. As they were eating, Talia started the conversation, "What I would like to do today, if you're all right with it, is to visit the Basel Historical Museum. I think, for most people, it's hard to imagine living hundreds of years ago. My dad was a history buff, and I'd like to have the chance to go through it, for my dad. We didn't get to visit it when I was young, and I know it's something he would have enjoyed." Little did she know there's more history.

"Talia, I'm good with whatever you'd like to see. My mom is the one in our family who enjoyed history. And, believe it or not, I actually wouldn't mind doing that with you today. I can do this for my mom. So, when do you want to do that, this morning or this afternoon?"

"I'm thinking, when we finish with breakfast, we could walk there. I have my trusty map in my bag here. The museum doesn't open until 10:00 a.m., and we can take our time getting there. Do you have your *BaselCard?*"

"Oh, you mean the card all of us guests get to use for trams, buses, and for discount things?" he replied with a smile, nodding, and pulled out his wallet to show her his *BaselCard*, and then she saw the top of another card with blue on it. The top portion looked like it could be the medical symbol "Star of Life" on it. She wondered why he might have a card like that, unless it had something to do with him being a paramedic.

"Yup, I got one of those too. So, are we about ready to start this day?" Jason asked.

With a map in hand, they headed out the door. They went through the *Gate of Spalen*. Even though Talia had already walked through it on Sunday, she wanted to share it with Jason. They headed through the huge gateway, looking at and talking about the structures, windows, what was inside those shops, and the architecture of the buildings. It's even better the second time around when you share it with someone you care about.

Even though it wasn't mid-morning yet, the street was becoming filled with people chatting and laughing, and looking in windows, then going inside. Many shops opened early for the tourists. A large group of people came toward Talia and Jason, and he instinctively grabbed her hand in his to keep her close to him and not get separated, much like he had done in Colorado Springs and one or two other places. Once they were through the crowd, he didn't let go, and neither did she.

As they approached the intersection of *Petersgraben* and *Leonhardsgraben*, Talia would need both hands to get the small map out and open it up to look at, even though she didn't want to let go of his hand. Looking at the map, they saw that they could follow a couple of different streets, but decided on a street called *Heuberg* that would lead them down easily to the museum. As they started to cross the street, Jason took hold of her hand again. Once across, he let go of her hand, and she looked at him.

"What?" Jason asked with a grin.

Talia replied, "I liked you holding my hand, that's all. I remember a few other times when you did that."

He looked at her. He didn't think she remembered. "Um, do you want me to continue holding your hand?" he asked.

"If you have to ask, then maybe you shouldn't." She pursed her lips together with a sarcastic grin and eyes wide. At that moment, he stopped and gave her a quick kiss on the lips, surprising her. And with that, he took hold of her hand again and didn't let go until they were at the museum. It was a wonderful walk, until she all but fell by tripping over a crack in the sidewalk near the museum and almost went down. Jason pulled her hand up and grabbed her waist to stop her fall. All she could do was laugh at herself. She could envision how silly that would have looked to bystanders.

Even taking their time walking, they still had about fifteen minutes before the doors would open. They found a place to sit and relax. Other people were doing the same, just waiting for the doors to open. Talia then asked Jason, "I saw the card in your wallet showing a portion that was blue. Was that the 'Star of Life' symbol on it?" He looked at her and then realized she would know what they called the symbol, with her mom being a nurse.

He pulled out his wallet and pulled the card out, giving it to her. It was his international identification card showing him to be a paramedic/firefighter. Jason said, "If I am ever questioned in a particular situation, I pull this out and show it. It's my international ID card. We all have them. It has all my contact information on it and the unit I work for. There have been a few times when I didn't have my uniform on, and people weren't trusting that I was someone who wanted to help them or who knew what they were doing."

"So, you've had to pull this out and show it," Talia said, looking at it and then at Jason. She handed it back, and he put it away.

"Maybe, sometime, while we're still here, you can tell me about your job. I'd like to know more." He got quiet, looking at the ground, and she wondered if it was something she said or if there was more to it that he wasn't saying.

After looking at his watch and seeing that the museum doors would open, he said, "Let's go look at some history."

They entered the huge building. They were given a pamphlet to help guide them to different periods. It was fascinating to see all these pieces and read about their history. Talia knew her dad would probably have spent a whole day here. As they went through, they would agree about different pieces, and which parent might have found one piece more interesting than the other one and why. It would be something they both would treasure, especially spending this time together.

Chapter 6

Looking at his watch, they couldn't believe the time they'd spent in the museum. It was about 2:30 p.m. Now it was his stomach that was growling. Talia said she was ready for some lunch, too. They looked at the map and saw an American/Caribbean place called, *Papa Joe's Basel*. They agreed it would be a good place to eat, and it was about a five-minute walk. They could sit and eat, and relax a bit before venturing off to the next thing, which entailed them doing more walking.

There were so many places, she thought to herself, that she would love to visit, but they would take a lot longer than a week. There was just so much, and that's not even counting wanting to see Austria, and Germany, and France. Time and money are usually a big factor for most people. At least while she's here, or they're here, they can use their *BaselCard* for free transportation and get discounts, a nice perk most hotels offer their guests.

After arriving at *Papa Joe's Basel*, it was nice to see some American food or something close to it. They ordered, and talked more about what they had seen at the museum, and then the next thing to do was the Downtown Walking Tour. Lucky for them, the Tour was close by and would only take five to eight minutes to walk to it.

After leaving *Papa Joe's*, they headed toward the start of the walking tour. There were benches to sit on, so they sat until the tour was to start. That gave them about twenty minutes to enjoy the scenery and each other's company.

"Can I ask what made you want to be a paramedic/firefighter?" Talia asked Jason, looking at him.

He thought for a moment, sitting back on the bench, and said, "I think it came about because of my mother being a critical care nurse." He looked at Talia, and said, "Your mom was a surgical nurse, right?" Talia nodded. Jason continued, "My mom would come off a shift from the hospital exhausted sometimes, but feeling like she made a difference that day. She'd bring home stories about what emergencies had occurred. Ambulances and paramedics would bring people into the ER. If they're stable enough and didn't need surgery, they're admitted. Most others needed surgery first and then sent up to ICU. She was one of a dozen critical care nurses. She's head nurse and might have ten patients on her end of the floor, helping all of them along with other nurses. They might work ten- to twelve-hour shifts.

"She'd talk with the patients' family members, reassuring them they were all doing their very best to get their family member well so that they could go home. Sometimes it didn't go so well, and a patient died. Sometimes the family members would yell at the nurses more than at the doctors and ask why they let them die.

"For other patients, she'd be in those rooms, constantly checking on them, watching their vitals, and administering medication when needed. She wanted to provide the best care she knew how to. It was great when a patient got better, getting moved to a regular room for whatever time they needed to still be in before being released to go home. Sometimes, when she lost a patient, she would struggle with why she couldn't be the one to save them. She had the knowledge and the know-how along with the doctors.

"I would hear her in her bedroom, crying because she'd had a patient that she was so damn sure would make it. They'd get a code blue, but the patient died. It was worse when it was a young person. I didn't always know what I could do for her. Sometimes I left her alone, and sometimes I went into her room, and I'd sit on the bed with her and hold her, and let her cry until she fell asleep. It almost broke my heart that I couldn't help her get through some guilt of that young patient dying. She was strong, but I know it affects both doctors and nurses.

"I wanted to help in any way I could. I wanted to be one of the first people on that scene or home or office, wherever it was, and provide medical treatment as soon as possible, reducing the chance of them dying alone before getting to a hospital. I wanted to be the one giving them a fighting chance to survive. After all those years of listening to her talk about her patients, that depth of caring and knowledge, I wanted to be one of those that could make a difference in someone's life.

"I started in my senior year of high school as a volunteer first responder. I couldn't do much regarding the medical part, being in high school, but I could physically help and usually mentally able to help. There was an accident or two that I lost it, because of how bad it was, and I threw up all over the place. But getting to the scene as quickly as possible and providing medical help, in whatever way, watching these first responders, EMTs and paramedics do that, I felt this was what I was to do.

"It required lots and lots of hours of physical, mental and medical training, along with a lot of education. Over the years, I went through all the programs. I've been a paramedic for a lot of years, and it's something that I enjoy doing, and I'm good at it. So, it was because of my mom, seeing and hearing what she did every day. I wanted to be that someone who made a difference to someone else. I also wanted to be a firefighter, so I trained, and now I'm a firefighter. Do you remember that my dad was also a volunteer firefighter?" Talia nodded.

"Wow" was all Talia could say at the moment. She just looked at him, then leaned over and kissed him on his cheek. She didn't know what to say. He closed his eyes with an ever-so-slight shake of his head. There was something he wasn't saying or couldn't say she thought, *Maybe, if, and when he's ready, he'll tell me. I won't ask. It's up to him.*

Talia placed her hand on his knee. "Are you okay with going on the walking tour, or do you want to pass on it or do something different?" Talia asked.

He looked at her with a slight shake of his head. "No, I'm good. We're here, and I want to do this with you." He looked over toward a bunch of people and said, "Should we walk over to where all those people are? I'm assuming that's where it starts, besides the fact that the sign over there says, 'Downtown Tour Starts at 4:30 p.m.,' and it's about that time." He looked at Talia with a smile. She giggled and nodded her head yes.

They stood up and headed toward the *Tinguely Fountain*. Jason put his hand on Talia's back, guiding her around some people in the group. The tour guide came and introduced himself in his strong French accent. He explained that the tour would take approximately one and a half to two hours. He gave a brief list of the things they would see, and asked if anyone had questions before getting started. There would be lots of opportunities for great photos. Jason and Talia took many photos between the two of them of buildings, people, cars and each other enjoying the tour. It was fun and interesting to learn about the history and culture.

The tour ended at the *Mittlere Brücke*, otherwise known as the Middle Bridge, and it was now 6:30 p.m. Both were getting hungry. There was an Indian Restaurant that Talia had passed Sunday afternoon when she headed to the *Café VonKutch*; its name was New Bombay and it was also not that far back to the hotel.

Chapter 7

By the time they had finished eating at New Bombay Restaurant, it was around 8:00 p.m. It had been a wonderful, but long day, and she wanted to relax. She knew the hotel had a pool and thought it would be a good way to end the day. As they were heading back to the hotel, she brought up her idea about the pool and said with a slight smile, "It's been a long day, and I'd like to relax. The hotel has a pool and I'll be taking advantage of it. I know I'll sleep well. You can join me, if you'd like, but that's what I'm going to do."

Jason was quiet for a few moments and said, "I think I will join you. It has been a long day, and that's a perfect way to end it."

Once back to the hotel, they headed upstairs to the second floor where Jason's room was. Talia said, "I'm going to go change and head down to the pool. I'll see you there in a few?" And she headed up the stairs.

Jason replied, "I'll see you down there."

Talia changed into her one-piece swimsuit. She never cared much for wearing a two-piece; she didn't think they fit her body right and looked unattractive. Her suit was black with a few swirls of white off to one side, accentuating her waist. She looked at herself in the mirror and smiled, looking at the front of herself and then side to side. She liked the way she looked. She put on the robe and slippers the hotel provided, stuck her room key in her pocket, and headed down the stairs, again forgetting about the elevator. Quite a few people were enjoying the pool and hot tub. She found an empty lounge chair, took off her slippers, and then untied the tie from around her waist, taking off the robe.

With the number of people in the pool, she didn't see Jason and figured he wasn't down yet. The pool was huge. Even though she didn't see him, he was already in the pool near the deep end, on the opposite side, where he could watch her come through the door. He made his way through the people toward the pool steps. He watched her walk toward a chair, take off her slippers, and then untie her robe, taking it off.

By the time she took hold of the handrail, he was there in front of her, looking up at her. She remembered the first time their families met; she thought he was cute. And the times they all got together after that first vacation; he became more attractive. But now, he's just plain handsome. She took a few steps down, testing the water with her feet. The water was warm and felt good. Even before stepping down the last two steps, Jason reached up with his hand.

She stopped a moment, looking at him. He is this kind, caring, strong, all-around good guy, and she gets to spend time with him. She took the last two steps down, reaching for his hand before taking the final step onto the pool floor while looking at him. Neither said a word.

Stepping further into the water where it now came up past her waist, she was glad for the cover of water, even though you could still see through the water and it didn't cover anything. They walked toward the deep end, or at least as far as she could before it reached her shoulders. She had to take a step back, letting go of Jason's hand, using the palms of her hands to help guide her back a bit. He turned toward her, realizing how high the water was on her. Jason was tall, so the water only came up to his upper chest. He took a step toward her and motioned for her to lean against the pool wall. He did the same thing, looking around the pool.

He spoke first. "This was a good idea, and the water is warm, and you look amazing." He turned and looked at her.

"Thank you. You... also look... great. You're right about the water, and I don't know why I feel so awkward with you," she said. She felt like she was blushing; it was getting warm in there.

"I'm sorry, I didn't mean to make you feel like that or to make you blush. But you really do look amazing." Jason looked toward some other people.

When he looked back at her, Talia was looking at his chest. He looked down to see what she was looking at. "What, do I have something on me?"

"No," she said, giggling now. "Growing up, my dad always told me not to drink beer."

He grinned at her. "Really, why is that?"

She stated, matter-of-factly, "He said, 'If you drink beer, you'll grow a hairy chest,' and I didn't want that to happen to me. So, I never acquired the taste for beer." They both laughed. "My dad liked beer, and he had a hairy chest."

Still smiling, Jason replied, "Well, I don't mind drinking a good beer now and then, so that's probably why I don't have a lot of hair on my chest." This seemed to ease the situation, a good icebreaker while the two stood in the pool all but half-naked.

Not sure why, but the huge pool made her think of another vacation their families went on. "Do you remember the vacation trip to the Porcupine Mountains?" she asked, her mind wandering.

He looked at her, wondering where that came from. "I do remember it. You thought it was funny that they called it that, thinking we would see lots of porcupines."

"OK, so we didn't see a lot of them; only two," she said, smiling.

"Do you remember why they called it Porcupine Mountains?" he asked.

She nodded, turning around and putting her arms up on the edge of the pool. "Something about all the trees and how they looked like those poor little rodents from a distance." He grinned at her.

"Do you remember the scenic view where we saw Lake Superior? That was an incredible view; it looked like a mini ocean. And do you remember the cabin where we all stayed?" he asked. She turned toward him and nodded. "Three rooms and a small bathroom. Our parents each got one of the small bedrooms, and you, me and Kurt slept in sleeping bags on the floor. That's the first time we slept together."

"In separate sleeping bags," she said, grinning and looking at him.

He said, "Well, ya. Your bag was sandwiched in between Kurt and me. Do you remember what else happened?"

She nodded and said, "You reached over and took my hand, and just held it until I fell asleep. I liked it. That was a good week." She continued to look at him.

"As long as we're remembering trips, what about Wyoming?" he said, looking around the pool, then back at her.

"Devils Tower in the Black Hills; that thing is humongous," she said wide-eyed, remembering how insignificant she felt looking at it.

"Did you know that from its base to the summit, it's 867 feet tall, which makes it well over two hundred feet taller than the Arch in St. Louis?" he said. She was looking at him. "And it's about the size of a football field in diameter."

She said, "We were all going to go walk around it. I thought that would take a long time, especially when you got up close to it. When we started on the trail, my mom wasn't feeling well and thought it better that she didn't go, so your mom stayed with her. Then it was just our dads, you, me and Kurt. I remember stopping to look at the chipmunks. They were so cute."

"We were about half-way round. Kurt was keeping up with our dads. Every time you saw a chipmunk, you wanted to stop, hoping one would come close enough for you to touch. Do you remember something else that happened?" he said, lowering his head a little, looking at her lips.

"Ya," she said with a shy smile. "It was my sixteenth birthday, and I said to myself in a whisper, 'sweet-sixteen, and never been kissed.' And before I knew it, you kissed me and made me blush." She was feeling herself blush again. "I never told anyone. Not my mom, not Kurt, not my best friend. No one."

"Why not?" he asked.

"Because, I wanted to keep it a secret. Something special only I knew about. I didn't want to share that with anyone," she said.

Jason said, "Well, someone else knew about it."

She looked at him. "I never told anyone. Who did you tell?" she said, feeling a little betrayed.

Seeing the look on her face, he said, "I didn't tell anyone either. When I kissed you, and then we started walking, you had your head down. Kurt was watching us. He told me later that he was supposed to come back and see where we were and that he saw us. He promised he would never tell anyone, and neither did I. It was a special moment, just like now." He leaned over and kissed her.

"You remember when we were in Yellowstone, seeing Old Faithful and the mud pots?" he asked.

She started laughing and took a step away from the side of the pool, bobbing up and down. Jason also moved away from the side, lowering himself into the water to warm his shoulders. "Oh, geez. Kids were running on the wooden boardwalk, and there were signs saying, 'No Running on Boardwalks.' I was following you and Kurt, and kids went running by and shoved me into the back of you," she said, giggling now. "You stopped and turned around and looked at me, and I said, 'I'm sorry, one of those kids bumped into me.' You gave me a look, and before I knew it, you picked me up and threatened to toss me into one of those smelly mud pots. It scared me, and I thought you would do it, so I put my arms around your neck and hung on."

The only ones left in the pool now were Jason and Talia, plus one other couple who were engrossed in each other. Jason took a step toward Talia and scooped her up in his arms, with Talia giving a little scream, putting her arms around his neck and giggling more. He carried her toward the center of the pool and closer to the deep end, but not going any further. He just wanted to hold her, and knowing she couldn't touch the bottom of the pool, this was the best way. He also figured she knew how to swim, but was hoping she wouldn't try to leave his arms.

He could tell, holding her body, that she was much more at ease, not trying to get away, and he liked that. He started slowly turning around in the water and said, "Maybe we could talk about what the rest of your time looks like here, what your plans are and where you want to go?" He looked at her, "If I don't become too much of a pain, I'd like to spend it with you."

With Talia's one arm around his neck, she took her other hand and slowly scooped up water, letting it trickle over his shoulder and chest, and then wiping the droplets of water away. She did it again, looking at him, and nodded her head. "I would like that. I planned on heading down to Bern and then Villars, doing more sightseeing and then coming back up to Basel. I'll be leaving from here to head back home next week."

"And I'll be heading back up to Stuttgart, that's where we flew into, and after that week is finished, I'll fly home with the guys," Jason said.

Still having one arm around his neck, she slowly laid back in the water where it covered her ears. She took a slow, deep breath, closing her eyes, knowing Jason was holding her up. He continued to slowly turn with her in his arms. He had a look of content on his face, as he held someone very special that he loved. He didn't want this to end.

As she continued lying against him in the water, it was a few more minutes before she tried sitting up to speak. "Then I guess I'd better check with the hotels and see if they have any spare rooms for another guest," she said, looking at him. "I plan on taking the train down tomorrow afternoon to Bern. I'll spend at least a day or so there, and then another train down to Villars for a couple of days before heading back here."

"So, what if they don't have any spare rooms in the hotels you're staying at? Would you find one close for me, or maybe there might be a possibility that we could share a room?" Jason asked with a tilt of his head.

Talia took a moment to reply, and with a raised eyebrow and a slight smile, she said, "We'll see. If we're going to be heading out tomorrow, I'll need to repack and make some calls." Talia tried getting out of his arms to head toward the shallow end of the pool, when Jason started walking further toward the deep end, with her laughing and squirming until he had to let her go, making the both of them tread water.

"What are you doing?" she laughed, still treading water.

"You're the one that wanted to come to the swimming pool; I just wanted to make sure you knew how to swim. Otherwise, I'd have to rescue you and possibly perform CPR. You know what that means; mouth-to-mouth," he said, laughing. She splashed him and started swimming toward the shallow end with Jason in tow. They both got out of the pool, taking some towels to dry off before putting their robes and slippers on, and then headed for their rooms.

Jason walked Talia to her room. She turned to tell him she had a good time today, and before she could say it, he kissed her, and she returned the kiss. "I was going to tell you I had a really good time with you today, and to thank you for sharing it with me."

"You're welcome. I had a really good time sharing it with you. I'll see you in the morning. Sleep well." And with that, Jason turned, heading down the hallway. She watched him go, and as he turned to go down the stairs, he looked back at her, giving her a nod.

Chapter 8

With everything packed and the hotels called, it was time to get some breakfast before heading to the train station. She'd come back up for her bag before checking out. Opening her door, Jason was standing in the same place he had the morning before. No bag, so he also must have left his bag in his room. He turned to her and said, "Good morning." He held out his arm for her to take, and they headed downstairs.

Once they were seated and eating, she started telling Jason about the hotels. "I called both hotels, and they have a room. The one in Bern is for one night, and the hotel in Villars is for three nights. It's less expensive than many of the others, and has that alpine look and feel. They also have the continental breakfast, and there's a shuttle or a bus that runs toward the center of the city." She saw the look he gave her regarding the cost.

"Sounds good to me," Jason replied.

She stopped eating and looked at him with an elbow on the table and one hand covering her mouth. "What? Are you all right?" he asked with a worried look.

"When I booked this trip, I wasn't planning on anyone being with me. I thought I was going to be by myself. I booked inexpensive hotels, finding free things to do, cheaper places to eat, and transportation not costing a lot. I know I made a birthday wish, not thinking it would come true. And if it did, I didn't consider what the cost might be to someone else. I'm sorry," she said.

"And what birthday wish would that be?" he asked.

Still looking at him, she said, "That I'd get to spend it with someone I knew... like you." Her voice trailed.

"I don't want you to worry about this," he said with a confident look. "I'm good on both, and I'd like to enjoy this trip with someone special. I'm thrilled to share it with you. Okay?"

She looked at him, thinking he was just saying that so she wouldn't feel bad. She didn't know what else to say except, "Okay." But she was still thinking otherwise.

Seeing her doubt, he responded. "I'm not worried about any of this, and I don't want you to be." With a little smile on his face, he said, "So, there might have to be a little change here and there. It will work out the way it's supposed to. I'm ready to see where this adventure takes us." He leaned over, kissing her on the cheek.

She thought, *A little change, uh, like maybe robbing Peter to pay Paul.*

"So, once we check out, do we take a shuttle or a tram to the train station?" Jason asked. All she could do at that moment was look at him, wondering. And yet, she was feeling lucky to share all of this with him.

She'd never seen him as anything but laid back while they were in each other's company so long ago. She didn't know if he got upset or angry and could probably knock someone on their butt, which he looked like he could easily do. He had the build for it. And since they've been together here, as adults, he seemed to be this very loving and caring man; just go with the flow of things, play it by ear. She thought, *Is this really who he is?* "Ya, there's a shuttle we can take and get train tickets there. Trains run about every thirty minutes," she said.

"Why don't we go get our bags and check out." He looked at her with a smile. She nodded, and they got up. Getting ready to check out, Talia confirmed that they would be back Sunday and check out the following Tuesday. They made their way to the shuttle, which would take them to the train station. There, they purchased Swiss Travel Pass Flex tickets for travel to Bern and Villars and back to Basel. The train ride would be a good hour to Bern, a nice amount of time to sit back and look out the window. After boarding the train and finding the racks for their luggage, they took their seats. There was plenty of legroom, and the windows were overly-large, allowing you to look toward the sky.

The train started moving, and they were on their way. Talia was happy to sit next to Jason. She looked out the window, watching everything go by. It wasn't long before Jason asked, "Are you OK? You're quiet."

"I'm OK. Just enjoying the ride and view." She looked at him with a slight grin and a nod and looked back out the window.

He took her hand, lifting it to his lips, and kissed the back of it. She turned and looked at him, then looked toward the seat across the aisle and saw an older couple looking and smiling at them. They smiled at her, and she just smiled back. Jason saw this and gave a little wave with his free hand, but he kept hold of Talia's hand. There wasn't much talking between the two of them, except to comment on what they saw out the window.

The train pulled into the station and stopped. As they were getting out of their seats, Jason allowed the older couple to leave first and then had Talia go next. The older couple had some difficulty getting their luggage off the center rack, so Jason helped them and then got their bags off the top rack. Once they were off the train, they checked about getting a shuttle or tram to head to their hotel; a tram would drop them off across the street from the hotel entrance. Once they arrived and checked in, getting their keys, they headed up the stairs. Jason took Talia's bag, instead of her lugging it up the three flights. Had they thought more clearly, they could have taken the elevator.

Finding their rooms, Talia took her bag and opened up her door, walking in. Jason held the door open to look inside. It looked very nice, a good-sized room with a large window and only one bed in the room, plus the bathroom. He watched as she put her bag on the luggage stand and put her small bag on the bed. She turned to look at him and grinned. "What, checking out my room to see if yours will be the same or slightly smaller? Or, to see how many beds were actually in the room?" He knew she had to be feeling better for that to come out of her mouth.

"I was just looking, no clear reason," he replied. "I guess I'll go to my room." And he started to leave.

"Wait a second. I'll go with you," Talia replied. She grabbed her hotel key and small handbag, following him. After opening his door and going in, yup, it was the same. He placed his bag on the luggage stand and then walked over to the window, opening up the curtain to look outside.

"I think we got the back side of the hotel," he commented. She walked over to the window to look out, as she had not opened up her curtain in her room. "All I see are mountains," he said. He turned to look at her.

"Smarty-pants," Talia said. She stood next to him, looking at the view. The mountains were breath-taking. That's something she could get used to looking at, besides the man next to her.

"You know, I could stand here most of the day looking at those mountains, but there are probably a few other things we could go look at. Do you know what you'd like to do first?" Jason asked.

"I'll let you know in a moment." Talia just wanted to soak up the view. Jason didn't push. As she looked out the window, she said, "I'd like to do the clock tower tour. I read about it, and I think it would be interesting. We could do that before lunch." She turned toward him and hugged him, resting her head against his chest, looking out the window. He was a little surprised, but liked that she hugged him at that moment because, if she hadn't, he was going to hug her. He put his arms around her, and they just stood there. He felt more accepted by her, feeling she could trust him. He closed his eyes for a moment, holding on to that. "Thank you for being here with me," she whispered. He kissed the top of her head, placing his chin where he kissed her. They stood there looking out at the view.

She finally looked up at him and said with a smile, "I'm ready to go see some stuff."

Picking up a tram schedule at the desk, they headed out the door. It looked like they could get close to the clock tower. The next tram would arrive in a few moments. They received a *BernCard* like the one used in Basel from the hotel. It almost didn't seem real, being in Switzerland. Everywhere you looked, there was an incredible amount of history of hundreds and hundreds of years of architecture, structure and culture. Bern would have been another place her dad would have loved to visit.

Chapter 9

The tram stopped within a few blocks of the clock tower. Talia knew about it, had read about it and saw photos of it, but now she was standing here looking at it. Jason took her hand, and they joined the tour group, listening to their guide talk about the history of the famous *Zytgloggeturm* (Clock Tower). Talia had a hard time pronouncing the name. It was fascinating seeing the inside. They climbed the stairs to the top, looking out over the city. Someone offered to take Talia and Jason's photo by the window. These would be memories for a lifetime.

The tour ended right at lunch. There was a bar and grill across the street from the clock tower. They headed over and had lunch, totally enjoying the food and the atmosphere. When they finished, they started walking. There was so much to see. They stopped in various shops to look, and then more walking, again checking out the structure and architecture of the buildings. Just like in Basel, you would need a good week or more to see what's here. Time was already moving swiftly. It was middle to late afternoon.

"What do you think about seeing the city from high up?" Talia asked Jason, looking at him.

"OK, and where would we go to see this fantastic view?" he asked, raising an eyebrow.

"Gurten," she said.

"Gurten," he replied with a silly look on his face and nodding his head. "What is Gurten?"

"It's a place. We'd take a streetcar from the main station to the Valley Station; it takes about fifteen minutes to get there and then ride up in a Gurten fu-nic-ular to the top." She laughed because it sounded funny when she was trying to pronounce it. "I heard another tourist talking about it while you were indisposed. Apparently, the view is spectacular, and it's something I'd like us to do."

"So, where is this main station that we would ride on a streetcar?"

She pulled out of her bag the map she'd been carrying. "We're here, and this is the main station, and here is Gurten. There's a tram about a block away that we can take to the station, and the rest is history," she said with a giggle.

"What was in the coffee you drank?" he said, with the same silly look on his face, enjoying the way she explained things. "OK, I'm game. Let's do it."

After getting on the tram and heading to the main station, they were soon riding on the streetcar, No. 9, heading for Gurten. It was an enjoyable short, fifteen-minute ride to the Valley Station. They also didn't have to wait long to take the funicular to the top. It's 858 meters above sea level, looking out over the *Bernese Oberland* region. She'd never ridden in a cable car like this one before.

As they were riding to the top, the view was something else than where they had started. Now at the top, looking back, it was incredible. "Wow. Look at that view," Talia said, looking out over the valley. Jason agreed, but he was looking at two different views: the one out there and the one standing next to him. "I want a picture of us with that view in the background." There were quite a few people around, so Talia asked one of them if they would take a picture of the two of them. They took two different photos, with each of their phones, with the view behind them: another beautiful memory.

Jason looked at her with this look of content. Talia turned to look at him and asked if everything was all right. He responded quietly with, "Yes. Thank you. Because of you and your trip here to Switzerland, I've seen and done some wonderful things that I probably wouldn't have done on my own. Seeing all this through your eyes has made me appreciate so much more." They both turned and looked at the valley below. They could see the sun ever so slowly lowering behind the mountains.

It was time to head back down. In the mountains, it gets dark sooner. Jason commented, "Why don't we head back to the hotel? They have a restaurant, and we can relax and enjoy it."

"I like that plan," she responded.

Back on the tram, they were now heading toward the hotel. The air was chilly, and Talia was getting goosebumps, as she forgot her sweater in her big bag. Jason saw her rub her hands up and down her arms, trying to warm them up. He had her scoot toward him and he put his arms around her to keep her warm.

Arriving back safely, and before going to the restaurant, they cleaned up a bit, giving themselves ten to fifteen minutes. Opening her door, she thought Jason would be standing outside waiting for her. He wasn't there, so she walked down to his room, getting ready to knock on his door, and she felt a tap on her shoulder. Turning around, she saw Jason was standing behind her. She smiled at him and saw he had one arm behind his back. "What have you got behind your back?" she asked with curiosity.

"Wait a moment," he said with a smile on his face. Her eyes got big, and he saw her nostrils flare, and she closed her eyes. He knew she could smell them.

"Lilacs, but from where?" Talia said.

He brought his arm around and handed her the small handful of lilacs he'd been holding. She took them and promptly put them up to her nose, inhaling the scent of them.

"I noticed a bush around the side of the hotel this morning. It still had some late blooms on it. After we got back and changed, I went down to the front desk and asked if I might take just a small sprig of them for you. At first, they weren't going to let me, but then said I could as long as it was a small sprig. I promised."

"That was so sweet. Thank you," she said.

They headed down to the restaurant, where the hostess took them to a table. There, sitting on the table, was a small vase with lilacs in it. Talia looked at Jason, thinking he had them do this. He looked at the hostess, and she said, "We heard you love lilacs. Your waiter will be with you in a moment. Enjoy your evening."

Talia thanked the hostess. Jason pulled out her chair to sit down and then seated himself across from her. Their waiter came and introduced himself, handing them a menu, most of which was in French, and told them about the list. He asked about drinks. Talia wasn't a wine drinker, but would try one. She asked the waiter about them. He chose a wine for her and said he would also bring her water, which you had to ask for. Jason asked about their beers and then ordered one. After ordering it, he saw Talia looking at him, remembering about drinking beer and putting hair on your chest.

"So, you want to add a few more hairs on your chest than you already have." She laughed, remembering his chest from the swimming pool.

"Maybe. Or, if you like, I could shave off the ones I have," he replied.

Shaking her head, she said, "No, I kind of like the ones you have." He smiled at her.

Once their drinks arrived, they ordered their food. While eating, they talked about the next day's plan.

"I want to know what you'd like to do. I feel like we've been doing everything I want to, and you're just going along with it. I'm feeling a little guilty about that," Talia said.

"I have been enjoying all of this. I don't know that I would want to do any of it by myself, and if I were by myself, it would be hard to pick what things to do and see and how to get there. I would probably enjoy myself, but having someone to share it with is...." His voice trailed.

"Is what?" Talia asked.

"Special. And you're right; I have been going along with it because I see how happy this is making you. Honestly, I'm just feeling happy and content being with you and seeing all of this through your eyes, and sharing it with you." Jason paused a moment. "And, yes, there is something I would like to do, but it will have to wait until we get to Villars."

"You can tell me," she replied.

"You can ask me about it tomorrow when we're on the train," he said with eyebrows raised and a slight smile. "How about we enjoy our food, this atmosphere, and each other."

"OK, but I'm going to sneak in that I would love to see the Rose Garden tomorrow morning," she stated. He smiled and nodded.

Somehow, she knew he was going to get her back for all the walking tours and in and out of shops and up mountains. She just wasn't sure how.

The fresh mountain air had made her tired. As they were getting up to leave, the hostess came to their table and told Talia it would be all right if she wanted to take the vase of lilacs to her room. Talia shook the hostess's hand and thanked her. The hostess said she hoped they enjoyed their meal and their evening.

She then looked at Jason, who was looking at Talia, and in German, she softly said, *"Für jemanden, der sehr geliebt wird,"* and left.

They headed toward their rooms. Jason stood at Talia's door, looking at her. He placed his hands on either side of her neck, bending down and kissing her slowly and gently. He didn't want to leave her, even to go down two doors. He finally took a step back and headed to his room.

Chapter 10

Opening her eyes to the bit of light that was shining in through her window made her smile. It was going to be a new day of adventure. The scent from the lilacs was still fresh and made her feel warm all over. Thinking about Jason and the time they'd shared the last few days was like rekindling an old friendship that never really got started.

She felt the chemistry between them and liked it a lot. She was getting deep feelings stirring inside of her, but was also scared that it might not last through this trip. And if it did, once they parted, she'd be heading home and he'd head back to Stuttgart; things would fizzle. Their lives would pick up just like before they met on this trip, and that made her sad because she cared so much for him and even felt like she could fall in love with him, if not already. She felt there was a space that needed to be filled, but she didn't know how to do it.

Even though he'd commented several times that he was happy and content to be with her, and the way he would look at her and kiss her, she thought, *How long would this last? What if he had someone else in his life? What if it was just the romance of being in Europe, a fling? He's a paramedic/ firefighter, and I'm a designer, both having busy lives. Would there be time for us? How would I know what he was feeling deep down? Would I be able to say those three little words to him; would he be able to say those three words to me? Can't exactly ask him point-blank, can I?*

There was a light knock on her door, and then another. She looked toward the door and got out of bed, looking out the peephole; it was Jason. Not looking her best upon waking up, her hair going every which way, needing a shower, makeup and to get dressed, she thought, *Well, this is me in the morning. Just open the door. He'll either walk away or laugh at how I look first thing in the morning.* She unlocked the door and opened it partway. He stood there looking at her. "The early bird catches the worm."

"Uh," she replied.

He asked, "Is it OK if I come in for a moment instead of standing here in the hallway? I couldn't sleep. I was up early and went out for a walk. It's quiet out there."

She stood looking at him and then opened the door further, letting him in. She wasn't fully awake. She'd left her curtain open just enough to let in some light to help wake her up; otherwise, she'd still be sleeping in an almost dark room. She walked over to the window, moving the curtain a little further open, looking out. The sun was up, the sky was blue, and it looked like another beautiful day. She turned and saw that he had sat down on the edge of the bed and was looking at her.

She wasn't sure what to say at this moment, except to say, "I'm awake. I didn't realize how tired I was." She plunked herself down where she had slept, pushing the covers she had moved back. She sat with one leg curled up, and the other leg was hanging over the edge with her foot touching the floor. She put one of the extra pillows on her lap and yawned into her hand.

He sat, looking at her. "We've been doing a lot these last several days, and maybe it's all just catching up to you. I wanted to let you know that, when you're ready, I am too. No hurry. I know you'd like to go to the Rose Garden this morning. Hence, the early bird catches the worm. You know, garden stuff. So, we can play it by ear."

And once again, she heard it. It was her stomach telling her it was time to eat. She looked at him with a goofy look. "I'll take a shower, and get dressed and get my bag repacked. Could you give me about forty minutes? I am a girl, and I need time to look my best."

He replied with a smile, "I'll give you all the time you need." And with that, he got up and headed toward the door. "I'll be in my room when you're ready." He opened the door and headed out, but not before turning around and telling her to lock the door behind him. She got up and locked the door.

Her bed looked very inviting, but she knew she would feel better after taking a shower. Whatever she was going to wear, it would be for the whole day until they got to Villars, so comfortable clothes and good shoes. She put her hair up, brushed her teeth, put her makeup on and got dressed. Then she repacked her large bag and put what necessities she needed in her smaller one she carried with her. It rarely took that long in the mornings to get dressed, as she was always ready for a new day. She figured she might as well put her large bag in Jason's room.

Feeling good about the time it took her to get this all done, she was under her forty minutes. With her small bag over her shoulder, she grabbed her room key and the large luggage bag and looked around the room one final time before opening her door and heading out. Pulling up the handle, she wheeled her luggage bag two doors down. She stood at the door for a moment before knocking. She took a breath, not sure why. Maybe because it was Jason's room. She knocked on the door, waiting for him to open it. Once open, he looked at her with her big bag.

"I figured I'd just leave my bag in your room until we're ready to check out and head for the train," she said.

"OK. Bring it in. Are you ready for breakfast?" he asked.

"Yes, I'm hungry," she replied.

After having breakfast, they walked over to the tram that would take them to the Rose Garden. There, you could freely wander all around, looking at the flowers and plants. Because it was getting into fall, the colors were also slightly changing, which were beautiful. Her mom would have liked this, and the botanical garden in Basel. Talia watched the kids playing in the park on the premises. Jason watched her as she smiled, watching them. There was a big, red wooden dragon. It looked like a lot of fun; they were having a great time climbing and swinging, and balancing on a low beam. She thought someday she'd like to have a child and bring them to a place like this. Nearby, a lily pond and fountain were sitting in the open.

"I remember you standing by a lily pond in your flowy skirt, and top, and sandals." He smiled at her, remembering how she looked. She smiled back at him. He wanted to tell her she wouldn't have to kiss any frogs to find her prince because her prince had found her. They continued wandering, and he took her hand. After spending a good hour there at the garden, they headed for the *Barengraben*, otherwise known to the locals as the Bear Park. It was within easy walking distance. When they arrived, the Bear Park was closed. It was very close to the *Aare River*. They had several hours to go before heading back to the hotel to check out and head to the train station. Walking across the *Nydeggbrucke* Bridge, it took them back to the older part of Bern. There were several small art galleries, a museum, and a church dating back to the 14th century.

It was past lunchtime, and they headed back to the *Restaurant Rosengarten.* It would be the perfect place to end this portion of the trip. It also provided an excellent spot for a few photos with Bern in the background. They took a selfie or two sitting on the Albert Einstein bench. After enjoying some good food and the view, they found a tram taking them back to the hotel. Their train would leave at 4:06 p.m. They headed up to Jason's room, collected their luggage, checked out, and then got back on a tram to take them to the train station.

After boarding the train, they placed their luggage on the luggage rack and found some seats. Talia told Jason, "You can sit by the window; it's your turn."

"It's OK. You can have it," he replied, expecting her to sit near the window.

Talia got this look in her eye and said, "Don't argue with me. Sit." He looked at her like he could pick her up and set her there without even trying.

"OK, I'm sitting," he said. She smiled with an authoritative grin and sat down in the aisle seat.

"Comfy?" he asked.

"I'm good, thank you," she replied.

"So, how long does it take to get to Villars?" he asked.

"It's less than three hours," she replied.

They could feel the train moving; it was right on schedule for leaving.

She waited until the train was well underway before asking him the question that she wanted him to answer last night. He had said she could ask him when they were on the train, so, here they are.

"OK, so tell me about it," she said.

"Tell you about what?" he replied, looking at her, not sure what she was saying.

"You said, and I quote, 'Yes, there is something I would like to do, but it will have to wait until we get to Villars,' to which I said, you can tell me, and you said, 'You can ask me about it tomorrow when we're on the train.' So, we're on the train heading to Villars. Now is as good a time as any."

He turned toward her, contemplating whether he would tell her just yet, and figured he might not win this argument with her. *Might as well talk about it now.* He thought to himself, *What is she going to do if she doesn't like the idea, get off the train? OK, just say it.*

"Hiking." There, he said it. A few moments passed as he waited for a response, raising an eyebrow while still looking at her. *She's not saying anything. Why? Crap, what is it with women, and what is it that will come out of her mouth?*

"Hiking." She nodded her head, looking straight forward. "I remember a young girl on vacation with her mom, dad and brother one year. They headed out to the mountains of Colorado. On this trip, they got to see a lot of things and do a lot of things with another family." He thought he knew where this was heading.

"And toward the end of this vacation, the adults decided that there was one last particular thing they still wanted to do to top off this vacation, in which everyone was going to partake." She turned and looked Jason right in the eye. "Well into this adventure, after following everyone across a creek, this young girl stumbles and falls into said creek. Once they fished her out of it so she wouldn't drown in a foot of water, they proceeded to go back down the trail. And then it wasn't long before this young girl trips over a stump and twists her ankle, having then to be picked up and carried back down the mountain trail looking like a drowned rat with a twisted ankle.

"And you know who it was that carried her down the trail? It wasn't her father, and it wasn't her brother, but the son of the family they vacationed with. Any of this ring a bell?" She tilted her head. "Do you remember who that girl was?" she asked with her eyes wide, looking at him. "I'll give you one guess!"

Jason started laughing, covering his eyes. It was hard keeping a straight face as she was retelling what happened. And it was true; he remembered carrying her down the trail. "I'm so sorry. Thank goodness you were light, even after being soaked to the skin."

Talia opened her mouth in disbelief at what he just said.

"Well, that was then. I have hiked since then and on my own two feet, staying away from creeks and stumps. But if this is what you want to do, I am more than willing to go hiking with you," she said.

He took her hand and kissed the back of it before saying, "Thank you. I honestly didn't think you would even remember that. You have to admit, we did a lot of fun things on that trip."

"Ya, we did. So, what made you want to go hiking here?" she asked.

He looked at her and sighed, putting one arm on the back of their seat and crossing one ankle over his knee. "This last Sunday, I rode the train back with a friend who is a doctor in Basel. His name is Jéan-Paul Lemaitre. I first met him back in the States, in Colorado. He was a visiting physician working with one of our hospitals. It turns out he wanted to work with paramedics to get a better understanding of what we did, that first contact in an emergency. So, over a two-year period, he would come for a week at a time, a couple of times a year, working in the hospital and working with us.

"When I told him that I had signed up for this work abroad program, he was excited and hoped that I would be one paramedic he would work with in the German paramedic program. He had told me about his job at the hospital in Basel, and about his wife, Suzanne. He said that he loved to hike, but she didn't. He has a place not far from Ollon. So, when he needs a break from everything, he heads down there for a long weekend to hike and relax, then takes the train back up to Basel.

"He said, if I ever get the chance, that I should head down toward Ollon. There are some excellent hiking trails and some beautiful scenery. He provided me with a map of the paths and his place. And he told me I was most welcomed to stay there whenever I wanted or needed. He was there two weekends ago.

"And, when I learned from your brother you would be here, that I was this close to you, I wanted to see you. I told Jéan-Paul a little about you and your family on our way down. I wasn't sure where or when I would have that opportunity to see you or find you, and then when I saw you standing near the river last Monday, I couldn't believe it. I told Jéan-Paul that you were standing right there. He and his wife turned to look at you just as you picked up the calico cat.

"We were getting ready to stand up when I leaned back and looked at you. I didn't know if you would even recognize me and maybe stay put. I wanted to get up and walk right over to you. You put the cat down, and next thing I know, you were headed back toward the buildings, and then was gone. We said our goodbyes. And as you said yesterday, the rest is history."

"So, I wasn't seeing things. It really was you," she said, looking at him and feeling hurt. "As soon as you saw me and knew it was me, why didn't you stand up and come to me?" Talia asked quietly, now looking straight ahead. Her thoughts were now rambling in her head. She turned her head slowly, and said, "So, what were these last four days? Why did you want to see me? We haven't seen or spoken to one another in what, fourteen years? And then here you are." She adjusted her body in the seat, turning and looking toward the front of the train.

Jason wasn't sure what just happened, but wanted to explain to her that this wasn't just some fling or that it would end when they parted. He saw the hurt in her eyes and distrust, and now the uncertainty about where this relationship might have gone or should have gone. Not what he wanted at all. He didn't know if she would sit still long enough for him to explain about the first time he saw her, that it was love at first sight. And each time they all were together, how excited he was to see her, be near her, and to touch her. He wished now he would have told her back then, but it scared him; maybe things would have turned out differently.

These last four days, he wanted to tell her how much he loved her, that he never stopped. She was right; it had been a long time, and he should have found a way to talk with her and be open about his feelings for her. Even though Jason had revealed a few times to Kurt how he felt about Talia, Kurt said nothing to her. It scared him that she wouldn't feel the same way about him. They were young. But she was always the one, and it just never seemed like the time was right. Maybe he just needed to have been upfront with her, now, from the very beginning.

Jason sat more upright and turned toward her. She was still staring toward the front of the train. "Talia, I'm sorry. I never meant to make you feel this way or hurt you. And this thing between us, these last four days, has meant the world to me. Each day, being close to you, holding your hand, giving you hugs and kisses, my heart felt so much love for you." He was trying to get her to look at him; she kept her eyes straight. He could see the glisten in her eyes and began to wonder if she actually might have feelings for him. "From the first time I laid eyes on you in Basel, you were nine, and I was fourteen. It was love at first sight for me. I couldn't believe that I had to be in Europe to fall so hard for someone from back home in the Midwest." He took a moment, still looking at her, hoping she was listening to him and what he was confessing to her.

Chapter 11

"Do you remember the Basel Zoo?" he asked. "We were all standing at the elephant enclosure, and you kept staring at them. You had this longing on your face. You told your mom you wanted to see all the zoos everywhere. It took a bit of bribery to head to the next enclosure. Your mom had asked my mom where we were from and what kind of work they did. Learning we were all from the same part of the Midwest, and that our moms were nurses, was like fate to me.

"Our parents had saved up for this trip to Switzerland for vacation, not even knowing one another. When it was time to leave to head home, I was so sad, and I didn't want to leave you; your family left a day later. So, I made it a point to keep in touch with Kurt. It just seemed easier, more comfortable to talk with him and bring up your name. You were young, and honestly, I didn't want you to think I was a creep. When plans were made for a vacation to Michigan, Porcupine Mountains, I changed what I was doing because I wanted to see you and be near you."

Jason continued to look at Talia, and she slowly turned her head and looked at him. His eyes then looked past her, out the window across the seat, with sadness. He cleared his throat and took a moment before continuing. "When I lived in Colorado, I met someone, and we dated for a couple of years. We were best friends, and I loved her. I could never get to that next stage with her; it was me, not her. There was always this empty space in here." He tapped his chest.

With a little shake of his head, she saw his eyes were glaring over, and she wondered what had happened. He continued. "Well over a year ago, while I was on duty, we had a call come in that there had been a horrible accident. Jéan-Paul was working with us that day. Everyone was called out: fire trucks, EMTs and us." Talia saw a tear roll down his cheek. Her eyes now had tears. "The weather was not good. We're responding to the call. We arrive at the scene and see that a car had tangled with a semi. It had gotten shoved hard up against the median barricade wall. It was such a mess. You couldn't tell the glass from the ice on the pavement.

"The firefighters had to go through the truck's passenger door to get the trucker out. He was injured but would be all right. The car was a different issue. It was sandwiched in so tight, we knew whoever was in that car died on impact. The guys worked on both front and rear windows. They were so twisted, and it seemed to take forever. Jéan-Paul was standing next to me and said he'd seen nothing like this before. He'd never been on the scene after an accident happened. And being a doctor, he just wanted to get in there and see what he could do to help, but..." His voice trailed.

"The rear window was removed, and we moved in while they were trying to remove the front window. The airbags were deployed in the front; there was no airbag in the back. We could pull the passenger out of the back seat. He was an older gentleman, had blood all over him, but he was dead. EMTs took him. Then Jim and I, and Mike and Jéan-Paul, we all jumped over the median and got around to the front of the car. Once we removed the airbags and saw the two women...," more tears fell from Jason's eyes, "I just stared at them. I couldn't believe my eyes: it was my best friend, Amy, and her mom. There was blood all over. I heard Jim say, 'Oh my god.' I yelled so loud, I lost it and started crying." Tears were falling from Talia's eyes. "Everyone stopped what they were doing and were looking my way. Jim told them who these people were. It was Jéan-Paul that grabbed my coat and pulled me away, staying with me. There was nothing anyone could do for them. They were gone." Tears were streaming down his cheeks. "I lost my best friend and her parents that day." Talia couldn't even imagine any of this, what he went through. Her heart ached for him.

Jason slowly shook his head back and forth. "I swore at everything holy that day. I was so angry, hurt and scared. After that, I quit dating because I never wanted to get that close to anyone and go through that kind of pain again." Wiping his tears away, he just stared at the seat in front of them. "Over time, I threw myself into my work, just wanting to be as busy as possible so I wouldn't have to think about the loss I was feeling, but still trying to be the best paramedic I could be, to be there for someone else. And I was good at what I did, and I still am." He turned to look at Talia. "I know how it feels to lose someone, just like you lost your dad."

"But I didn't lose him in a tragic accident and then have to see it," she said, with tears streaming down her cheeks.

"It wasn't until Kurt called me several months ago, out of the blue, and we talked about the accident and life. He told me about your dad's passing six months ago. I knew how close the two of you were, and I knew you were hurting, and I wanted to reach out to you. And I didn't. I couldn't. I wasn't ready, even though I just wanted to tell you I was sorry." She took hold of his hand.

He got a weak smile on his face, remembering, and said, "Turns out, Kurt's a darn good listener and friend. It must have been after your dad's accident, and he told me the two of you talked about things. I also didn't know if he had ever told you about the accident of my best friend." Talia shook her head no. He rubbed the palm of his free hand on his jeans. "I wondered if he brought up my name in your last conversation. I always wondered what it was the two of you were telling each other. And because he knew, I wondered if he ever told you how much I cared about you, and loved you." He slumped a little in his seat, leaning his head back, looking toward the roof of the train.

"I would think back to the times when we spent vacations together." He smiled, remembering those vacations. "I remembered your mom telling Kurt to stay close to you or hold your hand, and he'd pretend not to hear her, and then she might say, 'Jason, Kurt isn't listening to me, would you mind watching out for Talia,' and I got to be the one that watched over you, staying close and getting to hold your hand." Jason looked at her now. "It was me. Kurt would look at me with a grin. When I carried you down that trail in my arms, I was your protector and I was going to keep you safe." He turned his head toward the seat in front of him. "I didn't know if you ever asked questions about me or if you even cared that much. During those vacations, maybe you thought I was just someone that had to watch out for you because your brother didn't want to.

"During this last conversation, I told Kurt about the program in Germany and that I was one of five guys heading over. I was looking forward to the break, giving me a different focus. I told him I would do one week with the first two guys and then do the second week later when the other two flew in. They had families and didn't want to be gone from them more than that, so I was willing to split between the two of them. I didn't have a family to worry about, and I was all right with it. After telling Kurt this, I thought he forgot I was on the phone. I asked if he was OK, and he said yes, but he needed to tell me something." Jason looked back at her.

"That's when he told me you would be here, that it was your birthday gift you were giving yourself and you planned on being here for business and taking time for you. Kurt said, 'Jason, after all these years of you and me talking, knowing how you feel about Talia, if you ever wanted a chance at all to be with her, then you need to find her there.' He gave me the names of the hotels you were staying at, but honestly didn't know what your plans were. Maybe finding you and spending time with you would help lessen the pain of losing my best friend so tragically." He looked at her, thinking how that sounded coming out of his mouth. "This past week was NOT to replace what I had lost, but hopefully, to find the one that I thought I had lost and now found."

Tears fell from her cheeks. All Talia could say was, "I'm so very sorry for your loss." At that moment, she didn't think about anything else. She leaned into him, putting her arms around him, and placed her head on his chest, listening to his heartbeat. He placed his arm around her shoulder, taking her hand and kissing the back of it. They both now looked out the window.

☙

There was more than an hour to go. They sat like this the rest of the train ride to Villars. It took a lot of energy out of Jason, telling her this, and then not knowing for sure what their relationship would be like after it. He felt exhausted, almost emotionally spent, something that hadn't happened for a long time. Most men have been taught not to show emotion, to keep it inside, be a man; but here it came out, making him feel vulnerable. He didn't know what was going through Talia's mind, but it would have to keep. If all he had with her was this moment, he was taking it.

It was not the train ride she had envisioned. She had hoped for good conversation, just not this kind. It was hard for her to wrap her head around being the one to see someone you love taken so tragically, to see it with your very own eyes. *How does anyone do that? How do they get past it?* It was becoming darker outside because of the season and the mountains. No words came from either of them. And they both drifted asleep.

Jason woke to feel the train slowing down. They were pulling into the station and coming to a stop. Talia was still sleeping, nestled against him with her head drooping. "Talia." He gently nudged her. "Hey, love, we're here," not realizing what he just said. She opened her eyes and sat up, now trying to get the kink out of her side from leaning on him. Jason had stretched his arm out, as it fell asleep after being in the same position wrapped around her shoulder.

There weren't a lot of passengers on board this car, for which he was grateful. Hopefully, no one heard the long conversation the two of them had. It was around 6:45 p.m. They stood up and headed to get their luggage from the luggage rack, and soon stepped off the train. They found a shuttle that would take them to their hotel.

They hadn't eaten since early afternoon. Both were getting hungry and looking forward to having a bite to eat. Once at their hotel, they were checking in, when the desk clerk said they had a situation that they were not aware of until that morning, and sorry to inform them of this: the rooms had been overbooked because of a wedding, and the extra room Talia had wanted was no longer available. He was very sorry about this, and would check for other accommodations for the second party that would be with her, and that the hotel would provide compensation.

The clerk said that the room Talia had initially reserved had a big bed in it, but they could switch her with another guest where the room had two beds; she could decide. Talia just stood there for a moment, trying to think. Jason started to tell him he could check for other accommodations, but he was interrupted by Talia. She said, "No, just stop a minute. We can share my room; it's fine."

"Talia, are you sure about this? I'm OK with him checking for other accommodations." He wasn't. He didn't want to be separated from her. The desk clerk waited for her answer.

She looked at Jason and then the desk clerk, and calmly answered, "I'm all right with this; he's staying with me. I have this room for three nights, correct?" The clerk responded, yes. After getting them checked in, he gave her two room keys and told them when breakfast would be. Talia asked the clerk about the car that she had reserved for tomorrow. He said the vehicle would be delivered to the hotel in the morning and she would be given the key to it. So that time wasn't wasted in the morning, if she provided her driver's license and passport now, they would photocopy them for their records. The clerk asked if she was the one to do all the driving, and Jason said he would probably also be driving the car. The clerk then asked for his driver's license and passport as well; since both would drive the vehicle, both were placed on the insurance.

They headed up to their room, which was on the fourth floor, this time taking the elevator. They were quiet riding up. After entering the room, they saw that the room was a lovely size. Besides the large bed, there was one large overstuffed chair with an ottoman, a table, and two chairs. There was the usual dresser with a television on top, and the bathroom was a nice size.

Jason let Talia put her bag on the luggage stand; he put his bag on the ottoman. The silence between them annoyed Jason. Trying to make light of the situation where they would share the room and the bed, he said, "I can sleep on the floor or the big fluffy chair."

She sat on the edge of the bed and looked at it, and then back at him. It was a huge bed, and very fluffy. Hopefully, he didn't move around a lot when sleeping. She knew she didn't, or at least didn't think she did, and then she said with a half smile, "No, you're not sleeping on the floor. The only reason you might sleep on the floor is if you toss and turn, and then I kick you to the floor." He looked at her, nodding in agreement.

They were both tired and just wanted to get a bite to eat, so they headed down to the small restaurant attached to the hotel. They each ordered, and had a light conversation about what they would do tomorrow. Jason asked, "What time do you want to get up and leave for Ollon?"

"I checked the map. It's not that far from here, and we've got all day. I'd like to see what's in Ollon, and I know you want to go hiking. I'm thinking of waking up at around 8:00-ish. We could have breakfast, and then be on our way," she said, looking at him. "Oh, I don't have any hiking boots with me. Didn't know I was going to be that adventurous on this trip."

"Well, when we get to Ollon, why don't we see if we can find a hiking boot store and get you a pair," he said. She smiled and nodded.

When they finished eating, they headed back up to their room. She thought that sounded strange, "their room," but in a small way, also liked the sound of it. Jason walked over to the window, thinking it was just a window with a curtain. When he pulled the curtain open, he saw a sliding glass door leading to a small balcony with a little table and two chairs. Talia walked over as he opened the door and walked out. The air felt good, and you could see the outline of the mountains. There were so many stars. Jason stood next to her, both touching the balcony rail, and asked, "Do you have a preference for which side of the bed you want?" She turned and looked at the bed, saying, "I'll take the side near the bathroom."

"Thank you for letting me share your room. I promise to be on my very best behavior," he said, looking at her. It surprised him when she placed her hand on top of his.

After a moment, Talia said, "I'm going to get ready for bed. It's been a long day, and I want to feel fresh for tomorrow. I'll hurry in the bathroom." She turned and walked back through the balcony door.

He turned and called after her, "There's no hurry. I can wait."

While Talia was in the bathroom, Jason changed into a light pair of sweats, laid out the clothes he was going to wear, and then turned down the bed. He had pulled out the small backpack that he was going to take with him. It had some necessary medical supplies, including scissors, bandages, stethoscope, and a blood pressure cuff that many paramedics carried when they were not actually on duty.

Talia came out of the bathroom in what Jason thought looked like short shorts and a t-shirt. He liked what he was seeing. While traveling, she wanted to feel comfortable. It was what she had been wearing, and now Jason saw it. She looked at him, with his light sweatpants on and no shirt. She thought, *There's that bare chest again.* He saw her look at him with a questioning look, and then said, "I rarely wear a shirt to bed. I can put one on if you want me to."

Still looking at his chest, she said, "Um, no, whatever you usually wear."

"When I travel, I wear light sweats. Otherwise, when I'm home, I wear nothing." He just looked at her with a half grin. With that, she saw that he was putting things in a small bag, and had his clothes laid out neatly. "Do you always lay your clothes out so neatly?"

"It's a habit of being a firefighter. And the backpack is the paramedic bag that I'll be taking along."

"Oh. Well, that will be a good thing to bring along just in case someone trips over a stump and scrapes a knee or elbow. Although, it probably wouldn't do much good if someone falls into a creek," she said, remembering the last time it had happened.

"Exactly. Then, I'm heading to the bathroom," he said.

She looked around the room and saw that the patio door was still open. It had felt good, but there was now a slight chill, mostly because of what she was wearing. She closed it, and went to her side of the bed. She got under the covers, bringing the blanket close to her chest. The bed felt wonderful, and the pillow was soft. Her eyes drifted shut, and soon she was fast asleep.

Jason came out of the bathroom and saw that she was already asleep. He stood at the edge of the bed, just looking at her; she looked so peaceful, lying there. There was just enough light from the half-moon coming through the balcony door, and it shined across the bed. Turning off the lamp, he got under the covers, bringing the blanket up just past his waist. He turned his head to watch her sleep, wondering how amazing it would be to wake up next to her every morning. And with that, he fell asleep.

Chapter 12

Jason woke up and stared at the ceiling, then toward the balcony door; it was still dark outside. He looked at the clock on the nightstand and saw that it was only 5:30 a.m. He turned onto his right side toward Talia, who had turned on her stomach and now facing him. His eyes adjusted to the dark room, and he saw her long hair half draped over her face. She was still, but breathing steadily. He wondered, if he were to move the hair from her face and move it back over her shoulder, if she would wake up startled and punch him out of defense. He grinned to himself. He felt if he could move the hair from her face, she might breathe better but didn't know for sure; he'd never had long hair.

He was getting ready to move her hair, when she rolled almost over on her back, putting her left side closer to him, and all but hitting him with her arm which now lay next to him. After rolling over, the blanket partially came off, exposing her now twisted t-shirt. She was so close to him. He could feel the heat from her body, and he just wanted to cradle her in his arms, but this would have to do. He laid his head back down and closed his eyes, breathing in the scent of her, and fell back asleep.

They woke up simultaneously at about 7:30 a.m., the light coming through the balcony door. Talia was in the same position he saw her in earlier this morning before he fell asleep. She was now half-awake and started to roll herself to the left, turning into Jason. Not remembering he was there, her eyes opened more fully, and she looked at him. He was looking back at her with a half grin on his face and raised eyebrows, looking at where she was, and he liked it.

Jason adjusted himself, placing his right arm down with his hand cradling his head. He looked at her, his eyes scanning down her partially uncovered body and back up to her face. He whispered, "Good morning."

"Good morning," she said.

"Did you sleep well?" Jason asked.

"I did. I slept like a log, uh, not a log," she replied. Jason chuckled because they had talked about someone tripping over a stump.

"We could get up and get dressed, or we could stay here longer." He preferred the latter, but knew that would not happen. Talia looked at him with not much of an expression. "Would you like to use the bathroom first or should I?" he asked.

She sat up and looked back at him. "I think... I'll let you go first," she said slowly. "You already have your clothes laid out; I don't. I have to figure out what I'm going to wear."

"OK." He got out of bed and headed for the bathroom. She heard the shower running, and thought she best figure out what clothes she was going to wear. She rummaged through her bag, finding her jeans, a top, her camisole, and bra and underwear. She laid out her sweater and light jacket, just because she figured it would be on the cool side in the mountains, and she took out some socks to wear. Jason said they'd have to buy her a pair of hiking boots. She hoped they wouldn't do too much hiking, as she would be wearing new boots that wouldn't have been broken in yet. With clothes laid out, waiting for him to get out of the bathroom, Talia walked over to the balcony door and opened it up. "Wow, chilly air," she said.

She didn't hear Jason coming out of the bathroom. "Ya, just a little chilly." She promptly closed the door, and turned around to see him with just a towel around his waist. His chest was still a little wet from his shower, and so was his hair. All she could do was look at him standing there, and then she started walking past him. She stopped and looked at him. "You're enjoying this just a little too much," she said.

"You think?" he said with a grin, looking at her.

She continued toward the bathroom, picking up her clothes. After getting dressed, and with the bathroom fan on, she opened the door to let fresh air in. She put her hair up so she could start applying her makeup. As she looked through her makeup bag, she saw him out of the corner of her eye and glanced his way. He was leaning against the door frame of the bathroom, just watching her quietly. She asked him, "Are you going to stand there and watch me put my makeup on?"

"Would it bother you if I did?" he replied.

"I've never had anyone watch me put my makeup on, so I don't know if it would bother me or not. It's a process most women go through to look nice and feel good about themselves, and it takes time," she answered.

She started applying her makeup, and he took a step toward her, watching her. She stopped for a moment, a slight smile forming on her face, took a breath, and then continued. He stood there watching her for a few moments longer, taking a last step inside the bathroom, giving her a quick kiss on the side of her head, and then turned around and left the room. She finished her makeup, redid her hair the way she wanted, and brushed her teeth.

Taking the clothes that she wore to bed, she put them in her large bag, organized it and then closed it. *Now I'm ready*, she thought to herself.

Jason had opened the balcony door, and was standing just outside of it. She walked toward him, putting on her sweater. She stepped out onto the balcony, walking to the railing, and took a deep breath; the sun felt good on her face. She turned around, and again he was looking at her. "I'm hungry. Let's get breakfast," she said, and headed back inside, walking toward the bed and picking up her bag and light coat. Jason closed the balcony door, locking it. He picked up his jacket and backpack and followed her out.

They got their breakfast and found a place to sit down. Talia saw the bananas and apples, and thought that she should grab those before they headed out; she wanted the extra fruit. Before they had finished, the desk clerk that helped them last night came over to them and asked if everything was all right with the room. Jason looked up at him, and said,

"Yes, it worked out perfectly. Thank you." The desk clerk smiled and said, when they were ready, they could pick up the keys for the car; it was sitting outside, ready for them.

After finishing breakfast, Talia got another coffee and grabbed the fruit, sticking them in her bag. She turned to see Jason looking at her like, *'what are you doing?'* She looked back at him, and gestured with her hand for him to turn around and go. He shook his head, grinning. Standing at the front desk, Jason said there was a car waiting for them and could they get the keys? Since this was a new person on duty, they asked for identification to match the paperwork. Jason pulled out his license and passport. After matching them up, the desk clerk gave Jason the keys and a receipt for the car, reminded them that they also drive on the right-hand side of the road, and then told them to have a pleasant day.

Their rental car was a Silver Audi A6 four-door. Jason liked this already. It's been over two weeks since he's driven, and he missed it. Putting on their seat belts, Jason started the car. There was a full tank of gas that she had paid for beforehand. They put in the GPS the address for the *Boothaus* in Ollon; it would take them on *Route de Villars*, showing their driving time. It didn't seem so far.

Leaving the hotel, they followed the directions out of town. It was smooth driving, with Talia getting to see more of the scenery than Jason. He tried doing more looking, and Talia told him to keep his eyes on the road, which didn't seem fair to him; a hard thing for drivers to do when they also wanted to look. It's a perk for any passenger, and even those back seat drivers.

The roads here were narrower than the roads in the U.S. They were passing through a small town, and soon the first hairpin curve appeared, making Jason slow down considerably; and then there was a second hairpin curve. Not knowing these roads, he went a bit slower. Trying to look around would not work. He needed to pay attention to what was in front of him. Traffic was light.

Jason said, "Tell me about your shopping trip on Monday." She thought maybe he just needed some noise in the car, but she was happy to tell him about it. "Well, I left that morning and took the tram through town. It stopped close to the first fabric store, and I only had to walk across the street." (She made sure she said, 'fabric store.') "I told them who I was, and that I had ordered from them online, and they had shipped to me.

"There was so much to look at and touch. Then I had to decide, and that wasn't easy. But once I made my purchases, they were more than happy to ship those for me. I was glad I didn't have to carry those bolts around, as I would have looked silly, and there was no little red wagon I could put them in to take them with me. And besides, they were heavy, and how would I have carried those on a tram, much less an airplane." She stated and glanced at him, and he seemed to be listening. He had a slight curl of his lip, but she didn't think he was that interested. Soon, they came to another hairpin curve, which was sharp; he had to slow way down.

Once they were past that curve, she continued to tell him about the next store while looking out the window. "So, I walked to the next two; it would have been silly to take a tram three or four blocks away. Anyway, it was called *The Sempiano*." She tried to spell it out and giggled. "This was a high-end fabric store." She emphasized that it was 'high-end' fabric, and then, *Whoa*, here was another hairpin curve. As they made it around that one, she started again, telling him about the kinds of fabric, "There was a large selection to choose from; so many tweeds, gorgeous silks, beautiful brocade, and lots of fine linen and cotton. I wonder where all these fabric stores get their supplies from; that would be interesting to find out, don't you think? You probably wouldn't care. Most men don't, and perhaps most women don't care either." She looked over toward him to see if it was getting annoying yet with the noise in the car, but he just kept looking and driving down the road.

So she continued by saying, "This store was also happy to ship for me, which was great, because I honestly didn't know how I would even get these bolts on the plane, plus the ones I bought earlier, and I didn't want to have to purchase a third seat for them." She looked his way once again.

This time, he turned his head toward her, glancing at her, and then his eyes were back on the road. She stopped talking for a moment, and here came two more hairpin curves. She saw that the GPS showed the road would be straight for many miles after those two.

She waited a moment before starting about the last store. "My last stop was *R. Carrington.* It was awesome, so much color. I had to take my time and look at everything, including the trim and ribbon in every color. And because I bought so much, they would ship those for me. I could have probably taken all those with me, but I didn't have enough room in my bag, and it would be so much to carry onto the plane." She wondered if he was going to tell her enough with the talking now. It was the look on his face every time she started with another store. It was rather funny to her. And then he slowed way down, and she looked to see if there was something ahead or another curve.

"Are you finished talking about the fabric stores?" he asked.

"For now," she said. "You wanted me to tell you. At least you heard that I was talking about fabric stores. Does that mean you were paying attention?"

"You're lucky I didn't pull this car over and kiss you so you would stop talking about the fabric stores," he said.

"Oh, in that case, I can tell you all about the ones back home," Talia said, laughing. He then pulled the car over, stopped abruptly, unhooked his seat belt, leaned over, and kissed her. With eyes wide, she didn't think he'd actually stop the car. He just looked at her with one eyebrow raised. She whispered, "Do you want peace and quiet?" He leaned over and kissed her one more time. She loved it.

After putting his seat belt back on and shifting the car into drive and accelerating, she quickly said in a whisper, "You want a piece of fruit," and started laughing, trying to be quiet. He slowed down again, and this time she covered her laugh with her hand and did a "zip the lip" motion. She didn't say another word. As they approached the town of Ollon, there were just a few curves he had to slow down for, but not like the last five or six.

The GPS took them straight to the *Boothaus*. Jason found a parking space in front of the store. Shutting off the engine, he unbuckled his seat belt and opened his door. Talia unbuckled her seat belt, and Jason told her to stay put. She didn't know why, and looked around to see what was going on. Jason came around and opened her door, taking her hand, and helping her out. She stood looking at him with a closed grin, as her mouth was still on lockdown. She moved so he could close the door and then lock the car. While still looking at him, she pointed to her closed lips and pretended to unlock her mouth. He shook his head and said, "Now who's the smart-alek," and kissed her. Still holding her hand, they both walked into the *Boothaus*.

Once inside, a well-dressed man came over and started asking in Italian, *"Benvenuti alla Boothaus, Posso aiutarla?"* Jason just looked at him.

Talia replied, *"Lei parla inglese?"* Jason looked at Talia.

The clerk turned and said, *"Si,"* then asked one of the other attendants, *"Puoi aiutare questo cliente."*

Jason asked, "What did he say?"

Talia said, "He said, 'Welcome to the *Boothaus*, can I help you?' and I asked, 'Do you speak English?' And then he said, 'yes' and asked if someone would help us." She looked at him.

"I'm not even going to ask how you know Italian," Jason said.

A female attendant, who had been standing at a cash register close to the front door, then came over, and in reasonably good English asked, "What can I help with?"

Talia replied, "I'm looking for a pair of hiking boots." With that, the attendant took them over to that section for Talia to look at and try on some boots. There were so many. They were on the expensive side. Talia tried on several pairs of boots and finally found one pair that she liked, and it was reasonably priced. As they headed up to the register, Talia got her bag and started to open it. Jason had already pulled out a card to pay for them.

"Jason, no. I can pay for my boots."

"Talia, I have no doubt that you can, but I'm the one who said we needed to get you a pair of hiking boots, and I intend on paying for them," he replied quietly.

She started to object, and he lowered his head a bit with a raised eyebrow, handing his card to the attendant. Talia just pursed her lips together. Once the boots were paid for and as she was giving him the receipt, the attendant said, *"Innamorato."* Talia looked at her, picked up the bag with the boots in them, and walked to the door. Jason said thank you to her and followed Talia out.

"Talia, what did she say?" Jason asked.

"What?" She pretended not to hear him, stepping off the curb toward the car.

With a tilt of his head, he said, "I asked a simple question: what did the attendant say? If you didn't know, I don't speak Italian."

She stood there a moment, looking at him, and then said, "'In love.'"

He stood a moment, and then unlocked the door. "Oh. She referring to you or me?" He opened the door so Talia could get in, and then went around to his side. She put her package on the floor.

Once they were both inside, with their seat belts on, Jason started the car. Talia turned toward him and said, "Since this is your day, do you want to head to the place where Jéan-Paul told you about the trails now, or is there anything else you'd like to do first?" He looked straight ahead with a cheesy grin, and then turned toward her and said, "Well, let's see. Since it took you a while trying on boots, and it's close to lunchtime, maybe we can find a place to have a bite to eat and then head for the hills."

"Oh, geez." Talia rolled her eyes. "Well, why don't you ask Google where the nearest restaurant is so we can go there. I'm putting on my boots."

Jason asked Google where the nearest restaurant was. It responded with *"Si prega di ripetere"* in Italian. "OK, what, no English, huh? What did it say?" He looked at Talia.

"It said for you to please repeat," she replied.

"How do you know what it said?" Jason asked gruffly.

"I've been taking Italian classes, and my instructor always said that phrase until we finally got it, and it stuck," Talia said.

"OK, miss smarty-pants, why don't you ask Google about the nearest restaurant."

"Dove si trova il ristorante più vicino." And it came up with a few. Then Talia said, "Why don't we find a grocery store and pick up a few things, maybe cheese and crackers, some bread, and fruit, and some chocolate that we can take on the hike, and something to drink? I like restaurants, but I'm getting a little tired of them."

"I hear you. And you already have fruit in your bag," Jason said. "OK, so where might a grocery store be here?" He started looking out the window.

"Google, *negozio di alimentari più vicino?* Oh, nice, there's one close by." She plugged in the address.

Jason just looked at her. He drove right to the store. Parking, they got out and headed in. Finding several kinds of cheese, crackers, chocolates and bread, they walked by the fruit so Talia could at least look. She spotted something she wanted to try, and then they found bottled water. She also spotted condiments, plastic silverware and napkins. With food in hand, they headed for the counter. There were good-sized canvas bags that would hold your goods and zipped. After making their purchase and placing them in the bags, Talia said, *"Grazie,"* and they headed out the door. Jason figured that meant, "thank you."

Chapter 13

Placing their goods in the back seat, Talia asked, "Where's the information Jéan-Paul gave you about his hiking trail?"

"It's in my backpack," he said. Talia reached for it, giving it to him. Finding the map and information, he opened it up to look at it.

"OK, here is the map showing where his place is, and the trail that he goes on is here. It looks like maybe a couple of miles apart. His place is on the way back to Villars." Jason started the car and proceeded to head out of town. Once they arrived at the parking area, they saw that Jéan-Paul had circled where the trail began that he used. There were two different trails, both equivalent in distance. One was more scenic than the other, which is the one he took often. Jason folded the map, and put it in a zippered pocket on his sweatshirt. Talia left her bag in the car, but took the canvas bag with the food. She grabbed her jacket, put it on, and was ready to go. Jason grabbed his jacket, also put it on, and then his backpack.

"OK, let's do this. Jéan-Paul said the trail was pretty easy to follow and had good markers for about eight or ten miles. Each marker is a mile."

"We're hiking ten miles? Do you know how far ten miles is in the mountains?" Talia asked. Jason turned around and nodded with a smile, fully aware they wouldn't be doing the ten miles; that's twenty miles round-trip, kind of payback for all the walking tours he did with her, and totally enjoyed. He wondered how far she would get.

"Oh, good lord, why did I agree to do this! I was thinking maybe four or less round-trip," she said under her breath.

The trail started at an even level. They saw open fields and birds and some deer. They had been slowly climbing and now had passed Marker 2. They came across a scenic station and stopped to enjoy a picnic, eating some of the cheese and crackers and chocolate they had purchased. It was beautiful up there. Lots of wildflowers were growing, and the mountains were amazing, and now she got to hike in them. Jason stopped for a moment and told her to turn around and look at the view, and to also see how high they had already come. They continued on. The higher up they went, the air got cooler, and she was getting a little out of breath, but she wasn't going to tell him that. Talia was glad for her sweater and light jacket she was wearing as well as her new boots.

They had passed Marker 3 and were almost to Marker 4, which they could see fifty feet in front of them. They also saw clouds moving in. It was supposed to be nice the whole day, but the clouds showed the possibility of rain. They decided it would be best to head back down to their car. Approaching Marker 3, it started misting pretty good. Before reaching Marker 2, it was light rain. By the time they got to Marker 1, it was coming down steadily, and they still had a mile to go. Reaching the car, they got inside quickly, soaking wet, and no towels to dry off with. And here it was, their rental car, now getting the seats wet. Jason started it, putting the heat on so they wouldn't chill.

Not knowing these roads, and the fact that they were narrow with lots of hairpin curves to maneuver, he took it more slowly. He'd driven the mountain roads in Colorado when the weather wasn't bad, and that was scary enough. These roads were a little nerve-wracking dry, and now they were driving on wet pavement. Following the main highway south and then heading northward toward Villars was going to take a bit longer. With it getting dark due to the rain, the headlights came on, and the wipers were clipping along. They came to the first curve, which was sharp. All of Jason's focus had to be on the road. Talia kept silent.

There were some stone walls for protection if you slid, but once you passed those, it was at your own risk. There were no other cars on the road; nothing behind them, and no one in front of them. Here, people knew to stay off the roads in conditions like these. As it continued raining hard, he also had to ride the brakes in some areas because they were actually heading downhill. Then came a very sharp curve, making Jason very nervous. He told Talia to pull out of his right pocket the map Jéan-Paul gave him. She opened it up to see where they might be, putting on the visor light.

Knowing they just did two sharp hairpin curves, she followed it and told Jason that Jéan-Paul's cabin was about two miles ahead and on the right. He didn't say anything. After seeing what happens to vehicles on Colorado mountain roads, he wasn't taking any chances trying to make it back to Villars, which was at least another fifteen miles. He had precious cargo sitting next to him. Remembering the road that they had taken this morning, heading for the cabin would be the smartest thing to do.

Jason had also been watching the odometer, clocking the two miles. Knowing they should be able to turn on the road to the cabin in just a moment, he almost felt a sense of relief, but couldn't. Not yet. Not until he was able to turn on the road. Once they reached it, they had to check the address number to make sure it was correct, and it was. He turned and headed up the road, slowly noting there were many ruts from previously being driven on when it rained and then dried that way. Approaching the cabin, there was a slight incline. Jason was trying to get the car up it with no success, but at least they were here. They would have to make a run for the porch.

They couldn't just sit in the car; they were both soaked and could easily get chilled and get sick. Jason grabbed his backpack, while Talia grabbed her bag and the food bag. "OK, are you ready to run to the porch?" he asked.

"Do we have a choice?" she said.

Because it was raining so hard, the ruts had filled with water. They both opened their doors and started running for the porch. Neither of them saw the ruts made by a previous car; Talia's foot went down into one, and she fell. Jason was at the porch, and turned around and saw that Talia wasn't behind him. He dropped his backpack and headed down toward the car, seeing that she was on the ground trying to get up. He helped her up and saw that she was limping, and promptly picked her up while she held the bags.

She yelled, "What do the mountains have against me?"

Once on the porch, he sat her down on a chair he saw. He looked where Jéan-Paul told him the key would be, and found it. Unlocking the door and feeling for the light switch on the inside, he turned the light on, picked Talia up, took her inside and then went back for the bags. It felt later than what it was due to the rain and being in the mountains, and it was dark outside. It was only 5:30 p.m.

Taking off his soaked vest jacket, Jason quickly took off his boots and then helped take Talia's boots off. First, the left one. She winched having her right boot taken off, grabbing his arm so he would take it off slowly. She tried to move her ankle a bit, thinking it felt better just getting the boot off. He helped her take off her jacket and sweater. Both were soaked, and her jeans were muddy and soaked.

He knew he had to get her wet clothes off so she wouldn't chill and get sick. They didn't need that, being so far from home, and her hair was dripping wet. Jason then took off her wet socks to get a better look at her right ankle; there didn't seem to be any swelling yet. He knew he still preferred to put some ice on it. "I'm going to the kitchen to see if there is ice." He left, then brought back a towel with ice in it. He put it gently on her ankle, having her hold it in place. He didn't see any swelling or redness, but it might still appear. He also had a couple of kitchen towels so they could wipe off their hands and face.

"Are you feeling any pain?" he asked.

"No, I don't think so. Maybe a slight headache, and I'm cold."

"I know. We'll get that remedied in a moment. Are you hurt anywhere else?" He was checking her legs and knees, making sure she wasn't injured.

He grabbed his bag and pulled out some ibuprofen, and then grabbed the food bag with their water in it, pulling her bottle out, and she took them. "OK, I'm heading into the bedroom to find blankets and clothes, and I'll get a fire started. We'll be able to drape our wet clothes over the chairs, and the warmth of the fire should help dry them." He headed to the bedroom.

❧

Talia was thinking out loud: "Geez, there's nothing worse than looking like a drowned rat, and spraining my ankle at the same time. This already played out once before, remember. At least I didn't fall into a creek; no, I just had the sky open up and dump on me. And instead of tripping over a stump or log, you cover up a rut with water that I don't see and trip into it. Thanks a lot."

"Talking to someone?" Jason had been standing there when she made her speech to whomever it was that she was blaming.

"Maybe. What is it with me and mountains, anyway," she said, making it more of a statement.

"Jéan-Paul didn't have a lot in his closet. And there are no womens' clothes because Suzanne doesn't come up here with him. But I did find these: a couple of long-sleeved shirts and a pair of long pants. Sorry, but I think I'm going to need the pants since mine are also soaked. Here are several blankets, and I have one for you on the back of the chair." He saw she was shivering. He dropped the other blankets on the floor near the fireplace.

"Let me look at your ankle." He still wasn't seeing any swelling, only a slight redness. She was very fortunate, because that rut was pretty deep. "OK, let's see if you can stand on it at all." He helped her up slowly. She put a little weight on it and stood for a moment and took a breath in. She moved her ankle, testing it, and then taking a step or two.

"It's just sore, but I can stand on it," she said.

Looking at her, he said, "You take the long shirt and get out of those wet clothes, and take the blanket with you. I'm going to start a fire and get out of my clothes. We'll drape them over these chairs."

She took the shirt and blanket, and slowly hobbled to the bathroom. She turned to ask, "Do you know if there is hot water?"

"I don't know. If you want to take a shower, you'll have to test it," he said.

She thought having a hot shower would help warm her up and get the dirt off after falling. She started the shower, and soon it was hot, or hot enough. She took her clothes off and stepped in. She was still shivering, but slowly warmed up. She didn't want to take too long, just in case Jason wanted to take one as well, not knowing how much water there might be. She finished up, drying herself with the towel that was in the bathroom. She checked her clothes to see how wet they were. Her jeans were soaked, her t-shirt, cami, and bra were wet, and her underwear seemed to mostly escape it. She put those back on, then put the long shirt on, buttoning some of the buttons. It came down to her knees. *Jéan-Paul must be a tall man.*

She wrapped the blanket around her, picked up her clothes, walked out of the bathroom back to the living room where Jason had a good fire going. His clothes were draped over one of the chairs, and another chair was placed closer to the fire. She draped her clothes over the back of the chair, making sure her jeans hung separately, letting the legs hang down, giving them more space to dry. She sat down on the big overstuffed chair, feeling the warmth of the fire and stared into it. She looked around the room. The living area had a huge, thick woven rug on the floor and a second large chair with a small round table sitting between them. She saw a small bookcase with some books in it. There were no pictures that she could see. There was a table sitting next to the large window near the front door with an empty vase sitting on it. The chairs that went with it were now being used to drape clothes over. There was a pair of snowshoes that hung near the front door and a large winter coat hanging on a door rack.

Minutes had passed, and she was now getting warm, and a little tired and thirsty. She picked up her bottle of water and drank some, setting it back down on the floor.

She thought the cabin looked smaller from the outside than it actually was on the inside. Looking toward the bedroom, she wondered if Jason went to lie down for a bit, tired after driving on that road and in the rain. Those roads were crazy; it made her tired, and she was just a passenger. She got up, leaving the blanket draped over the chair, and walked to the bedroom to see if he was in there. She looked in, and a little lamp was on, but he wasn't there. She left the door open.

There was another room on the other side of the cabin. She saw a dim light coming from the partially closed door, so she walked toward it. Slowly opening the door, it made a little sound. She stood quietly in the doorway. She watched his strong arms as they were moving back and forth, sanding some wood. She saw that he had put on the long pants and the other shirt, much shorter than the one she was wearing. He had the sleeves rolled up.

She started to walk slowly toward him and then stopped. Just being near him, she could smell the faint scent of the aftershave he used that morning. It smelled so good. She saw that it was a long wood bench, and wondered why he was working on it.

She looked around the room. It was about as big as the other one, and she wondered if this might have been an extra bedroom now turned into a workroom, especially since Jéan-Paul was the only one who came here. Maybe this was a hobby, woodworking. There were shelves with tools on them, and little boxes, probably holding sandpaper and nails and other miscellaneous things needed when working on wood. She had all but turned around, and when she turned back toward Jason, he was looking at her. There were two of those workhorse benches, and Jason was sitting on one of them. He didn't say anything but motioned for her to come closer. She took the steps that would take her right to him. He looked her up and down.

"You look good in that shirt. I'm kind of sorry I made you go hiking. If we hadn't, maybe we wouldn't have gotten caught in the rain, and you wouldn't have stepped into the rut." His voice was soft and gentle. "While you were in the bathroom, I called the hotel and explained what happened, and that we would be back tomorrow. And I called Jéan-Paul to let him know we were here."

She nodded. "So, what are you doing in here?" she asked.

He replied, "Jéan-Paul says it helps him to relax when things haven't gone well at the hospital. He would do some hiking, and then spend time in here. He's done this for years. He knew I was also interested in woodworking, and he told me that if something was troubling me, I should do this. Working with wood seems to help."

"So, do you have something that's troubling you?" she asked, looking into his eyes. "Who or what is troubling you?" He was quiet, looking back at her. She was thinking that he still misses "her" and decided to leave the room. She started to turn away, and he took hold of her arm, bringing her back to him.

Softly, she said, "I know you must still miss her. It takes time to heal, and you don't just get over it. When you were with her, Amy, you said you could never get to the next stage with her; there was always this empty space in here." Talia touched his chest. "What needs to fill that space so that hurt goes away?"

He pulled her close and slid his warm hands inside her shirt, bringing her to him, and leaned his head against her chest. He heard her heart beating more rapidly, and then her arms wrapped around his shoulders and neck, holding him. In a quiet, gentle voice, he said, "I did love her, but I wasn't in love with her. That space that you want to know what will help make the hurt go away has been slowly filling up for the last five days." He took a moment and looked at her.

"It's not my heart that needs filling, but yours. Yours is the one that's slowly been filling. The moment I saw you near the river, my heart was overjoyed and filled with so much love for you. With all that I have in me, I want to fill that empty space so that your hurt goes away." He took his right hand and slowly slid it around against her skin under her breast, placing his hand over her heart. Still looking at her, he felt her body lightly trembling and saw the tears rolling down her cheeks. "I told you, from the first time I laid eyes on you, I knew I loved you. That love has never gone away. And each day that I've spent with you, I've fallen more in love. That empty space in here, I can fill that so it overflows, if you'll let me."

Chapter 14

Jason slowly rose, bringing his hands to her face to wipe away her tears, and kissed her. He whispered, "As much as I want you, I won't do that to you until you're ready. Love doesn't hurt." He moved past her, and walked out of the room, leaving her to stand there.

Minutes pass. He was bent down, adding wood to the fire. Embers rose and fell as he stared into the flames. He felt her presence behind him, and slowly rose and turned toward her. She looked into his eyes, a look he hadn't seen from her before. She raised her arm up and slowly held out her hand to him, still looking into his eyes. He took her hand, waiting for her to take that first step. It needed to be her move, not his. He waited patiently. The fire behind him crackled, taking the chill out of the room. It was the only light besides the soft glow from the bedroom.

She raised her other hand to the buttons on her shirt, slowly unbuttoning each one, leaving her skin exposed to the warmth of the fire, and him. Still holding his hand, she took that step toward him, and they were inches apart. She knelt to the floor, drawing him down with her. She unbuttoned his shirt and then removed it from his shoulders, letting it fall behind him. He slowly removed her shirt, letting it fall to the floor. She reached up to his face, cradling it in her hands, and gently pulled it to her as his hands took hold of her waist. She kissed his lips softly. He looked at her lips, and she formed the words, "I love you." Three beautiful words.

He lowered himself to the floor, drawing her down to him. He wrapped his arms around her, kissing her gently while caressing her body, then up toward her breast. With a gentle touch, she caressed his body, moving up to his chest, up his strong arm and to his face. He gave her all the love he has always wanted to give her.

The light from the fire was dimming. Jason held her in his arms, looking at her, never wanting to let go. The blankets he had dropped on the floor earlier were now wrapped around them as they lay on the thick-woven rug. She looked at the small embers floating in the air, her arm draped across his chest. Her hand caressed his skin, and she could feel his heartbeat, a steady rhythm. She understood now about filling that space so the hurt would go away. She felt him kiss the top of her head, and they fell asleep on the floor.

☓

Still covered in the blanket, Talia could feel the warmth; it was the fire burning a little brighter, the only light in the room, and she could hear the crackling of the flames. She looked to where Jason had been lying next to her, and then turned to see him sitting near her legs, just looking at her. She gave him a small smile, and her stomach fluttered as she looked back at him and put her hand out. Not a word was spoken as he moved back to his place next to her. Once again, he took her in his arms, kissing her deeply and loving her so she would never forget that love doesn't hurt.

When Talia opened her eyes again, the room was lighter, more from the outside world, the room still feeling comfortable from the fire. Jason was still lying beside her. She smiled, looking at him, seeing that he was looking at the logs that burned, providing the soft glow and warmth. His arm was still wrapped around her, holding her close with his shoulder as her pillow. She again had draped her arm partially over his chest, feeling the steady beat of his heart. He turned his head toward her, giving a kiss on the forehead and then kissing her gently on the lips. It soon would be time that they would have to get up and head back to Villars. "I don't want this to end," she said.

As he looked at her, he said, "It doesn't have to end. I have wanted you in my life for so long. I want to share my life with you and continue to see things through your eyes, the way you've shown me this past week. I love you so much."

She rose and leaned over him, giving a kiss first on his chest and then on his lips. Talia whispered, "I love you. I didn't know how much. Each time we saw each other growing up, the crush I had on you was getting stronger, and I locked it away for that someday, rainy day, if it were ever to show up. I get it now, all the times you held my hand whenever you could, wanting to be close to me." She smiled. "Who knew falling into a creek and tripping would put me in your loving and protective arms. And yesterday, getting rained on and stepping in a rut again brought you to me, in your loving and protective arms. Lying beside you, still in your loving and protective arms." He raised his head toward her and kissed her, not wanting this moment to end either.

She lay back on his shoulder and, after a few moments, was smiling and remembering the trip to Colorado. He saw the smile, and asked, "What are you remembering?"

She took a slow deep breath, looking into the fire. "Do you remember when we all took the cog train up to Pikes Peak, the sound of the cogs on the rails as we were heading toward the summit?" She looked at Jason as he smiled back at her, remembering. "The view just kept getting better and better; the one sitting next to me. It was getting colder; we all had on light jackets. There were so many people on the train. Our parents had their seats, but Kurt, you, and I shared a seat. Kurt sat on the aisle while you sat next to the window, and I was sandwiched between the two of you. Someone had opened a window a little, and the cold air came in before someone asked if they'd close it. I was shivering. You put your arm on the back of our seat, shifting yourself and then had me move closer to you, keeping me warm."

"I remember it very well. You know, I had that planned," he said, still looking at her with his smile. He was waiting for her to continue.

"Even before we reached the summit, people were pointing out their windows looking at the bighorn sheep, cell phones and cameras clicking away. Once we reached the top and got off the train, we walked over to a scenic point, looking at that incredible view." Jason remembered the view standing next to him. "It was so clear and windy that day, and I was getting cold. Our moms were heading into the gift shop, and I followed. There were so many people inside, you could lose track of anyone in there," she said.

Jason said, "Yup. We almost lost you. I wasn't too far from your mom and Kurt when she turned to show you something and you weren't beside her. She asked Kurt to find you. He didn't seem to enjoy the experience of bumper-to-bumper people trying to get past them. And I started looking for you. Maybe being close to six feet tall had some advantages while looking for someone who's only about five foot five." He smiled at her. "I saw you across the room and headed toward you. I took hold of your cold hand, telling you your mom is looking for you."

"Oh ya, they were so cold, and yours weren't," she said.

Jason said, "Once I got you back to your mom, I thought, *'I'll have to let go of your hand,'* even though I didn't want to; I didn't want her to see me holding her daughter's hand. You looked up at me, like, why did I let go, and then you saw your mom looking at us. She didn't say a word, but started telling you about some jackets or zip-up sweatshirts." Talia moved her arm, sliding it down a little, playing with some hairs on his chest.

"We must have been up there almost an hour before taking the train back down." She got a big grin on her face, looking at him. "I remember Kurt sitting by the window, and you were now sitting in the aisle seat. You put your arm on the back of our seat with your other hand, holding onto the seat in front of us. I imagine so that you wouldn't fall off onto the floor. You almost did, and I couldn't help but giggle. Your face was like, 'don't you dare laugh if I do end up on the floor.'" She giggled now, remembering his face.

"I wondered if there were parts of that trip you would remember," Jason said as he continued looking at her. He took his free hand and placed it on top of hers, lying on his chest, then lacing their fingers together. "Do you remember the Air Force Academy?" he asked, and she nodded yes. "Seeing the beautiful Cadet Chapel, inside and out, there's nothing like it anywhere. I'm sure your dad was thrilled to see it, with him being an architect. But do you remember hearing why we went to see it?" She shook her head no. "My dad was in the Air Force as a mechanic. I think seeing it brought back good memories for him. I remember him telling us about the time he spent there. He looked delighted that he could share that with all of us that day. I know it meant a lot to him."

As he lay there looking at her, he didn't want this to end, but they would have to get up. The room was cooling down, and they would have to leave soon. He breathed, "I would love to lay here with you the whole day, but I'm afraid we have to get that car back."

She smiled at him and gave a nod. "I know," she replied. "Do you suppose our clothes are dry?" They both sat up, and she reached for the shirt she had worn, putting it on, not buttoning it. He reached up to the chair that was holding her clothes and felt them. He took hold of her jeans, giving them to her. They were dry, but had some mud on them. Then he pulled down her shirt, cami, and bra, looking at her as he handed them to her. She gathered all of her clothes before standing up, kissed him, and walked to the bathroom.

When she came out, Jason was dressed. The blankets were folded and lying on the chair, along with the pants and shirt he had on. She placed Jéan-Paul's shirt on the chair. Jason was in the kitchen, and had put the cheese and crackers, bread and fruit on the counter with two plates. He had a teapot on the stove, and there were two cups and two spoons. He pointed to the two small packets on the counter and asked, "Which one do you want? The Snickerdoodle or the Amaretto?"

She giggled and asked, "Where did you get those? Those aren't from here in Switzerland. Did you bring those with you?"

"No. Your brother sent them to me in Germany. He asked if I remembered which ones you liked. I said I did, and if he could send them, that would be great," he replied. She walked around and kissed him, taking the Snickerdoodle one and opening up the packet, pouring the contents into a cup. When the teapot whistled, Jason took it off the stove, shutting it off, and pouring the water into their cups for some delicious hot chocolate. They sat munching on the cheese and crackers, toast with jam, and taking sips of each other's hot chocolate. Once they finished breakfast, together, they did the few dishes they had used and put them away and then cleaned the counter.

Talia stood looking out the large window that was at the front of the cabin. It was a magnificent view of the mountain, something she could never tire of looking at. Not that she didn't mind living in the Midwest, but there was just something about being in the mountains. She felt a calm and peace she hadn't experienced before, but knew it had everything to do with the man she loved. Coming up behind her, Jason put his arms around her, and the two stood there looking at the same incredible view.

"Someday, I want to come back here with you," she said.

He replied, "I'm more than happy to bring you back; you just name the date."

Then after putting their socks and boots back on, Jason made sure the fire was completely out and that everything was the way it was when they came in. Talia put her sweater back on, but her jacket was still lightly damp, as was Jason's. They gathered all their things as they stepped out onto the porch. Jason locked the door, putting the key back where he found it. They looked toward the car and driveway, noting that the ruts still had water in them, but at least they could see the tops of them and where not to step. They both walked toward the car, slowly stepping around them, and got inside.

With their seat belts on, he started the car and then put the heat on, as it was chilly inside the car. Putting it into reverse, he could back down a little way without getting stuck, turning the wheels and backing up to a small clearing. He put it into drive, and headed down the short road to the highway. Stopping before turning onto the highway, he thought he could remember exactly how to get back to the hotel, but had Talia put the address of the hotel into the GPS anyway. Then pulling onto the highway, they headed back.

Chapter 15

It was a different route from yesterday morning's; it was the south route from Ollon back to Villars. There were some curves in the road, and then a decent stretch before coming to a hairpin curve. Remembering from yesterday, Jason took them slowly. There was light traffic on the road now, and people were going faster than Talia thought they should, but they lived here and knew these roads. Another short stretch, and then two more crazy curves would come up. She was just glad to be getting back to Villars, except for having to leave the cabin. They had ten or twelve miles to go.

A half-mile in front of them, they could see the car that would soon approach a sharp hairpin curve. The taillights came on as it started slowing down. Jason and Talia were also looking at the hairpin curve ahead, but also noticed to their far left, across to the road they would soon be on, was a car that would head in their direction after rounding this curve. The vehicle should have been going slower. Maybe the driver was going to take a wider turn, not paying attention to oncoming traffic?

They saw what was about to happen to the car in front of them, and Talia said in a loud voice, "Jason." She grabbed her door handle. He said, "I know, I see it." He started slowing way down to give the car room as it came around the curve without sideswiping them. The oncoming car must have over-corrected, and then sideswiped the vehicle in front of them, shoving it off the shoulder and onto a field. Had it hit them any harder, it could easily have pushed them another twenty-five feet into some trees. Talia's heart was now racing as she was witnessing this, and she felt sick.

In moments, Jason pulled over within a safe distance of the two cars, putting on his emergency flashers. He was out of the car, grabbing his bag, and told Talia to call 911. She grabbed her phone to call 911, but remembered it was a 112 or 114 number here. After trying to explain to the operator what happened, they finally understood and would send out help. Talia walked closer to the car that caused the accident, where Jason was checking on the passengers; it was two young males. After trying to open the driver's door, which was stuck; he went around and opened the passenger door, checking the young male out; he smelled alcohol.

The driver was trying to shove the airbag out of his face, muttering. As long as they stayed put, they should be all right. Jason needed to check out the other car. He started to walk away from them and turned around to see the young male trying to get out of his seat belt, fidgeting with it. Jason told him to stop and stay put. Both boys just looked at him, and then Jason turned toward Talia, "Tell them to stop and stay put, don't move." She approached the car and could smell the alcohol herself, and this made her angry. She yelled at them, *"Fermare. Non muoverti!"* (Stop. Do not move!)

Jason was now heading to the second car sitting on the field. There was a car approaching and pulling in behind theirs. The driver got out of the vehicle, yelling something about calling for emergency help. Talia nodded, motioning that she already called, holding up her phone. They didn't come any closer, who knows why. Jason approached the car that was in front of them. The driver's door was smashed in near the hinges. He tried pulling the door open, but couldn't. He saw two airbags deployed. He went around the other side, opened the door, removed the airbag. The passenger was still seat belted in, and he saw it was a female. She looked to be about thirty years of age, and about six months pregnant. Talia came and stood on the other side of the door, watching Jason. The male was not moving.

Jason left the seat belt on, as it was holding the woman in place and it was best for her safety. He checked her for a pulse, her pupils, respiration, and then pulled out of his bag a stethoscope and blood pressure cuff, placing it on her. He had a notepad, writing down the vitals. He started checking for any head and neck injuries and checked her arms and legs. He knew he needed to keep her seat belt on, as he didn't know what internal injuries she may have received, and to move her might cause harm to her and her baby. He couldn't get to the husband because it was a two-door car, but he could reach over to see if he could feel for a pulse; he was alive. All he could do was watch and wait. Talia was close by, wanting to help, but knew she would be in his way. She thought, *It has to be frustrating for him, having to wait until help arrives.*

A car coming from the other direction had pulled onto the shoulder on the opposite side of the road. Talia looked at the man getting out and was glad that maybe someone could help Jason. After approaching the car, Jason heard his name being called, and it wasn't Talia's voice. "Jason."

Jason knew that voice, and turned to the one calling his name; it was Jéan-Paul. Jason just looked at him as he came toward him. "How did you know it was me?" Talia looked at Jason and the other man, confused.

Jéan-Paul said, in his thick French accent, "I saw that beauty standing close to you and knew it was you, my friend. What have we got here?" Jason started going over the vitals he had taken on the woman, then told him about the accident and that he couldn't get to the husband yet, but he was alive. Jéan-Paul started checking the woman over while Jason tried the driver's door again with no success. The woman began opening her eyes and crying and yelling for her husband. Jéan-Paul talked to her in Italian, telling her he was a doctor and this was a paramedic helping her, that they would get to her husband in a moment and that he was alive, and she needed to calm down. Knowing Jason would have called it in, he asked what the ETA was, and Jason looked at Talia who then said she called it in.

"I called just after it happened. They should be here soon," she said.

Jéan-Paul looked at her, and then Jason. "And they understood what happened? She speaks Italian?" He looked back at Talia, and then Jason looked at Jéan-Paul and then at Talia and said, "Ya, somewhat."

Jéan-Paul smiled. *"Ah. Buon per te"* (Good for you), to which Talia replied, *"Grazie"* (Thank you).

They heard the sirens of the police, firetruck and two ambulances and saw them coming, heading around the first curve before getting to the second curve where they were.

Jéan-Paul asked Talia if she would go to his car and pull out the blanket in the back seat. As Jéan-Paul was checking over the woman again, the police, firetruck, and both ambulances had arrived. Talia brought the blanket back to Jéan-Paul. He told the men he was a doctor and that Jason was an American paramedic, and to let him help. Once the woman was unbuckled and carefully taken out of the car, being placed on the gurney, she was covered with the blanket and strapped on. The woman looked up at Talia, babbling in Italian, reaching for her hand. Jéan-Paul told Talia to hold her hand; she felt more comfortable with another woman.

Jason got into the front seat and was checking out the husband. Talia took her hand, and said in what she hoped was Italian, *"Sei al sicuro adesso"* (You are safe now). The woman clutched Talia's hand, and Jéan-Paul looked at Talia and nodded with a smile. The men worked on getting both drivers' doors open. The ambulance attendants started taking their female patient to the ambulance. The woman continued to hold Talia's hand and wouldn't let go; she was getting scared again. Jéan-Paul was standing at the end of the gurney as they were getting ready to put her in the ambulance. The woman yelled at Jéan-Paul, telling him she wanted the woman to come with her and wouldn't let go of Talia's hand. Jéan-Paul knew it wasn't all that far to the hospital in Villars. With the husband also on a gurney, he was taken to the second ambulance. Jason came over to see what was going on.

Jéan-Paul said, "The hospital in Villars is only sixteen kilometers away. In this woman's condition, having Talia with her may keep her calm. Too many men, and she's frightened."

Talia looked at Jason and said, "I'm going with her if that helps." Jason stopped her quickly and kissed her, saying, "I love you."

"I love you too," she said, and continued with the woman into the ambulance. Jéan-Paul told the crew they would meet them there. The ambulances turned around and headed toward Villars, with sirens going.

It was time to check out the two young men thoroughly; they had been drinking. The police had been questioning the boys and soon came over to Jéan-Paul and Jason to ask questions. Jason looked to Jéan-Paul to help translate, and then he started explaining what happened. Jéan-Paul told them that he was an American paramedic. They wanted to see his ID, so Jéan-Paul told him what they wanted as Jason pulled out his ID, giving it to them. Jéan-Paul also showed them his own ID; they nodded. The police asked Jéan-Paul about the boys, and he said they were just shaken with a few minor cuts. The police went back to the boys, taking them out of the car and placing them in the back of theirs.

Jéan-Paul told Jason to follow him to the hospital. Once there, Jason found parking not too far from the ER door, and he followed Jéan-Paul in. Jéan-Paul asked about the pregnant female brought in by ambulance, stating he was the doctor on the scene along with this paramedic. They knew who Jéan-Paul was, and lead him down a short hallway to a large exam room. Talia sat in the big waiting room, which was nearby. She watched who was heading down the hall and saw Jéan-Paul and then Jason. Jéan-Paul went into the exam room, closing the door. Talia stood up and put her arms around Jason, and he held her. She was shaking, and scared about what she had witnessed. But having seen Jason take action immediately, she could see why he did this, and she was so proud of him.

They sat down and waited. About twenty-some minutes later, the door opened with the hospital bed being moved out and the doctor headed back to the nurse's station. The husband was also being taken to a hospital room. Jason and Talia stood up, his arm going around her. Jéan-Paul came out and said, "Well, Ms. Rose, a name most fitting a beautiful woman, thank you for coming with her. She was scared, and you helped her very much."

Talia just nodded and asked, "Will she be all right?"

"Yes, they are taking her to a room. She will stay for a while to make sure that she and the baby are all right. She should then be able to go home after that. And how are you doing? All right, yes?" he asked.

"I'm OK, just a little shaky," she answered.

"Jéan-Paul, what were you doing on the road this morning? And how did you know it was me?" Jason asked as they were heading back out toward their cars.

"After your phone call to me, I took the train here early and decided I was going to drive down to the cabin, and hopefully the two of you would still be there, and we could go hiking. Good thing we now have crossed paths, but in a way that you would not always want to meet." Jason nodded.

Jason asked with a grin, "You would have called first, right? We might not have been decent." Talia's eyes opened wide, blushing, and she turned her head toward Jason's arm while covering her cheeks. Jason hugged her.

Jéan-Paul said with a smile, "Talia, I'm a doctor. And I know love when I see it. He loves you very much, yes?" She nodded and looked at Jason. "Besides, I am a Frenchman, and wanted to see this woman that he talks about before she left for America and I didn't have the chance to meet her." He looked at Jason, "And I knew it was you after you sent me the two photos from Gurten. As soon as I saw her standing near the car, and saw you, I knew you were doing what you were trained to do. Sorry, no compensation for this job."

"I'm just glad I was there, but that could have been us. Before leaving your driveway, I stopped to make sure we put the directions to the hotel into the GPS," Jason said.

Jéan-Paul said, "There is a nice little place we could go eat. Please allow me to take you to lunch and talk. I will not take no for your answer, my friend." Jason looked at him and nodded, the two of them shaking hands.

Jason said, "We would like that. But first, we have to get the car back to the hotel. We were supposed to have it back last night. They'll be waiting for it."

"Then why don't I follow you to your hotel, and I take you with me, OK?" Jéan-Paul said.

Chapter 16

After following them back to their hotel, Jéan-Paul parked his car next to the rental and waited for them. They retrieved all their items and headed inside. After speaking with the desk clerk and handing the keys back to them, they headed up to their room. After laying their things on the bed and washing their hands, they headed back down to Jéan-Paul's car. Once inside, he said, "I thought, since you know some Italian, that maybe a good Italian pizza would fit right in." Talia smiled, nodding from the back seat, and said, "Oh yes." Pulling into the Pizza House, they got out of the car and headed in. It smelled so good. Talia's stomach made a noise, and she grabbed it, thinking it would help quiet it.

Once seated, a waiter came over and asked about drinks. Jéan-Paul and Jason both ordered a beer, while Talia ordered a soft drink. What goes better with pizza than either beer or a soft drink? After deciding on the pizza, they placed the order. Jéan-Paul said, "Watch as the cook takes the dough and tosses it in the air, turning it, before preparing it for the oven." Talia loved it. She'd seen it done on TV, but that was all.

While waiting for their pizza, Jéan-Paul told Talia, "Jason told me you are a designer, but didn't tell me what kind of designer. Which are you?"

"I'm a fashion designer," she replied.

"And you went to university in the States?" he asked.

"Yes, I went to ISU or Iowa State University. I received my BFA," she said.

"Ah, Bachelor of Fine Arts, yes?" he stated. She nodded.

"Why did you go there? Why not come over here?" he said with a big smile.

She giggled. "That would have been wonderful, but that would have been out of my reach, financial-wise. I was looking at three different schools in the Midwest, in three different States. I didn't want to be that far from my family, and I loved it at ISU. And I love what I do now."

Jéan-Paul then asked, "You speak Italian, yes?"

"I've been taking classes, when I can, over the last year or so. Italian is a beautiful language," she said, and Jéan-Paul smiled at her.

"Ti piace fare un'escursione?" Jéan-Paul asked.

Talia looked at him, and hoped she said it right, with a questioning look, *"A volte quando non piove."*

Jéan-Paul laughed, *"Molto bene."* Then, he looked a little more serious looking at her and asked, *"Lo ami?"* Jason watched, and wondered what was said.

Talia looked at Jason and replied, *"Sì, molto,"* holding her hand out to Jason, and he took her hand.

Jason said, "OK, you both know I don't speak Italian; I'm feeling a little left out here."

Jéan-Paul looked at Talia, and said, *"Gli dici."*

Talia nodded and said, looking at Jason, "He first asked me if I like to hike, and I said, 'sometimes, when not raining.' Jéan-Paul then laughed and said, 'very good.' Then he asked me, 'Do you love him?'" She looked at Jason with loving eyes, and took his hand and said, "Very much." Jason took her hand to his lips and kissed the back of it.

Their pizza came; it was huge. They continued talking about many things, and laughed. They must have been there for a good two hours.

Jéan-Paul said, "My friend, I will take you back to your hotel. I plan on going down to my cabin and do some hiking. It gives me a couple of days before taking the train back up to Basel, and then we head back up to Stuttgart for the next week. Shall we go now?"

Returning to the hotel, they all got out. Jason and Jéan-Paul hugged and shook hands, and then Jéan-Paul turned to Talia and kissed her on both cheeks. "You keep on him if he misbehaves." Talia nodded. *"Continua ad imparare l'italiano."* Looking at Jason, he said, "I tell her to keep learning Italian."

"Lo farò. I will," Talia replied.

Jéan-Paul said to her, "It was a lovely treat, spending time with you, and a pleasure to meet you." He held her hand.

Talia replied, "It was a pleasure meeting you. Now, I'll know who Jason is speaking about when he says your name." He raised her hand and kissed it. Again, the two men shook hands, and then Jéan-Paul got into his car and left.

"This was so wonderful, meeting Jéan-Paul and spending some time with him. He seems quite the character," Talia said, watching his car drive away, and then she turned toward Jason.

Looking at her, he said, "He is a wonderful man, and a great doctor. I've been grateful for the time I've spent with him these last two years. He's also taught me a lot, which has helped me become a better paramedic. We've become good friends. I'm really happy that he showed up this morning and helped at the accident, and then getting to meet you."

"I know he was there helping, but it was you. As soon as we stopped, you were so focused on what had to be done. You were doing your best for all those people with no help from anyone, not until Jéan-Paul showed up. I was so impressed by what you did, how you handled it, and not even in our own country. I'm so proud of you," she said.

Jason took a step closer and hugged her. "Thank you. That means a great deal to me." He kissed her. "Well, it's been quite the day so far. What would you like to do this afternoon and evening?" he asked.

"I wouldn't mind just wandering around Villars and seeing what there is. But, I-- we have been wearing the same clothes since yesterday morning.

I feel grungy, my jeans are muddy, and I want to get cleaned up before doing anything else. And then we only have a few days left before I have to leave and head home...." Her voice trailed off, and she looked at him. Jason looked at her, seeing the sadness in her eyes. He felt it too. "I know that you'll be heading home. I want you to listen to me, OK; I'll only be gone that next full week, and then I'll be home. You can text me or call me whenever you want. I want us to be together. It took a long time for us to get to this point. I'm not letting you go. I promise."

"*Ti Amo,*" she said, looking into his eyes.

He tilted his head. "*Ti Amo?*" He repeated it, not sure what she said, except he knew it was Italian.

"*Ti Amo.* Three beautiful words, in any language you say to someone who you give your heart to: 'I love you'!" she said. Jason gave her the biggest hug and a deep kiss.

"I'm going to have to learn Italian," he said. She giggled. They turned and headed inside. Once in the room, they took off their shoes. Talia headed toward the balcony; she just wanted to stand there and look at the mountains. Jason followed her out, leaning against the balcony door frame, looking at her. Minutes went by before he said, "So, we'll head back to Basel in the morning on the train. We have until Tuesday before you have to leave, and I head out with Jéan-Paul for Stuttgart. When does your flight leave?" The moment he said that, he wished he could take it back. He closed his eyes with a little shake of his head. "Talia."

Not wanting to think about it, she said, "I don't want to talk about it," and turned. "I'm going to go take a shower and put clean clothes on." She walked past him.

While Talia was in the shower, Jason was glad he had the quick opportunity to call up to the *Hotel Spalentor* where they were staying their last two nights. He needed to speak with either Sophia or Laurel. He told them to cancel one of the reserved rooms, and there was also something he wanted to do Monday afternoon, and he needed their help. But he told them that when they arrived, they could say nothing to Talia.

He came back into the room, closing the balcony door, and then opened his large bag. He took out clean clothes and laid them across the chair. He heard the door to the bathroom open up, and started walking toward it. Talia came out, half-dressed. She had on some straight-legged jeans and her bra, but no shirt. It was lying across her bag. Her hair was up in a towel, and he looked at her with a smile; she looked so adorable with the towel wrapped around her head. "No shirt today?" he asked. She looked at him with a half-smirk.

"My hair is wet, and if I put on my shirt and then take the towel off, the back of my shirt will be wet, and I'm running out of clothes. This is what I do," she replied. There was a counter on the outside of, and one inside of, the bathroom. The blow dryer hung on the wall on the outside with a very long cord.

He loved the way she stated things and said, "Gotcha." He stood there watching her as she bent over, rubbing her head with the towel, and then stood upright.

He would love to watch her, but feeling somewhat grungy himself, he continued toward the bathroom to take a shower. He gave her a quick kiss on her wet head. He left the door partially open. Talia found her comb, then took the blow dryer off its hook and turned it to medium heat and fan setting as she began drying her hair, first with her fingers as a comb providing more space for quicker drying, and then using her comb to make sure there weren't any snarls.

As she stood there drying her hair, she closed her eyes, feeling the warmth of the dryer as she also aimed it at her arms and chest, then back to her hair. With eyes still closed, she put the dryer on a lower fan speed. When she thought it was dry, she opened her eyes and saw in the mirror that he was standing behind her with only a towel wrapped around his waist.

"How long have you been standing there?" she asked.

"Long enough to see the ritual of blow drying your hair with your eyes closed," he said. He shook his head, releasing some water that was in his hair, shaking it toward her. She gave a screech of laughter and aimed the dryer at him. He took hold of her waist, pulling her toward him, and kissed her before walking away. She wanted to put on fresh makeup, but had to get her makeup bag. She walked around the corner to see Jason facing the balcony, just pulling his jeans on over his backside. He turned around while zipping up to see her watching him, and then asked, "How long you been standing there?" He had a grin on his face. "It's not like we haven't seen each other in the flesh."

She looked him up and down with a half smile, then grabbed her makeup bag and headed back to the bathroom. He came and stood near her, watching her, not saying a word. She glanced at him as he pulled a long-sleeved polo shirt over his head, and then pushed up his sleeves, revealing his watch. She asked, "What time is it?"

He looked and said, "It's just after three-thirty." She nodded. When she finished, she turned to walk past him, and he put his arms around her, looking at her with a boyish grin and asked, "What would you like to do the rest of the afternoon?"

She looked up at him with a big smile, knowing what he was thinking, and prophetically said, "Shopping." He tilted his head back and laughed, and shook his head, then hugged her. "OK," he said.

"I want to see what Villars has. I haven't gotten anything for myself, and I would like to see what I might find as a remembrance of this place, besides being with you. I'd also like to do the same in Basel tomorrow or Monday," she stated.

He nodded. "Well, I guess we'd better get to it then. But you are going to put on a shirt first. I really don't think I could stand having any men ogling you," he said with a raised eyebrow.

"Oh, ya, I forgot. I should put one of those on." She gave him a sassy look.

She grabbed her shirt, and pulled it over her head. Once it was on, she straightened it out and grabbed her hair from inside her shirt. She sat down on the bed and put her shoes on. Quickly looking at herself in the mirror, she then picked up her light jacket and handbag. Jason had the key card. He opened the door, waited for her to precede him, and he then followed.

ɞ

Walking down the street, not knowing exactly where they were going, they wandered, checking out all the various shops. Some roads were narrow, so when they were walking on the sidewalk, Jason placed himself next to the street; not that anything would happen. They stopped in a couple more stores and browsed. Talia found some new pants she liked, and a couple of tops. She also found some earrings and a necklace. Jason even found a new pair of pants and a shirt. They looked at shoes, but nothing jumped out at them. Wandering more, they came across a *gelato* store. You can't leave without having some. It was so delicious, and hit the spot.

They had walked all around, and were headed back toward the hotel. They knew that they weren't far from the Pizza House where they had lunch with Jéan-Paul. They walked into a quaint-looking shop and saw several people inside looking and talking. Talia saw something near the front window she wanted to check out. Jason wandered toward the middle of the shop and heard the voice of an American woman asking about a sweater she wanted to purchase. The store owner, an older woman, was speaking in Italian and almost in tears because she didn't understand. Then the other American was asking about some shirts, and the owner just looked at them and kind of shrugged her shoulders, saying, *"No Inglese, no Inglese"* (No English). Jason was watching them. The two men, more than likely husbands to the women, stood back quietly; either they were embarrassed or didn't know how to get their wives out of the store.

Talia was slowly working her way toward the center of the shop, when Jason said, "Talia, need a little help here." The women turned toward Jason, hearing his English, and they asked, "Are you American?"

"Yes," he replied. By then, Talia came and stood next to him. He whispered in her ear, "Things just keep getting better and better today." She nudged him in his side.

"Hello. How are you?" Talia said.

"Hello. We need help here, and this woman, I guess, doesn't speak English."

Talia said, figuring they didn't know any better, "She's probably from the old country." She looked at Jason.

Jason mouthed the words to Talia, "The old country?" with a slight grin, and raised eyebrow.

The owner was watching, not knowing what was going on in her shop. Talia said, "I do speak some Italian. I'll see if I can help, all right? Just give me a moment." Talia spoke with the owner. *"Ciao"* (Hello), to which, the owner stood a little straighter and replied, *"Ciao."*

Talia then asked, *"Lei parla inglese?"* (Do you speak English?)

The woman replied, *"Non parlo inglese"* (I don't speak English). She continued saying that her niece was to be here that day, but got sick.

"Va bene" (That's all right). Talia continued the best she could without messing it up. *"Parlo un po di Italian.* (I speak a little Italian), *Cerchero di aiutare"* (I'm going to try to help).

The woman took Talia's hand, shaking it, *"Grazie"* (Thank you).

With the two American women looking on and listening, Talia asked them what they needed help with. One woman took Talia's hand and walked her right over to the sweaters, and wanted to know what they were made of and how much they were. The shop owner followed. Talia said what they were made of and then asked the owner, *"Quanto costano i maglioni?"* (How much is the sweater?). The shop owner told her the cost, to which Talia told the women. She continued helping the best she could.

Jason was just standing there, watching and listening. The husbands of the two women came over to Jason and told him thank you that his wife could help. Jason liked the sound of that: "wife." They told Jason that they were with a tour group from North Dakota, touring France and Switzerland for a week. They'd never been outside the United States. It was pretty, and they got to see castles and some museums and such, but they were ready to go home; they were leaving tomorrow. They were staying in Villars. Since this was the last free evening, some of them wanted to find a place to eat, maybe something a little more American. They didn't like some of the food because they weren't used to it.

After Talia helped the ladies with their purchases, they came over to their husbands and stood there, waiting.

Talia turned toward the shop owner, and learned her name was Caterina. She told her, *"Grazie"* (Thank you). The owner said, *"Prego"* (You're welcome).

When Talia joined Jason and the others, she said to them, "Her name is Caterina. Why don't you tell her 'thank you'?" They looked at Talia. Talia said all you have to say is, *"Grazie,* Caterina."

So, the two women replied together, *"Gra-zie,* Caterina." Talia looked at them and smiled.

They started walking toward the door when Caterina said loudly, *"Addio"* (Goodbye).

Once out the door, Jason took Talia's hand and waited for the people to go where they needed to. But then these Dakotans turned and asked, "Where is a good place to eat that's a little more American?"

Not knowing that Jason just wanted these tourists to go on their way, Talia spoke and said there was a pizza house just ahead and around the corner. She felt Jason squeeze her hand, and she looked at him with questioning eyes.

The group thought that was a great idea, and that they wouldn't take no for an answer, that they would like for Jason and Talia to join them just in case they needed a translator. And to thank Talia for helping them, it was their treat. One of the women, Carol, took Talia's hand and started walking in the direction that Talia said. She just looked back at Jason. Then they all followed.

Once inside the Pizza House, they were taken to a large table to be seated. The waiter spoke reasonably good English, for which Talia was grateful. He asked what they wanted to drink, and the ladies asked for soft drinks. The men asked Jason about beer; they wanted to try some. So, Jason suggested what he had earlier today, but didn't tell them that. Then they ordered pizza. Talia told them to watch the pizza maker as he tossed it in the air, which delighted them, and they took out their cell phones for pictures.

As they were waiting for the pizzas, they asked what Jason and Talia were doing in Villars, to which they replied, "Doing business and some vacation." They then asked what kind of business. Talia said she was a fashion designer, and had purchased bolts of fabric, having them shipped home. The ladies thought that was so wonderful that they get to eat with a fashion designer, and took some photos of her. Talia just smiled.

Then they looked at Jason and asked him what he did for a living. He looked at Talia and then said that he was a paramedic/firefighter. He spent time in Germany with a work abroad program, going out on calls with paramedics and learning about their protocol. The North Dakotans didn't know people could do that, and found that marvelous. The ladies took a couple of photos of Jason. As the pizza was getting ready to come out of the oven, they just wanted to thank Talia for being so helpful and kind in that shop today. Since Jason and Talia sat next to each other, the ladies wanted to take a photo of the two of them. They would show friends back home about the designer and paramedic they shared pizza with, in Villars.

The pizzas came, and they enjoyed eating, drinking, and talking. When they were all finished and didn't have any more to say, it was Carol that said they should get back to their hotel and get things packed; they were leaving early in the morning. As they all got up to go, Carol said she would like a group photo. The waiter had come over to clear some plates, and Carol asked if he would be a gem and take their picture as a group. So, both ladies handed him their cell phones and he took a picture with each.

When they headed out the door, there were three other people from their tour group that spotted them. Apparently, Carol texted her friend Lana about the pizza place and who they met. As Lana approached with the others, Carol yelled at her friend, "Lana, get over here; this is the young woman who speaks Italian. She even has an Italian sounding name. Maybe that's why she can speak it. Thank goodness she did, or we wouldn't have been able to buy anything. And then they showed us this great pizza place; real Italian pizza." Lana looked at Jason and smiled. "I must say, you Italians are so good-looking." Looking back at Carol, she said, "How come you didn't tell us about having pizza? We would have loved to have joined you." She stood looking back at Jason.

Carol said, "Lana, he's not Italian. Jason and Talia are both from the States, the Midwest."

"Oh, you look Italian. Are you sure you're not Italian?" Lana asked, looking at him. Carol and Jolene, the second woman from the shop earlier, each gave Talia and Jason a hug, and then Carol took Lana by the hand, turning her around as they started heading back toward their hotel. The men shook Jason and Talia's hands and thanked them for their help, and then followed their wives.

"What just happened this evening?" Jason asked, looking at Talia.

Talia replied, "Well, I got to use a little more Italian, and we got a free dinner." She giggled, then, taking hold of Jason's hand, started casually walking with him.

Chapter 17

"You do look a little Italian." She grinned.

He said, "Well, if I have the look of an Italian, you'll have to teach me some phrases so I can at least sound like one." He continued, putting his arm around her waist, "I was impressed that you could help that shop owner. When I first heard them speaking to her, I could see she was getting frustrated and all but had tears in her eyes. And I didn't want her to think that all Americans are, should I say, pushy."

"I'm just glad that I could help her. Her niece speaks English, and was supposed to be there today, but she was out sick," Talia said.

"Well, I'm proud of you for stepping up and doing what you could for all of them. And I'm glad they invited us to dinner. As you said, it was free. And besides, I like their beer. Should we see if I've grown any more hair on my chest?" he said with a big grin. He leaned down and kissed her. They could see their hotel; it wouldn't be much further now. The streetlights had come on over three hours ago, and it was getting chilly out. Talia was glad she had her jacket.

When they got to their room, Talia plopped down on the bed, dropping her shopping bags and taking off her shoes. She looked at her large travel bag and knew she would have to reorganize to make sure everything fit. She already had a smaller bag that contained souvenirs from walking through the *Gate of Spalen*, and she had picked up a few things for her mom, Kurt, and her staff of two. She just stared at the bag now. She knew it had to be done because she didn't want to have to do it in the morning; time would be short.

Jason set his shopping bag down near the big chair, then took off his shoes and came to sit on the bed beside Talia. He could see her mind was off in the distance as she stared at her large bag, not blinking, and he wondered what it could be. Checking his watch, he saw it was nearly 10:00 p.m. He knew that today had been a long day. They were up early, and then headed back here to Villars. Then they came across the accident, which had shaken Talia, then going in the ambulance with the pregnant woman. Then with Jéan-Paul, and then the people from North Dakota. It had just been a very long day. Jason got up and drew back the blanket on the bed.

As he sat back on the bed and looked at her, her eyes were closed. He quietly said her name, "Talia. Why don't you get yourself ready for bed? We can repack in the morning." She opened her eyes and looked at him, not saying a word. She got up and took out what she had worn to bed all the other nights, and then headed to the bathroom. She came out, laying her clothes on her bag. Jason had shut off the lamp on her side of the bed. He had taken off his shirt and put on the light sweats. He then went to the bathroom. When he came out, she had already crawled into bed with the covers up near her shoulders, her eyes closed; she was sound asleep. He got into bed, shutting off the light on his side, and scooted next to her. He wanted to hold her and make her feel safe, so he gently placed his arm around her waist, pulling her closer to him and whispered, learning from her, *"Ti amo, I love you."* And he fell asleep.

℈

Jason woke to the feel of Talia's legs moving, and then they quit. Within moments, they started moving again. He felt something was off, and was more awake. Her arms were moving, and her body was lightly shaking. "Talia," he said softly, feeling concerned. He could feel her breathing was a little more substantial; she made inaudible sounds, and her heart was racing. He heard her mumbling quietly, "No, no, move... too fast. Mama, baby, NO." She woke up, sitting up and crying. He sat up and turned on his lamp, and put his arms around her. She held his arm, tears falling.

"Talia, I'm here," he said, holding her and rocking her. He still felt her body shaking. He figured it was a bad dream regarding the accident earlier. "Everyone from the accident is safe, including the mama and baby; and we're safe. Shhh, everyone is safe," he repeated, giving her a few moments. He gave her a light kiss on her damp cheek and said, calmly and quietly, "Talia, look at me." He lifted his hand to her chin, turning her face to him. "Everyone is safe. I want you to take a slow, deep breath for me, all right." She looked at him, nodding, taking a slow, deep breath.

"It felt so real. But it was all in slow motion, the car coming around the curve and then hitting the other car in front of us, and seeing that pregnant woman still seat belted. You left it on her, keeping her safe so she wouldn't fall out. That could have been us," she said, with more tears coming. "I don't know what I would do if I lost you."

"And I don't know what I would do without you, my love." He held her tight, remembering those feelings, and that loss. He didn't want her to see his tears, but that was about to happen. She looked at him and saw his tears, and knew what he was feeling. That picture of their bodies still clear in his mind. He'd lost one tragically that he loved, and it most certainly scared him to think of possibly losing Talia today, knowing how deeply he loved her. Had the other car not been where it was, and had they been any closer, they would have been hit head-on.

"I'm sorry," Talia said.

"Why?" he asked.

"Because of your best friend; and then the thought of possibly losing me," she said. "I guess no one knows what might happen in a split second. Life is so precious."

"Yes, it is. How are you feeling?" Jason asked, as he saw that her eyes were getting heavy. He turned to shut off the lamp.

"Leave it on, please," she said, and then laid back down with Jason's arm behind her. He held her close and placed his other arm around her. She turned toward him, laying her head against his chest, and fell back asleep. Jason just looked at her, closing his eyes for a moment, then opened them.

He looked at her once more, hugged her, kissed the top of her head, and then closed his eyes. They didn't know then that there would be another time and place when life became uncertain.

Talia opened her eyes, feeling rested, and took a slow, deep breath; she was still in his arms. He had rolled over slightly onto his back, still with one arm around her. She watched his stomach go up and down with his breathing. She laid her hand over his heart; it was beating steadily. He then put his left hand over hers and turned his head toward her with a simple smile. Slowly, he rolled over toward her, where she ended up lying on her back with him placing himself half on top of her. He teased her with his kisses, looking into her eyes, but then kissed her on her forehead and laid back down. She turned her head toward him, half sitting up, wondering why he stopped.

"Are you all right? Why did you stop?" she asked.

"Because, my darling," he held his watch in front of her face so she could see the time, "we have approximately an hour and fifteen minutes before our train leaves, and we need to be there at least ten minutes before the train leaves. We still have to repack and have a bite to eat. I think we overslept."

"Holy crap!" she said.

He chuckled, and watched her get out of bed and head to the bathroom. He got up himself, starting to change into his jeans, when he said, "Are you taking a shower? I know how long it takes for your hair to dry." He heard the toilet flush, and then listened to the sound of running water from the sink. He was a little worried for a moment.

He headed for the bathroom as the door was opening up. "Why didn't you wake me up earlier?" she asked.

"I would have, but I didn't wake until you put your hand on my chest. I thought I had more time to love you more appropriately when I rolled on top of you, and then I saw my watch," Jason grinned. He headed to the bathroom, closing the door.

Talia didn't know which to do first: reorganize her bag or get dressed first. She meant to reorganize her bag last night and lay out her clothes. So, she put on the jeans she had on yesterday evening, then moved her bag to the bed, giving her the space needed to half-empty her bag and reorganize. She took off the top she wore to bed, putting her bra on and laying out one of her new shirts. Jason came out, watching her reorganize her bag. He walked over to his bag and also did a little shifting around of clothes, and then placed his paramedic bag on top. He put his deodorant on, placed it back in his bag, and then put on a pullover sweater.

After sitting down to put on his socks and shoes, he then got up and zipped his bag closed, laid his jacket on top, and sat down on the chair to watch her. She was finishing up putting things in their place, but took out her makeup bag and headed to the bathroom. It looked like record time for her to put her face on, but then he'd only seen her do this a time or two. Placing her makeup bag back in its spot, she then put on her deodorant, sliding her shirt over her head and then putting on her sweater. She sat putting her socks and shoes on, then stood up to zip her bag, which she had to shove down with her hands. She grabbed out of her small bag a small tube of toothpaste and her toothbrush, and went back to the bathroom to brush her teeth.

Jason sat watching her, feeling like he was watching an old Charlie Chaplin movie; lots of movement, but no noise. When Jason was very young, he would spend time with his grandmother, and she liked to watch Charlie Chaplin movies.

When all was done, she sat down on the edge of the bed for a moment. She had to do this before when running late, and it annoyed her then.

"You have everything done you need to?" Jason asked.

"Yes, I think so. I don't like being hurried, feeling like I'm going to miss the boat, or in this case, the train," she replied.

"Well, we have about fifteen plus minutes to get some breakfast and get out to the tram," he said. They both stood up. Talia grabbed her small bag and jacket, lifted the handle on the large bag and rolled it out the door. Jason followed her, carrying his bag and jacket.

After having a quick breakfast, Talia grabbed some fruit, putting them in her bag. They checked out and headed toward the tram. They were there fifteen minutes before the train was to leave for Basel. Other people were standing around, chatting, saying goodbye to family or friends, and then getting on the car they were riding in. Talia and Jason stepped up and walked inside, again placing their luggage on the rack. Talia started heading for a seat, waiting for Jason. He motioned for her to sit down next to the window; she didn't argue. They noticed there were more people on this train.

The train started accelerating. It would take under four hours, which put them into Basel well after lunch.

Chapter 18

There was a couple on the train, one seat up from Talia and Jason, across the aisle. They had a little girl with them. She looked to be about five years old. She was sitting on her dad's lap, holding a doll. Talia just looked at her, smiling. The little girl smiled back, and then gave Talia a little wave. Talia waved back. The little girl looked at Jason with a smile, and then waved to Jason. Talia glanced at Jason and noticed the look on his face. There was sadness in his eyes, and he gave a little wave then lowered his eyes to the seat in front of them. The little girl moved to her mother's lap, looking out the window. They hadn't seen too many kids, except the ones at the Rose Garden in the playground area, but with school in session, that was probably why.

Talia turned her head, looking out the window. Jason looked at Talia, wondering if she ever wanted to have kids. He knew he did, at least one or two, maybe a boy and a girl. He also knew they had to be watched over carefully, not taking your eyes off of them. "Do you ever think about it?" he asked.

"What? Think about what?" she replied, looking at him.

"Having kids someday," he said, also looking at the young family.

"Ya, I do. I wonder what it would be like to have a family and have them grow up the way I did, hoping I could someday be a great mom the way my mom was with Kurt and me. And having someone who would be a great dad for my kids," she said, looking back at the young family.

"Maybe... someday, that could be you and me," he said, looking at her. She smiled at him and took his hand. He knew she would be an awesome mom, and was sure he would be a great dad, to be there and love them and protect them.

"Maybe," she said, looking at him, raising his hand and kissing the back of it.

They sat quietly for a while, looking out the window. Talia leaned her head back against the seat, looking up at the mountains as they moved swiftly past them. She could see quite a ways up with the high windows.

"So, you asked the other day how I got to be a paramedic, and I told you. What made you want to go into fashion?" he asked.

She took a slow breath, looking toward the far windows on the other side of the train. "I think it started when I was young, not even in high school yet, and we visited my grandfather. He'd see me daydreaming, looking at something, and ask me what my dreams were. I must have told him when I would watch television and see what people were wearing, 'I couldn't believe someone made that outfit.' Some I liked, and others just looked stupid or the colors didn't seem to go together. I thought I could do better if I were to come up with something fashionable and not too expensive for people. He looked at me, nodding. And I told him sometimes I doubted myself, and that other people would tell me what I should or shouldn't do. I didn't think I was deserving or worthy of having something so wonderful in my life. He looked at me and said, 'Don't allow other people's writing to be on your wall.' I looked at him, wondering what he meant, and he pointed to my head." Her eyes teared up, but a little smile was on her face.

"Then, when I was in high school, my sophomore year, I took a Family and Consumer Sciences class. I was kind of on the shy side. I was good at some sewing projects, and then I started doodling and drawing what I wanted to see someone wear. My good friend, Linda, hated that class. She asked me if I would sew a skirt and top for her that looked great together. I came up with something for her, and she liked it, so I made it for her.

"Then there was a dance. I went, but didn't dance with anyone; I sat back and watched with a few friends. I got to thinking how nice it would be to create an amazing design for prom dresses. I had done more drawings throughout my junior and senior years, and I could sew a few items for some girls, which got me noticed from more of the kids. They liked what I made, and they told me I should become a, quote, "'fashion designer.'" She smiled a big smile. "I even had one of the female teachers ask me to make her a skirt or something, and she liked it."

"You told Jéan-Paul that you chose ISU. Was that the best school?" he asked.

"It was right up there with a couple of other schools that had excellent design programs. I didn't want to go that far from family. But I learned a lot, and totally enjoyed my time there. Once I graduated, I found a company that liked my designs and hired me. I worked hard for them; I was with them for almost ten years. And then some new management came in and started acting like jerks with several of the staff, including me. I thought to myself, I was tired of giving my time to someone else. I was good at what I was doing, and I decided I wanted to be my own boss, give my time back to me, allowing me to be more creative. I knew I had talent. I remember my grandfather telling me that too.

"About five years ago, we were visiting him; his health was failing. I wanted to tell him what I had been doing before I didn't have the opportunity again. I told him that someday, I'd like to have a shop of my own." Her eyes were tearing over. "He listened to me. And he said, 'Whatever dream you have, design it. Be open to it. What is the outcome you want for you and your life?' He looked at me and gave me a hug and a kiss on the cheek. We talked more. And then he asked me, 'So sweetheart,' that's what he called me, he'd say, 'Sweetheart, what is the name of your shop?' I smiled at him and said, 'The T.E. Rose Shoppe.' I told him it had to have two p's in Shoppe because it looked cool. He laughed at me, but I knew it was in a very loving way. I thanked him and told him I loved him. That was the last time I saw him. I wish I would have made the time to go see him more often."

With tears still in her eyes, she said, "Less than a year later, he died. I miss him. He left me an amazing gift of not only believing in me, but making sure I believed in myself, that I could do it. In his will, he left me enough money to open up my small shop. My grandfather's name was Theodore Earl Rose. He and I have the same initials, but of course, my name being, Talia Elizabeth Rose. So, I wanted it to be named for both of us, because he believed in me. I've had my shop for almost four years. It's not large, but it doesn't have to be."

Jason looked at her with such loving eyes. "You are such a strong woman. I am so proud of you and what you've accomplished. Your grandfather was very wise." She leaned on him.

They had eaten breakfast quickly, and now Talia's stomach was talking to her. She opened her bag and brought out one banana. She looked at Jason. "Would you like the other banana?" He smiled, and she gave it to him. She had several napkins to put the peels in. There were small trash bins near each door entrance on each car. When they were finished, not thinking, instead of going to the one behind them, which would have been closer, he headed up the aisle to the one they were facing and put them in that one. As he was walking back, he saw the little girl sleeping in her mother's arms, her dad's arm behind his wife, and holding the little girl's hand. Jason sat down and just looked out the window. He was feeling different; he remembered another little girl.

His thoughts turned back to the entire last week, spending it with Talia, seeing things through her eyes, and falling more in love with her. They shared a lot; happy, and sad times. They laughed and cried together. At the cabin, they shared a very intimate and deep love that connected two people when giving themselves to one another. And he thought about all the years he lost out on by not having her in his life that he could have had if he weren't so afraid. He wished he could have said something to her each time their families were together. He wasn't exactly sure what he was fearful of or what held him back. He didn't know. He knew he couldn't look back, which was hard not to do, regretting things from the past. That was then. He had this day, and all the days to come, to have a beautiful life with this woman. And he intended to do something about it. The timing was right, and it felt so right at last.

He felt Talia's head on his shoulder; she was sleeping. After having that bad dream, she probably needed this rest before they arrived back in Basel. About an hour and a half to go yet. He was going to close his eyes for a few minutes.

It was Talia that opened her eyes as she felt the train slowing down. She looked at Jason, who had fallen asleep, thinking she could get used to waking up next to him every morning. She leaned up and kissed his cheek. He opened his eyes and sat up, stretching in his seat. The train came to a stop, and the passengers gathered their things and were heading out the door. The couple with the little girl got up and headed for the door nearest them. Her father held her. She turned toward Jason and Talia and waved to them with a smile.

℣

Jason let Talia go first as they headed down the aisle to retrieve their luggage. Once off the train, Talia took hers, pulling up the handle and pulling it behind her. Jason did the same. They headed to catch the next tram that would stop near the hotel. With it being Sunday afternoon, they had until Tuesday before she was to fly out and head back to Des Moines; Jason would head back up to Stuttgart with Jéan-Paul by train.

Once the tram stopped, they got off and crossed the street to the hotel. It was Sophia at the desk. She told them welcome back. She was happy to see them both. She looked at Jason with a raised eyebrow, remembering the conversation they had on the phone. His eyes got a little big, and then he closed his eyes, remembering he had forgotten to speak with Talia about it.

"Um, Talia, I have something to tell you before we check-in."

"Really. What might that be?" she said, looking at him straight-faced and then looked at Sophia, who took a step back from the desk. He saw Sophia take a step back and then looked at Talia.

"Well, after we finished having lunch with Jéan-Paul yesterday afternoon, and got back to the hotel so we could get cleaned up, you headed into the shower, and I may have called the hotel here and canceled one of the rooms that were booked for tonight and Monday night."

"You may have called the hotel; you don't remember calling the hotel?" she said, still straight-faced.

"OK, I called and canceled one of the rooms, for both nights." He took a breath. "It's because I don't want to spend any nights away from you that I don't have to," he said slowly.

"Um, I see," she said, nodding her head. "OK." She turned toward Sophia and winked at her. Sophia gave a slight smile to Talia, which Jason caught. He looked at Sophia and then back to Talia.

"Wait a minute, you just winked at Sophia, and she smiled at you. Oh, I see. You were going to let me squirm, weren't you? You knew?" He just stared at Talia, tilting his head with a furrowed brow and a half grin, which Sophia caught. She let out a little giggle, covering her hand over her mouth.

Still giggling, Sophia asked in her best composure, "May I check the two of you in?"

Talia said, looking at her, "Yup."

"Would you like to know when our breakfast is open? I can tell you again," still giggling. Sophia apparently couldn't help herself. Once she checked them in, she handed the room keys to Talia and told her they would be in the same room that Talia was in last time, Room 47. As they started pulling their bags behind them, Sophia knew that when they were there before they would take the stairs, so she called after them. "You can always take the elevator; it will get you to your room much faster." They could still hear her giggling.

They took the elevator, walking down the hallway to their room, where Jason first kissed her.

Once they were in the room, and the door was closed and locked, Jason dropped his bag, making Talia turn around and look at him. With a raised eyebrow and intent look on his face, her eyes got big, and she started to giggle. "Were you going to say anything to me about this?" Jason asked, his head tilted down. "How did you know that I canceled one of the rooms?" He had a questioning look.

"I'm a mind reader?" she replied with a cheesy grin.

He took a step toward her, slowly staring into her eyes. "How did you know that I canceled one of the rooms?"

With a sheepish look, she said, "When you were in the shower, I called here, telling Sophia to cancel one of the rooms; that we'd be sharing a room because I didn't want to spend any nights away from you. And that's when she told me you had called to cancel one of the rooms as well. I was going to tell you, and then I thought I'd see how long it would take you to tell me. And then yesterday, there was so much going on, and I forgot to tell you until we walked in the hotel door, and I saw the way Sophia looked at you, and then you forgot you were to tell me and..."

"I have half a mind... but I think I'll wait until later when we can pick up where we left off this morning." He looked at her, taking a closer step, and bent down, placing his hands along either side of her face, and gave her teasing kisses. She put her hands on either side of his face. When he stopped, still holding her face, he took a small step back, looking at her. She still had her eyes closed, and then she slowly opened them up. "We will continue this later," he said with a sultry look. "Why don't we go for a long walk and see where it takes us?"

"OK, maybe later this evening we could also go for a swim and relax," Talia said. Jason nodded.

They headed out their door, taking the stairs down to the main lobby. Sophia saw them walk by the counter holding hands, and she smiled. They walked across the street toward the *Spalen Gate*, passing through and wandering past all the shops, stopping in quite a few of them. Talia found a few other little gifts. They stopped by one store she hadn't seen before just to browse. There were many interesting gifts, but nothing she wanted. They were getting ready to leave, when someone tapped her on the shoulder. She was thinking it was Jason, wanting to call her attention to something he had seen. Turning around, she saw an older woman look at her like she knew who Talia was, then asking, *"Sei Maria Rizzo?"* (Are you Maria Rizzo?)

Talia replied, *"Mi dispia, non sono lie"* (I'm sorry, I'm not her).

Jason came and stood beside Talia, and asked, "What is she saying?"

"She's asking if I'm Maria Rizzo, and I told her I'm not her," Talia said. She looked back at the older woman and asked, *"Lei parla ingles?"*

"Si, yes. Maria is a good friend's daughter who has been gone many years. She left home, never to return, until I see you and think you are her. You look very much like our Maria. I would have told my friend good news, but now I cannot."

Talia just looked at her, thinking, here this woman thinks she found her good friend's daughter and could return her home. "I'm so sorry. I hope she returns home soon and you can all be happy once again." Talia took her hand and held it a moment.

The woman asked, "What is your name, and where do you come from?"

"My name is Talia Rose, and I come from America; just visiting," Talia responded. The woman looked at Talia, patted her hand and then left, looking back at Talia as she walked out the door. Talia watched her walk away and said to Jason, "I wish this family's daughter would come home to them soon, wherever she is, if she can. That has to be hard not knowing where their child is, if she's safe or what kind of life she might be living." Talia shook her head a little, and they headed out the door. Jason took hold of Talia's hand as they continued to walk. They'd been wandering, and then found themselves near the small restaurant they had eaten at earlier in the week. Not realizing the time, they were both getting hungry; it was close to 6:00 p.m. They went inside the restaurant and had dinner, not saying much.

Jason asked, "Do you still want to go for that swim?" Talia nodded yes. They got up and walked back to the hotel. After changing into their suits, they put on the robes and slippers provided by the hotel and went down to the pool. Walking down the steps into the pool, Jason went first, turning around and taking Talia's hand as she took the final step walking onto the pool floor. They headed toward the side, standing. Jason lowered himself in the water so it would go over his shoulders. Talia looked at a few families that had been swimming, seeing their kids having fun.

"When I have kids, I'm going to make sure they know how to swim," she said. Jason turned toward Talia, picking her up in his arms, meandering toward the deep end, then stopping, again where he could continue to hold her and she couldn't touch the bottom. They stayed here a bit longer. She looked at him, putting her arms around his neck, and kissed him. "Years ago, I had kissed one, maybe two frogs, and they stayed green, obviously not turning into my prince. And then a week ago, my birthday wish came true," she said.

Jason smiled, "And then this frog kissed you."

Looking at him, she said, "My prince has been in front of me ever since my sweet-sixteen kiss. I just wasn't as aware of him as he was of me. It's taken a long time for me to open up my heart. I wish I'd done it sooner." Jason let her legs go, wrapping both his arms around her, holding her close. He started walking toward the shallow end, picking her legs up again. As they neared the steps to go up, he had to put her down, as there were several people in front of them with their kids also leaving, and the kids were looking at Jason and Talia. Heading back to their room and once inside, Talia headed for the bathroom to take off her suit. She wanted to take a shower and get the chlorine smell off of her skin. She put her hair up and turned on the shower, waited for it to get it good and warm, and then stepped into it with the water spraying down her body. She soon felt his arms around her waist, and his body against hers. She leaned her head back against his chest as he caressed her, then he turned her toward him, giving her gentle kisses. He turned off the water, took a towel, and wrapped it around her; he grabbed the other one for himself and led her out to the bed. He was going to finish what he started that morning.

Chapter 19

The streetlights illuminated the room just enough as she looked at the man lying next to her, loving him so much. He was this strong, compassionate and extraordinary man who had made her feel worthy and deserving of everything that life had to offer. Her thoughts turned back to all the times their families spent together, remembering how often she would catch him looking at her and that he would try to stand or sit close to her, and when possible, he'd hold her hand. She remembered when he had given her that first kiss, which stirred a feeling in her she'd never felt before, and being carried down a mountain, feeling safe in his arms. All he ever wanted was to be there with her and love her. But why had it taken her so long to get it, and let love in?

Jason stirred next to her. She looked at his chest, placing her palm flat against it, feeling the rise and fall of his breathing and his steady heartbeat. Talia eased her hand down slowly past his stomach. She was the one now that wanted to make love to him, feeling butterflies in her stomach. She started to rise and lean on him, looking at him and saw he was looking back at her. He must have read her mind as he pulled her closer, bringing her on top of his body.

ℂẁ

It was now getting lighter out. She felt a tear fall from her cheek down to his chest. She looked into his eyes, kissing him. With his strong arms around her, he rolled her over gently, looking down at her and returning her kisses. They would have at least twenty-four hours before she was to leave. She wished for more time. As they lay in each other's arms, they must have been thinking the same thing. With a few more tears in her eyes, she said, "I don't want to go back without you. What if something happens?"

"What do you think will happen?" Jason asked.

"I don't know. Sometimes I feel like this is just a dream, and I'm going to wake up and none of this will have happened. And I won't know where you are. I won't know how to reach you. I don't want to leave you tomorrow."

Hearing some fear in her voice, he wanted to reassure her. "I promise you, I will always be there for you, and with you. Remember I told you, it's only one week and I'll be home, and we can be together. You can call me and text me, and I'll get back to you as soon as I can. This program is something I signed up to do, and I need to complete it. I also wish I could go back with you, but I need to be here for just a little longer. You know I'll be working, right?" he asked. She nodded. "Think about all the bolts of fabric you have being shipped home." He saw her smile. "I can see your design mind powering up. After being here and seeing so much, I can't wait to see what you come up with. You are a strong and talented woman. Remember the things you and your grandfather talked about. And besides, today will be an incredible day. It will only get better," he said with a smile. "Look how we started it." He smiled and raised an eyebrow, bending down to kiss her. "The photos on my phone, I'm going to send those to you so you can look at this face anytime you want until I get home." She put her arms around his neck and shoulder, giving him the best bed hug.

"OK," she said. He wiped her tears away.

"Something I would like to do today is take another walk with you through the botanical garden, and then for lunch, go back to the New Bombay Restaurant, and then walk by the river. And then we play it by ear later this afternoon and evening, OK?" Jason said.

She replied, "I'll do whatever you want today, as long as I'm with you."

"I'm going to go take a shower. We might have missed breakfast, so I thought I would check to see what was maybe left. You can then take a shower and get dressed. Would you do me a favor and wear your long flowy skirt and top and sandals?" he asked.

"I guess I can. Any particular reason why?" she asked.

He said with a smile, "Because you look beautiful in it," giving her another quick kiss. He got up and headed for the bathroom. She lay in bed longer, thinking about what he said, that it was going to be an incredible day. How can it not be a great day? Any day was, being with him. She had to let the sadness go, knowing he was right. It was only a week, and she would be fine. There would be plenty to do when she got home, and she could text or call him.

She got out of bed, putting her robe on, and walked toward the window, looking out. It had been the most amazing week of her life. She thought, *You do have to be careful what you wish for; it just might come true.* She felt his arms wrap around her, and she leaned her head back on his chest. "I'm going to get dressed, and go check out about some food. I'll take a key with me," he said, kissing her on her neck. She nodded and then headed to the bathroom to take her shower.

When she came out, he hadn't yet returned. Her hair was still up in a towel. She got partially dressed, putting on her flowy skirt and bra, but didn't want to put the top on yet because it would get wet from her hair. She brushed her teeth, then took the towel off, rubbing her head, and then began to blow-dry her hair, again closing her eyes and periodically aiming the blow-dryer over her arms and chest and back to her hair, going through it with her fingers.

Talia opened her eyes, and there he was, standing behind her, watching her. She loved seeing him behind her, and she smiled. She shut off the blow-dryer, combing through her hair. As she applied makeup, he stood watching her. She noticed he had on the new pants and shirt he bought in Villars; he looked so good in them. He noticed that she eyed him up and down in the mirror and smiled back at her. He put his arms around her waist, kissing the top of her head, and then went around the corner.

When she finished, she sat on the bed, and then put on her sandals. She picked up her top and put it on. Looking at herself in the mirror to make sure everything looked good, she turned to him and said, "What do you think?"

"Gorgeous," he replied.

"You're looking handsome today with your new pants and shirt," she said, smiling at him.

"Thank you. If you are ready, my lady, we can head down and get a bite before heading to the garden." She picked up her small bag and turned toward the door. He opened it, and she headed out, and he followed. They found a few things to eat and some coffee to drink. Then they walked past the counter. Both Sophia and Laurel were behind it. They smiled, saying, "Have a good morning," and, "We'll see you later." Talia thanked them and headed toward the door. Jason looked at them, and they both winked at him, and he nodded.

Heading across the street to the botanical garden, Jason took Talia's hand. The warmth of the sun felt good, and the sky was a beautiful blue. Everything seemed somehow more vibrant, but maybe that had something to do with the joy Talia was feeling and the love in her heart. They walked inside the garden, following the different paths and looking at all the plants and flowers and little waterfalls. They heard the birds singing, and came across the lily pond where Jason first spoke her name. This time, standing side by side, she looked toward the lily pads, closing her eyes, remembering the first time he said her name. And now, she heard her name being said again, "Talia." She opened her eyes, turning to look at Jason, and with no hesitation put her arms around him, holding him tightly as he wrapped his arms around her.

❨❩

They'd spent a couple of hours wandering around the gardens, and it was already lunchtime. "How about we head for New Bombay," he said. They headed down the street, arms around each other, not saying much of anything. They didn't need to. She felt like she was getting used to walking around Basel, remembering all the various shops and the museums, plus the restaurants. They headed inside and found a seat near the window, looking out while enjoying their food with some light chatting. Jason was ready to get his week going. The sooner he started, the sooner he got home to her. His two comrades would fly in tomorrow morning, and he and Jéan-Paul would take the train north. He saw some sadness come back in her eyes and lifted her chin up so she could look at him, and he said, "No sadness today; it's not allowed. Time will go quickly for both of us." She took hold of his hand and kissed it.

Jason paid the bill, and they got up and headed toward the river. They came around the corner and could see it. Talia was ready to walk closer to it, but Jason stopped her. She looked at him, wondering why. He asked her, "Do you remember where you were standing when I saw you, and you thought you saw me, last Monday?"

Talia replied, "Yes, I was standing about here, I think. Oh, I remember the kitty walking up to me."

"Yes, it did," Jason smiled at her, nodding.

Talia looked toward the bench where Jason sat with the man and woman, knowing now that it was Jéan-Paul and his wife, Suzanne. Jason watched her face as she looked toward the bench, looking at who she thought was Jéan-Paul. But this time, they were facing her and Jason. She looked back at Jason and asked, "Do you know that looks like Jéan-Paul sitting there?"

Jason replied, "I asked him if he would be here."

"All right, I'm confused, and I don't understand. I thought he was hiking this weekend. Why is he here?" She looked at Jason.

Jason took hold of both of her hands, bringing them to his lips, holding them there, and he closed his eyes for a moment. He felt his heart beating faster.

Talia looked up at Jason and had a slight frown, not sure what was going on. "Jason, what's wrong? Please tell me. You're scaring me. Jéan-Paul's a doctor, and he's here. Has something happened to you?" She glanced at Jéan-Paul and assumed that Jason would tell her that he was sick or something.

He saw the tears in her eyes and lowered their hands. He took one of his hands and placed it along the side of her face. "Oh, my love, no tears. Not today. There's nothing wrong with me. Everything is right. I love you so much. From the first moment I laid eyes on you, and each time I saw you after that, my love for you has grown stronger. Remember the first time I told you on the train, when I saw you standing here in this spot; my heart was so full of the love I feel for you.

"At that moment, I wanted to walk over to you and grab you in my arms and hold you tight, never letting you go. It had been so long, and I didn't know how you really felt about me. I knew I had to give you a little more time being with me to see if what I felt from you in the past was real. When you told me that you loved me at the cabin, my heart soared.

"I won't let any more time slip away from us. I want you in my life, and I can't imagine you not being beside me anymore. I want us to go on this incredible journey together." He looked at her, and let go of one of her hands, reached into his pocket, and pulled out a small velvet, navy pouch with a small gold drawstring. Letting go of her other hand, he opened it, holding it upside down against the palm of his hand. She looked up at him, her heart beating faster, then she looked back at the palm of his hand. Out came a beautiful white-gold ring with sapphires encircling a diamond. He took a breath and looked at her, saying, "This was my grandmother's engagement ring. Sapphires are her birthstone; the same as yours." She looked up at him, and he kneeled before her. Looking up at her, he asked, "Talia Elizabeth Rose, would you do me the honor of joining me on this journey, by my side, as my wife?"

Her heart spilled over with love. Tears filled her eyes as she looked into his, and said, "Yes, I would be honored to be your wife." He took her left hand, placing the ring on her finger, and then stood up, putting his arms around her, and kissed her deeply.

There was clapping from Jéan-Paul and his wife Suzanne, who had walked closer, and Sophia and Laurel, plus many other people who witnessed the proposal. Talia looked at them, wondering where they all came from. Jason motioned for them to come closer. The girls had their cell phones out, recording and taking pictures.

Jason said, "I want to explain why the girls, Jéan-Paul and Suzanne are here. I wanted them to be a part of this, since we don't have any other family here. The girls were more than willing to take photos and record this for you so that you can share it with your family, if you want, before I get home. And Jéan-Paul has been my amazing mentor, and he feels like family. They're all special people."

The girls gave Talia a hug and best wishes for an amazing life with this man. Jéan-Paul hugged Jason, as did Suzanne. Jéan-Paul then kissed Talia on both cheeks, and then took her hands in his and kissed the back of them, wishing her a beautiful life. He introduced Suzanne to Talia, who kissed Talia on each cheek and wished them both a long and joyful life. The girls continued clicking away, excited to send them all to Talia and Jason. Jason asked someone in the crowd if they would take a photo of the six of them, and it delighted several people to help. They took Jason's cell phone and the girls' and clicked away.

ଔ

Everyone became quiet. Jason told Talia, as he looked into her eyes and held her hands, "I have a song that I have listened to so many times over the years, and it's what's in my heart. It was recorded in the '80s by a wonderful and talented artist. In a movie, he was a poker player back in the old west, a befitting gambling man." He smiled at her. "This song made me think about us from the first moment I laid eyes on you until this very moment. Now, granted, I don't have a horse and no armor, but I am your prince, and I found you, here. And I love waking up with you next to me. You are my lady."

ଔ

He looked at the girls to play the song, and he asked her, "Talia Elizabeth Rose, would you dance with me?" She looked at him with tears in her eyes, and hearing the start of the song, she knew exactly the song that was being played. He took her in his arms and started dancing to the music. As they slowly turned, she saw Jéan-Paul dancing with Suzanne, and so many others in the crowd started dancing with the Rhine River as their backdrop. Laurel and Sophia danced with each other. Talia had such joy and love in her heart. As the song ended, everyone clapped and cheered, making her feel like a princess.

The crowd became quiet again, and Jéan-Paul walked over to the both of them. He took out of his coat's inside breast pocket an envelope and said, "I would like to give you a pre-wedding gift, that you take a short cruise on our lovely Rhine River this afternoon." Both Talia and Jason just looked at him. Talia gave him a big hug, and kissed his cheek. Jason hugged his good friend.

"Thank you, Jéan-Paul," Jason said.

"You will find your tickets in here. You leave in thirty minutes." He grinned at them. Everyone laughed and clapped.

As the crowd left, the girls came up quickly with another hug for both Jason and Talia, saying they'd see them later. Jéan-Paul and Suzanne would also leave; Jéan-Paul told Jason he would meet him tomorrow at the *Spalentor.*

Chapter 20

Looking at the tickets Jéan-Paul gave them, they headed to the boat dock. Once there, they presented the tickets and boarded a small ferry. It was a late afternoon river cruise that took about two hours, and then they would come back to this same dock and get off. They found some seats near the front. The cruise would get started soon. "I can't believe Jéan-Paul did this. It's an incredible gift. I absolutely love it. It was part of my birthday wish," Talia said, as she sat looking out toward the front of the ferry. She turned to Jason. "I get to cruise on the Rhine with my love beside me."

"So do your wishes often come true?" he said, smiling at her.

"I guess I've had a few in my life, but this past week, more of them came true," she said, smiling, reaching up to kiss him.

Jason turned toward his bride-to-be, looking at her. "I can't wait to make you my wife," he said. "I love how that sounds: my wife."

She turned to Jason, "And I can't wait to make you my husband." She looked at her engagement ring. "This is so beautiful. I don't know anything about your grandparents. Are they all still living?"

Jason said, while holding her left hand, "The only one living is my grandmother Jean. I talked to her so many times about you over the years. She's the one that listened to me go on about you like we were already dating or something." He smiled. "She kept telling me to be patient, that timing is everything. She was married to my grandfather for fifty-three years. He died about ten years ago, and she still misses him; so do I. When I told her about this work program and that I would come here, she was so happy for me to see another part of the world and experience it, and that more was in store for me. I just looked at her. She smiled at me. After Kurt called me, telling me you were going to be here, I called Grandma Jean the next day and told her. She's been my confidant all these years." Talia watched him, seeing how much he cares for her.

"Her name for me is Jay, and she said, 'Jay, you get yourself over here. I have something for you before you go. Now don't you dare forget to see me before you leave; it's important. You promise?'" Jason chuckled. "I remember the tone she used with me. So, a couple of days before I left, I went to see her. She's still in good health, which I'm grateful for. She had me sit down next to her and then handed me this little navy pouch and told me to open it. I just looked at her, and she raised her eyebrow at me. I knew I better not disobey her." He shook his head lightly. "I opened it as I did with you, and the ring came out into my palm. I looked at it, and then I looked at her. She said, 'This was my engagement ring, and I want to pass it onto you. Do you remember me telling you to be patient and that timing is everything? You take this with you; the timing is now. I know your heart is full enough for the both of you. Just know, she'll come to you this time.' She looked me square in the eye with a smile. I don't know how she knew this. It's so uncanny." He looked out the front of the ferry. "She also seems to know some things before they happen."

Talia said, "I think it's wonderful how our grandparents know things and are so wise. I love her already, and I haven't even met her."

"You would love her. I know she already loves you, from everything I told her about you until I came over here. You have something in common with my grandmother, besides me. She loved sewing; she doesn't do it anymore." Jason chuckled. "On our road trip to Ollon, you were driving me nuts about fabric. I saw what you were doing, and each time you would look over at me, I just wanted to stop the car and kiss you," he said.

"Oh, you picked up on that. And you wanted to? You did, twice. Remember?" Talia giggled. Jason put his arms around her and kissed her. They looked at some homes in the distance, and could see castles that still stood proud in their grandeur.

"I'd still like to have you teach me some Italian," he said, looking at her. "So, the next time you talk with someone in Italian, I'll know what you're saying or at least try to understand, or even look like I might understand. I do know this much," he said, *"Ti amo"* (I love you).

"Ti amo," she responded.

They enjoyed their short river cruise, seeing more castles and vineyards, and watching the sun slowly going down. It was so beautiful. By the time the ferry docked, it was after 7:00 p.m. The memories they shared this past week will last a lifetime. Walking back to the hotel, they realized they hadn't eaten since lunchtime. Jason said, "I'm hungry, but I'm not. What about you?"

"I'm the same way," she replied. "Would you be willing to split a sandwich at New Bombay? I know we've been there twice already."

"I can do that, *fiancée,*" he said, smiling. And they walked around the corner to it. They ordered a sandwich, having some coffee, and then shared a dessert of chocolate cake. It hit the spot. As they were walking back to the hotel, they saw the outside garden of the botanical center and stood near that entrance. They didn't go in, but stood there looking at it one last time. They wrapped their arms around each other. Talia could hear Jason's heartbeat as she put her head against his chest, and she could feel hers syncing with his. *It's said that when you are in love, heartbeats and respirations will match.*

Jason felt Talia shiver. He rubbed her arms up and down, then hugged her and kissed her, and then they headed for the hotel. Once inside, Sophia and Laurel greeted them with big smiles.

"Ladies, you have charming smiles on this evening," Jason said, smiling at them.

"It was so wonderful this afternoon, the way you proposed to Talia. We loved it. Thank you for letting us share in it," Sophia said.

"Thank you for recording it and taking photos. That meant a great deal to me, to us," Jason replied.

"We have something for both of you." Laurel set on the counter a wrapped box.

"Oh, thank you," Talia said. "Can we open it now?"

"Yes, please do," Laurel said.

Talia unwrapped the box and turned it around. "We wanted you to have something to put all your digital photos in so you can see them anytime, without looking at your phones. It's a digital picture frame and has room for a lot of pictures," Sophia said. "And of course, there are a couple of us in there as well. We already uploaded the photos from our phones so you would have them."

Giving it to Jason, she walked around and hugged them both, and then Jason did the same. "You two have been such wonderful guests, we loved having you here, and we did something else," Laurel said.

"What did you do?" Jason asked.

"Well, we want you to have this for the next time you come here, which we expect you to do soon, maybe?" Laurel handed them an envelope.

Jason opened up the envelope, looking at them and then back to the envelope, with Talia looking on. It was a gift certificate for a three-night stay at this hotel, and no expiration date on it. Jason showed Talia. There were happy tears all around and more hugs for everyone. "Ladies, will we see you in the morning before we have to leave?" Jason asked.

"Yes, you will," Sophia replied, tears already in her eyes.

Jason and Talia headed up to their room. It had been an extraordinary day, waking up next to the one she loves, getting engaged, having a pre-wedding cruise on the Rhine River, and spending at least one more night with her prince.

"I can't believe they gave us two such beautiful gifts," Talia said. They sat down on the bed. She knew how the digital frame worked, plugging it in, and pulled out her cell phone to load her pictures onto it. She took Jason's phone and did the same thing. This one also supported video. "Do you want to take it with you tomorrow and bring it home?" she asked.

"I would love to, but I don't want something to happen to it here and get lost or left behind. We have a lot of beautiful memories in there now. I want you to take it home and keep it safe with you, and this gift certificate, which we will use soon," Jason said. "I have my photos here, and you can send yours to me so I can look at your beautiful face anytime I want to and show you off to the guys here. A little jealousy never hurt anyone."

Talia giggled, and Jason grabbed her around her waist, laying her back on the bed. "Do you know how much I'm going to miss you?" She put her arms around his shoulders and placed a hand on the side of his face. He took her hand and kissed it. He kissed her neck. He had a small gift he wanted to give her so she could pack it carefully. "I have a little something for you," he said. He got up and went to the little box sitting on the table. She hadn't seen it there before.

"What is it?" Talia asked. He handed it to her.

"I saw this in the last little shop we were at. I asked them if they would please deliver it to the hotel this afternoon; I didn't want you to see it until now," he said.

Talia opened the box, which was well packed, and slowly drew out a small snow globe of the *Gate of Spalen*. She shook it and watched the snow inside, floating. "I love it," she said, looking at him. "I don't have anything for you."

Jason stood up, moving the picture frame and their phones off the bed and pulling down the covers. He took off his shirt, looking lovingly at her and said, "Yes, you do."

Ϩ

They both lay there, awake, with the soft glow of a distant streetlight coming through to the other side of the room. Jason's arm was around her, with his hand caressing the small of her back. The blanket was down around their waists with their skin exposed. She let her fingers gently caress down his arm and back up again and then slowly across his entire chest, resting her hand over his heart. Jason turned his head toward her, taking a slow deep breath, watching her. She raised her head, leaned over him and kissed his chest in several places while her hand moved below his stomach. Before she could go any further, with both hands, he raised her and pulled her on top of him, knowing what they both wanted.

☙

It was early morning, around 5:45 a.m., when Jason woke. He held her close, not wanting her to leave this morning. He took a deep breath and knew he would have to wake her. He also had to remember that it was only a week, and then he would be home. He'd come so far to find her, and he was feeling sad, like the very first time his family left to head home, leaving her behind with her family. His comrades would arrive this morning at Stuttgart, and he and Jéan-Paul would leave on the train thirty minutes after he would have to say goodbye to her. He took another deep breath; he needed to be strong. "Talia," he spoke softly to her. "My love, it's time to get up." She stirred, turning her head toward him, and smiled. "We have just a few hours before you…" He couldn't say the word "leave." She opened her eyes more fully, looking into his, both their eyes glistening now with tears knowing what he was going to say. He drew her to him, just wanting to hold on as long as he could. He knew he had to be strong, but sometimes men aren't always able to; and that's all right.

She whispered in his ear, "I love you so much; you showed me how. We both can do this, be strong for the other."

"Before I let you leave today, I want us to decide when we're getting married," he asked.

She looked into his eyes and said, "The week before Christmas." He chuckled.

"So glad I got to help with that decision. I love it," he said. "The week before Christmas, it is. Are you sure you don't want Halloween or Thanksgiving?"

"No," she said.

"Which year?" He smiled at her, knowing sooner than later.

"This Christmas, celebrating all our little miracles," Talia said.

"I like the sound of that, and I'm so looking forward to calling you 'my wife.'" He kissed her. "When is your flight?" Jason asked.

"I have to be at the airport before 9:00 a.m. My flight leaves at 10:00 a.m. It will be a long one going home —about seventeen hours. I have two plane changes before getting into Des Moines around 9:00 p.m. Kurt is picking me up."

"OK. I want you to text me when you get to the airport, and before your flight leaves, and when you get home. It will be early morning here, but I want to know you're home safe," Jason said. Talia put her arms around him and hugged him.

"It won't take long for me to repack. I'm going to take a shower. Come with me?" she asked.

"I'd be happy too," he replied.

❧

With just over an hour before she had to leave, taking the shuttle back to the airport, they were both dressed and bags repacked. They stood at their window, looking out. Jason's phone was ringing; it was Jéan-Paul, checking in. He told Jéan-Paul that Talia would take the shuttle to the airport in under an hour. They were going to have some breakfast downstairs and then walk over to it. Jéan-Paul said he would come to the hotel, as their shuttle would take them to the train station less than thirty minutes later.

"Did you pack your snow globe carefully?" he asked.

"Yes, I wrapped some of my clothes around it to help cushion it. It should be safe in my luggage. And I have the digital frame, the gift certificate, and my passport in my shoulder bag. I'm good, for the most part." She looked at him.

"Why don't we head downstairs, then, and have some breakfast," Jason said. Talia wasn't really hungry, but knew she needed to eat something. There would be a meal served on the plane. When they finished, they walked over to the counter to check out. Both Sophia and Laurel had sad faces. "No long faces. We need to keep in touch. I want you each to have one of my business cards," Talia said, as she gave them each one. "You can email me and Facebook me, OK?" They looked at Jason and asked if he used

Facebook, and if he had a card. He said yes, to both. They looked relieved. It was a connection they wanted to keep.

They came around the counter, giving both of them hugs. Other people were arriving for check-in and were looking at them. Jason perked up, saying, "Oh, just saying goodbye to family."

They walked over to wait for the shuttle. Jéan-Paul was standing close by. He walked over to the two of them, hugging Jason first and then kissing Talia on each cheek along with a hug. Jason noticed that Jéan-Paul did that a lot with her. He commented, "You be careful there with my *fiancée*, you hear." He chuckled.

"Don't you forget, my friend, I'm a Frenchman, and we love the ladies, especially beautiful ones. You are blessed to have this one in your life, yes?" Jéan-Paul said.

Jason put his arms around Talia, looking at her and said, "Yes, I am," He kissed her.

It wasn't more than ten minutes, and the shuttle came. Jéan-Paul told her to have a safe journey home, and that he would take good care of this man until he returned home to her. He hugged her, and took her hands and kissed them one last time. With the shuttle there, she turned toward Jason, tears in her eyes. They hugged, and he kissed her deeply, telling her, "I love you so much," wanting to be strong. He reminded her to text him. She took her bag and boarded the shuttle, finding a window seat, and then looked out at him. Holding her hand against the window, the shuttle headed for the airport. Jason stood, watching it leave his sight.

Jéan-Paul saw how hard this was for Jason, and was glad he would be with him throughout the week. He also knew that Jason's two comrades should already be in Stuttgart, which would help him focus on the week ahead.

Their shuttle arrived, and they headed for the train station. By the time they arrived, Talia had texted him that she had made it through customs and was now waiting to board. Jason texted back that they arrived at the train station, which would leave before her plane did, but wanted her to text him anyway.

Talia heard over the loudspeaker that her flight would be on time and would soon board. It was getting close to 10:00 a.m. She texted Jason that they would board in a bit, but would text him again just before she had to shut her phone off. Her phone buzzed, a photo of Jason and Jéan-Paul sitting across from one another on the train. Jason had his hand to his mouth, showing he was blowing her a kiss. She returned a text doing the same, only sitting among a bunch of other passengers. It was time to board. She found her seat next to a window, almost the same place she sat when she headed over. Before they told everyone to shut off all electronic devices, she texted Jason quickly to let him know they were taking off, and she had to shut off her phone. She texted: *I Love You!* with a heart beating emoji.

He returned it to her, including the same heart beating emoji. She then had to shut off her phone.

Chapter 21

Jason and Jéan-Paul arrived back in Stuttgart, heading to the hospital first. That was where they would meet up with Paul Daily and Jim Peters, the other two paramedics. Paul hadn't been outside of the United States; Jim served in the military, serving overseas. Jason and Jéan-Paul arrived at the hospital, which Jason had been to several times the first week. He was familiar with the layout. They headed to one of the conference rooms, walking in. They saw Paul and Jim, both equally glad to see Jason. They greeted each other with a hug. Seeing Jéan-Paul, they also greeted him with a hug.

Jason asked the both of them, "How was your flight over?"

Paul replied, "Having never flown before, I'm not sure I want to do it again. The only problem is, I'm going to have to if I want to get home. But, who knows, maybe in time. I see planes all the time flying, and I think, *'There are people in that little tube flying across the sky.'"* The four of them chuckled.

Jim replied, "I was in the military, so I've flown plenty. I like flying; it's amazing looking out the little window and looking down at the earth below. I think our flight was smooth. The food could have been better, but other than that, I'm glad to be here and see you. Jéan-Paul, it's good to see you as well."

Jéan-Paul replied, "It's good to see you both. We have a full week. But we are first to look at some ER rooms. Jason is familiar with them. You can see their set-up and speak with some doctors and staff. We'll do that in about thirty minutes." Just then, Jéan-Paul's name came over the speaker system. He excused himself and said he'd be back soon.

"So, what have you been up to the last week or so?" Jim asked.

Jason replied with a huge grin, "I got engaged yesterday." Both Paul and Jim looked at Jason with eyes wide and mouths open.

"What do you mean you got engaged yesterday? You've only been here a week or so. How did that happen?" Jim asked, shaking his head.

"Paul, you wouldn't know about Talia, but Jim does," Jason said, looking at his best friend. Paul just looked at the both of them, confused.

"Talia is here?" Jim asked. Paul looked from one to the other, still confused. "Boy, you best not mess with me." Jim looked at Jason. Jim was this strong, tall Black man who was always there, ready to help in whatever situation arose. He was kind and compassionate with everyone. He was thinking back to what Jason had told him years ago about meeting her the first time, along with other family vacations, and remembering his best friend Amy. He was there.

"Who's Talia?" Paul asked, wanting to know. "Does she live here? How did you meet her?

Before Jason could say another word to Paul, Jim asked, "Did you tell her about Amy?"

Paul was perplexed, and both Jason and Jim seemed to have forgotten that Paul was in the same room.

Jason explained just a little while they waited for Jéan-Paul to come back. Looking at Paul, Jason explained, "Talia flew back to the States this morning. And if Jim didn't tell you already, he's from Colorado. I lived in Colorado for several years and had joined the fire station where Jim was a paramedic/firefighter. I was hired on as a paramedic first and then joined as a firefighter. I had a best friend, Amy. We were getting close, but it just really never got any further. One day, we got a call," (pointing to Jim), "about an accident up in the foothills. A car and semi tangled." Paul could see where this was going and put his head down, shaking his head. He'd gone on calls like that.

Looking now at Jim, Jason continued. "Long story short, once the car's front windshield was removed, and I saw who it was, I lost it. Jéan-Paul was there working with our unit. He had to pull me away. My best friend, Amy, and her parents died that day. It was only a couple of months later that I moved back to the Midwest. Jim and his family moved after I did."

"Jason, I'm so sorry. I didn't know," Paul said. "But, where does this Talia fit in?" Just then, Jéan-Paul came back in.

"Paul, I will let you know throughout the week," Jason said. "But, she's this amazing fashion designer from back home. I have photos of the two of us from this past week; I'll show them later. I can tell you that when I first saw her, she was nine and I was fourteen."

"OK, this I want to hear about," Paul said, now really wanting to know about this mystery woman.

"And gentlemen, then he will become one of us, married," Jéan-Paul said with a smile. "She is, indeed, a beautiful woman and speaks Italian as well."

"What?" Both Jim and Paul said it at the same time. "You didn't tell me she spoke Italian," Jim said.

Jason said, "Well, I didn't know until I first heard her speak it in the *Boothaus* in Ollon. Didn't know what she said at first, but it sounded sexy." They all laughed.

"All right, gentlemen, if you'll follow me, let's head to the ER," Jéan-Paul said. Upon entering the ER, there wasn't much going on. Jéan-Paul introduced Jason, Paul and Jim to two of the ER doctors who welcomed them with solid German accents. It was a little hard to understand them, so Jéan-Paul translated. They explained that this was where they would bring patients. The three Americans were asked if they all had their uniforms, to which they all replied yes. Just then, the ER doors swung open with a paramedic and a hospital staff pushing a gurney to one of the rooms. The two doctors went to work. Jéan-Paul was not needed, so they headed back to the conference room to collect their bags. Someone from the fire station came to the hospital to pick them all up.

One fireman, Adrian, recognized Jason from the first week and welcomed him back. Jason then introduced Paul and Jim. Driving to the fire station would take them about twenty minutes. Adrian started going over some duties they would do alongside the others. They would eat and sleep at the station. Since all three Americans were also firefighters, they would go on those calls as well.

Jason decided to text Talia about arriving in Stuttgart and meeting up with Paul and Jim. They were being driven to the fire station where they'd be staying the entire week. He told her to sleep well, and to text him when she arrived at the airport. *"Tell Kurt, hello. 'Ti amo.'"* She wouldn't get the message until her plane landed, around 9:00 p.m., but he wanted to be the first to check in. It would be 4:00 a.m. the next morning for him.

Paul had glanced over, watching Jason text, and saw the foreign language. He said, "What's *Ti amo?*"

Looking out the window, Jason replied, "I love you."

☙

It was already a long flight, and they hadn't even been in the air that long. Looking out the window, she could see the ocean. There was a lot of water down there. Electronic devices could now be turned on, and she took out the digital picture frame. She had let it charge fully throughout the night. She missed him so much already and just wanted to see his face. She turned it on and started looking at all the photos from the beginning of the week, grinning from ear to ear. She had earbuds on so she wouldn't disturb anyone else, and hopefully, no one would talk to her. Seeing his face, she touched the screen, a tear falling. When it came to Jason's proposal, she watched intently and listened carefully. The girls, Sophia or Laurel, did an excellent job recording the whole thing. When it came to the video of the dance and the song they danced to, more tears fell. She wanted to feel his arms around her and his kisses. She pressed two of her fingers against her lips, kissing them, and then touched the screen.

She was seated next to an older couple. The woman sitting next to Talia said, "Excuse me, miss?"

Talia looked at her, wiping the tears from her eyes, and slightly smiled. "I don't mean to impose, but you seem a little sad. I was watching as you were going through your photos."

"It's all right. I just got engaged yesterday to this amazing man. He had to stay back in Germany," Talia said.

"Oh, is he in the military?" she asked.

"No, he's a paramedic/firefighter," Talia said. Seeing the woman wonder, she had no problem explaining. "Jason, that's his name. He's part of a work abroad program in Germany. Two of his comrades flew over last night from the Midwest. That's where we live."

"My husband and I are from Georgia," the woman said. "My name is Rosalind Kaden, and this is my husband, Marcus." He gave a little wave.

"My name is Talia Rose."

"So, did you meet him in Germany?" Rosalind asked.

"Not exactly. I was already in Basel for business and vacation, and he came down from Stuttgart with a friend. He'd been working the week before with the German paramedics, and then had a week-long break before heading back to Stuttgart this morning. We've known each other for a very long time," Talia said.

Rosalind said, "You must be very proud of him, being a paramedic/firefighter."

Talia replied, "I am very proud of him. He's this strong and amazing and wonderful man. Just this last weekend, we were heading back to Villars and came across an accident. I called it in while he attended to the people. There was no one else to help him for a little while; just him. He was doing his job." Talia didn't mind boasting about him at all. How could she not be proud of what he did, and the man himself?

"I have a grandson who wants to be a fireman, but that can be a dangerous job," Rosalind said.

"It can be. But there are a lot of jobs that can be dangerous. I hope that if that's what he wants to do, he should. He can at least start as a volunteer firefighter, get into one of their programs and see where it takes him. You should be proud of him if that's what he wants to do. They save a lot of lives," Talia stated.

"And what line of work are you in, Talia?" she asked.

"I'm a fashion designer," Talia said.

"That sounds interesting. Have you been doing it long?" Rosalind asked.

"Close to fourteen years. I've owned my own business about the last four," Talia stated.

It was close to lunchtime, and the flight attendants were checking with all the passengers about what they wanted for lunch, telling them their choices, and taking meal orders. Talia, and Rosalind chatted for a little while until their food came. Talia was glad for the food; she was getting hungry, and it provided a break in the conversation area. She just wanted to eat now and go back and look at all the photos again.

When they finished eating, Talia excused herself, stepping over Rosalind and Marcus to go to the bathroom. When she came back, she put her seat belt on, then her earbuds, picking up the digital frame and going back over the photos. With the sun coming through the window, it was making her warm and tired. She closed her eyes to the hum of the plane's engines.

Talia woke to the sound of the wheels of the plane coming down and locking into place. She'd change planes in Detroit with a two-hour layover before heading home. Tired of sitting for such an extended time, she was glad to get up and move. After disembarking, she walked to the next terminal where she would need to be. She looked up at the flight boards to make sure her flight would be on time. She'd get to do a little more sitting, waiting for her next flight to take off, but knowing where she needed to go now, she could wander and people watch.

She purchased a cup of coffee and took her time walking around before heading back to Terminal C. She found a place to sit. Just another thirty minutes. She decided to text Jason. When she turned her phone on, there was a message waiting from him. It made her smile. She texted him back: *I'm sitting in Detroit. I only have to change planes once instead of twice. The next flight leaves in thirty minutes. I miss you terribly, but looking at our photos helps. Sleep well, or at least the best you can without me. I love you so much! XOXO.*

The announcement came that they were now boarding and for passengers to come forward, please. She was glad to be closer to home. She found her seat, got comfortable and then put her seat belt on. She texted Kurt quickly and let him know that her flight was about to take off from Detroit and when her flight would be arriving. Kurt texted her back and said he would be waiting for her at the airport.

Talia told Kurt he could stay at her place after picking her up at the airport instead of driving home that hour and a half. He could have stayed at their mom's, but he didn't want to do that. He would be tired, and she had space. Kurt had been thinking about moving back to the big city for a while, but just hadn't gotten around to it. He liked his job, but wanted a change and didn't want to leave Caren, his girlfriend. So maybe having a day or two with Talia, he could figure things out a little better. And if he and Jason kept in contact, the way it sounded from Jason, she was going to see about getting some information out of Kurt. She was curious now about what they talked about, with her being the main news.

When her flight landed, it was just before 9:00 p.m. She headed to the baggage claim and watched for her bag. She texted Jason quickly: *We've landed. I'm waiting for my luggage, and Kurt is waiting for me. I'm so tired. I hope your day is good tomorrow. Love you. XOXO.*

She got a text back; it was Kurt, and he was waiting right outside for her. Picking up her luggage, she headed out to the car. Kurt opened the trunk, put her luggage in and closed the lid. He gave her a big hug, welcoming her home. As they left the airport, Kurt asked, "So, did you enjoy your time in Basel?"

Being dark outside, he couldn't see her face very well. "Yes, I did. A lot of wonderful memories were made," Talia said. She was waiting for Kurt to prompt her about Jason, because she knew he was dying to know. She waited for his next question. She smiled to herself.

"How did your shopping go for your fabrics?" he asked, hoping she would fess up and give him some interesting information.

"Oh, it was terrific. I went to three different stores, the ones I had special ordered from before. It was nice meeting the clerks. When they learned who I was, they became helpful, and of course, shipped for me. I loved being there. It was a good experience. I'm looking forward to seeing the bolts in my shop. I hope they arrived, I meant to check with Chloe, and then I got sidetracked, and we were planning--" She stopped abruptly.

"What were you going to say about 'we were planning', who's 'we'?" Kurt asked, waiting for her to spill the beans. He had now pulled into her apartment's parking lot. He shut off the car and waited for her to tell him. She looked ahead, and then turned to him.

"It's been a long day. Can we maybe talk about it tomorrow? I know you want to hear about Jason. You are my big brother, and I also have questions for you, but not tonight, OK?" Talia said.

"OK," Kurt replied. He popped the trunk. They headed into her apartment. It felt good to be home, but it was missing one thing, and he was across the ocean. At some point, she and Jason would have to decide where they would live once they got married, whether it was her place, his or a new home. But she was ready to start a new life with him.

She brought out blankets and a pillow for Kurt. She had a hide-a-bed sofa, and got it made up with his help. She changed for bed. She came out and told Kurt thank you for picking her up at the airport and staying with her. They hugged, and she headed for bed, leaving him to either go to bed or watch television. She was glad he was there.

"Good night Kurt," Talia said.

"Good night, sis," Kurt replied.

<h1 style="text-align:center">Chapter 22</h1>

The buzz of her cell phone woke her. She didn't hear it the first time, which was 6:00 a.m. for Jason, but 11:00 p.m. her time. She must have been zonked. It was just a long, emotional day. The first text message she saw was: *Good morning, fiancée!* She grinned, loving the greeting. The second text message was sent at 7:00 a.m. from him: *Only seven more days. We're having breakfast, and then we have a class to attend at 8:00 a.m. going over their protocol, and then 'chores,' just like we do back at my station. So far, all is quiet. Love you much.*

It was 7:30 a.m. when she texted him back: *Good afternoon, fiancé!* Then the following text: *Have miscellaneous things to do here at home first before going to my shop to see if my purchases arrived. I have to get moving on my winter line; I have eight designs I plan on finishing before saying, 'I do.' Love you.*

Talia took a shower and then got dressed. She missed not being able to plan another adventurous day with Jason, seeing something new. But who knows, maybe they'll get to go back within the next year, and he can show her some places he's seen in Germany. Talia came out of her bedroom, feeling much better about everything. She started a list of what she needed to accomplish in the next several days, and she needed to get a load of laundry done. After putting a load in the wash, Talia headed to the kitchen to make breakfast. She could see Kurt was up and had the television on, watching the news. Kurt turned around, looking at her, and said, "Morning."

"Morning, Kurt. Did you sleep, OK?" Talia asked.

Kurt shut off the TV and picked up the blankets and pillow he used, and put the sofa bed back the way it was supposed to be. "I did. Did you sleep, OK?" He looked at her. She noticed the way he was looking at her. She had a feeling she wasn't going to get by with not telling him about her and Jason. He was the one that told Jason where to find her. She set the small table for the two of them. She started the coffee and then made pancakes and scrambled eggs. Kurt came and sat down at the table, waiting for her. As they were eating, he noticed the ring on her finger, mostly because she didn't wear one on that hand, and said, "That's a beautiful ring. A souvenir from Basel?" She knew he was fishing, and it was going to be hard not to tell him almost everything that happened.

She looked at the ring and said, "It's my engagement ring." Then she looked at Kurt. It was the way he was looking at her. He seemed different, almost like a peace came over him. She expected him to be stern with her about getting engaged so soon, and not even dated the man she was going to marry. She could hear the questions now. But looking at him sitting there, not saying anything, she couldn't stand it. She and Kurt had been close throughout their lives. It's only been in the last three or four years that they didn't talk as much as they used to. She cared about what Kurt thought honestly of Jason, and maybe they just needed to talk.

"I don't know what you're thinking about right now. I half expected you to be upset with Jason or me. Maybe you have questions or something you feel you need to tell me. I'm not sure where I should start, but I want you to know that I love Jason more than I ever imagined," Talia said to Kurt.

"I knew a long time ago how he felt about you. I didn't catch on when we first met in Basel. I mean, you were nine, I was twelve, and Jason was fourteen. We were all young; different families on a fun vacation, meeting and getting to see things with another family from back home. And when Mom and Jason's mom got to talking and realized they were both nurses in the same town, just different hospitals, it was cool. It gave Mom someone to talk to because Dad didn't always want to listen about what she dealt with being a surgical nurse. But Mom and Mary Ann Porter formed a friendship. I remember the next vacation after that, the way Jason looked at you. I started watching him more closely. I liked him, but I didn't trust him, and I wasn't going to let anything happen to you. You're my little sister, no matter how old we get," Kurt said.

"You never told me this, all these years that we've talked, and his name came up that you didn't trust him, why? Why couldn't you tell me?" Talia asked. "So, what changed here? He told me that you called him and that if he wanted a chance with me, where to find me. I'm a little confused here."

Kurt got up from his chair and walked over to the sofa, and then back to a window, looking out. "He's very much in love with you. I was the overprotective brother. I've listened to the crap in the locker rooms, what guys say, how they'll look at a girl and wonder if they tried this or that, and it scared me." He looked at her. "Your name came up, and then they would see me and laugh. I wondered if they knew how foolish they were. What would they do if it was their sister who was hurt? Would they do something about it or laugh to fit in with all the other morons? They were jerks, but I was going to make sure you were safe.

"When we were on vacation up in Michigan, and I saw how Jason looked at you or would stand near you, I think it was the first day, and I was going to nip it in the bud with him. I told him I wanted to talk to him, so we walked off on the other side of the parking lot where people couldn't hear us. He wanted to know what was going on, and I told him I was watching him. I saw how he was always looking at you or tried being closer to you. I told him I remember how the guys were in the locker rooms and the crap they would say and that he wasn't going to hurt you; that he was older than you, and I didn't think it was right, and that I would punch him out if I had to." Kurt sat back down on the kitchen chair. "Jason just looked at me, appalled. We had a long talk. It was then that he told me when he first laid eyes on you in Basel; it was love at first sight. I thought he was kidding, and I told him that.

"He said he didn't understand it, how you can look at someone at a young age and know if you love them or are in love with them or even what love looked like. He thought maybe it was just an infatuation, but it wasn't. We'd had a lot of talks over the years, and I could hear it in his voice or see it in his eyes when he would look at you, wherever we were on vacation. I didn't know what he was talking about until I met Caren, and then I understood. More than anything, he wanted to be there to love you, and protect you and keep you safe if I couldn't. He swore on his little sister's grave that he couldn't possibly hurt you and have someone feel the pain of losing a sister. Talia, he fell in love with you." It took Kurt a moment to realize what he had just said. He had promised Jason he would never, ever tell her that. "You were never supposed to hear that." Kurt looked mortified.

Talia just looked at Kurt, trying to process what he just told her, tears forming in her eyes, "Wait! You're telling me Jason had a sister. He swore on her grave." She got up from her chair and walked to the window, turning around, looking at Kurt. "He HAD a sister?" She just stared at him, taking a moment before asking in a quiet voice, "What happened to her?"

Kurt knew there was no turning back now. He closed his eyes and lowered his head, then he got up and walked to her. He wanted to be close, just in case.... Talia just looked at him, her heart beating more quickly. "His sister was about five-years-old. They were all at a park one day. He said they took their eyes off of her for only a moment. Someone grabbed her and ran with her toward the street when they were both hit by a pickup truck. She died on impact. The man who took her had internal injuries; he later died at the hospital. Her name was Amy," he said with tears in his eyes. He knew of Jason's best friend, Amy, as well.

"Oh my god." Talia burst into tears, her heart aching for Jason losing people he loved. Kurt grabbed her as she dropped to the floor. All he could do was hold her and sit on the floor with her. Kurt couldn't imagine losing Talia at a young age, going through life without her. They sat for a while. There were no words. All she wanted to do was go to Jason and hold him. It just doesn't make any sense what human beings are capable of, what they do to others. Talia slowly got up from the floor and just stood there, unsure what to do or where to go. Her brain seemed to disengage. She wandered over to a big overstuffed chair and sat down. Kurt got up and walked over to the sofa.

She just sat, staring at the coffee table. "Jason and I did a day trip to Ollon. He bought me a pair of hiking boots because I didn't have any, and we were going to hike up on a trail that Jéan-Paul told Jason about. We'd gone about four miles, and then the weather changed on us, and we had to head back down; we were both soaked. It was about fifteen miles before we could make it back to Villars, but it was raining so heavily, and the roads were narrow and weren't safe with all the hairpin curves. Jéan-Paul had a cabin close by, so we stayed there. The next morning, when we left, we stopped at the end of the driveway, and Jason had me put in the address to our hotel in Villars. It took all of five minutes to put it in, and then we were on our way.

"There was a car about a half-mile or less ahead of us. They were slowing down for the curve. We saw a car that would take that same curve toward us from the other direction, but they didn't seem to slow down. I mean, why wouldn't you slow down for a dangerous curve? We witnessed the car in front of us getting sideswiped and getting shoved onto a field. My heart dropped, and I felt sick to my stomach. Jason pulled up close to the cars, getting out and grabbing his paramedic backpack that had medical supply stuff in it, yelling at me to call 911. He ran over to the car that caused the accident first. Two young males, in the middle of the morning, had been drinking; stupid. He went over to the field." She spoke with tears in her eyes again, this time rocking, still staring at the coffee table. Kurt got up and sat next to her, putting her arms around her.

"He couldn't get the driver's door open, no matter how hard he tried. Then he went around to the passenger side and got that door opened. It was a woman; she still had on her seat belt, and she was about six months pregnant. The husband's airbag had been deployed. Jason didn't know if he was dead or not. He couldn't get to him; it was a two-door car. Jason started taking her vitals; she was alive, but he had to leave her in her seat belt. He stood up, looking around for help, and there wasn't any. He looked at me and then re-checked the woman. He had four people that needed help. I wasn't of any use. I didn't know what to do. Then a car pulled up on the opposite side, and a man got out. It turns out it was Jason's mentor, Jéan-

Paul; he's a doctor. Finally, the police and fire trucks and ambulances came. I went to the hospital with the woman, because she was terrified. I tried speaking Italian to her to help calm her.

"After arriving at the hospital, they took her to an ER exam room. About twenty some minutes later, Jéan-Paul and Jason arrived. I was so glad to see him. He came over to me and held me. When Jéan-Paul and the other doctor finished with the woman, Jason told Jéan-Paul that that could have been us. We would have been in that spot, but because he stopped and had me put in the hotel's address, that probably saved our lives. I told him I didn't know what I would have done had I lost him, and he told me he didn't know what he would have done if he'd lost me. That could have been us, something could have happened to me, and that would have been three people he lost," she said, looking at Kurt with tears.

Kurt hugged Talia, giving her a few moments. Maybe it would lighten the mood, or she might tell him to go home, but he asked, "Talia, um, when did you learn Italian?"

She looked at him with a slight grin, shaking her head. "I've been learning it off and on for the last year. I got to use it in Ollon and Villars. I need to move my clothes over to the dryer."

Chapter 23

It was around 5:00 p.m. in Stuttgart. There was some downtime before dinner was served. Jason, Jim, and Paul were sitting in the lounge around a table when Paul asked Jason, "So, you have any photos of this Talia you're engaged to? With a name like that, she sounds kind of *Mediterranean.*"

"Well, her family originated somewhere between France and Italy, I believe. I remember when we first met. It was her mother who spoke French, helping to translate for us." Jason looked at Jim with a quirky grin. Jim knew the whole story about his first encounter with Talia and her family. Jason pulled out his phone, and the guys pulled up chairs right next to him so they could see the photos better. Jason was feeling sandwiched in as he looked at the guys, one on each side, ready for viewing. He pulled the photos up and started going through them, telling the guys what they were looking at. Paul asked, "You had this whole week. Were these things you had already planned on seeing? What made you go down to Basel?"

As Jason looked at Talia in the photo, standing by the historical museum sign, he said, "To find her."

Paul looked confused and started to ask Jason a question, but Jim looked at Paul and shook his head. Jason continued showing them some photos, stopping to tell them briefly about what they saw and did. He didn't have as many pictures as Talia, but he got the essential images that he wanted; of her, and a few others to remember. "I'm not sure what I would have done last week if she weren't here. She wanted to see so many things in a couple of cities, and I was just happy to be with her and see them through her eyes. We went through what's called the *Gate of Spalen*, built in the 1400s.

I liked the Historical Museum, fascinating to see all this history in person. I wanted to see it for my mother; she loves history, and Talia's dad loved history. He was an architect. We spent several hours there. We had lunch and then a two-hour downtown walking tour. That was just the first day. I'll tell you guys, I've never done so much walking, but I got payback." Jason grinned, looking at the two of them.

Just then, Adrian came in and told them dinner was ready. Jason told Paul and Jim to go ahead; he was going to text Talia really quick: *Getting ready for dinner. It depends on who cooks if the guys like it or not; lol. Learned that the first week I was here. I'll check in later before we have to call it a night. I Love You.* Then he headed into the dining room.

⊗

Talia did the dishes and cleaned the kitchen. With her laundry dried, she folded and put it away. Checking her phone, there was a text from Jason saying they were having dinner, and he'd check in later. She wanted to text him back to tell him how sorry she was about his sister, but then shoved it in the back of her mind for another time: *Did a few things around my apartment. Going to check in with Chloe and head to the office after lunch. I hope your day has been good so far. I woke up thinking about another place to visit, and then realized I was home and not with you. I'll also check in before heading to bed without you. I Love You.*

"Kurt, how long can you stay?" Talia asked him.

He replied, "Is it OK if I stay until tomorrow?"

"You can stay as long as you want. How's Caren doing?" she asked.

"She's doing well. She's visiting her cousin in Arizona and won't be back until this weekend. I miss her, and I love her a lot. We've texted several times. I called her while waiting for your plane to land last night. I'm hoping that, eventually, I can talk her into moving down here. I love Uncle Dave and Aunt Joan, and grateful to stay with them, but I want to get moved back here and bring Caren with me, if I can get her to. There's just so much more opportunity here for her," Kurt said.

"Give her time. Mom's still in the house. Maybe she'll let the two of you come to visit so Caren can get used to a bigger city and what it offers. She's lived in a small town her whole life. It's a huge change for anyone. I need to call Chloe and maybe go in for a bit this afternoon. I also have to get started on my winter line," Talia said.

Kurt asked, "How about I order pizza for lunch before you go?"

"Sounds good, although I wonder if it will compare to having an actual Italian pizza, which we got to enjoy; it was scrumptious," she replied. "OK, I'm going to go call Chloe."

⚃

Dinner was potato stroganoff with pork chops, and dessert was apple crisp. Adrian asked, "Jason, do you remember when you were here a couple of weeks ago, that sometimes the wives will make food and bring it in for us to eat for lunch and dinner? I think the wives feel sorry that we men don't always come up with good things to eat. Not that we would starve, but what some of us make here isn't delicious." They laughed.

"So, are you telling me this was made by one of your wives?" Jason asked, smiling.

"Yes. It was to be Jürgen's turn to cook, but he is not very good. Give him a good fire, and he's excellent at putting it out. And Niklas isn't much better. Their wives bring in food."

"You wait until you have a wife who cooks, Adrian," Jürgen said, laughing. "Your wife can bring food in sometimes."

"So, Jim and Paul, who does the cooking at your station in America?" Wolfgang asked.

Jim replied, "The guys don't do too bad with cooking. It's quite edible, although I have noticed that we pass the hat and collect money for takeout."

"What is 'pass the hat?'" Niklas asked.

"It means everyone chips in money for takeout, which can be pizza or Chinese or sandwiches. It doesn't happen real often, but we even tire of our cooking. But I like having wives bring in food. I think we ought to suggest that when we get back home, don't you think, Paul?" Jim said, then pointing to Jason, "Maybe after this man gets married, he can have his new bride bring in food as well?"

"You know, I don't know if she cooks. I never thought to ask her, and this past week, it was a lot of restaurant food, except at the cabin," Jason said with a slight grin.

Several of the guys raised their eyebrows, pointing at him. "Oh."

"I won't kiss and tell," Jason grinned.

Pretty much all the guys got up and headed back to the lounge. There were two big sofas and a couple of big chairs and a large table. There was a small bookshelf and a TV.

Paul asked Jason, "You care to show us a few more photos?" as he sat down next to Jason. Jim wasn't going to get left out, so he again sat on the other side of Jason.

"When did you first see her here?" Jim asked.

"I saw her on the Rhine River waterfront. She came around the corner and looked toward the water, and then this calico cat came up to her. She bent down to pick it up and pet it. I'd been sitting on a bench with Jéan-Paul and his wife, Suzanne. I couldn't believe she was standing there, only fifty feet away from me. I told Jéan-Paul that Talia was standing there. He and Suzanne turned to look at her. We were getting ready to stand up and say goodbye. Talia looked my way, but I didn't think she recognized me. I had my sunglasses on. And it'd been almost fourteen years since we last saw one another."

"Wait, why didn't you stand up and just go to her?" Jim asked.

"Honestly, I was afraid to, and I felt frozen. It felt awkward, and Jéan-Paul and Suzanne were there. It'd been so long, but my heart just about jumped out of my chest, seeing her. I wanted to get up and walk right to her," Jason said.

"Did you know where she was staying?" Jim asked.

"Ya, I did. Her brother Kurt had called me several months ago. We talked; I told him about this program, something we had signed up for long ago. He told me what hotels she'd be staying at and said it was up to me to find her if I wanted her. So, I checked at the first hotel she was staying at. It took some convincing with two of the hotel desk clerks, who are sweet. I checked to see if I could reserve a room there as well. Anyway, Talia was going to the botanical garden later that afternoon, and that's where I found her."

Jason pulled out his phone to show them a few more photos, and then the loud bells went off in the station, alerting them that they all had to go; rescue squad, and firetrucks. There was an explosion, and would take several stations to help with it. There were multiple injuries, and it would be many hours before they returned to the station.

Ↄ

After having pizza for lunch, Talia changed clothes and headed to her shop. The fabric bolts had come in, and she was excited to see them and her staff of two, Chloe and Jana. They had kept somewhat busy while she was gone. When asked about her trip, she couldn't help but smile and then presented her left hand. The girls looked at the ring, thinking it was beautiful and asked if it was a souvenir. Talia shook her head no and said, "It's my engagement ring."

Chloe and Jana shrieked, both saying, "WHAT?" Talia's ears were now ringing.

"You go overseas to buy fabric and take some time for yourself, and then you come home and you're engaged? How the hell does that happen? You need to spill the beans, girl," Chloe stated, "because you aren't leaving here until we get the low-down."

Talia was happy to share some of that week's events, but not all of them, as that was between her and Jason. She started with how they met at a young age and the various vacations and worked through the photos. She said the digital frame was a beautiful gift from two charming women from the hotel where they stayed. The girls then asked about the proposal, and she told them she would share that after they shared the news with their families. As she was going through the photos, they both got jealous, seeing Jason. He was hot, and it didn't hurt that he was a paramedic/firefighter. They wanted to know where they could get one of those.

❧

Throughout the week, there were lots of calls they went on. One day, Jason, Jim, and Paul didn't have to go out on calls. They were having breakfast, and Paul asked if Jason was willing to share other photos. So, after eating, Jason pulled out his phone and pulled up the remaining photos. He talked about seeing the clock tower in Bern. The name of the clock tower was long, and he couldn't pronounce it, but he enjoyed the tour. He showed some photos of the two of them with the view of the city behind them. It was taken looking out the top-floor window by someone else. He showed several photos of Talia being silly. He chuckled, remembering why she was giddy.

He told them about Gurten; there was a cable car that took you to the top. It's 858 meters above sea level, looking out over the *Bernese Oberland* region. It was a beautiful view, almost as gorgeous as the one that was standing next to him. He paused a moment, looking at the photo of the two of them, arms wrapped around each other. And if either Jim or Paul got the chance to come back, they needed to see a few of these things. Several of the German paramedics had gathered behind Jason, looking at her pictures, and razed Jason about how he got such a beauty. Jason just smiled and said, "Boys, you raze me all you want, but I got the girl." They laughed, stating they were jealous, especially a few of the single guys.

Adrian and Wolfgang, who were already in their uniforms, said they would take Jason, Jim, and Paul to a museum. They thought they would appreciate going through this one, but explained that they might want to put on their uniforms. Jason asked why, if they weren't working. Adrian said if they went with uniforms on, they would get in free. When Jim asked what kind of museum, they said to see a lot of beauties. The three of them looked at Adrian and Wolfgang, not sure if this was something they wanted to do, not knowing what type of museum it was.

Adrian said, he promised, it would make their trip there worthwhile. So, they changed into their uniforms. Leaving the station, Adrian headed toward the Porsche Museum. When they arrived, the guys' eyes got big, like kids in a candy store. Arriving at the front door, Adrian spoke to one employee in German, stating he had already called about visiting the museum and doing the factory tour. He said these were the American paramedics working with them this past week, and wanted them to see some real beauties. A tour guide came, introducing himself as Friedrick, speaking good English, welcoming them to the Porsche Museum and thanked all of them for their service to the community. Paul asked if they were allowed to take photos, and Friedrick took a moment to reply. "Only in the museum." They allowed no images in the factory. They all nodded that they understood.

As they walked through the factory tour first, workers were looking at them. Friedrick spoke German to them, and then they continued. Once they finished with the tour, they went through the museum. It was by far the coolest thing they had done since being in Germany, and they thanked Friedrick for this experience. He was sorry that they could not take one of these beauties for a drive, but of course, if something happened, the medics would already be on the scene. He said it with a smile.

Chapter 24

It was a hard and busy week for the three American paramedic/ firefighters. It seemed like they were on one call after another: rescues or fires, and back to rescues. And then both, more than when Jason was here the first week. It was Jason's, and in particular, Jim's gut instincts from the military that made a difference in many of the lives that were saved throughout the week, situations that almost seemed hopeless whether someone would die that day. There were some medical procedures the three of them had learned back home that also made a big difference to the ones they were attending at a scene, getting them to a hospital sooner. The Germans noticed, watched, and learned. They knew how valuable these three were to their department in the States. And if what they saw was across the board with American paramedics and firefighters, they wanted to learn.

Jason, Jim, and Paul each had reports to fill out and submit to Captain Karl Urich. They also sent their reports by email to Captain Michael Robins. Between both captains, they decided that Paul, Jim and Jason would leave a day earlier than expected. As much as the Germans wanted the three of them to stay longer, they felt what they had learned would make them better at their jobs, and it was only one day, but knew they missed their families in the States. Both sides learned a lot from each other. They formed great friendships that would last a long time. As with the military, they had become a band of brothers. The Germans joked that if they were ever to come back to Germany to visit, and a call came in, don't be surprised that they just might be put to work.

Jéan-Paul was called to come in and be part of a meeting the captain was going to have with all the guys before the three Americans left. It was 6:30 a.m. Captain Urich told them that he and Captain Robins discussed having the Germans spend a week in the U.S. at different times. They were going to get at least one to go over with Jéan-Paul, which would be a couple of weeks before Christmas, and get some first-hand experience with the Americans. They had details to work out, and then decide who would be the first to go. The captain let Jéan-Paul tell them about the times he spent in America the last two years, working at the hospitals and going out on calls with the firefighters and paramedics. There were things he'd seen in America that he had not seen back in either Germany or Switzerland. "It was an eye-opener," he said as he looked at Jason, nodding. The men looked at Jason and then Jéan-Paul. They didn't understand, but were sure at some point they would.

Jéan-Paul said that whoever went over would also stay at the fire station, as he did most times. These were great men, and he has been proud to work with them; he also learned a lot about trust and compassion from them. He hugged and shook hands with Jason, Jim and Paul. If the captain didn't need him anymore, he would go, but would get his travel times and documents to him within the next week. As he started to leave, he turned to Jason and said with a big smile, "Give your *fiancée* a kiss and a hug from me." Jason shook a finger at him with a smile.

They had their bags packed and were ready to head home. Their flight would leave at 9:45 a.m. There was a small gathering for them from all the crew members and some wives. It was a good German breakfast, so they wouldn't forget it was the wives that made it. Then the three were presented with a few simple gifts: a white German stein with the Star of Life on it, underneath were the words "Emergency Medical Services," a German Medic - Tactical Polo shirt, and two separate medic's lapel pins. They were told to ask their captain if he would allow them to wear the lapel pins on their uniforms. They had two small bags with the same gifts for the other two paramedics that came a couple of weeks ago, and if Jason would take these gifts to them. He replied, yes, that he would. They all shook hands with each other, some gave hugs, and then it was time to leave. Adrian would take them to the airport.

On the way, Jason texted Kurt for Talia's address. He didn't tell Kurt they were coming home a day early because he wanted to surprise Talia, and he didn't want Kurt to let her know accidentally and give her a heads-up. He knew it was around 3:00 a.m. when he texted, not expecting to receive anything back for quite a while. It surprised him when Kurt texted back with her address. He was glad Jason would be home in a day or so, because she was missing him terribly. He had to go back to his aunt and uncle's later that morning. Hopefully, soon, they would catch up about the adventures overseas with his sister, "lol." Jason smiled. If only Kurt knew.

They said goodbye to Adrian and hoped he would be the one to come to the U.S. first. They decided before heading into the airport to get a quick selfie of the four of them. Adrian wished them a safe flight, shook hands, and then headed out. Their plane would be leaving on time, and soon they began to board. The flight was full. Jason took the window seat, with Paul in the middle. Jim's legs were longer, so having an aisle seat made it more agreeable for him. Paul felt a little more at ease, having two buddies on either side of him, still not enthused about flying in a mini tube through the sky. They would arrive after 8:30 p.m.

He texted Talia, telling her he didn't have much time to chat, that things were moving quickly. She didn't know that he would have to shut off his phone in about three minutes, as they would be taking off. He said he was so ready to come home. He missed her terribly. Hours later, she texted back that she had designer block, kind of like a writer's block. She'd only finished one design and was half-way through another. She worked from home yesterday and was going to be home today and possibly tomorrow. She was feeling a little down, eager for him to come home, worried about him because of the calls they went out on. On his layover, he texted back that he had to go and would be home soon. Loved her with all his heart.

When they landed, it was just after 8:30 p.m. Their plane had made good time. It was the first of October. Paul's wife, Ally, was there to pick him up, and Jim's wife, Nadine, came to pick up Jim and Jason. By the time they all got their luggage and headed out, their rides were waiting. Nadine popped the trunk, getting out of the SUV, and walked around, giving Jim a big hug and kiss. She missed him. Seeing Jason standing there, Nadine gave him a quick hug, welcoming him home. They had met when they all lived in Colorado. After putting their bags in the back, Jim took over the driving. Jason gave him Talia's address, and he put it into the GPS. The guys were allowed two days off before they had to be at the station for work.

On the way to Talia's, there was conversation; mostly about the work they did in Stuttgart, the Porsche Museum, which was a highlight for them, and the nice gathering this morning. Jim also told her they would hopefully have one of the German paramedics join them in early December before Christmas. They were looking forward to it.

Arriving at Talia's apartment, there was parking close to her door. Jason was feeling nervous, although he wasn't sure why. She loved him, and he was so in love with her, and now they could finally be together. There were a few lights on as he sat for a moment, looking at her. He could see her through the blinds. Jim got out and opened the back, with Jason getting out. After getting his luggage, he and Jim gave a hug and shook hands. Jim put a hand on Jason's shoulder and gave a nod. Jim stood by his front car door, waiting. Jason was standing near the front of Jim's car, looking at Talia. He knew she was working on a design, or at least trying to. Jason took out his phone and called her as he was walking toward her door, getting closer. He can see her pick up her phone, answering. "Jason," she said.

"Hey, my love, how are you?" he replied.

"It's so good to hear your voice. I miss you. When are you coming home?" Talia asked.

"What are you working on?" He wanted to take a moment and watch her. She was wearing one of her short shorts and a t-shirt and nothing on her feet.

She throws her hand up in the air. "Well, I'm trying to be productive and work on my second design, and it's not going so well," Talia said.

Jason turned a moment and looked back at Jim, who saw it and smiled at Jason. "Talia, you may have a visitor soon, and I don't think you'll want to turn him away," Jason said.

"What do you mean I'll have a visitor? When, and who is it?" she asked.

"Sweetie, you might want to put that pencil in your hand down and come to the door," he said. He saw her slowly turning toward the door.

"How do you know I have a pencil in my hand? Where are you?" she asked, standing straighter, looking at her pencil.

"Please go to your door and open it," Jason said. He had placed his bag on the ground, then put his phone in his pocket. He saw her walk to the door and open it. With eyes wide and filling with tears, she shrieked and took two steps toward him, throwing her arms around him. He grabbed her in his arms, picking her up and kissing her. He set her back down and turned toward Jim, pointing to Talia with a big smile on his face. Jim waved back and looked at Talia, saying, "Hello, Talia, I'm Jim." She waved back at him, and then looked down at what she was wearing and covered her face in Jason's chest, and also realized she was getting cold.

Jason waved to both Jim and Nadine, and thanked them for bringing him home. Seeing how deeply in love Jason was with Talia, Jim smiled and got back in his car. They watched for a moment as Jason picked up his bag and walked inside with Talia. As Jim was backing his car to leave, he stopped a moment, looking back at them. He saw the two hug and kiss, and saw Jason wipe away her tears.

Nadine found it very loving and emotional, with tears in her eyes. She asked, "How did they meet anyway?" Jim watched Jason and said, "It all started when they were very young, and he fell in love at first sight."

Nadine took Jim's hand and held it while looking at the two of them through the window. As Jim looked at his best friend, he whispered, "Home at last - Alone is past."

Chapter 25

Jason again took her in his arms, not wanting to let go. She could feel his heart beating fast. Still not believing he was here in her apartment, she looked up at him and he once again wiped away her tears, saying, "No more tears unless they're happy tears." He bent down, holding her face in his hands, and kissed her gently.

She looked at him. "I can't believe you're here, in my apartment. I thought when you got back, you'd want to go home."

"I am home, if you'll let me call this home. I know we have a lot to discuss. I just couldn't go to my place. I wanted to be with you. I missed you so much," he said.

"I haven't been able to get very far on my designs because I worried about you, not only doing the job you love, but in another country. It was just too far away. I tried to keep my mind busy, and it didn't work out the way I thought it should," she said.

"So, maybe with me back now, and here, you'll be able to unblock your design door or whatever is in that little head of yours?" Jason said with a smile.

She took a deep breath and said, "Yes." She leaned up to kiss him.

"Would you like to show me around? Maybe we should close these blinds," Jason said. He walked toward all the blinds and closed them, knowing that if he could see in with it dark outside, so could anyone else.

"Well, you're standing in my large living room, as you can see. And way over there by that window is where I try to draw whatever inspiration comes to me, not always succeeding, by the pile of scrunched up paper you see on the floor. And where you must have seen me working, or trying to work with said pencil in my hand." She smiled at him. She took his hand and walked with him to the bathroom, which was a good size. "This is my laundry room and my open, spacious kitchen and dining area. Notice no walls.

"This is where I cook and bake. Sometimes I get inspired to try new and wonderful dishes, but they don't always look like the recipe I'm following, but I eat it anyway." Jason chuckled; he loved her narration. "My guest bedroom is that sofa over there, which is a pull-out bed. Not the most comfortable thing to sleep on; I've tried it and don't care for it much, but for any guest I have staying with me, it provides a place to lay their head. I also provide the pillow, sheets and blankets. And last, but not least, this room in here is my bedroom," she said as she walked with him into it. "So, are you going to be a guest staying here periodically or are you looking for something more permanent?" She grinned at Jason as she walked over to the bed with him, both sitting down. He turned toward her, giving her a kiss.

"I think I'll pass on the guest bed. It looks a little short, and my feet might hang over the edge and get cold. Then I'd have to get up, and stumble, and find a way to warm them up by crawling into bed with someone else just to warm them up," he said, smiling at her. "This room looks a lot more inviting." He put his arms around her, just wanting to hold her close.

"When do you have to go back to work?" she asked.

"Two days to rest up. Captain saw our reports. Our shift starts with three days where we also stay two nights, and then it rotates." He picked up her left hand, feeling and looking at her engagement ring, kissing her hand and then holding it against his chest. He was silent. He laid back on the bed, looking at the ceiling.

"What are you thinking?" Talia asked softly, seeing his mind was somewhere else. She laid back with him, and he put his arm around her. He took a moment to respond.

"I'm glad to be home, with you in my arms, safe," he said.

"What happened over there, in Germany?" she asked, leaning over, kissing his cheek.

He took a slow deep breath. "I do this job so that I can help provide the best care after arriving first on a scene, working with my partners on whoever needs our help. The first week I was there, it wasn't anything like this past week; it was crazy. Even though Jim, Paul and I were on the go constantly, we each worked with other paramedics; but it felt like we were doing time-and-a-half shifts. We didn't know where we were going; everything was in German, so you have the whole language barrier thing going on. Many people didn't speak English, and we didn't speak German. There was one point when I thought we were being tested as American paramedics. We had to wait a few times to treat someone until one of our German paramedics could come to help translate and explain that we were there to help and do our jobs. People were already scared in the first place. We weren't speaking their language, in different uniforms; they were unsure whether to trust us. It was frustrating. I almost wished it were Italian, and you were close to me to help translate. There were two incidents where we could have saved two lives, but because we also had protocol we had to follow, and traffic, two people died and I don't think they should have."

Talia looked at him as he continued, staring at the ceiling, his eyes getting heavy. "I'm sorry," she whispered.

He turned his head, looking into her eyes. He looked exhausted. "I just want to lie next to you and hold you in my arms," he said, giving her a kiss on her forehead. Talia stood up, pulling the blanket and sheets down on the bed. After she left the room, he took off his clothes, getting into bed, and soon saw lights being shut off. His eyes were partially closed. He was so tired. She walked back in, shutting off the lights, letting her clothes fall onto the floor, and climbed in next to him. He wrapped his arms around her, holding her close, and fell asleep. Before Talia closed her eyes, she placed an arm across his chest to his side, looking at him. Remembering her conversation with Kurt about Jason's little sister, she wondered if he also just wanted to feel safe in her arms.

Jason woke to a dark room after 2:00 a.m., but feeling the warmth of her body next to his, he half smiled. This is what he's wanted for so long, to belong to someone and to be with someone; to love deeply, and be loved deeply back. He smelled her hair, and it smelled of coconut. He felt like he was home, even though he had his own apartment. It was smaller; it didn't feel like a home, just a place to go to after getting off work, maybe hanging out with a few friends. This was home; comfortable, safe, and she was here. They would have to talk about their future together. Did she want to stay here for a while or maybe get a bigger place, one they could eventually grow into as a family? He guessed, in due time. He wasn't going to push; he had now. With the work he did, doing his best to save lives and knowing that life can be snatched away at any given moment, he would take one day at a time.

She moved in his arms, and he leaned into her, kissing her gently on her forehead, then her cheek and moving to her lips. With her eyes still closed, she moved her arm across his chest and kissed him back. He slowly rolled over, half on top of her, kissing her lips and neck as he placed one arm under her, pulling her closer to him. While she put one arm around his neck, she put her other hand on his hip, hoping to guide him the rest of the way onto her. Their heartbeats, now in sync; it was like their first night at the cabin, loving each other deeply.

☓

He could hear the rain against the side of the building. There was a flicker of lightning and the rumbling of thunder. He looked at the clock on her nightstand and saw it was 6:30 a. m. He would have all day today, tonight and most of tomorrow with her before going into work. He looked over at her, the sheet covering only half of her body, exposing her upper half. He watched her breathe, watching her stomach rise and fall. Sometimes, looking at Talia, he couldn't believe they had come full circle and were finally together. He had waited such a long time. As he looked at her, he slowly pulled the sheet up toward her shoulders.

Still looking at her, he thought about the little girl on the train, seeing her happy while holding her doll and sitting on her father's lap. He smiled now, remembering the smile she gave them and the little wave of her hand, and he remembered her moving over to her mother's lap, looking out the window. After eating their bananas, he had gotten up to throw the peels away. Walking back past the family, he looked at the little one sleeping in her mother's arms, the father's arm around his wife and holding his little girl's hand, keeping his family safe. It had made him ache inside. When the train had stopped, and they were getting ready to leave, he remembered how the little girl had looked him right in the eyes and smiled. She had pretty, soft brown hair and hazel eyes, like someone else he once knew.

He hoped that little girl would grow up in a safe world where she could raise a family of her own, unlike the sister he lost, who would never have that opportunity to love and be loved. It angered him for the longest time, thinking he was the one to blame for her being snatched and then killed in front of their eyes, and that's why he would never have anyone in his life because he didn't protect the one he loved. Then seven years later, a nine-year-old came into his life, and everything changed.

Talia moved onto her side, facing him. He looked at her sleeping and wondered, should he keep it a secret, hidden away for eternity, or share it with her? He had held onto it for so long, shoved so far down inside. Then, it was like a light bulb moment just now for him. He looked toward the window; he just realized, maybe that's why he'd been so afraid of loving Talia so much. Each time he saw her, wanting to hold her and tell her how he truly felt, it was like if he did, something would happen and he would lose her. So, in order to keep her safe, he would have to let her go because he didn't want anything to happen to her, and he couldn't go through that pain. Not again. Those memories coming back up to him, he wondered if the only reason it was coming up now was because of how that little girl looked at him, with knowing eyes.

CB

The flashes of memory from that day were rising now more and more, seeing Amy thrown in the air. Tears were in his eyes, and his breathing had changed, becoming heavier. And the thought of losing Talia, fear was taking over. What was happening? He felt his heart race. Talia opened her eyes, seeing a flicker of lightning and hearing the rain. It was light enough in the room, and sensing something was off, she looked at Jason. She saw the tears in his eyes and saw that his breathing was different. She half sat up and looked at him, her hand going to the center of his chest. She felt his heart beating faster, and it scared her. He looked at her with tears in his eyes, and slowly shook his head, and Talia said, "Jason, what is it? What's wrong? Please tell me. You're scaring me. I love you so much." He couldn't hold it in any longer, the fear and guilt. It was time to heal the ache inside. He partially sat up, looking at the end of the bed. He saw it all over again, like watching a rerun playing over and over.

He felt so vulnerable, but spoke softly and slowly. "When I was seven years old, my family consisted of my mother, my father, me, and my little sister." More tears came. Talia had tears, knowing what happened. "We enjoyed going to the park, swinging and sliding down the slide, like we did every Saturday. We'd go on the teeter-totter; I'd be on one side and my mother, holding my sister on the other end, and we'd go up and down and my little sister would laugh. It was infectious; you couldn't help but laugh with her." He had a half smile. Then the smile was gone.

"One Saturday, we went to another park. There was a sandbox that I was playing in with her, filling up a bucket and turning it upside down. My parents were just on the other side of the sandbox talking with some people. I was getting sand in my shoes, and I went to sit on the edge of the box, taking my shoes off to empty the sand, and the next thing I hear is a scream; it's so loud." More tears were flowing. Talia's heart was hurting for him. She sat more upright. "Someone came behind her and grabbed her and started running toward the street. A bunch of the people around wasn't sure what was going on until my mom looked down for Amy and she was gone. She was the one being taken.

"Both my parents took off running after the man who had her; Amy was still screaming. He had her under his arm, and he ran in between two parked cars, heading across the street when, in an instant, a pickup truck hit them. They went flying, and the screaming stopped." He was silent for a moment, remembering. "Everything went silent until my parents got to her, but the screams from my mother were deafening." More tears were running down his face. Talia was crying, shaking her head. "She died there on the street, my baby sister." He sobbed. He leaned on Talia, putting his arms around her, and she put her arms around him, holding him, slowly rocking him and crying with him.

"I'm so sorry for your loss. I'm sorry, I'm sorry." She continued holding and rocking him, tears still running down her face. She didn't know what else to say to him. She'd hold him as long as he'd let her. She whispered to him, "I love you so much. I'm sorry. I love you. I'm here." She scooted down a little and let him lay his head on her chest with her arms wrapped around him. All she could think was that here was a seven-year-old boy taking on the guilt of the world, feeling responsible for the death of his sister. It wasn't his fault, he wasn't to blame, but he took that on and carried it with him. He'd had two such tragedies in his life. There were people who have lost just as much, if not more so. The depth of that loss and guilt, she can't even imagine.

Feeling a little cold, Talia drew the blankets up and around the both of them, still holding him. She kissed the top of his head. Hopefully, his healing can begin just by releasing this guilt, finally. She wondered how often he might go to her grave to sit and chat with her, even though she wasn't really there. Sometimes it was just a comfort, seeing their name on a headstone or seeing a picture. It brought sadness, but maybe a piece of healing as well.

Jason was quiet, and she could see he had fallen asleep. She glanced at the clock to see what time it was, not that she had to go anywhere, and with what just occurred, she was going to stay put. Everything could wait. He was the most important thing to her. She took a slow deep breath and closed her eyes, gently and slowly rubbing his arm and back like a mother would with her scared child. She could still hear the rain and the rumbling of thunder in the distance.

Talia opened her eyes. It was still cloudy out, and she thought she could still hear it raining. Jason had moved from her shoulder, resting his head on his pillow. She looked at him, and he was looking back at her. He just wanted to hold her now. He slid one arm around the top of her shoulder and placed his hand on her side, pulling her close to him. Talia put her arm across his chest, resting her head near the top of his shoulder. He kissed her forehead and said, "Thank you."

She wasn't sure if she should dare to ask him about visiting his sister's grave, knowing it was probably a special thing for him. She looked up at him with questioning eyes, but then let it go for now. Jason noticed, and asked her quietly, "Is there something you want to ask me?"

"I don't know if this is the time to ask," she said.

"Try me. I might surprise you," he said.

She looked at him. "If you let me, the next time you go visit her, I would like to go with you."

Tears appeared in his eyes. He hugged her closer and said, "I would very much like for you to go with me. Maybe having you by my side will help me not miss her so much still." Talia buried her head in his shoulder, crying because it made her think of her dad and how she missed him. Feeling that sadness was awful, and it'd only been six months for her. She couldn't imagine carrying that hurt and guilt as long as Jason had. He lifted her chin so he could look at her. "This may sound silly, but when I've gone to visit her, even though I know she's not really there, I told her about you, about the first time I saw you, and how much I have grown to love you. But that I will always have a special place for her in my heart, and that I love her, and I'm sorry she's not here to get to meet you."

"I know she would be so very proud of you, the person and man you are. I know I am. You are so strong, and kind, and understanding and compassionate," Talia said.

He looked at her and spoke quietly. "I love you. No more sadness this morning. You bring me so much joy. Seeing things through your eyes, hearing your laughter, seeing the way you love me; it all fills my heart." He kissed her lightly. "I want to spend between now and the time I have to go to work with you, here or wherever you need to go." He paused, and then said, "I do have to ask one thing of you." He smiled at her.

"Name it," she says.

He got a big grin on his face and sniffled. "I really need to do some laundry. Can you help me with that? And, maybe we can figure out what to do about lunch, since we missed breakfast completely," he said. "It's about 11:30 a.m."

"I think we should order pizza in. It probably won't be as good as the pizza in Villars, but we'll have to make do. My food supply is a little on the low side. And laundry is not a problem, my love," she said, kissing him.

"Then, maybe we'll have to do a little shopping later; don't want either of us to starve," he said. "Maybe the first order of business is start laundry, then order pizza, eat pizza, finish laundry, get dressed and go shop for food?"

"Sounds like a plan," Talia replied.

Chapter 26

Jason got up, grabbing his jeans, and headed to the bathroom. Talia found her silky lavender robe, putting it on, and headed out to the living room. He came out of the bathroom with just a towel wrapped around his waist. She looked at him and said, "Did you want to take a shower before laundry?" He shook his head no.

Picking up his bag, he carried it to the laundry room. "These clothes have not seen the best washing in the last three weeks, and these jeans also need to be washed, so you'll just have to put up with me walking around with this frog towel wrapped around me," he said with a grin. She looked at him, smiling, eyeing him up and down. She rather enjoyed seeing him with just a towel on or, better yet, in the buff. Opening his bag up, he saw the gifts the German crew had given. There was a small bag for the other two paramedics at the station.

Talia saw the polo shirt and unfolded it, looking at it with a smile. She said, "I think you ought to wear that today after we wash it. It's well-earned, and I think you'd look hot in it." He smiled back.

He took out the cup, handing it to her, and the two lapel pins. "Captain Urich told us to check with our captain to see if it might be all right if we wore them. He might, then again, he might not. But five of us have them. I don't know what American protocol is about wearing something like this," he said with a grin, feeling very proud. They all worked hard and felt deserving. He felt honored for being given the pins.

"Well, I don't know what the protocol is, but you should be proud of the work you did those two weeks; all of you should. You're my hero, with the lives you save every day, and not just here, but the ones across the ocean. And I won't forget the accident we saw and what you did trying to help those people by yourself until Jéan-Paul showed up." She kissed him on the cheek.

Taking out his clothes and putting them in the washer, Talia started the machine. Before leaving the laundry room, Jason put his arms around her, giving her a hug and a kiss. "Thank you," he said.

"For what?" she asked.

"For being you. For your laughter, your kind heart, and for loving me the way you do," he said.

With her arms around him, she said, "I wondered a long, long, time ago if there would ever be a chance that someone like you would, and could, ever love a girl like me. But you've loved me from the very beginning. I just had some catching up to do, and I'm glad I finally did. You filled that space. I love you, and I am so grateful for you."

Walking toward the kitchen, Talia put on the light, and then her phone rang. It was lying on the counter; she put it on speaker as she looked for something in one of the kitchen drawers. It was Chloe, wondering if she might be in today. Talia replied, "No, I'm going to spend it with my man."

"What man? Oh, my god, is Jason home?" she shrieked. "Oh, then never mind, if anything important comes up, I'll... Well, I'll handle it until you come in. But I want to hear about all the good stuff when you come in." She giggled.

Talia had to cover her mouth so Chloe wouldn't hear her laugh. Jason was standing right there, smiling, and couldn't help himself. He bent closer to the phone and said hello in a soft voice, "Hello Chloe, it's Jason, and I'm just standing here in a beautiful frog towel."

"Talia, you have me on speaker, holy... now I'm embarrassed," she said. "I'm sorry, Jason."

"Don't be, I thought it was rather cute and," as he picked up the phone and held it close to his mouth, he kissed Talia so Chloe could hear, then laid the phone back down, continuing to say, "I don't know that Talia will kiss and tell."

"Bye, Chloe," Talia said, and giggled. Jason gave her a big hug and laughed.

"I think we should order pizza now, because I'm getting famished," Jason said.

"OK, so am I. Anything special on your pizza?" she asked.

"No, surprise me," he said. She called in the order. They would deliver within the next thirty minutes. It was a pizza place close by that she used when she didn't feel like cooking anything. They knew her.

Jason had walked over to her drafting table, not sure what he was looking at. Lots of lines and squirrely things, and colors blended in. "This is pretty; lots of colors. What is it?" he said. She walked over to see what he was looking at, kicking the scrunched-up paper on the floor rather than picking it up and putting it in the little trash bin.

"Oh, ya. I had an idea that came to me in Bern, and I had sketched it out quickly on a small notepad I keep in my bag. I just haven't figured out exactly what or how I want this to look, being here at home. It looked and felt different in my head there," she said.

"Then why don't you close your eyes and go back to that point and recreate it. You are very talented. The designs on your wall are amazing. It will come to you," he said.

"I guess I can do that. I just had other things on my mind, like worrying about you," Talia said.

"Well, no more worrying. I'm here now," he said.

The laundry didn't take long and was ready to be put into the dryer. Talia laid the money out for the pizza on a long, skinny table close to the front door, and then she headed to the laundry room. It had been almost thirty minutes, and then there was a knock on the door. Jason opened it to find a pizza delivery person standing there with their pizza. The man looked at Jason with his frog towel on and said, "Pizza delivery for Talia Rose."

"Good, we were getting hungry," Jason said, and taking the money from the table, he gave it to the delivery guy who tried peering in to see if he could see Talia.

He asked, "So, is Talia here? I don't live that far from work, and I walk by here. I sometimes see her working on stuff in the evenings at her table. She'd been gone for a while."

"So, you know, Talia?" Jason asked, now getting a feeling he didn't like.

"Oh, just from delivering pizza to her for the last year; I always ask if I can deliver it. She's really pretty. I thought about asking her out, you know. We'd have a good time," he said, still trying to peer in.

"Well, she's engaged," Jason said.

"Oh, that's too bad. You know who the lucky guy is?" he asked. Jason couldn't believe he was asking.

Jason took a step closer to the man who was shorter than he was, blocking his view, and looking him in the eye, and said, "Me."

"Oh, sorry, man, I didn't know. Thought I might have a chance at her," he said and took a step back.

Jason backed up, closing the door in the guy's face. Talia came out of the laundry room and saw the pizza in his hand, walking toward the counter. She got out some plates and glasses. Jason said, "You'll need to be more careful in the evenings with your blinds open."

"Why," she replied with a smile.

"Because your pizza delivery guy over the last year has walked by here, watching you in the evenings working, and I didn't like what he said or what he was thinking," Jason said, not smiling.

"That's Tim, and I think he's harmless," she said.

"That's not the vibe I got. He just tried peering in to see if you were here. He's wanted to ask you out on a date, and said you'd have a really good time. I told him you were engaged. He didn't seem to like that at all, and then he asked who the lucky guy was, with a smirk on his face, and when

I told him it was me, he backed up. I'm just asking that when it gets dark out to please close the blinds. No one needs to be looking in your window at you. And just be careful, too, when you go out. I don't want anything happening to you," Jason said.

Talia could see the concern in his eyes, and now it made her feel uncomfortable thinking people, or someone, has been watching her. She turned toward the windows, looking at them. And glad that it was Jason who answered her door. "I promise," she said, looking at him.

"OK, I love you, and I want you to be safe. I have shifts that won't allow me to be here with you. I know you've lived here by yourself for quite some time. Just, please be careful," he said.

Talia nodded. She opened the pizza box, and there was a little piece of paper folded in half under the cardboard plate. Jason took the note and opened it, reading it and then giving it to her. It said, 'We need to go out, you and me. Tim.' She got shivers up her spine and looked at Jason. He wanted it to soak in what may or may not happen with this character. Jason took out a piece of pizza and started eating it, sitting on one of the high-back chairs. Talia knew she needed to eat, but now she wasn't very hungry. She took a slice out, taking a bite and then laid the pizza down on her plate. Reality kicked in. She was feeling sick to her stomach. She turned and headed to the bedroom, closing the door.

After ten minutes or so, she still hadn't come out. Jason got up and walked to the door, tapping on it, and then opening the door to let her know he was coming in. She was sitting at the end of the bed, looking at the floor. He sat down next to her, putting an arm around her. "I'm sorry. I wasn't trying to upset you or be mean about this. You probably had no idea that he was looking in at you. Any number of people could have. It's hard for people to close their blinds or shades when it gets dark out so early. We like having that daylight and seeing out," he said, putting a finger under her chin so she would look at him.

"You're right. I like having my blinds open. I hate when it gets dark early. I feel like I can't accomplish as much feeling closed in. I hate putting lights on when I'm working; it's not the same as having natural sunlight. I will be more careful, especially when you're not here. I guess that's a wake-up call to me," she said.

"Just pay attention to what's around you, or who, is all I'm saying. If I'm not here, and you need help, you call me immediately, OK?" Jason said. She nodded, and he hugged her. "Maybe you would want to finish your pizza before it gets cold, although cold pizza is perfect too." The dryer buzzer went off, signaling the clothes should be dry. They got up and headed to the laundry room, taking the clothes out he wanted to wear, and then folded most of his clothes except for the two uniforms he took with him overseas. Before getting dressed, he told her he'd like to take a shower first before they headed out for groceries, and asked if she wanted to join him. He could see that the note still upset her and said it would be a quick shower for both of them to feel clean and refreshed. Maybe she could eat her pizza after a shower. She nodded, and they headed to the bathroom.

After getting dressed, Talia had her piece of pizza. Jason took another slice and then put the remaining slices in the refrigerator. She had started a grocery list the week before, but didn't get around to going to the store. There wasn't much on it. Jason saw her list and added to it, more than what she ever had on it, but then there were two of them now. He said he actually enjoyed cooking, but his baking skills were lacking. It was the opposite for Talia; she loved baking, but didn't always know what to cook, and sometimes she'd eat a bowl of cereal and call it quits. He told her what his favorite cookie was, and that his mother had made them often when he was growing up. He could make those; they were easy because it didn't require him to start the oven.

Talia would have opened blinds by now as she worked or cleaned, but she left them closed. With their list made out and jackets on, they headed out the door, locking it behind them. Jason didn't have his car, so Talia drove to the grocery store, the one she usually went to. As they walked down some aisles, Jason joked about getting different cheeses and crackers and French bread, making her think about Ollon.

Hoping again to say it correctly, but if not, Jason didn't understand Italian anyway, *"Oh, prendiamo del formaggio e dei cracker,"* she said (Let's get some cheese and crackers).

"OK, I think I heard cracker in there," he smiled at her. "Whatever you said, sure, let's get some." Talia laughed, and they picked up a few different kinds of cheese and crackers as well.

With groceries in canvas bags that Talia carried in her car, they headed to her vehicle, putting them in. The rain had quit, and it was partially cloudy out. They arrived back at her place, taking off their coats, and put everything away.

Chapter 27

After unloading all the groceries, Jason was the one to open the blinds up with the slats turning upwards. It made it just a tad bit harder for someone to see in. They sat down on the sofa, with Jason putting his arm around Talia. He had some things he wanted to discuss with her.

"I think there are some things you and I need to talk about or at least think about," he said.

"OK, I'm listening," Talia replied and turned toward him, giving him her attention.

"Well, first off, I need my car so I can get to work tomorrow. So, maybe we could get it this evening?" he asked, looking at her. "And then you can see my place; the lonely bachelor pad."

He took a moment to collect his thoughts as he looked at her, and she looked back at him, waiting patiently, and then he lowered his head, taking her left hand and playing with her engagement ring. "Here we are, engaged to be married," he said with a smile. "We've never officially dated, even though we've spent time together. It's hard to get to know someone when you have family around. But I knew what my heart was telling me. And then, while we were in Switzerland, I wondered if you thought that week might have been just a whirlwind romance, having had a wonderful and incredible week together." He looked at her. "Then I was thinking, was it by chance that I was in Germany and you were in Switzerland? Maybe. Had fate been unfolding its hand all along? Maybe," he said, tilting his head.

"All I knew was that I wasn't going to let you slip away from me again. I couldn't. So, after a week, and before you left, I asked you to marry me on the very spot that I saw you and I felt everything had finally come full circle. I wanted you to know that I am committed to you and only you. And the most beautiful part was that you said yes, to me. Then you headed home. I didn't want to let you go; it hurt. But knowing I would be home a week later, I started counting down the days. I then head home, and I show up on your doorstep, ready to move in. I didn't give you the opportunity to know if this was moving too fast for you." He looked at her, and in a quiet voice, he said, "Are you all right with me staying here with you, moving in, or do you want some time to think about it? I'll keep my apartment if you need your space. I mean, I show up last night and then I'm just here invading your space. I know in my heart what I want." He lifted her left hand, kissing it. "I'm just not sure how you feel about all of this, and I want us to be honest with each other."

She looked at him with eyes glistening. She intended to be honest with him and also trying to get clear in her head how to articulate what she wanted to say. "I guess I hadn't thought about it. It happened pretty quickly." She watched him lower his eyes, looking at their hands. "I know that you can't be here one hundred percent of the time because of your job," she said, thinking and looking at him. "Even though you were already overseas, and when you learned that I was going to be there in Basel, you came in search of me, simple little me, and found me." He raised his head, looking at her.

"You showed me how to fill that space with the love I've had for you for a long time, and to not be afraid, because love doesn't hurt," she said with tears as she placed her hand on the side of his face lovingly. "Jason, I love you so much. I think fate has been playing with us for a long time, when I look back at all of our encounters. I don't want to spend any more time away from you than I need to. I want you to stay here with me, to move in with me. That's what I want." He put his arms around her, pulling her close to him, and she put her arms around his neck. He kissed her cheek and her lips.

"I don't ever want to be away from you unless I have to go to work. Maybe over the next few weeks, I could move a few things at a time," Jason said, looking at her.

"Well, maybe I should see your place first. If it's bigger than mine, maybe I'll have to move in with you; and if it's smaller than mine and not as pleasing, I'll take pity on you and let you stay here," she said smiling, and he chuckled. "It won't be mine, and it won't be yours, but ours."

"Then, what if we were to head over to my apartment, and I can show you that my place is smaller than yours. I can get a few of my things and my car and then come back home," he said with a smile. She nodded, and they got up to get their jackets. It was already getting dark outside, which Talia hated. Jason's apartment seemed easy enough to get to, but a lot farther away. Talia's residence would be closer to his work and some conveniences. After arriving at his place, they headed inside. It was cold because he had turned the heat way down, being gone for over three weeks. He flipped the light on, and she saw how small it was as she looked around. It didn't feel homey. He looked at her and said, "Do you think you want to move here?" She shook her head no and half grinned. She said quietly, *"Troppo piccolo"* (Too small). He looked at her, but wasn't going to ask.

He headed to his bedroom, and she followed. It was at least one-third smaller than hers. The bathroom was small, as was the kitchen; nothing you could call dining space. The living room was OK, but not great, and not as many windows. She watched Jason pack a few more clothing items, some things from the bathroom and a few books. He didn't have a lot of furniture. There was a large book bag that looked like it had photo albums in it, more than likely memories he didn't want to leave behind. He closed the bag and gave it to Talia to carry.

After looking around, he said he was ready to go; he would come back later and check for other items. He wanted this to be a gradual move of his things into her place. What was important to him was standing there next to him. Then he grabbed his car keys. He had been picked up by Ted when they headed to the airport to leave for Germany, so he didn't need to carry them with him. After walking out the door, he locked it and then headed toward his car. It was an older Jeep Cherokee. He put his things in the back seat and told Talia he would follow her.

After arriving back at her— their— apartment, he found a parking spot. She waited for him to gather his things, and then they headed in. She turned on the kitchen light, which was bright. Taking his bag into the bedroom, she showed him the closet where he could hang some of his clothes. She would make room for some of his other things in a dresser drawer. She then headed to the bathroom. There was a nice closet with sheets, blankets and pillowcases, and towels, which he already knew about from getting the frog towel, and then some of her miscellaneous items. She cleared some space on a shelf for his things. There was plenty of room on the bathroom counter; she barely used half of it. Her bathroom was bigger, with a large mirror and good lighting.

After getting some things put away, they headed back to the living room to sit down on the sofa. Talia asked, "What's in the large book bag?"

He had set it down on the side of the sofa where he now sat. He pulled the bag up and opened it, taking out the albums, handing her the bottom two to hold. "This first one is family photos from a long time ago." He opened the oldest album first. She could see it was worn from being gone through many times. He started going through it, telling her who the people were and some places in the photos. Getting near the end, he stopped and looked at several of the pictures of a young boy and a little girl. "That's me when I was five, and Amy when she was three. It was her birthday party." He turned a few pages. "Then here I am at six, and she's four." He smiled, looking at several more pictures. Then he turned the page. "And then here I'm a seven-year-old; I was getting up there in years," he said, maybe trying to lighten his mood. "And here's Amy at five-years-old." He grew quiet, looking at the photo. "It was her birthday that weekend that we went to this new park." He just stared at the picture of them. Talia put her arm around behind him. She wanted to say how adorable Amy was, but didn't know what his response would be. She took a chance and told him anyway. And then he moved past to the last two pages and then closed the book.

It was about 8:30 p.m., and Jason asked, "Do you even want to see the other two books? You don't have to, although there may be a few in here you might recognize." She smiled and wanted to see them all.

"Jason, I want to see these. They're part of you. These are wonderful photos, and beautiful memories you'll cherish," Talia said.

He nodded his head and said, "You may see some other familiar faces in here as well." Kissing her, he opened the next album, going through the various photos. Toward the end, she recognized some people in them. She looked at him and smiled. There were some from the zoo in Basel; she was in several of the photos. He turned a few more pages with pictures from Porcupine Mountains. She laughed, remembering the place, and saw a couple of pictures of her with Jason standing near her. She looked at Jason. "Who took these?"

"My dad," he said as he and smiled at her. "But I took these four here." She loved it. She gestured for him to turn the page, again seeing several more now from the Black Hills and Yellowstone. There was her and Kurt, and then the three of them, several different ones probably taken by one of his parents. On the last page, she started laughing at one of Jason picking her up, ready to toss her over into a mud pot. It was even funnier now because she could see her expression, which was hilarious. She sat there laughing now, and had Jason laughing as well.

"What incredible memories. I love them," she said, wiping the laughter tears from her eyes as they talked about those adventures.

"Are you sure you want to see the last album?" he asked, teasing her.

"Yes, we're not going to bed until I see them," she said.

As he started from the beginning, she saw many beautiful pictures. "Did you take these?" she asked. He nodded. There were some from a shorter trip they had all taken, and then the next several pages were from Colorado Springs, Pikes Peak, the Air Force Academy, and the flower garden where the lilac bushes were. She saw the photo of her, Jason and Kurt, the one in his wallet, and many other images. The album was only half full. After looking at them, she wrapped her arms around him and hugged him, kissing him on the cheek. "I loved them all. So, no other photos to fill the second half?" she asked.

"No, not yet. But we could fill those remaining pages and then get a new album and put in some of our pictures we took overseas, adding as we go along. It's nice seeing photos on our phones, but having an album to sit down and look at is even better. You have the digital picture frame from Laurel and Sophia, right?" he asked.

"Yes, would you like to go through those? There's a lot on it," she said.

"No, maybe tomorrow. Right now, I want to sit here and hold you," he said, putting his arm around her. She put her head on his shoulder, turning to look at him. He took a slow, deep breath. He put his head back. "I have to be at work by 3:00 p.m. tomorrow. I sure hope it's quiet the next couple of days, but then it drags when we're not busy. I want you to text me anytime, OK, even if it's just to say hi, or 'I miss you' or 'I love you.'" He turned toward her. "Promise?"

She looked at him. "Promise. And you can do the same for me."

He looked at his watch and saw that it was 11:00 p.m. "Why don't we head to bed, my love." Talia stood up and then grabbed one of his hands to pull him up. He looked at her, tilting his head with a sultry grin. "Oh, you think I need help getting off the sofa?"

"What? No, I was pulling you up...." she saw the look in his eyes and started giggling. He stood up and picked her up, twirling her around, with her wrapping her arms around his neck, and then he headed toward the bedroom, flipping off the kitchen light.

Chapter 28

Before heading to work, Jason told Talia that he wanted her to meet his grandmother, Jean, and tell her first about their engagement. So, after his three-day shift ended, he had two days off. Besides seeing Grandma Jean, he also wanted to visit the cemetery where Amy was buried, and visit Talia's dad's grave. He wanted to be there for Talia, as it's not always easy. He used to go to Amy's grave about every other week. Then, over the years, it was once a month consistently.

They headed over to his Grandma Jean's house. Knocking on her door, it took a few moments, and then the door opened. She had a big smile on her face, telling them to hurry and get inside; it was cold out there. She gave Jason a big hug and a kiss on his cold cheek. Then she turned to Talia, looking at her and kissing her on her cheek. Jason watched with loving eyes. "Didn't I tell you timing was everything and that she would come to you?" Grandma Jean said, looking at Jason. Looking back at Talia, she said, "My dear Talia, you have no idea how this boy has longed for you to be in his life. He and I have had many conversations about you."

"Grandma Jean," Jason said.

"You hush up. I'm old, and I can say what I want. Now come in and have a seat, both of you," she said. Talia just looked at Jason with wide eyes like, *Wow, you better do as you're told.* Jason shrugged his shoulders and gestured toward the living room. They followed her. Talia saw many beautiful pieces of furniture: well-preserved chairs, a large beautiful rug in the center of the room extending toward the walls, but not quite reaching. There was a piano with many pictures sitting on the top, a large dining room with a large table and chairs set around, and a huge buffet full of china —no doubt many family gatherings here over the years. The ceilings had crown molding, and the walls were light; a beautiful shade of light green. Pictures hung on the walls. It felt like a home that was loved and filled with joy.

Grandma Jean sat in her favorite chair while Jason and Talia sat on the sofa. "So, Talia, I see that you are wearing a very special engagement ring. Did Jay tell you where it came from?" she asked.

"He did." She looked at Jason, smiling. She turned back to Grandma Jean. "He told me it was your engagement ring and that you were passing it down to him. It's beautiful, and I will cherish it always. He said you'd been married for fifty-three wonderful years, but that your husband passed about ten years ago. I'm sorry," Talia said.

"Thank you. It was a long time ago, and I still miss him. So, are your parents and grandparents living?" Grandma Jean asked.

"My grandfather, Theodore Rose, was the last of my grandparents to pass away several years ago. My dad, Thomas Rose, passed about six months ago. I still have my mother and brother living, plus an aunt and uncle up North," Talia said.

"I see. Something tells me," she looked at Jason, "the two of you have talked about Jay's little sister, Amy, and what happened to her?"

"Yes," Talia said quietly, then looking at Jason.

"Grandma, how do you know I told her?" Jason asked with a slight frown.

"There has been little over your lifetime that I didn't already know something about. Let's call it 'my little secret' how I know. And right now, you don't need to know everything. Even when you talked about this pretty young thing, I could see what would lie ahead for you. Your trip overseas was especially enlightening to me. Many good things are in store for the two of you, and life has a few twists. Your love is strong, and you hold on to it with both hands, you hear?" Grandma Jean said, looking at them both. Jason started to say something, and she interrupted him, holding up her hand for him to stop and not say another word.

"Now, I know the two of you haven't even dated yet, so Jay, go over to the dining room table and pick up that envelope," Grandma Jean said.

"Grandma Jean, what did you do?" Jason asked.

"Jay, get off your hiney and do like I ask. Go on, get up, or I'll make you watch my favorite Charlie Chaplin with me again," Grandma Jean said, smiling. Jason got up and walked over to the dining room table, picking up the envelope. He saw it was addressed to both of them. As he was walking back, he saw and heard his Grandma Jean. She smiled at Talia and said almost in a whisper, "He hated watching Charlie Chaplin with me. He'd roll his eyes, but just sat there. I could see the wheels in his head moving, trying to think of a way to leave." She looked at Jason and said, "You had a morning where you sat and thought you were watching Charlie Chaplin over there, didn't you?"

He went to sit down. "What is it with the women in my life? One seems to see things beforehand, and the other speaks another language," Jason mumbled.

"So, Jay, open the envelope," Grandma Jean said.

Jason opened the envelope while Talia watched. He pulled out several gift certificates. One was for dinner for two with dancing, a favorite place that Jean and her husband had gone to many times. "You and Grandpa, this was one of your favorite places, wasn't it?" Jason asked. A second one was for a musical theatre production, whichever one came to town, their choice, and the third one was for one of the museums in the city.

Jason looked at his grandmother and got up and kneeled beside her chair, giving her a hug and a kiss. Talia also got up and bent down, hugging her.

"What made you do this?" Jason asked.

"As I said, you two have never dated. You're doing things a little ass-end backward, so this is to get you started before you get married, and the rest is up to you. You try to do a date night at least a couple of times a month. Surprise each other. That's what your grandfather and I did for a lot of years," she said. "You have a lot of spice in you, and life is just too darn short. Jay, you see this in your line of work. We all take too much for granted, and we don't know if we'll be here tomorrow. People seem to have their lives all planned up until the day they die, but that could be tomorrow. You're my only grandson, and I love you with all my heart," Grandma Jean said, smiling. "That's why I'm doing this for the two of you."

"Thank you, Grandma Jean. I love you too," Jason said.

Talia felt a bit awkward, but also said, "Thank you. We will enjoy each of them. I like the idea of going out on date nights. I'm looking forward to all of this."

"Darling, you also call me Grandma Jean. You're family, and there's more of you to come," she said, looking at Jason with a knowing look. "And with your talent as a designer, Talia, I have some ideas if you are open and willing to hear me out. Sometime when you're free, I'd like to tell you about them. Maybe the three of us can do supper here. Jason, you still remember how to cook my favorite food?" She looked at him. He nodded with a smile. "I'm sure he told you that I used to sew a lot. I know I'm old-er, but I also have young ideas, things full of color that maybe you never thought of. That's what keeps me young and sassy, right Jay?" She smiled, looking at him. He chuckled.

"OK, then. I know the two of you have a few other things to do, so I won't keep you. You didn't tell her I'm a jabberwocky, did you?" She looked at him knowing he hadn't. He shook his head no and pursed his lips together. "I didn't think so. First impressions aren't always what they seem."

She started getting up, and Jason and Talia also stood up. They walked to the front door, Jason giving her another hug and Talia doing the same.

"I wanted to tell you, I think your home is lovely. There must be a lot of beautiful memories here," Talia said. "I look forward to hearing your ideas, and Jason's cooking."

"I'm happy to tell you about them. Now, the two of you scoot. I have a Chaplin movie to watch," she said, smiling at them both.

They left, heading for Jason's car. Once inside, Jason looked at Talia to see what she thought about Grandma Jean. "So, what did you think?" Jason was a little leery about what she would say.

"I found her to be a hoot and an absolute delight. Jason, I love her. She is one spunky old-er woman. She says what's on her mind. What I did find a little strange, and gave me goosebumps, was her knowledge about things like you said. How does she know things ahead of time?" Talia asked.

"I've been wondering that my whole life," Jason said.

Talia had to ask, "What did she mean when she said, 'Many good things are in store for the two of you, and life has a few twists. Your love is strong, and you hold on to it with both hands.'"

"Ya, I caught that too. I'm not exactly sure. But she's right about our love being strong," Jason said. He started his Jeep, and they headed next to her mom's house.

After visiting with Talia's mom, she was so happy for them. Watching them over the years, it was just a matter of time before the two of them would finally realize that they needed to be together. Whatever plans they made for their wedding, Elizabeth would help, but told them it's their wedding and she was just a helper. She welcomed Jason to the family but told him he was always a part of the family, even when they were young.

Next, it was time to see Jason's mom and dad and visit with them about Europe, and then letting them know about their upcoming wedding. They pretty much said the same thing that Elizabeth said, and wondered what took them so long. Jason's mom looked at him and said, "You need to know and understand that what happened to Amy was never, ever your fault; that lies with us. If you've carried that guilt inside all these years, afraid to love anyone for fear of losing them, then that's also on me because of the time you could and should have had with Talia. We know she's always been the one. You were meant to be together, and I am truly sorry. And I hope you can forgive me for never speaking up and telling you," Mary Ann said. She put her arms around her son, hugging him and holding him. She had tears in her eyes, as did Talia. Jason hugged his dad. And they told Talia, as Elizabeth had said to Jason, that Talia had already been part of the family, and they hugged her.

Mary Ann told them that they would have to come over and have dinner in the next few weeks. They wanted to make sure and invite Elizabeth as well. They left, deciding to call it a day. It was late in the afternoon. They would do a cemetery visit tomorrow. They got home and had leftover pizza. Jason closed the blinds as Talia walked out to the living room with the digital picture frame. She sat down next to Jason, covering herself with a sofa blanket. The next hour was spent going through their pictures, remembering how far they'd come and sharing so many special memories.

Jason's last three days proved to be busy ones. She could tell he was tired. As they sat on the sofa, he put his head back to rest his eyes and fell asleep. Talia wasn't tired, but let him catnap for a bit. Maybe it would have been better had he just gone to bed. She took the blanket that covered her and placed it over him. She worked on one of her designs. Turning and seeing Jason, she liked that he was in the room with her. It made her feel safe. She put the lamp on over her design table and began working away on one of her ideas from Europe. After a bit, she found it wasn't flowing for her at all. Her mind was busy with other things, and she had to stop trying to force an idea.

As she had done often when she got stuck for an idea, she paced, letting her mind wander; it seemed to help. This evening, it was taking a little longer. As her pacing began, she took a deep breath, walking around the kitchen counter, past the sofa, and around the coffee table, around the two big chairs, walking around the kitchen counter again…. She did this about three times, and it seemed like nothing was coming to her. After walking one more time around the kitchen counter, she saw the small clock on the microwave. It was 9:45 p.m. Now she was getting tired, and nothing was coming to her. She hated that it got dark early. She hated that they would have to change their clocks back an hour within the next coming weeks; someone ought to be shot. At the moment, she didn't care who. She was feeling tired and cranky. She headed toward her design table, looking at the design she tried working on, then threw down her pencil. She wanted to wake Jason and head to bed. She wasn't thinking clearly at all, so she might as well leave it for now. Shutting off the lamp, she turned to find Jason looking at her.

"I was going to wake you and tell you we should head to bed. My brain isn't working this evening, and I'm feeling frustrated, tired, and cranky," she said.

"Yes, I noticed. You've been walking for the last fifteen minutes or so, stopping at your table and then walking again. Do you do this often?" Jason asked. "As far as shooting someone due to the time change coming, it would be hard to pinpoint one particular person. They've probably been dead a long time."

"What?" Talia said.

"You were talking while walking. And yes, I've been watching you for at least the last fifteen minutes. We need to go to bed," Jason said. He stood up and took her hand, guiding her in front of him.

Chapter 29

Another three weeks had gone by, getting them almost to Halloween. They hadn't been able to get to the cemetery when they had first planned several weeks ago, as Jason got called into work; one of the other paramedics ended up having emergency surgery to remove his appendix. On Jason's last day off, they went to both cemeteries where Amy and Talia's dad were buried. Jason didn't have a lot to say about Amy, since she died so young. But Talia talked a little more about her dad's architect business and a few things he had on a bucket list, two of which he did before passing away. Jason listened.

They both worked. Talia's schedule was a little more open than Jason's. She could work from home with a bit more peace and quiet. The girls were great, but they could get chatty. She continued with her Italian audio course. There was just something about the language that was fun and beautiful. To her, speaking Italian was more natural than speaking French as her mother did.

Jason was working his three-day shift with two nights at the station. He wasn't home last night and wouldn't be back tonight. She had risen early this morning and finished design number three, getting started on number four, so only four more to go. She gave herself an early deadline to have them completed before Christmas and their wedding. She took a break and was in the mood to do some baking, making something for Jason and the guys down at the station. She learned from Grandma Jean that one of his favorite cookies was a no-bake cookie. It's an easy recipe, and she had all the ingredients, and no oven was required. She'd make enough so that he could share them, figuring they would appreciate it. Jason had told her to come to the station sometime when she could; he wanted to introduce her and show her off. He was so proud of her and her accomplishments. This would be a pleasant way to surprise him.

Making the cookies half the size of what an average-sized cookie would be, she came up with about three dozen. She placed two and a half dozen in a box with wax paper between the layers, and then she put the box lid on. She'd keep the other half dozen here for him. With that finished, she went and changed her clothes. She also wanted to head to work and take in the next design so the girls could get started on it.

It was getting close to 11:15 a.m. She could drop off the cookies, see him, and head to her office. She was going to have lunch with the girls. Putting on her coat and picking up her bag, she then grabbed her portfolio satchel and the cookies. It was brisk out, but the sun was shining and it was slowly warming up. She put the cookies on the floor of the car so they wouldn't get dumped if she had to make a sudden stop, and then laid her satchel down on the back seat. As she backed out, shutting the door, she sensed she was being watched. She looked around but didn't think she saw anyone. Jason had told her to know her surroundings ever since the incident with Tim and the pizza.

Arriving at the station, she got the box of cookies out, leaving her bag locked in the car. The station garage door was closed, but there was a large glass door not far away that she walked to and opened, walking in. She saw several men who were wiping down a firetruck and a rescue squad; another one was sweeping the floor. As she approached, some of the guys stopped and looked at her. She gave a little wave, stopping in her tracks. She was ready to ask if Jason Porter was there. Recognizing her from photos, Paul came up to Talia and said, "Hi Talia, I'm Paul. I was one of the paramedics in Germany with Jason."

"How did you know my name?" she asked, looking at him.

"Jason showed Jim and me your photos when we were over there," he said. And then one of the other guys came up and said, "So, this is Jason's lady, the one that looks *Mediterranean*." Ted was looking at her as he said it. Paul smacked Ted with the back of his hand, letting him know that was inappropriate. Ted was one of two single guys at the station, according to Jason. He didn't count himself as single anymore. But he did say that Ted and one of the other guys, *What did Jason say his name was, oh ya, Jack, were both single.* But Ted thought he was a ladies' man. Talia took a step backward.

Jim came around the corner, seeing the guys hovering and saw it was Talia. He walked up to her, reaching out to shake her hand and said, "Hello Talia, I'm Jim. I'm the one that dropped Jason off when we came back from Germany."

"Oh, I remember you now. Nice to meet you," Talia said.

"I imagine you're here to see Jason. He's working on some reports before lunch. Ted, let Jason know Talia is here," Jim said, looking at Ted. Ted just looked at Jim, but knew he best do as Jim asked. They'd already had one altercation. "So, you came to see where Jason works?"

"Yes, I wanted to stop by before heading to my office for the afternoon," she said.

Ted came back around the corner with Jason following. He gave her a big smile. "I'm so glad to see you," he said, giving her a big hug, and not thinking, kissed her in front of the guys, a couple of them clapping and laughing. The only ones to have seen the photos from Europe were Jim and Paul; the others were probably wondering what kind of woman Jason could have. "All right, guys, let's go into the kitchen," Jason said. He walked with Talia, his arm around her. Jason introduced Talia to everyone, including Captain Robins. They were getting ready to sit down and eat, when Jason asked, "Would you like to join us?"

"No, I'm heading to the office and going to have lunch with the girls," Talia said with a look on her face. She couldn't help herself, but had to ask, "What's that smell?"

Jason looked at the others who were waiting to sit down. Being the gentlemen they were, they stayed standing in a lady's presence. Jason said, then thinking she shouldn't, "Well, that's called lunch. And maybe you shouldn't eat with us. What's in the box?"

"Oh, I was in the mood to make your favorite cookie this morning after finishing design number three," Talia said. "I thought I would bring some down so you could share them. I have some at home."

Jason opened the box, smiling and smelled them, closing his eyes, savoring the smell. "Right now, I'd rather eat your no-bake cookies than eat what we have for lunch." Several guys tried seeing what was in the box.

Paul, who was standing closer looked, and said, "Those are my favorite cookie. I'm going to have to get Ally to make some. She's my wife." Jim, who also was standing close, could see them and agreed; he liked them a lot.

"Thank you. We will enjoy them. There may not be many left by tonight," Jason said, kissing her cheek.

It was Paul that brought up about the wives bringing food in, and said, "So, Jason, you tell her about how the Germans' wives bring in food so their husbands wouldn't have to eat their own cooking? And here she is, with goodies for everyone."

Talia took a moment, looking at Paul with a frown, the others seeing it. She looked back at Jason with the same frown and tilted her head. Looking at her, he slowly shook his head. "No, it never came up, and we don't have to go into that," he said, looking at Paul and then Jim. He had a feeling something was about to come up, but wasn't sure what would come out of her mouth. He remembered Ollon.

Talia decided right then to have a little fun with them and introduce some Italian. Her lessons were paying off, not that she had to speak it, but because she could. She tilted her head the other way, looking at Jason with a straight face. She could tell Jason was already kind of squirming and just waiting for something to come out. He squinted at her and raised an eyebrow and took a half step backward, giving her some space.

"Jason," Jim said, wondering why he did that. Jason glanced at Jim and back to Talia.

"Sweetie, we can talk about this when I get home, right?" Jason asked, nodding his head yes.

"Non me l'hai detto," Talia said (You didn't tell me).

"Le mogli cucinano?" she said, looking at Jason and then the guys (The wives cook?).

"I knew something was going to come out," Jason said softly, looking at her.

Paul and the others were watching Jason. "What language is that?" Paul asked.

"Italian," Jason said with a half grin. "Guys, don't get her started, because I don't know Italian and I have a feeling there's a guest sofa with my name on it."

He handed the cookies to Paul. "Uh, Paul, why don't you take these, quick, and place them over on the counter before she takes them with her. At least we'll have something to eat." Paul grabbed the box just in time as Talia was reaching for them.

"Didn't see that one coming," Jim said. "You mentioned she spoke some Italian, and I didn't believe you, and her mother speaks French." Talia half-turned, looking at Jim and then back to Jason with her arms crossed.

"Suppongo de portare del cibo?" she asked with raised eyebrows (I'm supposed to bring food?). Jason stood there looking at her, not sure what to think, and no idea what she was saying.

"Non cucinano bene," she looked at each of them with her palm up, panning her hand toward them (They don't cook well.). They all looked at her, wondering what she said.

"Tu cucini, mostro loro come," she said, looking at Jason. (You do cook, show them how.)

"You know I don't speak Italian. Are you going to at least translate for us?" Jason asked.

Taking Jason's left arm, she looked at his watch. Then she said, *"Sono in ritardo, Devo andare ora"* (I'm running late, I have to leave now). She gave all the men a final look, turning back to Jason, with a sassy grin and winked at him. She then told Jason, *"Piu tardi amore mio,"* touching his lips with her index finger and walking out of the room (Later, my love.).

Jason turned and called after her, *"Ti amo"* (I love you.).

"I thought you said you don't know Italian," Jim said.

"I don't. Those are the only two words I know," Jason said, walking to his place to sit down and have whatever it was being served.

"She do this often, speak Italian?" Jim asked as the others waited for his reply as well.

Jason replied, looking at Jim, "Sometimes."

Paul said, "I'm going to say that to my wife." He remembered what it meant from seeing the words on Jason's text message, and when he had asked, Jason was looking out the window when he said: "I love you." Paul looked at Jason, but wasn't going to tell them what it meant; that was up to him.

Mike spoke up and asked what the others were wondering. "How do you know what it means? And what does *ti-amo* mean?"

Jason looked at the door she went through and said, "I love you."

Talia headed for her office, smiling. She knew there might be a price to pay when he got home tomorrow, but for now, she rather enjoyed it. Arriving at her office, the girls were finishing up with one project and were ready for lunch. Talia put down her artist's satchel, and they headed out. After lunch, the girls went back to work with Talia, working on the next design she brought with her. Time went by quickly that afternoon, and before they knew it, it was well after 5:30 p.m. Talia told the girls to quit and go home; she was heading out herself in about five minutes.

Chapter 30

When she arrived home, one of the parking lot lights near her space was out. As she was getting out of her car, she gave a quick call to Jason because she wanted to tell him about the light. He was in the lounge with some of the guys. He answered, but she didn't say anything, and then he heard her asking someone a question. "Talia, are you there, hon?" He stood up with a concerned look on his face.

"What are you doing here? What do you want?" Talia asked the person.

"I just wanted to see you and talk to you." It was Tim's voice, the pizza delivery guy. Jason remembered his voice.

"Talia, answer me, please," Jason said. The guys were looking at Jason. He turned to Jim and said, "Talia's in trouble." Adrenaline kicked in. Jason turned to leave, with Jim right behind him saying he was coming and that he was driving.

"Look, you need to leave. I didn't order pizza. I need to go inside; I have work to do," she told Tim as she was trying to get past him.

He blocked her from walking toward her apartment. "Please let me pass. You're making a mistake," she told him.

"Hey, I told you, I just want to talk to you. You had some guy at your place. He said you were engaged to him. I hoped that wasn't true and that you and I could, you know, hang out, or maybe we could go out. We could have a good time. And he didn't look like your type," Tim said.

The cell phone still in her hand, she lowered her hand. Jason was listening to everything. "I am engaged. Look, I don't know you, except when you've delivered pizza." She just realized it. "You're the one that always seems to deliver my pizza. Why is that? Aren't there other people who can do that besides you?"

"There are, but I tell them I know you and you like having me deliver your pizza," he said.

"I'm not interested in going out with you; you need to back off. I told you I am engaged, and you need to leave." She tried getting past him, her heart racing. She was trying to be calm and think clearly. "It's getting cold out here, and I would really like to go home. So, if you'll just let me pass, you can be on your way. I'm sorry, but I'm not interested at all."

"Well, little lady, I am interested. You and me should take a little walk." He took a step toward her, making her back up against her car as he took hold of her coat, pulling at it. She was trying to push him away, and with his other hand, grabbed her neck, trying to kiss her as she screamed. It was Jason that grabbed him by the shoulder, swinging him around toward Jim, who grabbed him and forced him to the ground. Jason turned, taking hold of Talia, who began shaking and crying. He held her close, telling her it was all right now; he was here, and she was safe. His heart was beating fast, still with the adrenaline.

"Hey man, get off of me. You have no right," Tim said.

"No, you're the one who doesn't have a right to force yourself on someone. You just lost any rights you think you had, and right now, you're lucky to be alive," Jim said.

A squad car showed up with lights on, an officer coming over to Jim and taking the man into custody, placing him in the backseat. He then came back over to talk with Jim, telling him thank you for the call, and then saw Jason holding a woman and walked over to him. "Jason, I'll need to take this woman's statement."

"Ya, I know. Mark, this is my *fiancée*, Talia Rose. Talia, this is Officer Mark Ford. He'll need to get a statement, OK?" Jason asked her. She nodded. "Mark, is it possible to go inside our place, and you can ask her questions there?"

Jim said to Mark, "I can stay here until you come out. He's not going anywhere."

Mark then looked at Jason. The three of them have known each other for a while. "Sure." They headed to their apartment, with Jason unlocking the door, going in first and turning on some lights, as Talia and then Mark followed. Talia sat down on the sofa with Jason sitting next to her. Jason was going to help her with her coat, but she didn't want it off. She stared at the floor.

"Miss Rose, I need to ask you some questions," he stated. She raised her eyes to him and nodded. He asked her questions and wrote down what she was saying. Then Jason told him about the incident weeks ago with pizza being delivered and the note in the box. When Mark was finished, he said they might follow up with her. She again nodded.

Jason told Mark he would follow him out. "Talia, I'll be right back, I promise," Jason said, looking at her. She grabbed his hand, looking at him. "I'm not going back to the station, but I need to talk to Jim, OK?"

"OK," she replied. He kissed the top of her head.

"I'll be right back." He walked out with Mark, heading to the squad car.

Mark turned and shook hands with Jim and then Jason, telling them they knew the drill. Both nodded. "And to let you both know, he has assault charges against him. Guess he won't be delivering pizzas anymore." He got into his car and left.

"I'm not coming back to the station tonight. I need to be with her. I could have caused him some real harm if you hadn't been here with me," Jason said to Jim.

"I get it." Jim was shaking his head. "If I had the opportunity, I would have had him in a chokehold that could have cut off his air supply and not thought twice about it. I'll inform the captain as soon as I get back. You call me, OK?"

"I will, thank you, Jim," Jason said, and they shook hands. Jim left after Jason headed back inside.

Once Jason was back inside, locking the door, he saw Talia still sitting on the sofa with her coat still on. She was leaning forward with her head in her hands. He sat down beside her and just waited. She slowly raised her head and folded her hands, placing them under her chin, just staring at the floor. Jason wanted to help, but didn't know where to start, except sit with her and be there for her.

After several more minutes, she looked up toward her drafting table and the windows. The blinds had been closed since she left this morning. "I think I need to work on a design," she said slowly, taking off her coat. She looked at Jason, and he could see the anger in her eyes.

She then spoke slowly. "I want to know what the hell is wrong with men, thinking they have any right to do that to another human being, especially women and children. We are not objects or something to be owned and told what to do. I'm so damn pissed. If I hadn't been caught off-guard and then let fear get to me, he would have been on the ground, grabbing his so-called manhood." She stared at Jason. What he knew about incidents like this was that it could change people. It now had him worried about their relationship all because, as she said, some man wanting to hurt another.

He sat back, partially turned toward her, putting his arm around the back of the sofa, looking at her with his other hand resting on his lap. It was a wake-up call for him. Someone he loved so dearly and wanted to protect could have been taken from him. What if he couldn't get to her in time. He couldn't say he knew how she felt; he's never been assaulted. He just wanted to hold her so she'd feel safe. "Talia, I'm sorry you went through that," Jason said quietly. He knew it would take time for her to trust anyone, possibly even himself, and that scared him.

She took a slow, deep breath and then reached for his hand, taking hold of it. With eyes misting over, she said, "I'm just grateful you were there to grab him. How did you know I needed help?" She looked at him.

"You called me. Do you remember that? As soon as I heard you questioning someone, and you didn't respond to me, Jim and I headed over immediately. I heard his voice. I heard the whole thing," Jason said.

"Oh, I do remember calling you. I was going to tell you about the light outside being out, and then I thought, I didn't want him seeing my phone because I thought he would take it away from me. You must have driven like a bat-out-of-hell," she replied, looking at him.

"It wasn't me, it was Jim driving, and he knew I would be a maniac on the road," he said. She slowly leaned back against the sofa, not against Jason. She looked toward the ceiling, letting her mind wander for a moment or two. She took a deep breath and then sat up. She took his left wrist and looked at his watch, noting the time. It was close to 7:30 p.m. "Are you hungry? I could fix each of us a sandwich," Jason asked. He felt her distance, which made him sad.

She turned toward him. She tried to smile a reassuring smile for him. "You need to give me a little space and time to process all of this. I know you love me with all of your heart, and I love you with all of mine, but I just need a little bit of time."

He looked at her with sad eyes. "I feel like he took something away from us, from you, now not trusting anyone, maybe even me. I don't want to lose you. I want to be here with you. I'm sorry I didn't keep you safe. But if you feel so strongly about having some space, I guess I can go back to my apartment since I still have it."

Seeing the hurt in his eyes, and knowing how much he loved her and would do anything to protect her if he could, she said, "No, I don't want you going anywhere. And I don't want you thinking this is your fault. How could it? I don't want you going to that place where guilt took you before. I want you here; I need you here. You may not always be able to protect me, but I think we both know to be more vigilant, or at least I do, like many women do. Jason, I don't want you to go anywhere."

Jason had to ask. "Is it OK if I kiss you?"

She leaned over and kissed him gently on the cheek, telling him, "Just a little time is all I'm asking."

"I'll give you whatever time you need," he said.

"I'm going to go take a shower, and yes, I would like a sandwich, please," she said, getting up, looking at him, and then heading to the bathroom.

Jason stood up and was now pacing the floor. He called Jim while she was in the shower. Jim had spoken with the captain, and he told him to tell Jason to take tomorrow off, but to call him and they would talk. "How's she doing, Jason?" Jim asked.

"I wish I honestly knew. She seems distant, hurt and angry. I don't know who she thinks she'll be able to trust, including me. She wants time and space for a bit. I don't even know what that means; how much time, and how much space? I'm afraid the strong intimacy we've shared isn't going to be as strong as it was. I asked her if I could kiss her, and she kissed me on the cheek. I'm worried and scared that our relationship will change. Jim, will it ever be the same? I can't lose her," Jason said.

"Jason, listen to me, all right, change is inevitable, especially when something like this happens. But try to look at it as something that will strengthen you. The love you two have is strong, and you have to hold on to that, and don't you ever think any differently. The time and space she wants and needs, give it to her and be supportive of her in every way," Jim told him.

"Ya, well, how would you know? That's quite a message you're preaching to me," Jason said, feeling angry about the whole thing.

Jim took a moment, then said, "When I served in the military, we were stationed at a base here in the U.S. My wife was attacked, and I wasn't there to protect her because I was overseas, and that eats at me every day when I look at her. Even though that was a long time ago, we made it through, and we are stronger people. It made Nadine a stronger woman. That's how I know. If I had reached that pizza guy first, instead of you, it could have been a hell of a lot worse for him. I'll talk to you soon. 'Night, Jason," Jim said.

Jason laid down his phone and stood there. He couldn't believe what Jim just told him; he's never said anything to him about this. They've been best friends for a long time. His eyes misted over. Jason felt angry, but couldn't imagine what Jim went through, not being there to protect his wife. Jim is one of the strongest people he knows.

Jason went to the kitchen and made up two sandwiches and pulled out several cocoa packages, putting on the teakettle, thinking maybe this would help her remember how much he adored and loved her. Talia came out of the bathroom with a heavier robe on and her hair down, but still wet. He looked at her with a half smile. "Would you like one of these?" He pointed to the packets on the counter, as he looked at her.

She sat on one of the high-back chairs, pulling her plate over to her and pointed to the Snickerdoodle one, looking at him. She knew what he was trying to do. He opened up the packet and poured the contents into her cup. When the teakettle whistled, he poured the water. He picked up one of the packets and did the same for himself. Then, he sat down next to her, pulling his plate over. "You still have your uniform on. I thought you would have changed out of it," she said, looking at him.

"I guess I forgot; other things got in the way this evening," he said, actually not feeling very hungry as he looked at his plate.

Talia touched his arm so that he would look at her, and she leaned over to him and gently kissed his lips. "Give me a little time."

"I spoke with Jim a little bit ago. He talked with the captain, and I'll be taking tomorrow off. But I'll have to call him tomorrow. I want to see if I can do days for a little while; no nights. I want to be here with you," Jason said. Talia nodded.

When they were finished eating, even though it wasn't late, they headed to bed. Talia got under the covers, leaving her robe on and pulling the blanket up, facing away from him. Jason lay next to her on his side, facing her. Soon, she reached behind her taking his arm and placing it around her, holding his hand.

Chapter 31

Jason woke to look at his watch; it was 8:00 a.m. Talia's arm was across his chest, with the big sleeve of her robe draped over him. She lay on his shoulder, and his arm was around behind her. There wasn't any incident with her having a bad dream, although he heard the siren of the rescue squad driving past their place. Their apartment was only about a mile and a half away; that's why he and Jim were able to get to her so quickly. Sometime that morning, he figured he would talk with the captain, but Talia would need to take him over since his Jeep was still there.

He could feel Talia stretch under the covers, and looked at her. She opened her eyes, slowly looking at him. "Morning, my love," Jason said.

"Morning," she replied. She started to move her arm from his chest and roll over but then rolled back toward him, looking at him and kissed him before turning back toward her side, sitting on the edge. She pulled her hair from inside her robe. She sat there and shook her head. She took a deep breath and started to stand up, then sat back down. Jason sat up, asking, "Talia, you feel all right?"

"Ya, I just felt a little funny, more than likely from last evening. I'm OK; whatever it was, passed," she said. She turned toward him and said, "I'm supposed to meet with a client for a short bit before lunch today. Maybe we could have a bite somewhere. You said you were off today, right?" She reached for his hand, and he gladly took it and kissed it.

"I am. I do have to get back to the station so I can talk to the captain. You'll have to drop me off," he said.

"Not a problem." She stood up again, this time walking out the door and heading for the bathroom.

After getting up and dressed, they had some breakfast. Talia didn't eat much. She walked over to her drafting table and worked on a few things. Her phone rang, and it was Chloe, needing some information. Then about twenty minutes later, Talia's phone rang again; it was the client she was to meet with and wondered if it was possible to meet fifteen minutes earlier than what they agreed on, and she was OK with that.

"Are you all right, leaving in a bit? My client wants to meet fifteen minutes earlier," Talia asked Jason.

"Ya, not a problem. I'm ready to go when you are," Jason said. He walked over toward her to see what she was doing. He didn't know much about fashion design except what he liked to wear: his jeans, pullover shirts, and some dress pants. He loved watching her work; she was so focused on creating. She gathered up some papers and a design she was working on, sticking those in her satchel. She was looking for something else, then after finding it, put it in her bag. She looked over her table one more time, feeling she had everything she needed for her meeting. She turned and found Jason leaning on her drafting chair, which she had moved back, giving herself space to move freely. He was looking at her. Many times he would see her standing while drawing instead of half sitting on her chair.

"What?" she asked, tilting her head slightly sideways.

"Nothing. I love watching you work. I see those little creative wheels turning in your head. When things are going well, you have this look on your face like everything's going to be OK," Jason said.

"I love what I do," she said, taking steps to him, putting her arms around him. He put his arms around her, hugging her and holding her. She looked up at him like she's done before when wanting a kiss, and he gave her one. He knew she still needed some space and would give her all the time she needed; he wasn't going anywhere. She'll come to him when she's fully ready.

Talia dropped him off, and they agreed he would come to her office just before noon, and then they'd have lunch.

Jason walked into the station and saw Jim heading toward the comp room. Jim stopped and waited for Jason. "How are you doing?" Jim asked, shaking Jason's hand and giving a side-hug.

"I've been better. I'm sorry about what I said on the phone to you, about how would you know and preaching to me," Jason said. "You never told me, but then that's a pretty private thing, and you had no reason to."

In a low tone, looking around before replying, Jim said, "The only other person who knows is the captain, and of course, Captain Johnson back in Colorado. When I came on board here, he was going over my background in the Army, and he saw that I was also a medic; we talked about things I saw over there. He also served in the Army. He was a single man. He asked some questions that I was uncomfortable with, and didn't know what they had to do with this job. Then he explained about his good friend's wife and what happened to her. He asked me if someone I loved was in harm's way, what I would do. I looked at him and said, depending on the situation, if it was my loved one's life at stake, the person intent on harming wouldn't live once I got done with them. Part of the training in me, I guess.

"But, I sat there for a moment, looking at him and it came out about my wife's attack and my not being here to protect her, because I was over there helping to protect everyone back home, except the one person I loved and cherished the most. I felt guilty for the longest time. It was my job as a man, and as her husband, to love and protect her. I failed at one of those. Over time, our love grew stronger. I am a better man and husband because of that, even though she paid the price. Captain was quiet for a bit," Jim said with a smile. "He then hired me on the spot. So, it's not something you go talking about, not until you know someone that went through what Talia did. Her life was being threatened. You were able to get to her before anything happened." He paused, looking at Jason. "How is she doing?"

Jason looked toward the garage with the trucks and said, "She stared toward her draft table and said she needed to work on a design. She sat there for a moment, then looked at me with such anger in her eyes, I'd never seen her with such hatred." He looked back at Jim. "She said, 'I want to know what the hell is wrong with some men, thinking they have any right to do that to another human being, especially women and children,' Plus a few other words. I told her I'd give her the space she needs, that I could go back to my apartment. She told me no, she wanted me with her, just needed time."

"I know this isn't funny, but did you have to sleep on the sofa?" Jim asked with a half smile.

"No." With Jim being his best friend, he felt he could tell him. "She gave me a kiss on the lips before we headed to bed." He said, looking toward the captain's door, "She wore a robe to bed, maybe feeling vulnerable or it was a way to protect herself, I don't know. But she took my arm and placed it around her, holding my hand."

"Give her time. She seems to be a very strong woman, maybe on the quiet side, but those are the ones to watch out for," Jim said. Then, with a smile, "She could have dropped me to my knees just with the looks she gave us and speaking Italian."

Jason chuckled and nodded his head. "Oh ya, been down that road with her a couple of times. I guess I best go talk to the captain. See you in a bit."

As Jason headed toward the captain's office, passing by the lounge room, he saw several of the guys sitting at the table. It was Paul who asked, "Jason, is everything OK? You didn't come back." Jason stopped at the entryway, looking at Paul. Then Jim came and stood behind Jason.

"Did you tell them about last night?" Jason asked with a frown turning to Jim.

"Jason, Jim didn't say anything to us. I overheard him talking to the captain. I'm sorry, is Talia, all right?" Paul asked. "I don't know what I would have done had it been Ally." Ted walked toward the doorway, thinking he was going to leave the room.

"Well, he wasn't the only one that overheard. So your lady had a scare last night, you went to her rescue, and nothing happened, right?" Ted had a smirk on his face. The captain heard a commotion and headed down the hallway right about the time Jason grabbed Ted by the front of his shirt, shoving him up against the wall. The other men got to their feet; they'd never seen Jason like this before. Captain came around the doorway.

"You think you're such a ladies' man. You had better watch yourself around me. Maybe you should look inside yourself and ask why you have such a problem with women. They're not toys or things you own and then dump when you've had enough. Is this how you would want any female in your family being treated, like they don't matter, or is this how you already treat them? I can see why women have a hard time wanting to be around you. Part of wearing this uniform is that we also protect and serve, not to show off thinking that's how you get a woman. You're cocky, and that's going to get you into a lot of trouble," Jason said in a disgusted voice.

Jim looked at Ted, saying, "You and I can go another round if you're that intent on being an ass."

Seeing that Jason had Ted against the wall and the others were watching, the captain tapped Jason on the shoulder, saying, "My office." Jason released Ted. "And Ted, you're pushing yourself with me big time. You're a good firefighter, but you need to work on a few other things in your life. Most of the men you work with are married or will be married," he said, looking at Jason. "Maybe someday, you'll know what that's like to give your heart to another where you will do whatever it takes to protect them first." The captain turned, walking out of the room with Jason following.

Walking inside the captain's office, he closed his door. He gestured for Jason to sit down as he took his seat. Jason took a moment before sitting down. "Captain, I'm sorry about what happened in there. It won't happen again," Jason said, looking at him.

The captain slowly nodded. "I'm sure it won't, although I do understand. How is your *fiancée* doing?"

"She's scared, hurt and angry, not trusting others; it may include me, I don't know. She wants some time and space, but also wants me there with her," Jason said.

"Jim told me about the phone call you received, and then the two of you leaving here to head to your place. I'm glad to hear that she'll be all right."

"Captain, I'd like to ask if I can do some days for a few weeks before going back to my other shifts," Jason asked.

"I've looked at everyone's schedule, and I've already done a little shifting, but I will only give you two weeks with days, all right. You and Jim will have this same shift," the captain said.

"Thank you, Captain. I'll be here tomorrow," Jason said. Finding Jim, he told him he would see him tomorrow. Jim said he had already been informed. The two of them were partners, and Jim was OK with it; the others would have to deal with it. And Jim would have a few extra nights with his lovely wife. Jason said, "OK, then I'm off to have lunch with my beautiful *fiancée*."

☓

Jason found Talia's shop. She told him it wasn't huge, but that it didn't have to be. He was impressed by her sign: The T.E. Rose Shoppe. He remembered her telling him that Shoppe had to have two p's in it because it looked cool, and he had to agree. He knew her grandfather would have been very proud of her. Jason wished he could have met him, probably nothing like his Grandma Jean.

He walked inside and immediately saw a long counter, which he walked up to, and off to the side, saw two garment racks with some clothing hanging on them. Toward the far end, he saw a couple of draft tables like Talia's at home, and then saw a couple of sewing machines with fabric laid out. On another long table, he saw bolts of material, and the walls had designs taped to them and swatches of fabric. From the back, came two young women who looked to be around Talia's age. They must be her employees. They saw Jason standing there, and it was Jana who forgot to use her inside voice, so the outside one showed up. "Oh, you are tall and so good-looking."

Feeling a little embarrassed, Chloe nudged Jana on her side, telling her to use her inside voice, which of course, was now too late. They both just looked at him.

"Ladies, I take it you know who I am," Jason said, looking at both of them.

Jana replied with only, "Uh-huh."

It was Chloe that walked over to the other side of the counter and shook his hand. "I'm Chloe Chang, and this is Jana Woods, the one who forgot to use her inside voice. You're Jason, the *fiancé*." He nodded, smiling at them both.

"Chloe, Jana, it's nice to meet you both," Jason said. "Is Talia back from her meeting yet?"

"No, not yet, but she should be back soon," Chloe said. "Can I get you some water or coffee, Mr. Porter?"

"Please call me Jason. And no, thank you," he said.

"So, you're the paramedic and firefighter. She told us that you met in Switzerland, like, when you were little kids," Jana said.

"Actually, not so little, but we were young," Jason said. "How much did she tell the two of you?" He could tell they had become flustered.

"Well, she maybe told me more stuff than Jana because Jana doesn't have an inside voice," Chloe said, looking at Jana. "And things spill out where they shouldn't spill out." Chloe took a deep breath. "Talia and I have known each other for a long time. We became good friends in college, up at ISU. It wasn't until Talia could open this shop that she contacted me and wanted to see if I would work for her. I'm much happier, and so is she, especially since you...." Chloe's voice trailed. Now it was Jana who nudged Chloe in the side, as that last part was supposed to stay inside. They just looked at each other. Jason stood there, smiling at them, thinking it was rather cute.

"Especially since what?" Jason asked, raising his eyebrow, wanting her to finish her sentence.

Jana finished it. "Especially since you came into her life."

Chloe spoke up, changing the subject. "Talia showed us some of the pictures on the digital picture frame. It looks like you visited a lot of nice places. I wasn't born here, but since living here, I've never been outside this country, just a few states here in the Midwest. So what did you think about traveling over there?"

"I loved being over there. There's a lot to see, and seeing it through Talia's eyes made it even better. It was her enthusiasm that made every day amazing," Jason said, smiling at them.

"It's a beautiful engagement ring. She said it belonged to your grandmother," Jana said. Jason nodded.

They heard the backdoor open and knew it would be Talia coming in. She went through the same doorway the girls had come through, and after seeing them, she handed Jana one bag, telling her to pull the bolts these would match, and Chloe another. Seeing Jason standing there, she stopped a moment, looking at him, smiling. She laid down her shoulder bag and walked around to him, giving him a big hug which he gave back to her. With their arms still around each other, she looked up at him, and he knew she wanted a kiss. He gave her a long kiss and then a little one. He looked at her and then tilted his head toward the girls.

"I missed him, can you blame me," Talia said, looking at them, with a smile. "We are going to lunch, and I'll be back later."

"Oh, how much later?" Chloe asked. Talia didn't answer.

She grabbed her bag, and the two of them headed out the door. The girls quickly walked to the window and looked out, watching them. Jason opened the door for Talia, letting her get in her seat, giving her a quick kiss before closing her door, and walking around to his side. And then they left.

"Oh, *mama mia,* did you see that kiss he gave her," Jana said. "Be still, my heart. Where the heck are all the good-looking ones?"

"I don't know, but we better get some of this done before she comes back," Chloe said, walking to her table.

"What if she doesn't come back?" Jana said with a grin.

໕

Jason and Talia had a nice long lunch. They were off in a corner by themselves, sitting close together. "The girls seem nice, inquisitive about us. How long have you known them, and what all have you told them about us?" Jason asked.

Talia looked at him. "Chloe and I go back to our college days. Her family moved to the States when she was, I guess, eight-years-old. She apparently had a hard time in school, not speaking English, or at least well, but she learned quickly. Sometimes I think she speaks better grammar English than most Americans. She really likes clothes and fashion, something she didn't grow up with. In school, she took classes like I did, along with Family and Consumer Sciences. She was also pretty good in math and some science. But fashion was her dream. Her father was a carpenter, and her mother sewed. Chloe received some scholarships to help pay for school, otherwise, she wouldn't have been able to go. So, we met probably second semester of our sophomore year and hit it off. We talked about school and fashion and boys," she said, smiling at him. "And what our dreams were. So, there were very few things I told her about us growing up, about Switzerland and you, and getting engaged. But leaving some things out.

"Jana, I knew her from the job I had before. They didn't treat her very well at all. I saw she had talent and a few skills that I didn't have. So when I had the opportunity, I found her and offered her a part-time position with Chloe and me. I haven't really discussed much with her at all. Sometimes, she keeps to herself. She knows what needs to be done, and she does it. She's been kind of a loner for a long time, but she's opened up more since working with us. She's funny and kind and actually really smart. I showed them the digital pictures, talking about our time over there. But I didn't show them our proposal video, at least not yet."

Jason just kept looking at Talia. "What?" Talia asked.

"You. I wish more people were like you. You're thoughtful, and caring, and considerate of others even though some people are not kind. I don't think you could ever hurt anyone or anything," Jason said.

"That's not totally true," she said, biting her upper lip.

"Really," Jason said, tilting his head and raising an eyebrow.

"Yup. I have killed plenty," she said, smiling. "I've killed ants and spiders and even ran over a squirrel once. I saw it in my rear-view mirror flopping back and forth, and there wasn't anything I could do for the fuzzy little critter, and I cried going home. I felt sick for about a day. Why don't they just stay up in their tree and quit running across the road?"

Jason chuckled. "And your sense of humor and the way you narrate, I love those things about you. Remember, at the cabin, when you were talking to whoever was supposed to be listening to you? The creek and the stump, then the sky opening up and the big rut you stepped into. All those years, I think fate just kept pushing us toward each other and finally that night, when you said those three beautiful words to me." He took hold of her face now, kissing her with gentle kisses. When he stopped, her eyes were still closed, and then she opened them, wondering why he stopped. Out of the corner of his eye, he saw the waiter trying not to look, but wanted to give them their bill. He laid it down and left. Talia put her head down, and they both laughed. Jason put cash in the small folder.

They'd been there about two hours. Talia had to call a client back that afternoon, but wanted to leave early to spend time with Jason. They got up to leave and were winding their way to the door, when there was a lot of commotion several tables over. People were standing up and moving when Jason saw that someone was choking and needed help. He quickly went over, telling them he was a paramedic. He pulled the gentleman's chair back, getting him to his feet, and started doing the Heimlich on him. After five or six abdominal thrusts, the object was dislodged, and the man could breathe.

The wife was in tears. Talia stood beside her, putting her arm around the woman's shoulder and told her that her husband was in good hands; Jason knew what he was doing. Jason sat him back down and started checking him over, asking him questions. The man sat, answering the best he could, taking slow, and deep breaths as Jason asked him to. He suggested he should probably go to his doctor and get checked out. Jason told them what fire department he worked with, showed them his paramedic card, and told them it was his day off.

Someone asked what he was doing, and Jason told him the procedure he did. If they weren't sure how to do it, to call 911. Another older patron said he thought paramedic people only went to scenes of accidents. They were mighty glad that Jason walked by, because none of them knew what to do. After making sure the gentleman was all right, they left the restaurant. Jason took Talia back to her office. He then got out and went around, opening her door for her. She gave him a hug, and he kissed the back of her hand and then kissed her lightly on the lips. He said there were people watching from a window. She reached and kissed him back. Jason said he was heading home and would see her later. He waited for her to go inside, and then he left.

<h1 style="text-align:center">Chapter 32</h1>

It was after 5:15 p.m., and Talia told the girls to go home; she was heading out as well. By the time she got home, she knew she would have to work on the next two designs. Time was flying by. She parked her car, then got out while looking around at her surroundings. She knew this would be something she had to stay on top of. She didn't have a guard dog with her, and there would be many times that Jason would have to work and not be home. The parking lot light had been changed, so it lit up the area well. The time change had already happened that weekend.

Talia saw the lights on in the apartment as she was heading for the door. She opened it to find Jason sitting on one of the big comfy chairs, and then he stood up. She noticed two other people had also stood up, and recognized Jim from the station. Jason walked over to help her take off her coat, hanging it in the closet. She had her satchel in one hand.

"So, what's going on, Jason," she said with a half grin. "Did you invite them over for dinner and forget to tell me?" She looked at him. "Oh, the fire station lunch thing when none of you understood a word I said."

"No. I don't think anyone at the station will forget that. Talia, you remember Jim from the station," he said. She shook his hand. "This is his wife, Nadine." Talia shook her hand. "They arrived here about ten minutes ago. Nadine wanted to speak with you about the other night in the parking lot."

She turned and looked at Jason with a frown. "I don't understand. What did you say?"

"Talia, Jason didn't know we were coming over. And actually, Jim didn't know until about thirty minutes ago; it was my idea," Nadine said. "I'd like to explain."

"Look, I'm fine. I have work to do. Jason, I'm sure you'll help with dinner. I still have several pieces I have to get finished," Talia said, feeling cornered and nervous.

"I think I can help with what you're feeling," Nadine said.

"I told you, I'm fine," she said, walking toward her drafting table and laying down her satchel.

"No, you're not. You're scared and trying to hide it the best you can," Nadine said, taking a step toward her. "You were assaulted; plain and simple."

Talia turned around and was getting upset now. "Jason and Jim were there to stop him. I need some time to process it and get through it."

"You don't just get through it. I can help you better understand what's going on, the emotions that are going through you, and provide you support or anything else you need," Nadine said.

Talia started walking to the bedroom. "I think the two of you need to leave."

"No. I'm not going anywhere until you hear me out." Nadine raised her voice and started to follow. "I was assaulted on an Army base, where people are supposed to feel safe. It's a damn military base. I didn't ask for that; I minded my own business, just like you. But this person had been watching me for some time, and my husband was overseas. He wasn't able to come to my aid and protect me as Jason did for you. I wasn't so lucky." Nadine's voice cracked.

Talia stopped near the kitchen counter, slowly turning around, looking at Nadine with tears in her eyes. Nadine took several steps toward Talia, standing in front of her, holding out her arms. Talia put her arms around Nadine and cried. "Is that your bedroom?" she asked quietly. Talia nodded. "Could you and I go talk, please?"

They headed to the bedroom, closing the door. Jim and Jason sat back down. "This might take a bit. Nadine's helped many women who were in denial," Jim said, near tears, as he remembered being told all the details of her assault. "This is only the second time I've come with Nadine to talk with someone. I still feel the guilt because I wasn't here," Jim said. "I told you it's the silent ones to be careful of."

Jason shook his head, closing his eyes for a moment, then opening them, looking back at Jim. "I thought things were going back to normal a little too soon. You had to have been so angry, wanting to kill the S.O.B. I can't even imagine going through that," Jason said. "Then again, maybe I know just a little how that feels."

"Jim, can I get you something to drink; water, coffee, a beer?" Jason asked.

Jim replied, "A beer would be great." Jason got up, going to the refrigerator and getting two beers out. They sat and talked about miscellaneous things, periodically looking toward the bedroom door. It had been more than forty-five minutes.

About another ten minutes went by, and the bedroom door opened with Nadine walking out first and Talia following. Both had been crying. Both men stood up. Nadine walked to Jim, and he put his arms around her, kissing her. Talia stopped at the kitchen counter, looking at Jason, more tears coming. He walked over to her, embracing her, and just held her. He then took her face in his hands, looking at her, and kissed her lightly on her forehead and then her lips. "I love you so much," Jason said. She took the Kleenex that was in her hand and wiped the tears. Jason leaned back, looking at her.

Talia took a breath, looking up at him, and said, "I'm OK." Jason didn't know whether to believe her or not, but had to trust that Nadine helped in whatever way needed. She saw the way he looked at her. She reached up for a kiss from him. "I'm going to be all right. Nadine and I had a good talk, and she said I could call her anytime I want or need to, but told me I have this incredibly beautiful person in my life to talk to and share with. I love you, Jason Porter."

He grabbed her, picking her up, hugging her with a tear in his eye. He was afraid that part of her might have been lost to him.

"Jason, Talia, we should go," Jim said. They turned, walking over to Jim and Nadine. Talia gave both Jim and Nadine a hug, as did Jason. "Jason, I'll see you at work in the morning. 'Night, you two."

"Thank you, Nadine," Talia said, taking her hand.

"Ah, *Prego,*" Nadine smiled (You're welcome.).

"No, not you too," Jim said, looking at Nadine. Then looking at Jason, he pointed a finger. "This is your fault." He grinned.

"Looks like we'll both have to learn Italian," he said, standing there with his arm around Talia.

After they left, Talia and Jason went to sit on the sofa. "I have been worried and scared for you, for us, because of how this could so easily have changed you here and here," he said as he pointed to her head and heart.

"It could have if I let it. Nadine is an amazing and strong woman, and I didn't want to hear what she had to say. But I'm glad that she and I could talk. I'm sorry that I scared you. I know that I can trust you with my life, that you will always do your best to be there for me when you can. Sometimes that won't be possible. I know, that deep down, I'm stronger than I think I am," Talia said.

"I honestly didn't know they were—," he started to say, but she put her index finger on his lips.

"I know; she told me. She's done this to several people, and they don't know what's going to happen until she opens her mouth, is what she said," Talia replied. "Kind of like me."

"Why don't I fix us some dinner. I know you said when you came in that you had some work to do," Jason said.

"Sounds good. I'm going to go change real quick," she said, kissing him.

After she changed clothes, she got to work on another design while Jason made spaghetti. When it was ready, they sat down to eat.

"I think we should talk a little bit about our upcoming nuptials," Jason said, tilting his head, looking at her. "We know we want it to be small, with family and a few friends. Do we have an officiant? And do you know where it's going to be?"

"Yes. And I do," Talia replied. "I like saying that, 'I do. I do. I do.' I want it to be at the Botanical Garden. I know it's not as big as the one in Basel, but it's the place where you found me. I love the stairs that go up to the landing. It's simple, and I love the plants; it makes me think of my dad. He would have liked us having our wedding there. I want to marry you, and be your wife."

"I love it. It's perfect. And I can't wait to make you my wife," Jason said. "We're getting a new schedule starting tomorrow up through Christmas. I'm sure the Captain will allow me time off for my wedding. I've asked Jim to be my best man, and since Jéan-Paul will be here, I've asked him to be my groomsman. Who are you going to have stand with you?"

"I've talked to Chloe; she'll be my maid of honor. And then I've asked Kurt to be my man of honor. That sounds funny, but many people are doing that," she said.

"And what will you be wearing, might I ask?" Jason said.

"Um, I thought I might design some kind of flowy skirt, with a peasant top and wear funny-looking sandals. I mean, it's going to be inside; I won't be walking through snow. And if I have to go outside, you'll have to carry me," Talia giggled. "You can wear whatever you want."

"'Whatever I want.' Uh, that leaves it wide open for just about anything," he said.

After they finished dinner, Talia went back to working on her designs. Jason did the dishes and then picked up one of his books. For the next two weeks, he would have straight days working with Jim. After that, it would be back to three days, two nights, and two days off. He knew he had lots of vacation time, never really taking any. There wasn't any place he wanted to go unless it was to see the love of his life in that place. And he rarely ever used any sick time, so he knew he would be covered for whatever came up.

It was 10:15 p.m. He'd have to be at the station at about 6:30 a.m., so he was going to have to go to bed in a few. He had a hard time reading his book. He kept reading over the same three lines, and then didn't know what he was reading because he kept looking up at Talia. Every time he looked at her, he was so grateful she was finally a part of his life and they would get to spend their life together, and maybe even have some little ones. Talia shut off her light. She stood a moment, looking at Jason, and then walked over toward him, walking around behind him. She leaned over the sofa and whispered in his ear. He looked up at her. "Are you sure?" he asked. She nodded and took his hand.

Chapter 33

It was a wonderful Thanksgiving Day with family. The Rose and Porter families were together, including Grandma Jean. There was plenty of leftover food; maybe not enough to feed an army, but enough that Talia and Jason could take some home and have leftover casseroles and turkey sandwiches, including some delicious pie. They laughed and talked. Talia talked with Grandma Jean about some of her ideas and actually had one or two that something could be done with for many older people looking for a change in their wardrobe.

The afternoon wore on, and it was getting a little later. Grandma Jean wanted to go home, so Jeff, her son, took her home. Kurt was headed back to Mom's house to stay until Saturday; his girlfriend Caren was gone with her family in Nebraska, but she'd be back on Saturday. So Kurt would hitch a ride with Talia on Saturday to their aunt and uncle's up North. They wanted to catch up on all the news, including Jason. They asked Talia a week before if the two of them could come for a visit, but learned that Jason had to work; they had plenty of room. Talia remembered staying at their home many times and had made friends with a bunch of the kids in the neighborhood.

Unfortunately, Jason would be working a late shift on Friday until Sunday evening, so she might as well go spend time with them. She was looking forward to the visit, and was excited to tell them about the last few months.

Jason was given the day off after Thanksgiving, mostly because he had worked so many holidays in the past, so this would give him up until Friday afternoon when his shift would start. Even for those three days, he was going to miss her. When he was home, he would watch her work at her drafting table, and he'd try to read; sometimes succeeding, sometimes not. They'd had several date nights, like Grandma Jean told them to, including using one of their gift certificates from her. They were planning on using the other two before their wedding, which was now three weeks away. Talia said she wanted their wedding to be a week before Christmas, and then they'd celebrate it as husband and wife.

Jéan-Paul and Adrian were coming in on Saturday for a two-week stretch. Adrian wasn't married, at least not yet, so he was the chosen paramedic to join them to see how the Americans work. At least he wouldn't have quite the language barrier the Americans had being in Germany, not speaking the language, and seeing everything in German.

Talia and Jason headed home, taking their leftovers; it would be enough for the two of them until Talia left on Saturday. Then the following week, they could go to the store and replenish their refrigerator and cupboards; they weren't totally bare, but getting down there.

Once home, the leftovers were put in the refrigerator, and they went to sit down. Talia picked up the bottom two albums sitting on the coffee table and started going back through them. It was kind of nice to actually turn the pages. She laughed at several of the photos, because she hadn't looked that closely at them before. Jason asked, "So, what's so funny now?"

She pointed to two of the photos, giggling, "I just now noticed in this photo, and this one, your hair is sticking out in back like you stuck your finger in a light socket. And look at your eyes." For whatever reason, she got the giggles and couldn't quit.

"OK, so I was having a bad hair day," he said, grinning. And she giggled even more.

"On two different days, look at your clothes; you're not wearing the same clothes." The giggles continued for a bit longer.

"You're asking for it, young lady," Jason said, smiling at her and pulling her toward him.

Giving him a long kiss, she said, "I am, am I? And what are you going to do about it, my prince?" She was taunting him.

"I'll show you what I'm going to do about it; you don't get away with teasing me about my funny hair standing out and think nothing's going to happen, do you?" He stood up and pulled her to her feet, picking her up, and she shrieked and started giggling as he headed toward the bedroom.

❦

It was nice not having to go into work the day after a holiday, Jason was thinking, lying next to this beautiful woman. Soon he could introduce her as 'his wife.' Just a few weeks now. And he was also really looking forward to Christmas this year. He wanted to do something special for her, and would have to pay close attention to see if she would drop any hints. Sometimes she was a little unpredictable, as he had learned when anything came out of her mouth that he wasn't expecting, especially in a foreign tongue. He smiled.

His watch was showing 7:30 a.m. He looked over at her as she lay on her stomach with her hair covering her face, something he remembered from Villars. He wanted to move her hair and place it back on her bare shoulders. He turned on his side, facing her and holding his head in his hand, looking at her. He slowly moved her hair away from her face. Her nose wrinkled from him moving it, like a feather touching someone's nose or chin, and you can't help but chuckle because of the face they make.

She turned her body toward him, opening her eyes slowly to look at him. "Are you playing with my hair?"

"Who, me?" Jason asked, smiling at her and leaning down to kiss her. "Now, why would I do something like that."

"Because I have better hair than you," she said, grinning. "Sometime, when you least expect it, I'm going to take some of my hair and tickle your nose."

He laid back down, facing her, putting his arm around her and pulling her close. He couldn't think of anything better to do today than lay there with her. It would be two more nights before he'd get to do it again. Sleeping with her was so much better than a bunk room full of guys. He'd have to be at the station by 3:00 p.m. this afternoon.

She rolled onto her back, then, sitting up, quickly grabbed her robe and headed out of the bedroom. Jason thought maybe she just had to go to the bathroom. He got up, putting his sweats on, and walked out toward the kitchen. It wasn't until he heard her throwing up and the toilet flushing that he tapped on the door before opening it. "Talia, are you all right?" he asked. He saw her with a washcloth, wiping her face. She didn't look that good.

"I think maybe something I ate," she said. "I've just felt kind of off, nauseated, the last few weeks, but not all the time. Some foods I'm OK with and others I'm not. We've not changed eating habits. You and I eat the same thing, pretty much."

"Maybe you should go see your doctor before heading out tomorrow," he said. She walked past him, heading to the bedroom, and he followed. She sat down on the bed.

"You've been nauseated the last few weeks? How many weeks?" Jason asked.

"Off and on the last four or five weeks, maybe," she said, standing up to go take a shower.

"How's your menstrual cycle been since getting back from overseas?" he asked, wondering.

"I've never been regular, or what you would call regular for most women. I've had some spotting off and on," Talia said.

"Well, I think you should make an appointment to go see your doctor. Please?" he asked, looking at her. She nodded.

"I'm going to go take a shower," she said, starting to walk past him. He took hold of her waist, then put his arms around her to hug her. She put her arms around him.

"Would you like some company?" he asked. She seemed quiet.

"Sure," she said. He kissed her gently and then followed her to the bathroom.

After having a shower, they got dressed and had some breakfast. She would work on the last two designs there at home, hoping to get those finished up for Chloe and Jana to work on. She also wanted to start with a design or two for Grandma Jean. She had plenty to do without worrying about being sick in any way.

She worked at her drafting table, and Jason started a load of laundry. He knew how to do laundry; it just wasn't his favorite thing to do. He had a couple of woodworking magazines that he'd picked up a few weeks ago but hadn't gotten around to reading through them. As he sat down now, trying to read through one, he couldn't concentrate on reading it. He started wondering about Talia being nauseated for so many weeks, and then the spotting. He would wait for her to see her doctor and get checked out, but he just had a feeling.

It was now after 12:30 p.m. and he asked Talia if she wanted some lunch. She said yes; a turkey sandwich would be nice. She wanted to keep working. After making her a sandwich, he asked her to stop long enough to eat something. She grumbled, but he walked over to her and looked at her with his sad puppy eyes, and asked, "Pretty please, come eat your sandwich?" He looked so cute. How could she not eat the sandwich?

Jason would have to leave at about 2:45 p.m. His shift would end Sunday afternoon at around 3:00 p.m. He put the wash into the dryer and then headed to the bedroom to put his uniform on. He saw that she had finished her sandwich when he came back out.

He walked over to her, saying he would have to leave in about ten minutes. He reminded her to call her doctor's office and make an appointment. She stopped what she was doing, giving him a huge hug. He wrapped his arms around her, holding her, kissing her forehead and then her lips. "I'll check in with you later, all right?" he said. "I love you."

"I love you too," she said. "Tell Jéan-Paul I said hello."

"When he comes in, I will tell him that his favorite little Italian says hello." He smiled, grabbing his winter coat, and headed out the door. After he left, she locked the door and watched him out the window, waving at him, blowing him a kiss.

Throughout the rest of the day, she finished the seventh design, getting started on the eighth; she would drop off the seventh one tomorrow before she and Kurt headed to Uncle Dave's. They were expected for lunch, so she would have to get up early to pack for the weekend, drop off the design at the shoppe, and then get Kurt. She was glad for the distraction, as she had been stressing out about finishing up her designs and their upcoming wedding and Christmas. She needed to figure out what would give Jason the most joy he's had in a long time besides finding her.

Talia called Jason before heading to bed. He asked her about making an appointment, which she forgot. He asked if she could do it tomorrow before heading out. She told him there was a family doctor they used to go to back in her hometown where her aunt and uncle live, and she would call them in the morning; they had her family medical records. He asked her when her appointment was done to please call him. He wanted to know that she was all right. She agreed. He told her to sleep well, that he loved her and to be careful driving tomorrow.

Chapter 34

Talia's alarm buzzed at her, and she hit the snooze button, glancing at the clock. It said 6:15 a.m. It was still dark outside. "Just another ten minutes, please," she said to her clock. It buzzed again, and she hit snooze, thinking it couldn't have been ten minutes already. It buzzed again, and she yelled at it, "All right, I'm awake now!" She sat up and swung her feet over to the floor, thinking it would be so easy to lay back down under the warm covers. Her alarm buzzed again as if to say, 'get up and get moving.' She finally shut it off. She heard the furnace come on; they had it set at seventy-two degrees. It felt chilly in the apartment.

She had her overnight bag out on the chair near the dresser, and had already placed some things in it last night. It wouldn't take long to put other clothing in it. She wanted to take a pair of ladies' long winter undergarments for extra warmth under her jeans, but would also wear a pair and heavier socks. They'd had snow yesterday up north, and she was getting where she disliked winter altogether. She was tired of the blustery winds, the ice, snowstorms, blizzards, black ice, you name it; she hated it. People were always idiots driving on the road, thinking it must be a summer day. They can't seem to remember how to drive from one season to the next, much less from one snowfall to the next on any given day.

After showering and getting dressed, she had breakfast and then cleaned up the kitchen. She finished packing her bag. She walked over to her draft table to gather her seventh design, putting it in the smaller satchel, and then heard sirens going. She looked out the window in the direction of the fire station, wondering if they would drive by here. The sirens were becoming louder and then decreased in sound, so they must have gone in the other direction.

She felt very proud of Jason being a paramedic/firefighter. It can't be an easy job at all, with the risks involved. What they see every day varies with the call that comes in. She didn't think she could do Jason's job, especially seeing anyone, including his best friend Amy and her parents, in that tangled mess that used to look like a car and their dead bodies. She shuddered. Or the accident she and Jason witnessed in Europe, with the woman who was six months pregnant and her husband. He knew what he was doing, and he was good at his job, as they all were. And she hoped he'd never see anyone he loved again in such a place.

She had all her stuff ready to go; she had her heavy scarf, hat, and heavy parka and pulled out her thicker gloves and good winter boots. She was prepared with extra blankets, a snow shovel, flashlight, and salt. Some might think it was overkill, but life and weather are unpredictable.

She called Kurt to see if he was ready, which he was. She told him she would pick him up in about fifteen minutes and then stop at her shop, get gas, and then they'd head out. Talia's relatives live in west-central Iowa, a relatively easy drive to some of the bigger cities when you wanted to do some big-time shopping and getaway on those mini weekend trips. Driving north, it was bright out and darn cold. Heading back to her hometown was a good hour and forty-five-minute drive. As they got closer, there was more snow on the ground. She scrunched up her nose and stuck her tongue out at it, wishing it to go away.

Arriving at her aunt and uncle's house brought back many wonderful memories. It would be a nice weekend, visiting with them and catching up. And Kurt was eager to see Caren; her family would be getting home later that afternoon. Kurt's car wasn't working, so he would usually walk depending on where he had to go.

Talia texted Jason, letting him know that they had made it and that yes, she would call their family doctor. After arriving, Kurt got out and went in; she told him she had to make a quick phone call. She didn't need another male pushing her about calling. She had the clinic's number on her phone. She called before going in so she wouldn't get distracted and then forget. Jason really wanted her to see someone and make sure she was all right. Her appointment was for 4:30 p.m.

From lunchtime on, they had an enjoyable visit. She talked about Europe and finding Jason, or that he had found her. She looked over at Kurt, and he grinned at her. She told them she was engaged, and that their wedding was coming up. They looked somewhat surprised, and after she and Kurt explained about all the vacations and such, they just nodded. They thought they remembered hearing about those vacations. They asked about photos, and she looked in her big bag and realized she forgot to bring the digital picture frame; it was sitting on the coffee table next to the albums. It had so many beautiful photos on it, but she had a lot on her phone. They were still happy to see those. How exciting it must have been to be over there, and someone who loves you this much finds you. "It's like a fairy tale," Aunt Joan said, smiling.

Kurt and Uncle Dave got up and left the room. Talia saw that her appointment was in about twenty minutes and told her aunt that she'd made an appointment. It was just a checkup, and she would be back a little later. Talia made her way to the clinic, checked in, and waited her turn. Their family doctor had retired, but the new M.D. was a female, which Talia was more than happy to see. Going back over her medical records and then asking questions, Dr. Laura Nowden put all that into Talia's medical file. She updated the primary person to call, listing Jason Porter with his cell phone; Talia's mother's contact information was secondary. She then did a full exam. It was after 5:30 p.m. when Talia left the clinic. It was dark outside, and she sat in her car with the heat running, not moving. Not the news she was expecting. She just stared off into the distance. She'd have to tell Jason. He'll want to know. But she wanted to put it off until she got home, and they could talk.

Arriving back at her aunt's place, they were getting ready for dinner. Her aunt looked at her, but didn't say anything about the appointment. They chatted more and got caught up on all kinds of things happening in town, and about Talia's new clothing line. She wished her all the best and success. They talked about Jason's work as a paramedic/firefighter. She told them about his best friend's fatal accident, and the accident they saw and what he did by himself without help until Jéan-Paul had arrived. She told them about him as well, "quite the Frenchman."

Talia told her aunt and uncle that if they could come to the wedding, please come, giving them the date and where and the time; it was just a small wedding. She never wanted anything bigger. Talia was getting tired; it was after 10:00 p.m. Kurt had walked over to Caren's, spending time with her. She texted Jason, letting him know she had her appointment and that she's fine, but they had to talk. She looked at her bag with the papers in it from the doctor's office, giving test results. She'd let him look at them himself.

ᴄꙅ

Talia enjoyed the visit, but was ready to go home. She had hoped to leave in the middle of the morning, and that way, she could be back home by lunch. But now, she would get a late start because Kurt decided that he had to borrow her car and see friends at the local family restaurant west of town. With it being winter, the weather could be unpredictable, and it was not fun driving in wet, heavy snow or sleet. Even when it got misty out and collected on the road, if the temperature dropped just enough, then you would have to deal with black ice. And it's hard to navigate. You'd travel at a snail's pace, and the usual DOT warnings would be issued that, if at all possible, to stay off the roads. How many people heed that warning?

So, even though it was only mid-morning and the weather seemed okay so far, Talia didn't want to take any chances. The skies were light gray, and you could smell it and feel it in the air. Kurt knew all this and knew Talia wanted to head back early to avoid dealing with the weather. He said he would only be gone just a short while, whatever that meant, but it was turning out to be a good hour and a half, and that wasn't helping Talia's nervous feelings or her mood. Winter was just something everyone dealt with, and you learned to take precautions when it came to traveling anywhere. But, if at all possible, staying home was the smart thing to do.

"Come on, where are you?" Talia was getting quite annoyed and upset. She was looking out the big bay windows, looking down the street to see if her car would come around the corner, hoping that at any moment, she'd see it and could get moving. Pacing back and forth didn't help any. *"I wanted to get headed home before the weather changed too much. I told you to be quick about it. Grrr."* Her brother Kurt couldn't hear her at all.

Talia tried reaching him on his cell phone, but it was either turned off or he didn't want to answer, knowing more than likely he'd be getting the brunt end of a lot of yelling. After all, he wasn't the one who had to head back. She called the restaurant and was told he left. Finally, after another fifteen minutes, here he came around the corner. "About time!" Talia still had to get gas. Her aunt told her she could stay until the next day if she felt uncomfortable about the weather possibly changing. Talia just wanted to go home. Who knew what tomorrow's weather would bring. She didn't want to take time off because of weather unless a full blizzard moved in right now; then, she wouldn't have a choice but to stay put. She wanted to be home when Jason got home.

Once she had gotten gas and could finally get on the road, her only thoughts now were getting home before the weather started turning. Thirty miles down the road, and just as she had feared, she could see it was ever-so-slightly snowing, just teeny tiny little flakes landing on the windshield. *Crap!* She had turned onto Hwy 4 heading south. Even though she was going the speed limit, she decided to push it. She was on the back roads, which were not heavily traveled. She was still a good hour-plus from home. About six miles further down the road, little by little, the snow was coming down in bigger flakes, and it was now sticking to the car and the road. She knew if she could make it to Hwy 141, a four-lane highway, she hoped it would lighten up a bit and drive out of it. Snowplows would definitely be out clearing the more traveled highways. She listened to the radio on the way; the snow was supposed to be heading northeast, but she was thinking, *What does the weatherman know. He's not out in it, is he?*

Had she watched the weather on TV, she could have seen the band, and where it was coming from, and where it was going. Then she would have known for sure and stayed clear of it, if she could have, or go another route. The sky and ground were blending; it snowed that much. Her red car was getting covered, and the hood was covered, as she couldn't see red anymore.

Finally approaching the halfway mark, she could breathe just a smidgen easier, but still had at least another forty-five minutes to go. She had turned onto a four-lane highway, which she thought should help. It had already taken her well over an hour just getting to this point, which rarely occurred, and now needing to decide to either keep heading for home or return to her aunt's home. But she continued toward home. Traffic got lighter as more snow was falling. She had to reduce her speed down to at least thirty miles per hour. It was so slow-going. The last thirty miles or so would be the hardest driving. Talia felt she was an excellent driver, and usually did well during winter. If the weather was going to be bad, she didn't go anywhere if she didn't have to.

It was like she spoke too soon. It was getting bad now. Visibility was down to maybe the length of three semi-trucks, and the road was getting slicker. Not only that, but trying to see if she was even on the road was very difficult, as it was pretty well covered. She reduced her speed even more, now down to twenty miles per hour, pushing it beyond that would have been ill-advised.

Trying to keep her eyes on the road took all of her concentration, and trying to find any landmarks wasn't going to happen. It didn't help to look at the car's clock to get any idea where she could be. She didn't know now if she had ten miles to go or fifteen miles. It felt like she'd already spent several hours on the road. How many times now hadn't she thought, *I should have turned around and headed back to my aunt's, one of those "six of one, half a dozen of the other"* thoughts.

She was pretty much driving blind in a snowstorm. "Crappy, damn, snow anyway. You couldn't have waited until I got home, could you? No, you just had to do it in the middle of the day. Stupid snow. Now, how often can one yell at Mother Nature for messing up a perfectly fine Sunday afternoon driving home," Talia stated. "Shouldn't be that difficult, right?"

It had taken at least a good three hours or more — not too many other vehicles on the road that she could even see. One truck passed her, going much faster than he or she should have been going. It whizzed by her like she was taking a stroll. She felt a strong gust of wind from the truck, and she felt her car shift to the right after the truck passed her. She yelled at them, "How can you drive so damn fast, unless you have x-ray vision and see the road so clearly to know whether you're even on the road, is beyond me. You jack-ass!"

In a matter of moments, the right back end of her car started sliding and being pulled toward the shoulder. She knew she had lost control of her vehicle, as it was being pulled closer to the far edge of the shoulder, and the back end turned downward as her car tilted to the right, sliding down the embankment and then flipping over. Her screams would not be heard.

Chapter 35

The call came into the 911 operator at 2:51 p.m. "Police, Fire, and Medical. What is your emergency?"

"My wife and I just saw a car slide off the road down an embankment and then flip over. It's bad out here."

"Can you tell me what happened?"

"I just told you."

"Sir, try to calm down; I need a little more information so I can dispatch help to your location."

"We're all idiots for being out in this storm. Idiots, I tell you."

"Yes, sir, I hear you. We're all idiots for being out on roads like this."

The man sighed before starting to tell her. "Okay, there were a few of us on the road, all going slow. It's icy, and snowing, and blowing. There was a red car in front of us, about two semi-lengths, when a big pickup truck zooms past all of us like we're out for a Sunday stroll."

"Sir, if you give me your location first; then you can give me your information. I need to dispatch help now, then you can tell me what happened."

"We're heading south on 141. We just went past Timberbrooke Ln. We hadn't gotten to NE 18th Street yet. We're so close to home."

"Is this the only vehicle involved?"

"Yes." He heard the dispatcher put out the call.

"Sir, I'm dispatching help to your location. Stay on the line with me, all right? Because of the weather, it may take them just a little bit to get to you. Do you have your emergency flashing lights on?"

"Yes, me and the driver behind me."

"They're on their way. This will help the firetrucks and paramedics know right where you are. Stay on the line with me. Sir, can you tell me when this occurred?"

"It just happened. Well, now about seven minutes ago after all the questions. I tried calling 911 as soon as we could pull over, and the lines were busy. So, I kept trying and got you. Can I tell you what happened?"

"Yes, sir, go ahead," she said, after getting the pertinent information she needed.

"The truck created a gust of wind that pushed this car toward the shoulder, causing the tires to slide on the ice. As soon as that happened, the driver must have tried to correct, and the back end of the car started sliding down the embankment, and then it just started to flip over, I think. Had we been even a quarter of a mile farther behind this car, we would have passed them and never saw it go down. It just slid off the road. The driver behind us pulled over and got out to look. He saw I was on the phone and came to tell me what he saw. He said it looked like, after flipping, it landed on its wheels, and the front of the car is aimed up the hill with the headlights shining upwards. He thought the car was still running."

Once the call was dispatched, firetrucks, ambulance, and paramedics were on their way. The paramedics arrived first after getting the call fifteen minutes ago, with the ambulance and firetrucks close behind. Once on the scene, it was Jim Peters and Mike Hanson that accessed the situation better. With their gear on and making their way down the embankment, it would take them a minute or so. It was snow-packed and slick, and they were trying to get a better foothold going down without falling themselves. The car had rolled at least twenty-five to thirty feet down, being stopped by dense brush and a tree. Had those not been there, the car could have gone down another twenty feet or more.

Once they approached the car, sliding down some because of the snow, they tried opening the driver's door. It was not budging. Jim stayed on the driver's side, while Mike went around to the other side. The passenger front door was up against the tree, and the back passenger door on the right side wouldn't open. Jim could open the back door behind the driver's seat. Two airbags had deployed, and the driver's head was turned toward the passenger seat. The driver had a heavy winter coat on, a thick scarf, hat and gloves. There was a purse on the floor, so the driver was probably female, and the purse was closed; he couldn't see a cell phone. There was an overnight bag in the back seat, as well as two large blankets. Jim thought, at least they had the sense to carry blankets in their car.

He looked at the female; she was possibly in her 30s. She had some blood on her face. He moved the long brown hair out of the way, as well as the thick scarf, so he could feel for a carotid pulse. He felt it, and she was breathing. Jim tried to get a better look at the female and soon recognized her face. He knew who she was. "Oh, man," he said. Mike asked, "'Oh, man,' what? Jim, talk to me." He backed out of the backseat and turned to Mike. He could see the fire truck was there, and the guys were making their way down.

Mike asked again, "Jim, what?"

"It's Jason's *fiancée*, Talia," Jim said.

"What, how do you know?" Mike asked.

"You haven't paid attention lately, have you? Jason talks about her and has shown pictures of the two of them when they were in Switzerland. This is her."

"Oh my god, we'll have to call Jason once we get her out." Mike didn't know Jason would be with this crew; his shift should have ended an hour ago.

"That won't be necessary; Jason was helping one of the other crew who had to leave early. He said he'd stay on for a couple more hours. He'll be down here in a moment." They both looked up toward the incline; another crew gathered equipment they needed to extricate the passenger. Jason led them down, with Jéan-Paul not far behind, and Adrian, the German paramedic, following.

As Jason got to them, Jim told Jason to stay back. Mike was behind Jim, ready to help stop him if need be. Then Jéan-Paul and Adrian were behind Jason.

"What do you mean I need to stay back? These people need our help. You remember that's part of our job, right? Do we call this a fatality?" Jason said.

"No, Jason, I think it's best that you just back off and let the other guys handle this."

"I'm here to do my job; you need to let me get in there and assess this." Jason's voice was getting angry. Both Jim and Mike were now grabbing Jason's coat as he was trying to get closer to the car, and they slid because of the snow. He didn't understand what was going on. Jéan-Paul was looking and asked what was going on, taking Jason's arm out of Jim's hands. The snow was still coming down heavily, but the winds had lightened.

Jéan-Paul started walking toward the back door so that he could assess. "We have assessed this; it's a female in her 30s." Jim looked at Jason and said, "It's Talia." Jéan-Paul stopped, looking at Jim and then Jason.

Jason looked hard at Jim in total disbelief, then looking at the driver's door. "What? What are you saying? How do you know it's Talia?" His voice rose.

Jim said, "I got a good look at her; it's her. I'd recognize her anywhere."

"Talia!" he yelled, trying to push past Jim, and yelled her name again. "Talia!" Jéan-Paul and Adrian grabbed onto Jason's coat. Both Jim and Mike also had to hold him back, and it became clear to the firemen that had made it down who it was, hearing her name. It was Ted who had the jaws, looking at Jason, seeing the pain in his eyes. He finally got it.

"NO. This can't be happening. Not again." Jason sounded defeated as he tried once again to get to the car. Jéan-Paul and Adrian grabbed Jason's coat, and he kneeled to the ground. Jim yelled at Jason, "The guys will do their job and get her out. She's alive. She has a pulse, and she's breathing. Did you hear me, Jason? She's alive."

With help from a couple of the guys, Ted started using the jaws, working at prying the driver door open. Two other men looked at Jason, and Jim told them it was Jason's *fiancée*. They all gave nods and continued working to free her. Another firefighter brought the backboard with a neck collar and a blanket to cover her once she was out. After the jaws opened the door, Jim told Jason to stay put; he and Mike would get her unbuckled and remove the airbag.

Jason stood up and grabbed Jéan-Paul's coat for support. They couldn't let Jason help; his emotions were too high and would get the better of him. It was different when it was one of your own. Time was always of the essence for anyone. Several of the crew had been in Jason's shoes when something happened to one of their own.

There was only room for Jim and Mike to work. Mike was working from behind the driver seat while Jim worked from the driver's side. They would need the neck collar to keep her head stable while carefully pulling her out of the car. Her left arm was pinned underneath the airbag, so there was a possible broken arm, and her legs were also pinned because of the steering wheel getting bent down. One guy handed Mike the neck collar to be placed around her neck and protect it.

Jason wasn't always one to listen at the scene of an accident. He inched his way closer toward Jim, wanting to help pull her out. He just wanted to touch her. The guys brought the backboard closer. Everyone worked together to get her out carefully, including Jason. Once she was out, they covered her body with the blanket, strapping her on for the haul up to the ambulance. As the guys lifted her, Jason gave her a kiss, telling her he was right there with her.

Mike was holding Talia's purse as well as her blanket, giving them to Jason. Talia's face had blood on it. Jason placed the blanket over her body. He motioned for them to move. He was right behind the backboard, wanting to make sure that if the guys slipped, he would be there to catch her. Adrian stayed with the other crew, but Jéan-Paul followed Jason up. Climbing up the incline was more difficult. It was still snowing, but lighter now.

The ambulance was there, waiting for the crew to bring her up, as there was no way for them to get down there. The people who had called 911 were talking with the ambulance crew and watching. Once to the top, she was placed on the gurney, and strapped in again and positioned in the ambulance. Jéan-Paul got in first, and then Jason, into the back of the ambulance. Both men started working on her, taking vitals, and starting a saline IV. The other ambulance member got in the front seat.

For Jason, it seemed to take forever to get to the hospital; the roads were a bit better in town. The storm was moving north. Once they arrived at the ER door, things moved quickly getting her into an exam room. Both Jason and Jéan-Paul went into the room, but then one of the ER doctors told Jason he would have to leave; they would take it from there. Jéan-Paul could stay.

"Jason, I will make sure she is taken excellent care of. You know me," Jéan-Paul said, taking off his heavy fireman coat and helmet, giving them to Jason to hold.

"Jéan-Paul, with all the commotion at the scene, I forgot to tell you. Before they do any x-rays or anything, they'll want to do an ultrasound," Jason said, looking at him. He wasn't thinking clearly, but knew they would do that anyway as they do with all female victims.

"Why is that, my friend?" Jéan-Paul asked calmly, thinking he knew why.

"Because she may be pregnant," Jason replied. Jéan-Paul put his hand on Jason's shoulder and nodded.

"So, now we have two lives to keep alive and safe; mama and baby," Jéan-Paul said. He turned and went back into the room.

Jason took Jéan-Paul's coat and helmet, plus Talia's bag, and went to the seating area. He took off his coat and helmet. He'd be able to see when they came out. At the moment, Jason's mind just went blank. It was like a gray slate and nothing was on it. Then all he could do was picture them taking off her coat, boots and clothes, putting an ugly gown on her and covering her with a blanket. Again, it seemed to take forever to examine her; he saw hospital staff go in and out. He just wanted Jéan-Paul to come tell him what was going on. He was scared.

While he was waiting, Jason looked at Talia's bag, opening it. She texted him last night, saying she was fine but that they needed to talk. He saw an envelope with the clinic's name on the outside. He looked toward the door, then opened the envelope, taking out a sheet of paper. He read it, and then tears formed in his eyes.

Just then, the exam room door opened. Jason stood up, placing everything on the chair he was sitting on except for the paper he now held in his hand. Jéan-Paul came over to him and hugged him. He motioned for Jason to sit.

"She is a fortunate woman to be alive. This is your first miracle," Jéan-Paul said. "She is not out of the woods yet, as you say here. On the outside, she has multiple bruises on both of her legs and her arms. She has a lung contusion, and there may be a small brain bleed; won't know until a CT scan is done. For a moment, she opened her eyes, and I spoke to her and told her, *'Ti ama cosi tanto la mia ragazza Italiana,'* which means 'He loves you so much, my Italian girl.'" Jason looked at him with tears. "And then I tell her before she closed her eyes, *'Rimani in giro per lui e il tuo bambino.'*"

Jason said, "I don't understand."

"It means, 'You stick around for him and your baby,'" Jéan-Paul said. He leaned over and hugged Jason. Jason handed Jéan-Paul the paper he found in her bag. "This confirms what the ultrasound also showed. She is about eight weeks pregnant." Jéan-Paul smiled at Jason. "You will be a wonderful *pápa*. But your second miracle will be if the baby survives."

One of the doctors came out, asking for Dr. Jéan-Paul Lemaitre. Jéan-Paul stood up, walking toward the other doctor.

"Jéan-Paul, do you think she heard and understood you?" Jason asked.

He looked at Jason with his Frenchman's smile and said, "There is something very different about this woman of yours. She is strong, and your love for each other is strong. I have seen this, remember. I think she understood perfectly. Give her a little bit of time. The outside will heal much faster than the inside; the inside takes a little longer. Hold fast to your love for her. I will come and get you when they move her to her room, yes?"

Jason nodded.

Chapter 36

Jason needed to call Talia's mom and let her know what happened and where Talia was. It was going to be a hard phone call to make. He sat there and leaned over with his head in his hands, worried and scared. He heard someone pick up and move the coats and the helmets. He looked up to see who it was, and saw his mom sit down next to him. She had on her nurse's scrubs. His tears came, and she hugged her son and rocked him. He leaned back against the chair.

"Are you coming to work or leaving?" Jason asked.

"I've been here since after lunch. I work until eleven tonight. When I saw who was admitted a little bit ago, I told them I had to come down and see if you were still here. I told the girls that it was my future daughter-in-law they brought in," Mary Ann said. "Do you know what happened?"

"We got the call that a car slid off the road and rolled down an embankment. We headed out. I was supposed to be off an hour earlier, but one of the guys had to leave. I took his spot. We arrived at the scene; Jim and Mike were already down by the car. I headed down with Jéan-Paul and Adrian to assess, when Jim stopped me. He wouldn't let me near the car. He told me it was Talia," Jason said, looking at his mom. "I can't lose her too, or the baby."

She looked at her son. "What, 'baby?'" Mary Ann asked.

Jason looked at his mom. "Talia's eight weeks pregnant with my child," he replied. He looked at the floor. "Jéan-Paul told me, 'She's alive; this is your first miracle. But your second miracle will be if the baby survives.'"

"Eight weeks. About the time you were in Europe," she said, looking at him. "Well, you're a grown man." At the moment, she didn't know what else to say to him. It was his life and Talia's, and now a baby, should it survive. "If it's meant to be, just know that little one is nestled down inside her."

"Mom, I have to call Elizabeth, and I don't know what to say to her," Jason said.

"I'll call her," Mary Ann said. She got up and walked down the hall. A few minutes later, she returned; Elizabeth was on her way. She held Jason's hand.

"Jason, they are going to move Talia to her room now," Jéan-Paul said. Jason stood up, as did his mom. "Hello, Mrs. Porter, it is nice seeing you again." He took her hand and kissed the back of it.

"I see you must have been out with the crew today, Dr. Lemaitre," Mary Ann said. "So, you were there?"

"Yes, I was. It was hard to see the car, and then once we learned who was in the car, my heart went out to your son once again. And then it also affected me; she is my Italian girl," Jéan-Paul said.

"Why is she your Italian girl?" Mary Ann asked, not understanding, looking at Jason and back to Jéan-Paul.

"Because she speaks Italian, and she helped when we were at the scene of an accident near Villars. A woman who was six months pregnant was terrified and seeing another woman helped to calm her down. Talia spoke pretty good Italian to this woman and rode in the ambulance with her to the hospital. I've heard she has spoken it several times from Jason," Jéan-Paul said with a smile. "I was most impressed with her, so I call her my Italian girl."

Jason grabbed their coats and helmets and Talia's bag. They headed up to her room. It was on Mary Ann's floor. She was head nurse. As they walked by the nurse's station, a couple of the nurses stood and eyed Jason, carrying their coats and helmets, and his bunker gear on, as did Jéan-Paul, but they didn't look at him the same way. Jason saw them watching as they walked by.

His mom looked at her nurses and said, "Heel. He's my son, and he's betrothed to the young woman that just came up here. Behave yourselves."

Once in Talia's room, Jason laid the coats, helmets and her bag on the couch. He walked over to the side of her bed, pulling up the chair next to it. He leaned over and kissed her forehead, and gently rubbed her cheek with the back of his hand. He could smell the scent of apple in her hair. It must have been the shampoo she used that morning. "Talia, I'm right here, love. I'm not going anywhere without you." He sat down, taking her hand in both of his, bringing it to his lips and holding it there. She had the ET tube in and IV going. She had some scrapes on her face. Mary Ann was checking her stats and noting them on Talia's chart.

Jason saw that Talia's engagement ring was not on her finger. He asked his mother where it was. She had it in her pocket, and gave it to him. He put it in the palm of his hand, closing his fingers around it, holding it to his lips and lowering his head. He heard footsteps, and turned around to see Jim in the doorway, still in his gear, and holding his helmet. Jason stood up, walking over to him, getting a hug. Jim had Talia's overnight bag in his hand along with the blanket they covered her with from her car. He got it from the ER room. "I thought you might want her bag. Her car has been moved. I've talked to the captain, and he said he'd probably call tomorrow or stop by, but take the time you need," Jim said. "The guys send you both their best wishes for a speedy recovery." Jason nodded.

"Jéan-Paul, you ready to go back to the station?" Jim asked.

"Yes. Nothing more I can do here," he said, looking at Jason. "I will check in with you later, my friend," Jéan-Paul said, hugging Jason. He walked over to the left side of Talia's bed, picking up her hand and kissing the back of it, putting it under the covers. He then picked up his coat and helmet and left with Jim.

Jason sat back down on the chair, picking up Talia's hand. He placed his other hand over her stomach and gently rubbed it. "Jason, I'll find you some scrubs. You can't stay in here with your bunker gear on," Mary Ann said, and then she left the room. As he sat there looking at his beautiful Talia, all

Jason wanted right now was for her to wake up. He wanted to tell her he knew about the baby she was carrying inside of her, and to tell her he knew she was scared, and so was he.

Elizabeth Rose walked into the room, laying down her coat. Jason stood up. She saw his tears, and they hugged. He sat back down, looking back at Talia. She walked around the other side of her daughter's bed, looking at her, then back to Jason. He just stared at Talia. "I remember the first time I saw you look at her, the same way you're looking at her now. I was going to keep my eye on you," she said with a smile. Jason looked up at her. "It was after she started walking toward the elephant enclosure. Remember? She didn't want to listen to me, and I had to call her name twice; loudly, the second time." Jason smiled, remembering and nodding his head, looking back at Talia. "Even though she's always been on the shy, quiet side --oh, she could be ornery, like her dad--, she didn't always want to listen, wanted to do things her way or at least try. Kurt was more of a pleaser, kind of like I am.

"Tom could be ornery, and he also had a somewhat dry sense of humor. But it was the same for him as it was for you, love at first sight," Elizabeth said, looking at him and then pulling up the other chair. Jason looked at her. "Oh ya, you're going to think this is crazy. Let me tell you a story. My family and I had visited relatives off and on for years when I was growing up. They lived in a small village near *Ranspach-le-Bas*, France. And yes, *'je parle français,'* I speak French."

"That explains why you know French, and you could translate for us," Jason said. Elizabeth smiled. "I just thought it was cool, that this girl's mom knew French. We'd never met anyone who spoke another language until we spent time in Basel with you."

Elizabeth continued. "It was the summer after my first year in college that we had gone back to visit a couple of my remaining family. They were getting older, and we didn't know when we would see them again. Tom was doing a semester abroad with his architect program in Basel. He was a senior in college, finishing up, and had the opportunity to do this. It was at the Basel Historical Museum. He liked history and anything that dated waaay back to ancient times," she said with a giggle. "Well, maybe not that ancient."

"Wait, you met at the Basel Historical Museum? Talia and I spent several hours at that one; the one with all the history and culture displays?" Jason asked.

"The same one. I know the name is hard to pronounce, *Barfuesserkirche*." She said it so fluently.

"You make it sound so much better than I ever could. Wow, that's amazing," Jason said.

She continued. "He loved the structures and designs of the old buildings. My parents and I were walking around, and I had stopped to look at something. I stood off to one side in this large room, and my parents had walked a little further down. I turned around to show my father something, not realizing they went to the next exhibit. And not far away, Tom was standing there looking at me," she said, smiling. "I remember the look he gave me. And then I turned around, thinking he was looking at someone else, but I was the only one there. I turned back, and he was walking toward me. I got nervous; didn't know who he was, but he stopped about five feet from me and then introduced himself. Looking into his eyes made my stomach flutter. I thought he was awful darn cute." Jason chuckled, as did Elizabeth.

"He thought I was from there because he heard my mother speaking to me in French. I introduced myself, and he looked at me, asking where I came from. I told him I lived in the U.S. and was from the Midwest. He got this big grin on his face and told me that's where he was from: Iowa. Since I knew French and some German, we spent the afternoon together. My parents were heading off to go look at fountains or something and told me to meet them back at a certain place for supper. It was a wonderful afternoon, showing him different things that I knew about and translating. We were leaving a few days later, and he told me he wanted to spend more time with me, and asked if that was possible. I told my parents; they said if he could come and visit the village where we were staying, he was welcomed, but he would have to travel there, which he did. Tom still had another month before returning. We exchanged addresses and wrote, a lot," she said. "The rest is history."

Jason smiled. "I remember the day I saw her," he said, looking at Talia. "She had long brown hair, and it was in pigtails. She was so stuck on being near those elephants, and when everyone was moving onto the next enclosure, she didn't want to go. I think she started to cry, and all I wanted to do was hug her and tell her I'd stand there with her as long as she wished to look at those elephants. I knew we were young; she was nine, and here I was, fourteen. But she captured my heart. I had a girlfriend, but that didn't last long. I cared about her, but it just didn't feel the same way. When I got older, I had a best friend I loved, but I didn't feel that way about her either; I wasn't in love with her. And then she died," he said, looking at Elizabeth.

"I know, Mary Ann told me about it. I'm sorry," Elizabeth said. "I also know about Amy, your sister," she said. "Your mom and I had become best friends. We've watched the two of you the last--well, since you were young. Kurt's not always good about keeping things totally secret. I heard about a sweet-sixteen kiss." Jason looked at her with a guilty look, and she smiled at him. "I know the feeling, Jason. Remember Colorado Springs, when we adults decided to go hiking up in the foothills? Someone wasn't at their most graceful moment when she had a hard time crossing a single creek. We told her about a couple of those flat stones and how slick they were. But she was going to do it her way, and then she slipped and plopped into the creek." Jason laughed, remembering the look on Talia's face.

"I remember the look you also gave her. The look of 'I told you not to step on **those** ones, and you didn't listen, and look where it got you.'" Jason laughed along with Elizabeth.

"I told you she didn't always like to listen," she said. "And then the small stump she didn't pay attention to; she always enjoyed jumping over things. I remember thinking, if you can jump over big things, how is it you can't jump over a small stump and not trip and fall? So, here she is, wet, and now has a sprained ankle. Kurt looked at me and said he wasn't going to carry her down. Tom was annoyed with her because, not only once, but now twice that afternoon, she didn't want to listen, so…" she said, looking at Jason.

Jason smiled, looking at Talia. "I got to carry my girl down the mountain and keep her safe in my arms. And each time, I fell more in love with her and wanted her in my life. I didn't know for a long time how she felt about me. It wasn't until we spent the week in Europe, and she opened her heart to me, and then…" Jason raised his eyes to Elizabeth. She looked at him with a knowing look. He looked back at Talia.

"I can't lose her. She makes me feel alive," he said.

Mary Ann came into the room, giving the scrubs to Jason. He stood up so he could go change in the bathroom. She walked around Talia's bed, Elizabeth standing up, and they hugged. Mary Ann looked at the monitor and the IV drip. She looked at her son with a raised eyebrow and tilt of her head toward Elizabeth, who saw this.

"Is there something I should know about my daughter?" she looked at Jason.

He took a moment, looking at Elizabeth, and then looked at Talia. "Talia is eight weeks pregnant," he said, then looked back at Elizabeth. "She saw your family doctor this past Saturday. I only suspected when she got up Friday morning and threw up and told me she'd been nauseated off and on. I asked her for how many weeks, and she said four or five, telling me she thought it was what she'd eaten. But I had a hunch, and then I asked her about her menstrual cycle after we got back from overseas."

When you grew up with medical people in your family like Jason and Talia did, with their mom's being nurses, there wasn't that much about the body you couldn't talk about and didn't need to be embarrassed. "She said she'd never been regular, and that she had some spotting. I told her to make an appointment and see a doctor. I wanted to make sure she was all right."

Jason was ready for the yelling, but Elizabeth just looked at him, not saying a word. That was scarier than just having her say something or yelling at him for not being more careful or using protection. Deep down inside, he wanted to be a dad, and knew Talia would be an amazing mom. He would be there for her and however many kids they had, as long as he lived.

"Elizabeth, please say something," Jason said quietly, all but holding his breath. She walked toward the window, looking out.

Mary Ann spoke first. "I understand that Grandma Jean already scolded you for getting engaged even before the two of you dated. And now with a baby on the way before you're even married? Grandma Jean was right; you're doing things a little ass-end backward." She looked at her son.

"I'll be honest with you, Jason. I would have preferred you be married first to my daughter," Elizabeth said, turning around. "I get how deep your love is for each other," she said, walking over to him and looking at him. "Things happen in life. Call it what you want; chance, fate. I didn't have to wait anywhere near as long as you did, waiting to fill that space." She half smiled at him. "I became pregnant with Kurt before we got married." She saw Jason close his eyes. "You can breathe now." She took a moment and then said, "So my baby's going to have a baby.... She's in her 30s, not exactly a baby. But she'll always be my baby. I'm going to be a grandmother." She hugged him.

"That is, if the baby survives. Jéan-Paul said that would be our second miracle," Jason said. She looked at him.

"I know she's in good hands, and looking at her chart...," looking at Mary Ann, "I know she'll be all right. I just have a feeling about it. I'll be back in a little while to check on the two of you," she said, looking at Jason and then Talia. She bent down and said, *"Je t' aime ma princesse"* (I love you, my princess), and she left the room.

"I'm going to have to learn Italian," Jason said with a grin.

"That's not Italian; it's French," Mary Ann said, looking at him.

"Great, now it's two languages," he said. He started to head to the bathroom to change into the scrubs, and his phone buzzed again. He'd already had a busy morning at the station, and then the call this afternoon; he forgot to check it. Grandma Jean left Jason a message on his phone. He listened to it while his mom was in the room. He didn't understand it at all. He looked at her and played it for her: "'be prepared, but all is well.'" Grandma Jean's message was at 2:51 p.m. "What does that mean?" he asked his mom. "'Be prepared, but all is well.'" Then he looked at her. "I didn't even think about it; Talia texted me that she was leaving, and it was 11:51 a.m. The call came in at the station at 2:51 p.m. That's three hours. How does she know things? It's freaky."

Mary Ann replied, "She's done that to me many times, and I have no clue. Go change; I'll bring you something to eat."

Chapter 37

Sunday Evening

Since bringing Talia in, time passed slowly, sitting in her room. It was now late. Looking at his watch, it was nearing 9:45 p.m. It was somewhat quiet, except for voices over the loudspeaker periodically. There was no change in her condition. Jason sat at her bedside, looking at her and holding her hand, while his other hand lay across her stomach, gently rubbing back and forth, imagining her with a big belly that carried their baby. He wondered which it would be, a boy or a girl. He thought either would be awesome, look at his or her parents. He smiled to himself. He could imagine himself standing behind her with his arms around her, embracing her baby belly, with her hands on top of his, slowly swaying back and forth, and she's humming to the baby; or she would sit on a high-back chair as he used his stethoscope to listen to the baby's heartbeat, and then had her listen; it's beating so strong.

And then the smile went away, remembering what Jéan-Paul said, 'It will be a second miracle if this baby survives.' He stood up and stretched, walking to the window, looking out. The parking lot was well lit. You could see the tracks from cars in the snow. A few people were either heading to their car to go home or coming into the hospital, everyone bundled up with hats, scarves, and gloves and winter coats. Up in the sky, he watched the landing lights of planes, wondering where they were coming from. He also heard the sirens from a rescue squad and then saw an ambulance pull in. He closed his eyes, wishing the best for whoever was inside it.

He turned and walked back toward Talia's bed, looking at the monitor, and watching the ventilator breathe for her. This allowed her body and brain to rest and heal a little more quickly, but it still scared him. How will this affect her? What did the CT scan show? He saw the bag hanging that provided a drip to help lower her blood pressure, another scary thing attached to her. He sat in the chair, reaching over and holding her hand, hoping she would feel the warmth of his and squeeze it, letting him know she felt his presence. But there was nothing. He leaned forward, resting his head on the bed, placing his other hand across her stomach, and fell asleep.

Mary Ann came in to check on both of them. She touched Jason's shoulder, and he woke immediately, looking around. The room was dim. "Jason, you should go home and get some sleep."

"I'm not leaving her. I told her after we pulled her out that I'm staying with her until she comes home," he said.

"Then, at least put the chair into a reclining position or go over to the couch and lay down. The nurses will come in to check on her. If there's any change, they'll let you know. I'll bring you an extra blanket. I'll be heading home in about ten minutes, all right?" she said. "I'll be in around ten or so in the morning." Jason nodded, standing up and giving his mom a hug and a kiss on her cheek.

☙

Monday Morning

Morning came, and there was more activity on the floor. He got up from the reclining chair, stretching, then moving it back to an upright position. He looked at Talia, bending over her to kiss her forehead and cheek. "Good morning, my beautiful *fiancée*," he said. *"Ti amo."*

A nurse walked in, going around the bed to check stats. She looked at Jason and asked quietly what it meant, *"ti amo."*

He looked at the nurse and then back at Talia, holding her hand. "'I love you.' My soon-to-be-wife speaks Italian, and she taught me this," he said with a half smile.

"I might have to say that to my husband. I mean, I do anyway, but that sounds much more romantic. He's a police officer, and I worry about him every day," she said. "I see you're a fireman by the pants over there." Just then, Jim and Jéan-Paul walked in.

"Yes, I'm a paramedic/firefighter," Jason replied. "Here are two of my comrades, Jim Peters and Dr. Jéan-Paul Lemaitre." Jéan-Paul walked around the bed, taking the nurse's hand, kissing the back of it, saying, *"Buongiorno."*

"Oh," said the nurse looking at him.

"It means 'good morning.' It is a poetic language, isn't it, Italian." Jéan-Paul stated to the nurse.

"He does this with all the ladies; he can't resist." Jason gave him a silly grin, shaking his head. "He's a Frenchman, through and through. I think he enjoys speaking Italian more than he does his native language of French. And he also speaks German."

Jéan-Paul looked at Jason in scrubs and asked, "You are playing doctor now, yes?" He smiled.

"No, my mom brought these in last night for me to change into," Jason said. Jason excused himself and went into the bathroom. When he came out, the doctor had come in, making his rounds. Jason asked how she was doing. The doctor wanted to know who he was, looking at the scrubs, or was he family. Jason said he was her *fiancé*, that he came in with her yesterday and that he's a paramedic/firefighter, the same as Jim. And then he introduced Jéan-Paul as a doctor.

Jason also told the doctor who his mother was, and that she was a nurse on that floor. The young doctor didn't seem to recognize her name and shrugged. He went over a few things with Jason, and then let him know they would take her down sometime this morning for the next CT scan.

Jason looked at Jéan-Paul, and he nodded, giving him a look of "it's OK."

"We can take your bunker gear back to the station," Jim said as he looked down at Talia and the ventilator breathing for her. "We best head to the station, then. We'll check in with you later, all right?" Jim walked over to the couch and picked up Jason's gear.

As they were leaving, Captain Robins came into the room, looking at Jason. "Jason, I wanted to stop in before going to my meeting this morning. How's Talia doing?" The captain looked at her.

"Captain, this is her doctor, Dr. Mueller. They shook hands. Dr. Mueller was on the young side and didn't seem to have the best bedside manner. There was something about this young doctor that annoyed the captain; in his eyes, Dr. Mueller was a kid with a hospital badge and the letters "M.D." after his name. He didn't have enough experience yet with patients and families. He'd learn soon enough.

Dr. Mueller looked at the captain, with his coat and uniform on, and then briefly told him how she was doing. Dr. Mueller said, "There sure are a lot of you guys coming in. Maybe they can spread out their visits or just call." Captain liked him even less with his comment.

"When one of our own has something happen to them like this, we're all concerned, as anyone would be. Maybe we need to see for ourselves that they are getting the best treatment, and best bedside manner, from the doctors who are treating them. It's called caring and compassion. Many of us have been down this same road, more than once. We see your patients, before they ever get to you, at the scene of an accident. Maybe you should come do a trial run with some of these paramedic/firefighters and see what they see. We are what you might call a band of brothers and sisters, like the military. I'll send you some information, maybe even sign you up; it might just open your eyes. We already have one doctor that goes on calls with us because he cares and takes it back to his own country. That would be Dr. Lemaitre, who was just in here. You have a good day, doctor," Captain said.

"Jason, I'll stop by later today." He looked straight at Dr. Mueller and then left the room.

The doctor walked out, not saying a word to Jason. Since it was Monday, Jason would have to call Chloe and let her know what happened. Two orderlies came in to take Talia down for her second scan. He might as well call Chloe now. He had used Talia's phone. After talking with her, he wished he could put an arm around her as she broke down crying; she couldn't believe something like this happened. When she was coherent enough, he asked if she would let Jana know.

Jason walked again over to the window, looking out, not thinking much about anything at the moment; it was just time after all. Elizabeth had called Jason, asking about Talia's condition, which he said no change. She let him know she was on her way. The hospital she worked at was less than a half-mile away. As a surgical nurse, she helped with surgery that morning. Jason paced with his hands locked behind his neck, then stretched and walked back to the window. It had been about twenty minutes since they took Talia down for the second scan, but it seemed a lot longer for Jason, wanting them to bring her back up.

Elizabeth came walking in and saw the bed gone, knowing she'd gone for another scan. Jason stood at the window. It was bright out, with the sun reflecting off the snow; a good day to wear sunglasses. When Jason turned around, he saw Elizabeth in the room and then saw Kurt standing in the doorway. The tears fell from his eyes. Jason walked over to him and hugged him.

"It's my fault," Kurt said, looking at Jason.

"Why is it your fault?" he asked, taking a step back.

"I wanted to borrow her car for a bit to go see Caren at the Family Restaurant; she told me to hurry up about it. She wanted to leave mid-morning and get back before the weather changed, if it did, and before you got home. Time got away from me. By the time I got back, it was close to noon. She was ticked with me. She loaded her stuff and headed out. I just figured she made it home. I didn't watch the news or the weather. I should have gone home earlier; she wouldn't be here if it weren't for me," Kurt said. "Jason, I'm so sorry."

Jason looked at him, feeling angry with him, but that wouldn't undo what was done. Kurt was feeling guilty enough that he could have lost his sister. Jason thought, *How many people, and how many times, don't we all regret doing something that could have caused injury, pain and suffering to someone else? I guess reality will kick in soon enough when they bring Talia back up, and he sees her hooked up to a machine breathing for her.*

"Kurt, I do feel angry. And I feel sad. It was my station that got the call about a rollover. We arrived at the scene, not sure how many people may be injured or dead. Three of the doors wouldn't open; the door behind the driver was the only one. Jim was the one to tell me it was Talia." Jason saw more tears from Kurt. "I lost it, again, yelling for her. Seeing her in that car, crunched, with blood on her. That makes three accidents in my lifetime, with two dying, almost making it three, and I don't have it in me for a fourth. You have to let the guilt go; we can't undo this. But, also remember, it's Talia wanting to do things her way. It was her choice, taking that chance coming home. Did she watch the weather? I don't know. Did she absolutely have to come home? No. I would have much preferred her to stay put and be safe," Jason said.

He saw Kurt looking at him funny. "What?" Jason asked.

"You just said 'it makes three accidents in your lifetime, and you don't have it in you for a fourth.' What's that supposed to mean?" Kurt asked.

Jason looked at him for a moment. "Talia is eight weeks pregnant with my child. She found out on Saturday. She texted me she was fine, but that we needed to talk when she got home. I found the clinic's papers in her bag. We don't know if the baby will survive."

It was like a sucker punch to Kurt, realizing who he could have lost, and the life she was carrying. Talia was brought back in. Kurt turned around, seeing her lying in bed, with scratches on her face and a ventilator breathing for her. Now he lost it, and started to go down, when Jason and Elizabeth helped him sit on the couch. Elizabeth wrapped her arms around her son. Talia and Kurt had always been close.

Kurt asked about the machine. His mom said, "The first scan showed a small brain bleed. The machine allows her body and brain to rest and helps her to heal, and she also has a lung contusion because of the force of her seat belt keeping her in place after rolling." Kurt was quiet, tears rolling down his cheeks and shaking his head. The three of them sat quietly. It was close to 11:30 a.m. and Jason's stomach growled. He hadn't eaten anything since his mom brought in some food for him yesterday evening, and he still wore the same scrubs she brought him.

Mary Ann came in, looking at the three of them sitting on the couch, then walked over, checking the IV drip and the monitor. Jason stood up and walked over, hugging her. They both looked at Talia. She heard his stomach growl and looked at him. "You need to go get something to eat, unless I bring you several cups of Jell-O?"

"I like Jell-O," Jason said.

"Then you should go home and clean up, change your clothes, and bring my scrubs back," she said.

"I'll go to the cafeteria and eat, but other than that, I'm not leaving her. I'll call Jim. He was going to stop by later today. I have an extra set of clothes in my locker at the station," he said.

"Kurt, why don't we go grab a bite?" Jason said. Kurt stood up, looking at Talia, then his mom. She motioned for him to go with Jason and get out of the room for a bit; she'd stay until they got back. While having lunch, Jason called Jim, telling him to bring the clothes in his locker.

"She knows about Amy," Kurt said while eating.

"I know, I told her on the train," he replied.

"No, I mean your sister Amy," Kurt said.

"How does she know about my sister," Jason asked, taking a hard look at Kurt.

"I'm sorry. The conversation started with me asking about the ring on her finger, since she didn't normally wear jewelry. She told me it was her engagement ring from you and how much she loved you, more than I would ever know. I told her about Michigan and how I saw you look at her and that you would watch her. I told her about conversations I'd hear in the locker rooms, and a time when her name came up; they looked at me and laughed.

I was going to keep her safe. I told her that you and I had a conversation out in the parking area…," Kurt was saying.

"About you not trusting me and what my intentions were toward her," Jason said.

"Ya, that one. I told her I'd punch you out if I had to." He was looking at his plate, and then looked at Jason. "But you looked at me with such hurt, and then we had that long conversation. I told her it was love at first sight for you, that you only wanted to be there to love her, and protect her, and keep her safe if I couldn't. And that you swore on your little sister's grave that you could never hurt her and feel that pain again. I told her you fell in love with her, and then it hit me what I said. I told her she was never supposed to hear that. I promised you I would never ever tell her that, and I never did until that moment when it came out. Jason, I'm so sorry."

"What did Talia say?" Jason asked.

"She just looked at me. She got up, walked across the room, and then turned back around, staring back at me with tears, saying, 'he HAD a sister?' She asked what happened, and I knew she wouldn't let go of it. I told her briefly what happened, and she burst into tears and sank to the floor." Kurt and Jason both had tears. "We both know she wears her heart on both sleeves. What's there not to love about her?"

"She never said a word to me, so it was a secret she was going to keep." Jason looked across the room. "After getting back from Germany a day earlier, I had Jim and his wife take me to her place," Jason said, with a slight smile on his face. "You should have seen the look on her face when I could get her to open the door. I felt like I was finally home, and there she was, in front of me. What else could go wrong?"

Jason looked at his plate. "Loving her is so easy. It wasn't until the next morning, and the flashes kept coming at me like they'd done so many times before, of that day in the park. My heart started racing and I felt like I couldn't breathe, and I knew I couldn't keep it bottled inside of me any longer. She woke up looking at me, sitting up, wanting to know what was wrong. I had to tell her. So I told her everything about that day, and that it was Amy's last birthday." He closed his eyes now, softly saying, "She put her arms around me, holding me and rocking me, and we both cried until I fell asleep."

They sat for a moment longer and then got up, heading back up to Talia's room. Jason and Kurt walked in and saw Elizabeth sitting in the recliner chair, looking at a magazine. She looked up at both men, seeing their eyes. They both looked so tired. She said she was going to go home for a little while; they didn't live that far from either hospital. She asked Kurt if he wanted to stay or come with her. He decided to go with her. She would check in later, and knew Mary Ann was on duty. She felt that Talia would be all right, and then they left, leaving Jason to sit with Talia. He partially closed the door.

Chapter 38

Monday - Later Afternoon

Jason walked over to her bed, leaning over and kissing her forehead, then moving some of her hair down over her shoulder so it would look more like her. He smiled to himself, remembering last Friday morning when he woke up and looked at her lying on her stomach, her hair covering her face, like the first time he saw her lying next to him and how he had wanted to move it so she could breathe. It would probably take a lot of hair to make it hard to breathe. But now, he could move it or play with it.

It was funny when she had asked if he was playing with her hair, and he said, why would he do that. It's true; she had better hair. It was beautiful and soft to the touch. He picked up a handful of it, bending down to smell it. There was still the lingering smell of apple. They didn't have apple shampoo at home, and he decided they would get some. He liked the smell of it, just like the coconut. Looking at her lovingly, and then with a grin, he took several strands, tickling her nose. He wanted to see if she would feel the light sensation and twitch her nose; there was no twitching. He then did the same to his nose, and of course, it wasn't the same.

He sat down in the chair, picking up her hand and lacing her fingers through his own. She had small hands, and her fingers were long and delicate. As he continued to hold her hand, fingers still laced with his, he brought it to his mouth, cupping his other hand around them. He closed his eyes and pressed them against his lips. He kissed the back of her hand, and then gently rubbed it against his cheek, feeling the softness of her hand.

He knew she couldn't hear him, even though he wished she could so she knew he was sitting right there waiting for her to open her eyes and look at him. "Where are you, Talia?" he asked her. "Where did you go inside that head of yours? I need and want you to come back to me. We've waited so long to be together, all these years afraid to say what was in our hearts. I'm sitting right here, and won't leave you." Jason took a slow, deep breath. While still holding her hand, he leaned back in the chair, rubbing his thumb on the back of her hand. He closed his eyes, resting. Even with her door partially closed, he tried blocking out the sounds coming from the hallway of laughter and general conversation.

There was a tap on the door as it opened a little wider, and Jim was standing there. Jason motioned for him to come in. He stood up and hugged his best friend. Jim had brought Jason's clothes to him. Jason turned his chair toward the couch so he could talk to Jim, and then picked up Talia's hand again. "Nadine sends her best to you both," Jim said. "She wanted to come but thought she might intrude, and then thought maybe she would wait until Talia was awake and responsive." Jason nodded. "And all the guys are wishing and praying for a speedy recovery." Jim then chuckled, "I think they really want to come to your wedding, so she'd better get moving on getting better and out of here." Jason chuckled; that was good to hear. He needed something positive to think about.

"And I want to see them there to share in the joy and love I feel for her," Jason said. "It's been over twenty-four hours since they admitted her. It's been quiet in this room, for the most part, except when the nurses, the doctor, and family have been here. Right now, I'd be so happy to hear her talk about the fabric stores she went to overseas and go on about them. I wouldn't even kiss her just so she'd keep talking to me." He grinned.

"Be careful what you wish for; we've heard her talk," Jim said, smiling. "How long has she been a fashion designer?"

"She worked for a company for almost ten years, and then she was able to open her little shop with the help of her grandfather. She talked about him on the train when we were heading back up to Basel. I asked her what made her go into fashion; she said it was when she got into high school.

They'd visit her grandfather, and he'd see her daydreaming. He asked her what she was dreaming about, and she told him, and that she also doubted herself because of what people would tell her, and she didn't think she was deserving or worthy of having good things in her life." Jason stopped a moment, looking over at her.

"He told her, 'Don't allow other peoples' writing to be on your wall.' She said she didn't understand and asked what he meant, and he pointed to her head. So, it all started with her making and designing things for some classmates, even a teacher. It was about five years ago when they visited him. His health was failing, and she wanted to tell him what she'd been doing since graduating from ISU in Ames, because she didn't know if she'd ever have the opportunity again.

"She told him she would like to own her own business someday. He said to her, 'Whatever dream you have, design it, and be open to it. What is the outcome you want for your life and yourself?' He asked her the name of her shop, and she told him 'The T.E. Rose Shoppe,' telling him it had to have two p's in Shoppe because it looked cool." Jim chuckled, and Jason smiled. "His initials were the same as hers; his name was Theodore Earl Rose. He died about a year later. She said he left her an amazing gift of believing in her and making sure she believed in herself. He also left her with enough funds to open her little shoppe."

"He sounds like he was an amazing grandfather who loved his granddaughter very much, and giving her such beautiful gifts for her life," Jim said.

Jason agreed. "Ya, I would have loved to have known him and spent some time with him myself."

He then told Jim, with a smile, "I remember a couple Saturdays ago; it was in the afternoon, and Talia was busy working on another design. She'd given herself a deadline. She hadn't taken time out to eat. She had her large sketch pad on the table, with a pencil in one hand and a small jar of peanut butter with a long teaspoon in her other hand. She'd dip her spoon into the jar and get a little peanut butter on it and lick it off. She'd do this a few times. She was so involved in her drawing, and I think she forgot what she had in her hand, and stuck her pencil in the peanut butter, licking it." Jason chuckled, as did Jim.

"I heard her say 'ick,' setting the peanut butter jar back on the table, instead of putting it away. But I wasn't going to interrupt her. Then she wiped off that pencil, laying it aside and getting a different one. She has a couple of small jars with various pencils and colored pencils in them." Jason chuckled as he pictured her doing it. "She was just so focused on her drawings, and honestly, I was just happy sitting there watching her. It made me smile and love her more.

"Her eyebrows went up, and she'd tilt her head, and her lips crinkled at something she didn't like. There was a small pile of crumpled papers on the floor, like a hailstorm came through just in her little area. But when she finished with that piece, there was this big sigh as she looked at what she had completed. She put down her pencil and got off of her stool and did a little 'happy dance.' She laughed, which is infectious, and she came and sat down beside me with a big smile, raising her arms and waving them in the air, and said, 'OK, six down; two more to go.' She was so happy with herself. We kissed, and there was the taste of peanut butter, but I didn't mind one bit. I kissed her again and again.

"She got up for a second, putting one leg underneath her and turning her body toward me, and asked me about my week, looking at me and giving me her full attention. She wanted to hear." Jason said, "You know, it's all the little things that she does or says or her narrative on something; it's how she comes out of the shower with her hair all wrapped up in a towel. She'll look at me straight-faced, with her hands together in front of her and give a little bow and then go back into the bathroom. I'd laugh because it was funny. It's her happy dance when something goes right. There are some big things, but the little ones I love and cherish the most; the way she giggles and laughs and turns her head toward me with those beautiful eyes, the way she loves me. She makes my heart flutter, and makes me feel so alive that I want to be a better man and soon-to-be husband. Seeing things through her eyes gives me a whole new perspective on how life can and should be." He sat up straighter in his chair.

Jason's voice changed. "Then last week, she said she had just one design left. She was on target. We had Thanksgiving; I hadn't enjoyed a holiday like that for a long time because I was always working," he said, looking at Jim. "Her aunt and uncle asked if the two of us could come to visit them this past weekend. I said I couldn't because I was working. With me not being home, she decided to go and take Kurt with her since he lives up there. She said she could use the break from her work. Maybe she'd be inspired for the last design. I wonder if she'll be able to finish it now."

"Don't go there, Jason. She will come out of it. She's a strong, healthy young woman," Jim said. He saw the look Jason was giving him. "Nothing new has happened to her, right?"

"Well, actually, there is something new with her," he said, looking at his best friend. "Talia's eight weeks pregnant." The look on Jason's face was a somber one.

"Congratulations, 'Dad?'" Jim said, now wishing he hadn't said it so quickly. "What? I don't like the look on your face."

"Talia has been nauseated for weeks now, which I didn't know until Friday morning when she threw up. I asked her some questions, and I had a hunch she might be. I didn't want to say that I thought she might be pregnant, but I asked her to please make an appointment and get checked out, which she did with her family doctor back home. She texted me that she was fine, but we had to talk about something. At the accident, there was so much commotion. Then we arrived here, and I told Jéan-Paul they'd want to do an ultrasound. He looked at me, I think knowing full well, but I said she might be pregnant.

"Then he said, 'We now have two lives to keep safe; mama and baby.' He'd gone in, and when he came out, told me, 'She is fortunate to be alive. This is your first miracle.' He said she opened her eyes, and he spoke to her in Italian, telling her she needed to stick around for her baby and me. Then he said, 'Your second miracle will be if the baby survives.' The ultrasound confirmed what was on Talia's papers; she was going to show me when she got home.

"So, I made my wish for Christmas last night. The first miracle occurred; she survived. The second miracle will be that this baby survives." Jason closed his eyes.

Chapter 39

Monday Evening

Elizabeth came back, shortly after Jim left. Taking off her coat and laying it on the couch, she asked Jason if he had eaten anything since noon; he shook his head no. She told him to go down to the cafeteria and find something to eat. Anything. She would sit until he came back; she wasn't going anywhere. Before leaving, he kissed Talia on her cheek, telling her how much he loved her and that he would be back in a little while. He said with a smile, "Your mother told me I had to go eat." He looked at Elizabeth, and she grinned.

Jason walked out the door and past the nurse's station. They were looking at him again, leaning over the counter or looking around the doorway of their station, about four of them, and he thought, *Why not*. As he passed, he looked back over his shoulder and said, "Sorry ladies, I'm taken. And she's the love of my life." He continued walking down the hallway toward the elevators. The walls were painted in light earth-tone colors with large pieces of beautiful artwork. The floors looked clean and shiny, and white. As he passed the rooms, a few were empty; some had lights shut off except for the dimmed light over the bed. A few had lingering family or friends who were getting ready to leave. In one room, a family was crying because their loved one had just passed away. A comment from someone in the room: "They don't have to suffer any longer." It made him sad, and even uncomfortable.

Even though he was a paramedic/firefighter, he saw life and death firsthand working with his comrades. There usually weren't any family members around to see what they saw or hear the cries from the people in the vehicles who were still conscious, or to see them lying on the road. Some images couldn't be erased, no matter how hard he tried. It was only at the hospital where family and friends might be fortunate enough to have a loved one survive.

He didn't want to be here at all, but he wasn't leaving without Talia. Depending on the room you passed, there was a strong smell of someone being sick and then the disinfectant used; he could smell chlorine to clean work surfaces and equipment. A different cleaning product was used on the floors. All these smells combined could be nauseating and most unpleasant. He remembered his mom telling him that there was also a smell of death, which he's also smelled before due to his job.

Taking the elevator down, he got off and walked into the cafeteria. It was pretty quiet, with hardly anyone there. Jason found a couple of things to eat and then found something to take back to the room. He just wasn't hungry. He wanted to be home with Talia, where the two of them could cook and bake together, or he could watch Talia make his favorite cookie. He liked others, but the no-bake cookie was his favorite. He wanted to sit in their living room and watch her work or sit on the sofa just being together, holding each other and chatting, or not.

Working long shifts required the guys to sleep at the station. It was not always restful to be awakened in the middle of the night or early morning, going out on a call in all kinds of weather. He had worked in the bitter cold and snow, with temperatures and wind chills below the minus thirty degrees, the rainstorms, hot and humid days, and nights with highs in the low three-digit temps. Sleep cycles were thrown off. When you got back from a call, going back to sleep was hard, depending on the time. The beds weren't that comfortable either; nothing to snuggle up to. And the guys rarely smelled as lovely as a female with hair smelling of coconut or apple that you could cuddle up to. Jason smiled to himself. He wanted to go home and sleep in his bed, with Talia beside him, holding her and making love to her.

He headed back up to her room. Elizabeth was still sitting in the chair, looking at the same magazine. He wondered how far she had gotten reading it. It looked like the same page she was on last evening.

He placed the item he bought on the couch, then walked back to stand next to Talia, picking up her hand and holding it. Mary Ann was on nights, and came into the room. She checked the monitor and IV, making notes. Looking at Talia, she noticed her hair down and around her shoulder, near her neck. She started to reach over to move her hair when Jason took hold of her hand, moving it away. He gave her a look. She took Talia's chart, and walked around the bed, hugging her son, and placing her hand on Elizabeth's shoulder. Then, she walked out of the room.

He bent over, kissing Talia on her forehead and told her, "I didn't find anything that I liked in the cafeteria, except what looks like a prepackaged sandwich and a Little Debbie cake. No fruit that I could stick in my bag, if you remember doing that. So, I'll probably starve until we both get home."

"Did you, by chance, call Chloe and let her know what happened?" Elizabeth asked him.

"Ya, I did. As you can imagine, she was upset and crying. I wanted to hug her. It sounds like she and Talia have been close, going back to their college days," Jason said.

Elizabeth said, "Both Chloe and Jana are talented in what they bring to the table to get those designs completed for Talia. They both are good at sewing. They all work hard and love what they do, so it doesn't feel like a job. The three of them are a team. Even though Talia's line is small, it's getting noticed. I love her creativity and her good heart. And she told me about Grandma Jean and her ideas. I think Talia will make some pretty nice pieces for an older group of people. She wants to help everyone, you know that. She wants to make things better."

"Talia told me about her grandfather, Theodore. I wish I could have met him. He gave her a very valuable and precious gift, believing in her and making sure she believed in herself," Jason said.

"Yes, he did." She looked at her daughter and smiled.

"Elizabeth," Jason said, looking at her, and then Talia, "how do you think she's really doing? I want so badly for her to wake up and talk to me and tell me how she's feeling."

She stood up, laying the magazine down on the chair, then walked around it and hugged Jason. "Honestly, I think she's doing better than they expected her to. Most accident victims have a long road ahead of them, and so many struggles. Knowing how much she hates winter, anytime she's ever had to travel during it, she bundles herself up like the abominable snowman," she said, smiling. "I can picture her when she says, 'You just never know,' with raised eyebrows and tilting her head at me with a goofy look on her face, and she'd put her hands out with palms up.

"I'm surprised she could even fit behind the steering wheel. She probably looked a lot like the white Michelin Man for tires, that commercial we all love, a bunch of different-shaped marshmallows stuck together," she said, grinning. Jason nodded, with a big smile. "I have high hopes that she'll be off the machine by sometime tomorrow evening. But don't quote me on that, you hear. I'm just a nurse and her mother."

"What about after she comes off it?" Jason asked, looking at her.

"Her body will need rest. She may be here for a few more days, depends on her doctor and tests. Jason, we all know how much you love her and want her home. Be patient; we can't push her," Elizabeth said.

"What about the baby?" Jason asked.

She looked at Talia. "I don't have an answer for you there. Yes, I'm a nurse, but a surgical nurse. I don't work OB." She looked at Jason. "I can only assume. And right now, I don't want to get my hopes up too high," she said, walking to the couch. She picked up her coat and purse and walked toward the door. "I'm heading home. I'll be back tomorrow after my shift, OK?" Jason nodded. "'Night, Jason."

He felt somewhat hopeful about Talia getting off the machine later tomorrow. But, maybe Elizabeth told him that just so he could relax a bit. He turned back to Talia, picking up her hand in both of his, bringing them up as he bent down to kiss the back of her hand.

Jason put the light on over her bed and then walked over to the couch, picking up the big blanket. He flipped off the top light, turning the chair so it was parallel to the bed. He put himself into a reclining position and turned toward Talia, covering himself with the blanket. He took hold of her hand and fell asleep.

❧

Tuesday - Early Morning

It was around 3:30 a.m. The sound of staff awakened Jason; they were calling for a crash cart. His heart started racing as he sat up and looked over at Talia, thinking something happened. He took hold of her hand, holding it to his lips and kissing her fingers; she was all right. He took a quick deep breath and got up, walking to the door. He opened it a little, then peered out. It was the next room over. He raised his arm and leaned it against the door frame, tilting his head against his arm. His heartbeat was still rapid, but slowing down. He closed the door almost all the way, then walked back to the chair and resumed his position, again holding her hand.

Jason had a hard time going back to sleep, hearing every little sound, and then listened to the wails of a woman. He held Talia's hand more securely. He opened his eyes, looking toward the foot of the bed, staring blindly at it. Memories came back from past vacations, wherever they were. He loved watching her, and she made him laugh. When he wasn't watching her, she was watching him. The reason he knew this was because when Kurt saw her looking at Jason, he would give him a little tilt of his head toward Talia's direction and give a grin to Jason, so he knew that Talia was watching him. It was like a cat-and-mouse game, or a who's-watching-who teasing game, back and forth, with Kurt as a commentator, and it was only one-sided: Jason's.

And the latest vacation with just the two of them in Switzerland, he had her all to himself. He might have missed out on some sights because he was always looking at her, but she was there to nudge him or tell him to look at something and then laugh about it. But he could look at her any time he wanted. He could hold her hand, put his arm around her and kiss her, among other things. He wanted to share more of everything with her, including the possibility of a little one. Right now, he just wanted her to wake up and get better so he could take her home. He dozed, off and on, finally looking at his watch; it showed 6:40 a.m. He sat up in the chair, pulling the blanket back up around him.

He looked toward the window. It was dark outside, and he thought there should be some daylight showing, but it was winter. He didn't want to get up out of the chair just yet. He saw the magazine that Elizabeth was looking at and picked it up. It was some Country Living magazine. So, he flipped through it, seeing some beautiful homes that would be nice to live in. Hopefully, one day, he and Talia could have a beautiful home in the country where their family had space to grow, and it would feel and be peaceful, away from the hustle and bustle of the city. It was nice having amenities close for convenience's sake, but there was a lot of noise and lots of people, everyone hurrying up to get somewhere and then waiting. The door slowly opened, and in came his mom. He laid the magazine down in his lap. She bent over, kissing Jason on his head, and he took her hand, holding it. She asked, "How did you sleep?"

"Sleep, what's that?" Jason said. "I guess I did. Some, until I heard nurses call for a crash cart, which made my heart race. It scared me, and I thought it was Talia, so I looked over at her. Then moments later, a woman wailed."

"The woman's husband passed. He was in his early seventies and had a lot of health issues. We'd had him several times before. The man didn't like to listen about taking better care of himself. So, I see you picked up Elizabeth's magazine. Nice-looking homes in there, don't you think?" she asked, looking at him.

He looked up at her and nodded. "Maybe, someday. Home is living with this beautiful woman in our apartment."

"Well, just think. You let go of your old apartment and put that money—" She was interrupted by Jason.

"I'm two steps ahead of you. And when we're ready for that move, you'll be the first to know. Right now, the focus is on her." He pointed over to Talia. Mary Ann walked around the bed, putting information in Talia's chart.

"OK. I won't say any more about a you-know-what for family…" She smiled at him. "Dr. Mueller should be in soon doing his rounds," she said.

"Tell me, why is it, that nurses run their butts off doing all sorts of things for their patients, getting information, changing bags, cleaning up after patients, and of course, the list goes on. Then, some doctor with an M.D. behind his name comes in and reads the chart, looks at the monitors, glances at the patient, and then leaves?" Jason asked.

"Because when we all went to school, we learned that M comes before R, not the other way around. Do you need anything right now?" she asked.

"No. And, if I get hungry, I have my prepackaged Little Debbie to eat. Just not very hungry. Maybe later. But I should get up and go use the little boy's room," he said with a quirky grin. Mary Ann left the room. When he came out, he saw his captain standing just inside the doorway.

"Captain, good morning," Jason said. He reached for Captain Robins' hand, and they shook.

"Morning, Jason. How's she doing?" he asked.

"All right; there's been no change. And I heard from some good sources that maybe, later today, she'll get taken off the machine for a bit. I just have to wait. I don't want to get my hopes up," Jason said.

"I'm sure it's difficult. I've been very fortunate to have had nothing happen to any of my family like this. I know you have. I can't imagine going through that. You know some of the guys have gone through this," Captain said. Jason nodded.

"How's Adrian doing?" Jason asked.

"He seems to be doing well. He's learning from us as you did with him. He's a good man and a good paramedic. It's a good program, and I'm glad that some of you got to experience it. Ted played a little joke on him yesterday morning." He grinned, shaking his head. "Ted switched one of

Adrian's boots with one of Mike's boots. When a call came in, he jumped up to put his gear on, and all but fell over because one boot was bigger," he chuckled.

"Well, Talia did something similar to me on Halloween," Jason said. "I don't know when she did it, but she took my jeans and strapped them inside my hiking boots, so they looked like our bunker gear with play spiders on them. She knows I hate spiders." He shook his head as he looked at her. "Right now, I'd take another practical joke from her..."

"Jason, I have to go; keep us informed, please," Captain said, shaking Jason's hand.

"I will. Thank you, Captain, for stopping by," Jason said, and the captain left.

Doctor Mueller came into the room with Mary Ann behind him. He checked Talia's chart and a few other things: checked BP, looked at her pupils and listened to her chest. "It looks like this afternoon we should be able to get her off the machine and see how she does on her own. I don't know how, but her scans look clean," he said, looking at Jason. "I'll be back this afternoon." And with that, he left.

Jason looked at his mom and did a sigh of relief. She took his hand, holding it for a moment, and then hugged him. There was a tap on the door, and Jason turned around, seeing Chloe and Jana. They just stood there looking at Talia with tears. "Girls, it's all right, come in," Jason said as he walked toward them. "She's going to be all right. They're going to take her off of this machine and see how she does, breathing on her own. Chloe, Jana, this is my mom, Mary Ann Porter; she's been watching over Talia. Mom, this is Chloe Chang and Jana Woods; they work for Talia." They were quiet, still looking at Talia.

"Hi, girls. Talia is OK," she said, looking at them, thinking maybe they've never seen anyone up close with a machine hooked up like this. "Do you want to walk over to her?" Mary Ann asked. They both shook their heads no. "Jason, I'll be back later."

"Chloe, Jana, she's going to be all right," he said, walking over to Talia and picking up her hand, showing them it's OK to touch her if they wanted to. "It's OK. Why don't you come a little closer? See, I'm holding her hand." He motioned for them to come closer. "When someone has an accident, like Talia did, it's common to induce a coma and put them on a machine to help them breathe. This way, it gives their body and brain whatever time is needed to rest and heal more quickly." He looked at their faces.

Chloe took a few steps closer, reaching for Talia's hand. She'd been staring at the machine. Jason held Talia's hand so she could feel it. "See? She's warm. She needed some help for a little bit." Chloe held Talia's hand, placing her other hand over the top and gently rubbing it. She closed her eyes. "Jana, would you like to come closer?" Jason asked. She looked up at Jason and shook her head no; she stayed where she was. "It's all right. You don't have to."

Chloe turned toward Jana and gave her a little smile. "She feels warm," she said, taking Talia's hand and kissing the back of it. That prompted Jana to walk just behind Chloe and reach out to touch her hand, also feeling the warmth. Chloe asked Jason how long she would be here.

"I'm not sure. It could be a couple of days to maybe a week or more. I don't know; it's up to Talia," Jason said. Chloe nodded.

"We were afraid for her. I wanted to come yesterday, but then I didn't," Chloe said.

"It's OK. You came today. She'll be glad that you did. It's difficult seeing someone you care about like this. I will tell her that you were here," Jason said.

"We wanted to see for ourselves. Maybe tomorrow we can stop by briefly. Is that all right?" Jana asked.

"Yes, it's all right," he said. They started to move away from her when Jason opened his arms up to them for a hug. They both took a step toward him and put their arms around him. "She's going to be all right. We need to give her some time." They both then turned and walked toward the door, turning back to look at Talia.

Chapter 40

Tuesday Morning

After the girls left that morning, Jason walked over to the window. It was so cold out. He watched the exhaust coming from the cars, as well as steam from the vents on buildings. It made him cold, looking out, and he knew eventually he'd be back at his job, going out in this weather. He turned around with his hands in his pockets, leaning against the window, and watched the ventilator breathe for her; up and down, up and down, and up and down. For a moment, he wondered what that must feel like, pushing air into your lungs. He was anxious about having them get the breathing tube out so that she could breathe on her own. She'd be able to lick her lips if she wanted to, and swallow. She hadn't done those things since the accident. He thought about how everyone, including himself, took these things for granted, as well as walking, moving their arms, turning their heads, hearing, talking, seeing, smelling, and of course, the big one is breathing on their own without the aid of a machine.

With time to kill, Jason sat down on the sofa, picking up the little Debbie Cake he got from the cafeteria, checking it out. He looked at the rolled-up, small chocolate cake with its shiny white wrapper with the white filling displayed so nicely on the outside. He read the ingredients and the nutritional facts, wondering if he wanted to eat it. Looking at it, he mumbled, "You are not my friend." It was something maybe a female might say. Setting it aside, he thought, if he got really desperate, just so he won't starve until they got home, he'd eat it. He was getting hungry, though, but didn't want to leave Talia alone; not that she was going anywhere. He got up and paced the floor, then picked up the magazine he had started going through. He sat down on the chair, looking at some of the houses, and thought, *What if we could find a nice-sized house to call home? And what if it had a big yard with some trees and lilac bushes, and what if children were playing safely outside...*

❦

Tuesday - Early Afternoon

He leaned back against the chair, taking hold of Talia's hand, and closed his eyes for just a moment. He felt his shoulder being touched and woke up, not realizing he'd fallen asleep. It was the nurse whose hand Jéan-Paul had kissed. He looked at his watch and saw that it was 12:30 p.m. He didn't sleep well throughout the night. And he thought, *That's one way for time to pass, nod off for a moment; time flies when you're asleep.* She said that the doctor would come in at about one-thirty to start the procedure to remove the tubing. *Great, only another hour to sit and wait.*

Elizabeth came walking into the room and saw Jason sitting and holding Talia's hand, smiling at her, and her magazine opened up on his lap. He looked back at her and smiled. "This young lady tells me that the doctor will be in at about one-thirty to start the procedure of taking the tubing out," Jason said.

"Well, I'm here to tell you that it will probably be earlier, to be sneaky. Have you eaten anything?" Elizabeth asked.

He shook his head no, rubbing his eyes, and pointed to the Little Debbie on the sofa. "If I have to eat that thing, I will, but I'm not leaving if he's going to be in here early. I want to be here." He smiled at her.

And Elizabeth was right; Dr. Mueller came in, probably hoping no one would be in the room. Jason and Elizabeth stood near the end of the bed, waiting. As a paramedic over the years, Jason and his partner have had to intubate many patients, inserting an ET tube, inflating the cuff, and doing the two-person mask technique. He's also had to start many IVs. Another learning experience he'd see is the removal of an ET tube, the reverse of putting one in.

A nurse helped Dr. Mueller start the procedure. During this process, the air was removed from the inflated gasket on the tube, releasing the tie that held the tube in place and slowly pull the tubing out. They heard a little cough during this process, and Jason saw Talia's little finger twitch. He looked at Elizabeth, and she saw it as well. To give her a little support, she was given a nasal cannula. She was now breathing on her own. Jason had tears in his eyes, and turned toward Elizabeth and hugged her.

After they removed the tube, Jason took a deep breath. Once the doctor and nurse left the room, he walked over to Talia, kissed her cheek, and took hold of her hand as he sat down on the chair looking at her breathing on her own. He couldn't help but smile. Elizabeth was on the other side, and also kissed her daughter's cheek, leaning toward her ear, saying, *"Un pas de plus."* Jason looked at her, and she told him it meant "one more step." Now he really didn't want to go anywhere, afraid she would wake up. He wanted to be the first one she saw. Elizabeth saw this in his eyes, and told him she would get him something to eat. He didn't take his eyes off Talia. His first wish for Christmas had two parts: one, she would survive; and two, she would breathe on her own with no help.

After about twenty minutes, Elizabeth came back into the room with a covered tray. He could smell the beef. She lifted the cover, and on the plate was a hot beef sandwich with mashed potatoes, Jell-O in a cup, and a cup of coffee. She put it on the rolling bedside table, and Jason mouthed the words "thank you" to Elizabeth, then stood up and walked to it. He bent over, smelling it, and it made his mouth water. Besides Talia breathing on her own, this was the next best thing that happened today. Elizabeth said she had to get going back to work and would stop in later this evening; she always knew her daughter was in good hands. Jason hugged her, thanking her for being there with him. She walked over to Talia and kissed her on the forehead, telling her in English that she'd see her later, and good job.

Jason finished his lunch and covered the plate, taking his coffee and Jell-O, and a spoon, and returned to his chair. Two of his favorite Jell-O flavors were cherry and orange; something else they didn't have at home, but were going to get. Who knew you could start a grocery list just sitting in a hospital room. He watched her breathe, in and out, in and out, smiling because she was doing it on her own.

❧

Tuesday - Late Afternoon

He took hold of her hand, tracing his index finger around her fingers and back again. He smiled as he pictured the long hair from the cat gliding through her fingers so gently from that first trip. He remembered the stroll their families took near the river bank. Their parents thought they wanted to take a short river cruise, but time didn't allow for it. Their moms then sat down on a bench, talking. Both dads and Kurt walked closer to the river, watching a ferry, and Jason, staying close to Talia. Jason now asked Talia, "Do you remember the day we all walked near the river; you, with your long brown hair in pigtails, wearing jeans and a purple pullover top with tennis shoes on?

"You saw this long-haired cat walk your way, and you kept calling to it to come to you, saying 'here Swiss kitty,' in this cute little voice. When it didn't come to you, you tried it again, saying it louder, the way your mom called to you at the zoo, 'come here, Swiss kitty.'" Jason smiled, turning her palm upward and tracing the lines on her palm. "You started walking toward it, and it turned, running away. I laughed, and you turned and gave me this snarly look. Do you remember that? You sat down on the end of the bench, with your arms folded across your chest, looking at the ground, and soon that cat came walking back to you. You looked down at it and slowly picked it up, holding it in your arms, petting it, and running your fingers through the long hair a couple of times. It nuzzled your neck and rubbed your chin, and I heard it purr at you. You had such a gentle, loving touch.

"And this last time, when I saw you in Basel. You picked up that calico cat so gently and loving again, doing the same thing, holding it in your arms, petting it and talking to it." He pressed her hand against his lips. "You captured my heart all over again and made me love you even more than I already did." He placed his hand across her stomach. "I hope against all hope, little one, that you are nestled safe, and that you will survive here in your mommy's tummy and be all right."

Jéan-Paul had been standing quietly in the doorway, observing. He heard that they pulled the tubing and she was breathing on her own, which made him smile. He knew precisely what Jason was feeling, but the ordeal he went through was much longer than a few days. His beautiful Suzanne was once in this same similar place as Talia… his thoughts trailed. Jason heard a noise, and turned around and saw Jéan-Paul. He stood up and walked over to him, giving a hug.

"Jéan-Paul, good to see you. How was your day?" Jason asked. He noticed that Jéan-Paul was quieter than he usually was, looking at Talia.

"Little miracles happen all the time," Jéan-Paul said softly, still looking at Talia, slowly walking around her bed. "We always want the big ones and expect them, and when they don't happen, we are disappointed and sad. Many aren't looking at the little miracles." Jason didn't understand as he watched Jéan-Paul. "The two of you have had little miracles, or if you prefer, chance or fate, if you want to call them that, throughout your life, bringing the two of you together. You were meant to be together, but you already knew this." Jéan-Paul laid his hand on Talia's stomach, looking at Jason.

"Jéan-Paul, are you all right?" Jason asked, feeling a little concerned.

Looking back at Talia, he said, "Seven years ago, Suzanne and I were heading home from our stay at the cabin. She didn't want to be there. She did not like hiking, but I begged her to go with me; just a little way up, not too far, maybe to Marker 1. I wanted her to do something I enjoyed doing. On the way back to Villars, on those same curves that you and Talia were on, the car that was ahead of you was Suzanne and me." Jason closed his eyes, shaking his head. "We were hit a little harder than the car in front of you that day. We were shoved into that tree."

Jéan-Paul spoke quietly. "We spent weeks at the hospital. We also hoped against all hope. I also had only two wishes for miracles. That my beloved wife would survive, but also that my unborn child would survive. She was not yet five months pregnant and lost the baby because of complications.

You see, had we not gone up even to Marker 1, but left and headed home, we would have been home, and eventually, a little boy would have come into this world."

"Jéan-Paul, I am so sorry," Jason said, walking around to hug his good friend. Then he stood back, giving Jéan-Paul a little space.

He looked at Jason. "I have felt guilty about that for a very long time, but my Suzanne, she forgave me. So, when I want to go hiking, I go by myself where I can yell all I want, and the only ones to hear me are those animals in the mountains and the trees. Then I work on my wood projects and go home. I love my wife very much. She cannot have any other children," Jéan-Paul said, looking at Talia. "But you and this beautiful woman made a baby at the cabin that night." He looked at Jason with a knowing look and smiled at him. "I feel connected to you both. I see it in your eyes and your hearts. I think this little one will be a fighter."

Jéan-Paul saw the vase sitting on the windowsill with flowers in it. He walked over, looking at the lilacs, and then tried to smell and feel them. He looked at Jason with a grin. "These are not real."

"No, they are not. The real things only last a short while. Lilacs are Talia's favorite flower; she loves them. I'm having my mom bring in some candles that smell like lilacs, not to burn, just taking off the lid, and let the smell of them come out," Jason said.

"Funny thing is, my Suzanne also loves lilacs. I see the card here; looks very familiar to me." Jéan-Paul read the words: *"Für jemanden, der sehr geliebt wird.* You know it's in German, yes?" Jéan-Paul asked. "Do you know what it means?" He saw there was nothing written on the back.

"No. There was a waitress who had said this to Talia. She had placed a small vase of lilacs on our table, from their bush. After paying, she gave me my receipt and this little card. I've kept it in my wallet, but I don't know, maybe it was for good luck. I never got around to finding out what it means, and I wanted to put it with the flowers," Jason replied.

"May I write on the back of this card in English for you what it says?" Jéan-Paul asked.

"Yes, I'd like to know what it means, if it's good," Jason said with a smile.

After writing out what it meant, and before handing it to Jason, Jéan-Paul took out a small card from his wallet, holding it, while giving Jason's card back. Jason looked first at Jéan-Paul with his card in his hand and turned his card over, reading it. His eyes formed tears as he lowered his head for a moment, then read it out loud: "For someone who is very much loved."

"We must have had the same waitress," Jéan-Paul said, handing his own card to Jason.

Jéan-Paul asked if he could stay for a while. They talked about work and Jéan-Paul's favorite hobbies: hiking and woodworking; two things Jason also liked. They spoke of the Rhine cruise that Jason and Talia took, telling Jéan-Paul they loved it. Jason thanked him for that special gift.

Jim popped his head around the corner, with Nadine behind him. They came walking in. Jason and Jéan-Paul stood up, walking toward them and shaking hands, and Jason hugged Nadine. "I see she's breathing on her own. Jason, that's a nice little miracle," Nadine said. Jason nodded in total agreement.

Jim said, "Everyone will be glad to hear it. They've been asking. So, between Jéan-Paul and me and the captain, we've kept them in the loop."

"Any idea when you can take her home?" Nadine asked Jason.

"No, not yet. The doctor took the tubing out this afternoon. Hopefully, it won't be long. I'm ready to get the two of us out of here," Jason said.

Nadine looked at Talia and then back to Jason, looking at him, wanting to ask. He could see she wanted to ask about the baby. He knew Jim would have told her since they have kids of their own. He gave Jim a side glance.

"We don't know about the baby yet. I'm hopeful, but things happen." He glanced at Jéan-Paul. Jim noticed the look, but wasn't going to say anything. He knew how close these two were, just like his friendship with Jason was. Some things you keep to yourself. Nadine hugged Jason and walked over to Talia, the men watching her. She bent down and kissed Talia's forehead and whispered in her ear, then stood up, taking hold of her hand.

It was just before dinner time when Jim and Nadine came in, and Jim told Jason, "We need to head home. Some kids might think they are starving if we don't feed them. Jéan-Paul, can we take you back to the station or do you have somewhere you want to go?"

"If you could take me back to the station, I would appreciate it. I best not leave Adrian alone with Ted. He might switch coats or helmets around, and then Adrian will tell his comrades not to come to the U.S.; too many pranksters, although I have noticed that Ted isn't quite as arrogant as I've seen him in the past. Maybe there was an eye-opener for him, yes?" He looked at Jason.

Jason took a few steps toward the door with them, hugging the guys and thanking them for coming. He gave Nadine a hug and a kiss on her cheek, thanking her for coming, and told her that maybe they could have them come over for a visit soon. Nadine smiled and kissed Jason on the cheek. Then they all left.

Jason stood leaning against the door frame, crossing his arms, looking down the hallway. Patients were being walked in their hospital gowns and slippers, with their IV stands and a staff member walking with them. The halls were lined with wood handrails. Patients were being pushed in their wheelchairs back to their rooms, and he saw kitchen staff picking up trays from patients who were finished with their dinner. And he saw a few nurses at the nurse's station, probably charting. One would come, and then one would go to see what a patient needed.

He looked up at the bright ceiling lights. Again, he could smell that a patient had gotten sick, and a nurse would need to attend to them, and again, the smell of chlorine and other disinfectants. It made him all the more want to just pick Talia up and take her home, but he knew that was not an option, at least not just yet. He walked back into her room and stopped for a moment, glancing at her, smiling and so happy to see she was breathing all by herself. He walked to the window, looking at the vase with the plastic lilacs in it. He thought that if she woke up and saw them, she would want to smell them. And she would remember the few times in Switzerland that she received these same delicate flowers from him with all his love.

The card was in the little cardholder with the German words showing toward her bed, and the written English from Jéan-Paul facing the window. When she would wake and see the card and ask about the note, he would take it to her, telling her it was the card given to him by the hostess who had put the lilacs on their table. He would take her hand and help her turn it around so she could see what Jéan-Paul wrote. And then he would kiss her.

He turned around, looking at her, sleeping peacefully. He was thinking out loud: "Soon, my love. Soon I'm going to take you home." He looked at the couch with Little Debbie sitting there, eyeing him. "Don't give me that look," he said, and then walked back to the chair. He started calling it his chair, and he didn't even like the color of it.

Chapter 41

Tuesday Night

The evening seemed to move a little more quickly, more than likely because he wasn't feeling as anxious or worried about Talia. He felt hopeful that he would soon take her home, but then there would be the worry about the baby and her driving again. It's a trauma that accident victims have to take step by step, maybe getting back into a car either as a passenger or driver. There are all kinds of PTSD. He picked up the magazine again, looking at the outside, and then setting it back down. He didn't hear Elizabeth come in, or Kurt. Jason stood up when she walked to him, and he hugged her. Kurt stood looking at his sister, and Jason walked to him, giving him a side-hug.

"Kurt, she's going to be all right. She's been breathing on her own," Jason told him. Kurt nodded and walked over to his sister, taking hold of her hand as he sat down, bringing it to his lips. He closed his eyes.

He turned toward Jason and his mom, "What about the baby?"

Elizabeth said, "We don't know for sure, but I do have a good feeling about it. We just have to wait a little bit longer." Kurt looked back at his sister, still holding her hand. "I think Jason will get to take her home in a couple of days," Elizabeth said, now kneeling next to Kurt, putting her arm around his shoulder. "Kurt, she made a choice to drive. It scared the crap out of me too, the thought of losing her when I was told about her accident. She could have turned around and gone back to Dave and Joan's and waited another day. But Talia gets things in her head and thinks she has to act on it." Kurt nodded, remembering a couple of other times when she did something stupid, just not as crazy as this.

"I know," Kurt said. "I still feel guilty that I didn't get home sooner so she could have left. She told me when she wanted to leave, and that was mid-morning, not around noon. But I was also pigheaded; I didn't want to leave Caren." Kurt turned toward Jason, knowing what love can do to you.

"Kurt, why don't you and I get a bite to eat. I'm hungry, and Little Debbie just isn't going to cut it for me," Jason said, looking toward the couch.

Kurt looked over and saw it, then looked up at Jason. "If you don't want it, I'll take it off your hands. I mean, a man's got to have some junk food in his diet, right?" He smiled.

"Yes, he does, and you're welcome to it. It's just not for me, and I don't even know why I got it in the first place. Maybe it was because of sleep deprivation," Jason said. Kurt stood up, walking over to the couch, picking it up and then handing it to his mom so that he wouldn't forget it, and then headed toward the door with Jason following.

Elizabeth had left a new magazine on Jason's chair, giving him something else to look at and maybe actually read; it had to do with woodworking. This one Jason could get into. Throughout the afternoon and evening, nurses came and went, checking on Talia. They all said pretty much the same thing: she was doing much better than they expected, and that she might be able to go home in the next few days. Jason thanked each one. He figured he'd have to wait it out, one step at a time. Elizabeth said that they couldn't push Talia.

Jason looked at his watch and yawned. It was after ten-thirty. The light over her bed was on, and he walked to the light switch near the door, shutting it off. He grabbed the blanket from the back of the chair, then leaned over Talia and kissed her lips, not once, but twice, just for good measure. He hadn't been able to kiss her since last Friday before he headed off to work; he missed those moist lips. He moved the chair again, closer to the bed. He sat down, leaving it upright, and covered himself. He took hold of Talia's hand again and fell asleep.

☙

Wednesday - Early Morning

Jason woke to the feel of something on the outside of his thumb. He opened his eyes and turned his head, looking at his hand. It was Talia's thumb rubbing his. Keeping his hand where it was, he looked at her; she was looking at the ceiling, and he looked where she was looking. He then looked back at her, giving her hand a little squeeze to see if she would look at him. His heart was beating faster. She turned her head toward him, looking at him in the dim light from the bed's overhead light with no expression. He sat up a little straighter so that he could get a better look at her, and she could have a better look at him. He didn't know what she might think or remember, and didn't want to frighten her.

She looked at him, her eyes heavy, looking around his face, at his forehead, his eyes, then to his cheeks and nose, then his chin, and then his lips. He gave her a half smile giving her a moment to look at him. Inside his head, all he could say was, *"Please remember who I am, please remember who I am. I love you, Talia".* She continued looking at him. He slowly drew her hand up to his mouth and kissed the back of it. She watched as he kissed it. He saw her swallow, and she licked her lips. She drew her hand away, lifting it to her lips, touching them, outlining them with her fingers. She reached over to his lips and did the same thing with her finger.

Jason let his hand lay where it was, and then she put her hand back down, lacing her fingers into his. He moved the blanket around behind him, slowly standing up so she could see him better. She continued to look at him, and then a slow smile came to her lips, and tears formed in her eyes. "Jason," she said quietly. Tears formed in his eyes, and he nodded yes.

"Talia, my love, I'm right here." He leaned over her, carefully putting an arm behind her neck and shoulders, cradling them, and the other arm around her waist. He placed his head down on her upper chest, being careful not to bump her left arm or disrupt the nasal tube. She wrapped her right arm around his neck and shoulder, holding him, and carefully laid her left arm along his back. She rubbed his shoulder, slowly drawing her arm back. He backed up a little, looking into her eyes and then kissed her moist lips, with her kissing him again. More tears came to her eyes, and Jason wiped them away. "I'm here. You're all right and safe," he said quietly.

He started to move back a little, and she said, "Don't leave me."

"I'm not going anywhere, but that chair is very uncomfortable. I'm just going to reach for the blanket and lay here with you." He reached for it, lying on top of her blanket, placing his legs next to hers, and taking his blanket and covering them both. He put his arm around behind her so she was resting on his shoulder. He took her hand, holding it with his hand on his chest. She looked at him, and he kissed her forehead, telling her, "I thought I lost you. I love you so much." He looked at her. "You're safe in my arms."

The door opened slowly, and a nurse came in. Jason raised his head, looking at her. She looked at him and then pushed a button that would allow for weight change at the end of the bed. It had signaled that something was off at the nurse's station. She turned and shut the door behind her. They both fell asleep.

 C3

Wednesday Morning

There was light coming from outside the window, a combination of street lights and a little daylight taking its time to come up. Jason opened his eyes, glancing at his watch, and saw it was around 7:20 a.m. He looked at Talia; she was still sleeping. Under the top cover, he still held onto her hand, lying against his chest. Several more minutes passed, when the door slowly opened, letting in the hall light. He raised his head, looking toward the door; it was his mom standing there looking at him. Her shift had changed to days. She walked around the other side of the bed, looking at them both.

He looked at his mom, and then in a whisper, he said, "She woke up. I just wanted to lay next to her and hold her." Mary Ann placed a pulse oximeter on Talia's finger to check her oxygen saturation level. While waiting for it, she checked her blood pressure, respiration, listened to her heart and lungs, making notes. Talia's oxygen levels showed they were in the normal range. Mary Ann was finished, for now, telling Jason that Dr. Mueller would make his rounds in a bit, but was running late. She grinned at him and said, "Be careful how much kanoodling you do with her in here." She left the door partially open.

Jason laid his head down. He didn't want to move, and all he could think about was getting her out of here and going home. And the only way to get home was to have a vehicle, but his was still at the station since he came in the ambulance with her. Oh, well. He took a slow, deep breath, looking down at her with a half smile. It felt good to have her in his arms. He could smell her hair, which had lost the scent of apple, not smelling like anything except a hospital smell. She'd been in this bed for almost three days. Talia was sponge bathed, but her hair wasn't able to be washed. She'd be happy to have a bath or a shower and to feel clean.

He felt her legs move, which he hadn't seen her do since lying here. *She would need help walking at first, getting her sea legs strong enough to carry her. Then would she want to go to work or stay home and work? And then, she has no car; she loved her car.* All these questions and thoughts were popping up in his head. As he looked at her, he gently let go of her hand, placing his hand along the side of her face with his thumb rubbing her soft cheek. He gave her a light kiss on her lips and then watched her eyes slowly open. It took a moment, as she looked at him and gave a little smile, then turning her head into his shoulder.

She tried to reach over him and place her left arm around him but moaned, pulling her arm back. Jason rose, and took her arm, turning it over and seeing the bruising, and then laid it back down. That was the first he'd seen it, as it had laid flat with the IV, and he always held her right hand. Her left arm was bruised more heavily than her right arm as it had gotten pinned under the steering wheel.

A nurse came in, looking at Jason and mentioned that he might want to move back to the chair; the doctor would be in momentarily. Jason nodded, looking at Talia and said, "You know I'd rather be here next to you, but I wouldn't want them thinking I was, how did my mom put it, 'kanoodling' you too much under the covers." He gave her another kiss and then moved off the bed, leaving the blanket. He stood and stretched just as the doctor came in, followed by a nurse. Jason gave Talia a quick look and winked at her; she smiled back at him.

Dr. Mueller said, "I see you're awake. Good." He was going through and checking her stats and asked her basic questions about how she felt. Did she remember the accident? And he told her what was going on with her; the nurse was making notes. He said they would do another ultrasound later that morning. If she was up for some breakfast, some suggestions were made. Then, he asked if she had questions for him, otherwise, he would check back later, giving her some updates. At the moment, Talia's mind wasn't in a questioning mood. Then she remembered why she needed to talk to Jason when she got home after the doctor said ultrasound.

The front of her bed was raised so she could sit up after laying flat for so long. Jason sat back down on the chair, looking at her with a slight grin. She looked at him, then at her arms, holding them up and looking at them and seeing the bruising. Then she placed a hand over her stomach, looking at it. It was all coming back to her. He watched her and then asked, "Do you feel all right? Any nausea?" He raised an eyebrow and tilted his head slightly. He wanted her to tell him; this was what she had wanted to share with him. She swallowed, looking at him. Once again, she felt like she had done something wrong. She looked into his eyes; she loved him so much.

"You know, don't you. I feel like I've done something wrong, and I don't know how to fix it," she said with tears. Jason stood up and sat partially on the bed with one foot on the floor. Taking her hands into his, he looked at her. He then laid his hand on her stomach and nodded.

"I know. And there's nothing to fix," Jason said.

"I was going to tell you when I got home, but then this happened. How long have I been in here?" she asked.

"Only a few days," he said.

"I had a feeling weeks ago that there might be a possibility that I was pregnant. I didn't want to admit it to myself or think about it. It scared me. After throwing up again, and you coming into the bathroom, asking me questions about how often I was nauseated and my cycle, I got even more scared. I don't know why I didn't just talk to you," she said, looking at him. "You're the father."

As he sat there listening to her, he lowered his head a bit. "Then you had to have known with my questions or suspected why I was asking. But I wanted you to see a doctor first and then tell me what your test results were. I wanted you to share it with me, not have me come out and tell you I was pretty sure you were pregnant," he said with a slight grin, looking at her. "It was your news to tell me.

"When we brought you in, I forgot that they normally do an ultrasound on a female of bearing age," he said, shaking his head grinning. "I told Jéan-Paul to make sure they did an ultrasound, and he looked at me with a smile and said, 'Why is that?' I told him I had a hunch you were pregnant. And he said, 'Then we have two lives to save; mama and baby.'

"I sat in the waiting area and had your bag on my lap. I opened it and saw the envelope with the clinic's name on it." He looked at her. "I felt kind of sneaky going through your bag, but I thought if you had anything showing your results or if anything else might be wrong, I wanted to relay it to the doctors. I wanted to know, so I looked at your results. My heart felt such joy, and then I remembered you were in an ER, and then fear took over that I could lose you both. I made an early Christmas wish that two miracles would happen. The first one did; now I'm waiting for the second one."

She touched his face. "Do you know what they found?"

He nodded. "Your results matched what theirs did. You're two months pregnant." He leaned forward, hugging her. "But there is a big concern about the baby surviving." She placed her hand on top of his, still on her stomach. She leaned back with tears, looking off at the far wall. She rubbed the back of his hand and was quiet.

A nurse came in and told them they would take her down for her sonogram in about an hour. Talia would have to drink at least two eight-ounce glasses of water. Talia asked why so much water. The nurse told them it helped the technician get a clear view of the fetus and her reproductive organs. Having a full bladder made this possible.

"Great, I wake up after laying here for how many days? I really do have to pee, and now you want me to explode," she looked at Jason, who chuckled. "Can't he drink the water for me?"

"I'm sorry," said the nurse, "but this is how it works best." Talia nodded.

"OK, give me the water; down the hatch," Talia said.

While she was drinking her water, the nurse had Talia's chart and was asking various questions that needed to be asked. A few last questions came up about her previous cycle and sexual activity. Talia almost spit her water out, feeling embarrassed, and then blushed. She looked at Jason. He took Talia's hand, kissing the back of it, and got up off the bed, walking over to the window and turning to lean against it. He looked at her with his hands in his pockets. He let her tell the nurse what she needed to know. After the nurse had her information, she told Talia to drink all the water in the container, which was the amount she needed to drink. They'd come and get her in under an hour.

After the nurse left, Jason walked back to the bed and sat down, looking at her. "You're cute when you're embarrassed," he said, grinning at her. She looked at him with an evil eye. He leaned over and kissed her, telling her how much he loved her.

She did her best to drink most of the water. She couldn't drink anymore. She had to go pee, and now she had to wait until after the sonogram. Time couldn't move fast enough for them to take her down and get this over and done with so she could go pee. They finally came for her, and Jason followed. Once in the exam room, she laid down on the table. The technician applied a special gel and then placed a small wand on her belly, moving it to capture images. Then, had her hold her breath to capture other images. Talia took hold of Jason's hand, and they watched the screen. The technician pointed to the small image about an inch long, but saw no movement; it was still early in her pregnancy. When the exam was over, the gel on Talia's belly was wiped off, and she could then go pee.

Back in her room, Jason lifted her into bed, covering her with the blanket. She had also coughed several times since waking up because of the lung contusion; her chest hurt. That would take time to heal. She leaned back, feeling tired. Jason stood leaning over her with one hand near her head and the other near her waist. He bent down and kissed her.

Another nurse came in and said Talia could have lunch and gave her a list of what was on the cafeteria menu; there was no restriction on what she could eat. At the moment, she wasn't really hungry but knew she needed to eat; there were two of them, and helping this baby survive was a biggie. Mary Ann came in, giving Talia a hug. She was so glad to see her awake and told her she looked so much better, that her stats were good, and that this handsome man has not left her side except for a few times to eat something because he was told by her mother to do so. Otherwise, he was here. Jason was on the other side of her bed, and Talia reached for his hand.

"I hear you went down for a sonogram." Mary Ann said. Talia nodded.

"Yup, he or she," Jason said, "is no bigger than a peanut, which is pretty tiny."

Jason noticed his mom looking at the two of them with this look. He wondered what she was thinking. "OK, out with it."

"What do you mean?" she asked.

"I think you know; something Grandma Jean said." Talia looked at Jason and then Mary Ann. They didn't see Elizabeth standing near the doorway.

"Your relationship, as your Grandmother Jean said, has been ass-end backward. You got engaged and didn't even date. Then, even before you get married, she's pregnant shortly after getting engaged. And before you get on the defensive with me…" she said, seeing he's getting annoyed and ready to say something. She held up her hand to stop him. "I don't know how many people have waited as long as the two of you to come full circle. You have loved her for well over twenty years. For as long as we all can remember, each time you saw her and spoke her name, I saw it in your eyes. I could hear it in your voice, the hurt and longing for her. My heart just wanted fate to get its butt in gear and get the two of you together already."

Elizabeth came in, closing the door, and slowly walked toward Mary Ann, whose back was to the door. Mary Ann was on a roll, and Elizabeth wasn't about to stop her, as she had felt the same for a long time. Jason looked at Elizabeth, and Mary Ann turned around to see her best friend standing there. "I whole-heartedly agree with you," she said, looking at Mary Ann, then looking at Jason and Talia. "It's past-time that the two of you were together, dating or not; engaged or not."

She took a step toward Talia, looking at her. "You wondered for a long time if he could be the one. Your grandfather and I did some talking as well. You told him about all the things you were feeling for Jason." Talia felt Jason sit down next to her on the bed, putting his arm around her. "He told me what he said to you about designing your dream. It wasn't just about fashion, it was about your life; how you wanted to live it, and who you wanted to share it with." She looked at Jason, then back to Talia. "He found you in the very place he first saw you, Basel, and fell for you." She glanced at Jason, remembering she told him about Tom falling in love at first sight with her.

"It's been a long journey of love that has finally come full circle; I'm sorry that it took so long for the both of you. So, you may have done things, as Grandma Jean said, ass-end backward, but there may have been a reason. I don't know, but you deserve a life of health and happiness, the two of you, and hopefully with a little one joining you. Now, I've finished standing on my soapbox," she said with a tear coming down her cheek. She turned toward Mary Ann, who also had tears, as well as Jason and Talia. She looked at Talia. "We need to get some food in you and hopefully get you out of here in the next day or so. We have a wedding coming up, come hell or high water." She walked over to her daughter, hugging her. Jason came around and also got a hug. Looking at Talia, she said. "Grandpa would be very proud of you, except for the chronological order of things that happened." They laughed.

Chapter 42

Wednesday Noon

Talia's lunch would come up soon. From that list, she had checked four little boxes; the only things that appealed to her were the turkey sandwich, green beans, a cherry Jell-O cup, and maybe some milk. Jason told her that he would go down to find something for himself and bring it back up so they could eat together, even though it wasn't at home yet. He wanted them to get back to fixing meals together, things that they liked, especially her no-bake cookies. He'd had enough of hospital food, and he wasn't even a patient.

When Jason came back to her room, he had a small tray. On it was a small plate with a sandwich, a small bowl of potato salad, a cherry Jell-O cup, and a cup of coffee. They shared her bed table; it was lowered to the right height for eating. Jason sat opposite of Talia on the bed. As they were eating, Jason said that his captain had stopped in to see how she was doing that past Monday morning, giving her young Dr. Mueller a small earful. He didn't like his bedside manner, but said that he would learn. Then he told her about a prank that was pulled on the German paramedic, Adrian. It was Ted, who had switched one of Adrian's boots with Mike's big boot. They got a call, and when Adrian went to put his bunker gear on, he tripped because one boot was much larger than the other. It was funny, but then not, as it took time to get his correct boot back. When they finished their lunch, Jason moved the bed table back to the end of the bed with the trays on it, ready for pickup by the hospital kitchen staff.

A nurse came in to help Talia use the restroom and then brought her back to bed, covering her, and then left. Jason sat back on the bed, facing her, and then asked, "Do you remember the little prank you pulled on me on Halloween?" He looked at her with a sarcastic grin.

"Yup. It was early morning, and you had to go to work. You mentioned to me once that you didn't like spiders, and I couldn't believe that you, this strong paramedic/firefighter was afraid of spiders. They're just little things with a few more legs," Talia giggled. "But when you got up to get off the bed and stepped on your jeans and hiking boots, yanking your feet back up, you had a little girl's scream. Then, when you looked down at them and saw the spiders, I thought I was going to lose it." She laughed out loud with tears.

Jason chuckled. "It's funny now, the way you tell it, but at that moment it wasn't."

"You looked back at me, and I was doing my best to stifle my laugh in my pillow." She covered her hand over her mouth, looking at him. "You mumbled under your breath about getting even. I'm sorry, but it was Halloween. I've been waiting to see what you'll pull on me," Talia said.

Jason leaned forward and kissed her. "You are ornery and feisty when you want to be," he said. "I thought about what I could do to you. Then, when you came to the station and brought my favorite cookie, I thought here she is to redeem herself, however small the gesture," he said, smiling at her. "And then you turned around and used your Italian on me, and the guys listening. I still have no clue what you said, but I knew I would have to be cunning about payback. And time got away from me. But then the incident with the pizza, and Nadine's intervention and your accident, I thought better of it. Those things made me think twice because I could have lost you."

"Jason, I'm really sorry," Talia said, looking at him. He got up and turned, sitting next to her on the bed, putting his arms around her and holding her as she put her arms around him. "It was my own fault. Had I watched the weather channel and saw what it was doing, where the storm was heading, I wouldn't have been stubborn, thinking I could make it home. I should have stayed put. It would have only been one more day, but I missed you, and wanted to talk to you about my doctor's appointment and the results. I was feeling so many emotions, and then my head was swimming..." She laid her head on his shoulder.

"I know. Hindsight is 20/20," he said, looking at her. "I heard that you like to dress as the abominable snowman, though, when you drive in 'crappy weather' as I've heard you mention, and your mother." He was smiling at her now.

"Ya, well, maybe it's overkill. I hate winter. It's pretty if you don't have to be out in it. But when driving, I'd rather be safe than sorry, except look where it got me. I just remember driving so slow. I was sure I was getting closer to home. The shoulder and the road blended, and I didn't know if I was on the road for sure. And when that truck passed me going so fast, I got angry with them. I yelled at them, asking if they had x-ray vision and knew where the road was, and thought maybe they had specially designed tires to grip the road. But I felt a gust after he passed me, and then I felt the right rear tire being pulled onto the gravel of the shoulder. I tried to correct it, which only made my whole car slide toward the shoulder on the ice. I felt like I was tilting, and knew I had lost control, and I screamed as I slid and it started turning over and then the airbag..." Her voice trailed off, and she stared at the blanket covering her.

"The only thing I vaguely remember is you calling my name, and I couldn't respond to you. And then bright lights. I tried opening my eyes, and then I heard Italian being spoken," she said, looking at Jason. "The only person I know who speaks it is Jéan-Paul."

"He was with us on the call, and I think this accident scared him just as much as it scared me, the thought of losing you. Do you remember what he told you in the ER room?" Jason asked, wanting to see if she remembered and understood what Jéan-Paul told her.

She tilted her head back a bit, looking toward the window. She had a big smile. "He called me his Italian girl and said you loved me very much." She looked at Jason. "That I needed to stick around for this baby and you." She had tears, as did Jason. That's all he needed to hear.

Looking toward the window, she straightened up a little, then looked at Jason and then looked back at the windowsill. He saw where she was looking and got off the bed, walking toward the vase with the plastic lilacs in it and brought it toward her, but not giving them to her. "I can't smell them. Did something happen to my smeller?"

He smiled at her. "No, nothing happened to your smeller."

He brought the vase to her, and she felt them. "They're plastic. You couldn't find any real ones, huh." She made it more of a statement, and then noted the card. "This is in German."

"You know that's German?" Jason said.

"Ya, it's different from Italian, but I don't know German. Maybe a language I'll have to learn next," she said, smiling at him. He shook his head.

"Jéan-Paul was in to see you yesterday afternoon. We had a long talk. He saw the flowers sitting on the windowsill, then did the same thing you did. He couldn't smell them either. He looked at the card, noting he's seen it before and pulled one out from his wallet. He asked if I knew what it said and I told him I didn't, but hoped it was a good thing. He asked if he could write on the back what it said." Jason sat down next to her, taking the card and was going to turn it over when he heard Jéan-Paul's voice say the words: *"Für jemanden, der sehr geliebt wird."'* Both Jason and Talia turned toward Jéan-Paul as he walked in and walked to the other side of Talia's bed, giving her a kiss on her cheek.

"Turn the card over," Jéan-Paul said, looking at Talia.

She read the card out loud: "'For someone who is very much loved.' Where did this come from?" She looked at the front side. She closed her eyes and asked Jéan-Paul to repeat the German. Jason was looking at her, not understanding what she was doing.

"Für jemanden, der sehr geliebt wird," Jéan-Paul repeated.

"I remember someone spoke those words," she said as she looked at Jason. "It was the hostess at the restaurant in Villars. You had brought me a small handful of lilacs. You said you had asked them if you could take some, and when we went to eat, there was a small vase sitting on the table. Before we left, she had said those words looking at me."

"I told them how much I loved you and that your favorite flower was lilacs. After paying the bill, she gave me my receipt and this little card. I kept it in my wallet," Jason said.

Talia looked at Jéan-Paul. "You have the same card?"

Jéan-Paul took his card out, showing it to Talia. "I know this hostess. She does not do this for everyone, only very special people. My Suzanne and I were at this same restaurant many years ago, and she also loves lilacs. Did you know the lilac originated in Eastern Europe?" Talia shook her head no. Jéan-Paul just looked at her. "I actually came to tell you about some other good news I heard this morning. You remember the accident you came upon with the pregnant woman and her husband?"

"Yes. Wasn't she about six months along?" Jason asked.

"Actually, she was a little further along, but I have kept in contact with her and her husband. She had her baby last night, a little girl. She asked me if I ever knew what happened to the American people who helped her, and I told her I knew them very well." Jéan-Paul looked at them both with a smile. "She told me that if I were to ever see them again, to please tell them she named her baby girl after that woman who made her feel safe. She remembered your name." Tears appeared in Talia's eyes. "The baby's name is Talia Rose Rizzo."

"What?" Talia looked at Jéan-Paul. "The woman's last name is Rizzo?" She looked at Jason. "I'm sure Rizzo is a common name in that area. Jéan-Paul, is her first name by chance Maria?"

"Yes, why do you ask? Did she tell you her name?" he said.

"No, I never knew her name. What else do you know about her?" Talia asked, now wondering if there might be the slightest connection.

"She and her husband are from a small town south of Ollon. That is where he is from. She has family east of Basel. They were headed to Villars to take the train to visit them. She hadn't seen them in many years because of a family dispute after she graduated from secondary school, equivalent to your high school. She knew, with a baby on the way, she wanted to share this with her family and make amends. She also started a small business, so she did not want to change her name when she got married. Why do you ask this?"

Talia looked at Jason, and he understood why she was asking. "After we got back to Basel that Sunday afternoon, we went walking through *Spalen Gate*, and we stopped in a shop. There was a woman who tapped me on the shoulder and asked if I was Maria Rizzo. I told her I wasn't, and she said I looked like her good friend's daughter, who had been gone for many years. She hoped that she could tell her friend that she found her daughter. I felt sad for them, missing their child. The woman asked my name and where I was from, and I told her, then she turned to leave and looked back at me. It just felt strange."

"Look at what kindness can do for people you come across," Jéan-Paul said with a smile.

The three of them visited a little longer. Jéan-Paul saw that Talia was getting tired. "I will leave for now, but maybe when you get home, we can visit again, yes?" he asked.

"I think we would like that very much," Jason said. Jéan-Paul kissed Talia on her cheek and the back of her hand, being the kind Frenchman that he was. He gave Jason a hug and said he would see them later.

When Talia first woke up, it was very early in the morning, around four. They both then slept until after seven that morning. The rest of the morning went quickly. Even though it was only the middle of the afternoon, Talia was ready for a nap. Jason put the bed down some so she could rest peacefully. He was also tired, so he laid down next to her, and they both fell asleep.

Chapter 43

Wednesday - Late Afternoon

It was Talia who stirred and woke up, waking Jason up. She was feeling nauseated and couldn't reach the little kidney-shaped container. A nurse came in and helped her. Jason was going to take it to the bathroom himself to empty it; he'd seen worse. But the nurse said it was all right, that was part of her job. Once Talia felt better, the nurse said maybe having a 7-Up and some saltine crackers would help tame her stomach. Elizabeth peeked around the door and walked in, seeing the nurse taking the container to the bathroom to wash out. Jason was standing next to Talia. He'd put a damp cloth on her forehead. Jason mouthed the word 'vomit.' She nodded, knowing why.

Dr. Mueller came in and checked Talia over. He went over information with her as well as Jason and Elizabeth. She was cleared to be discharged tomorrow afternoon. He wanted her to make an appointment with her OB-GYN in the next week or so. He was going to schedule her for another ultrasound to see what progress the baby has made. According to the technician, there was no movement, and he wanted to make sure there were no problems. He would see her in the morning and then after lunch. Shortly after that, he left.

Talia asked Jason if he had called Chloe and Jana. He said he did and that they had stopped by yesterday morning to see her. It shook them both up, seeing her on the ventilator, but he told them it was to help her body and brain rest and get better sooner. If the girls did stop by again, Talia didn't want anything to be said to the girls about being pregnant until she knew for sure that the baby was all right.

No sooner had Talia said that, there was a tap on the door, and two heads came around the corner. It was Chloe and Jana. They wanted to stop in quickly and see how she was doing. They each took a side of the bed and hugged Talia. They were so glad to see that machine off of her. They had tears, telling her they missed her and would do what they could to help. If she wanted to come to work, one of them would come to pick her up. Talia said she would think about that. She could work from home; she only had one design to finish up, and maybe they could stop by and get it. But she knew she would have to rest awhile at home. She told them that perhaps that coming weekend, they could stop by and fill her in about what's been going on at the shop. Not wanting to stay and tire her out, they said they would call tomorrow or the next day. After giving her another hug, as well as Jason, they left.

Talia was now feeling a little hungry, and thought she'd like to have something to eat. With the menu sheet again, she looked at it. Yet the only things that sounded good were the turkey sandwich and green beans, if they had that, along with a Jell-O cup. She still had her 7-Up and crackers. Once that order was placed for the hospital kitchen, Jason said he would go down in a bit and find something for him to eat, bringing it back up, so they could eat together. He was so looking forward to taking her home.

They asked Elizabeth if she would like anything to eat and, if so, to stay and join them. She thought that might be kind of nice; Kurt had headed back home. He didn't want to miss any more time at work, and he missed Caren. She would be glad to join them, otherwise, she'd be by herself. When they heard that Talia's food was coming, Jason was going to head down. He asked what Elizabeth wanted and would get hers as well and bring up their food. After they had finished eating and visited a bit longer, Elizabeth said she was going to go home. She would be back tomorrow. She gave both a hug, and told them she loved them, and then left.

Jason settled in next to Talia. "So, remember when we went through the historical Museum in Basel?"

"Yes, it was so much fun going through that. I knew my dad would have liked it; wished he could have seen it," Talia said.

"Well, it sounds like he already did in his college days. He studied abroad in Switzerland. Did your mom tell you how the two of them met? I think it's a great story," he asked.

Talia looked at him and said, "No. I guess I never really knew where or how they met. They never discussed it with Kurt or me. I knew he'd gone to college for architecture, and it took several years. When did you learn this?"

"It was Sunday evening. I was sitting here looking at you, when your mom came in. She said she remembered the first time I looked at you, the same way I did Sunday evening. She was going to keep an eye on me, kind of like what Kurt said. She said your dad could be ornery. I see where you probably got that from." He grinned at Talia. She listened intently. "She said it was the same for your dad as it was for me, love at first sight. Your mom just looked at me, and then she pulled up a chair and said, 'Let me tell you a story.' She told me about her family living in a small village in France; then she said in French, that she speaks it. I told her that's why she could translate for us, and I thought it was cool," Jason said with a smile.

"She said it was the summer of her first year in college that she and her parents went back to visit family. They must have had a day or so doing the tourist thing, and they visited the historical museum. That's where your dad spotted her. He walked toward her, and she got nervous looking into his eyes." Jason turned his head and looked into Talia's eyes. "It made her stomach flutter, and she thought he was darn cute." Talia smiled, and Jason kissed her. "He introduced himself, and she did the same. I guess he must have thought she lived there because her mom spoke French to her. She told him that they were from the States, from the Midwest; he was from Iowa. They spent the day together, they exchanged addresses, and as your mom said, 'The rest is history.'"

"I've never heard that story from her. I wonder why she didn't tell us, or tell me." Talia's voice sounded a little sad. "I would have loved to have had Dad tell me about how they met, to hear it in his owns words, and now he's gone. I just wish I would have heard about it, and I never questioned how they got together. I know how much he loved my mom. I would have loved to have told him that you and I spent time at that museum where he and Mom met."

"I'm sorry, too, that you didn't get to hear it from him. She said it didn't take them near as long to get together as it did for you and me. It sounds like once he got back to the States, they got together. Remember how both our moms talked about how we didn't do things in chronological order? It sounds like your mom and dad didn't either."

"What?" Talia looked at Jason with a confused look.

"After your mom finished telling me this great story, my mom came in to check on you, and she looked at me, nodding her head toward your mom, like 'you best tell Elizabeth about the baby.' She saw this and asked what else she needed to know. I'm sorry, love, but I told her you were pregnant." Talia looked at Jason. "She didn't say anything. She walked over to the window, looking out. I told her you were nauseated for weeks. And I said that I asked you to make an appointment with your doctor.

"I was ready for the yelling from her, but she didn't say anything for a bit. It was my mom that spoke and said that Grandma Jean already scolded me, that I did things ass-end backward; getting engaged before dating and then getting you pregnant before we're married." Jason shifted his weight to look at her better. "Your mom, Elizabeth, turned around and walked up to me, that was scary, and she said things in life happen; that she became pregnant with Kurt before they were married. I'd been holding my breath the whole time. She gave me a half smile and told me to breathe. And I have a feeling that that was not supposed to be made known." He looked down toward Talia's hands.

"A little late for that. I wonder if Kurt knows," Talia said, shaking her head.

Jason looked back at her. "Talia, I'm so sorry. It just all came out." He got off the bed and walked over to the window. "You can't say anything to him." Jason turned to look at her. "I don't know if she did or didn't tell him. But she's right; things happen in life by chance or fate. There are no accidents. No one is perfect, not even our parents." He walked back and sat in the chair, looking at her. "They must have loved each other very much, just like you and me. To find that one that you want to spend your life with, sometimes people go through their entire lives not finding that kind of love at all. I wish everyone could have that. It is the most extraordinary gift, loving someone like that and being loved back.

"You think of all the ways you can make them happy because they are first and foremost in your every thought." He slowly stood up and sat on the edge of the bed, looking at her. "We don't think of our parents as being young and in love, holding one another or being intimate. We see them hug and kiss, but…. People are allowed to make some mistakes. That's part of being a human being." Jason took her hands, holding them and looking down at them. He then shifted himself, partially standing up and took out of his pocket her engagement ring, putting it back on her left ring finger. "Maybe your mom and dad made a mistake. But did they? They had two great kids they have loved with their whole hearts. Look at how we did things. Talk about the pot calling the kettle black. The only thing I would have changed about us is that I should have told you sooner how deeply in love with you I've been. I would do anything for you." As he looked into her eyes, the tears came. She took his face in her hands, drawing him closer to her to kiss him, and gave him a big hug, and he hugged her right back.

"It's getting late. I know you're tired, and so am I. We get to go home tomorrow, my love," Jason said. Talia smiled and nodded. He helped her to the bathroom, and then lifted her back into bed. He turned on the light above her bed and dimmed it way down, then closed the door and shut off the top light. He took the blanket he used to cover himself with on the chair and laid down beside her, covered them both, putting his arm around her letting her put her head on his shoulder. He took hold of her engaged hand and laid it on his chest, and they fell asleep.

Chapter 44

Thursday Morning

As the sun came through the hospital room window, Jason woke up. He was feeling calm about the whole hospital situation with Talia. She had shifted so that they were spooning, with Jason's arm around her waist. He felt so happy that he would get to take her home today. Some things needed to get done in the next few weeks before their wedding, and then he'd be able to call her his "wife." He felt a sense of peace.

There was a tap on the door, and a nurse came in. Jason looked over his shoulder and smiled at her. It was the same nurse that had received a kiss on the back of her hand by Jéan-Paul. She was married to a police officer, and had worries of her own about her husband's safety every day. Jason said, "I'm kanoodling my soon-to-be wife just a little." She smiled back at him.

"I hear that the two of you will get to go home today. There have been a few instances when maybe I shouldn't have been 'overhearing' things," she said with a sheepish look. "But I admire you both and what you've gone through. Your mom told me a little about your journey of finding one another. No one else, just me. I wish for you both a life of joy and happiness."

"Thank you," Jason said.

"Dr. Mueller will be in, in about an hour." She started to walk toward the door and then turned partially around. "He seems to have somehow matured in the last several days, a little more kind, perhaps. I wonder how that happened." She looked at him with a raised brow and then walked out the door.

Talia started to stretch and tried to roll onto her back, but Jason blocked her. Hospital beds weren't necessarily made for two people. She looked over her shoulder at him, smiled at him and said, "Good morning, *fiancé*." He leaned over her, kissing her on her cheek, as her lips were momentarily too far away. He scooted back just a little so she could turn toward him, thus making her lips available for a good morning kiss.

"Good morning, my love. How did you sleep?" Jason asked as he kissed her again.

She looked into his eyes and with a smile said, "Like a log, but a safe log." He chuckled. "We get to go home today, you and me."

"How are you feeling otherwise? Anything with your stomach?" he asked.

"No. It feels OK," Talia said. "I'm feeling hungry, though. Is there one of those menu sheets I can look at?"

"There is," he replied, sitting up and reaching for it on the bed table. It wasn't there last night when they fell asleep, so someone must have come in and laid it down. He gave it to Talia, and she looked and picked out some scrambled eggs and toast, and a pancake, plus milk. She had Jason place it back on the bed table. It was close to seven forty-five. There was another tap on the door. In came a food server, picking up the menu sheet. She just looked at the two and then left. "I wouldn't want people to think that there's anything funny going on here, so I guess I should get up and move to that chair. I don't think I'll miss it one bit."

Talia giggled and gave Jason another kiss before he removed himself from the bed. He headed into the bathroom and soon came out. Talia asked if he could help her off the bed so she could use it. She still felt somewhat weak, and when she coughed, her chest hurt.

Dr. Mueller came in some thirty minutes later and was pleasant, asking how she slept and various other questions. When he was through, he told her he would get the forms started for her discharge, and reminded her to make her OB-GYN appointment.

Breakfast would be coming soon, so Jason said he was going to find something to eat. He wished he had room service, so he didn't have to go down six flights. Good thing there was the elevator. When he got back up to her room, breakfast trays were being taken into the various patients' rooms. Talia's was brought in and set on the bed table, and again they shared the space. Jason also found scrambled eggs and toast with some American fried potatoes, a Jell-O cup or two, and some coffee.

"So, are you going to eat both of those Jell-O cups, or are you willing to share one of them?" Talia asked with a smile. "I think we need to add Jell-O to our grocery list."

"Really? I didn't know you liked it," Jason said.

"Yup, I do." She smiled at him.

When they finished breakfast, Jason sat back on the bed, facing her. They talked about what the next week or two would bring, as well as Christmas. Talia knew she was going to have to rest and not overdo it. She could work from home, and have the girls pick up the last design. And she wanted to show them the video from their proposal on the Rhine River waterfront. Jason thought that was a good plan. He needed to check in with the captain. Not that he wouldn't love to stay home with her for the next several weeks, but he needed to be doing something he loved to do: work. The hospital thing was getting old, and he was bored. He loved being home with her, but she had her drafting table and could work. Maybe he could work for several days, but no nights.

"Oh, shoot," Talia said. "When is Jéan-Paul and Adrian to head back?"

"Oh, ya. They're supposed to leave on the fourteenth. Talia, I wanted Jéan-Paul to be my groomsman. He'll miss the wedding." He saw the look Talia was giving him, with a raised eyebrow and tilt of the head.

"Not necessarily. Can you bring my bag over to me, please?" she asked.

"What?" Jason asked. He got up and brought her bag to her. She rummaged through it and found her cell phone.

"He's been an important part of your life for several years. He shouldn't miss out on this, and I want him to be there for you and me. So, what if we moved up the wedding by a week? We'll let everyone know there's been a slight change of plans. If they don't like it, they can miss out."

"But—," he started to say, but she pressed a finger against her lips.

"Just let me make a phone call or two or three." He looked at her, then got up and headed first to the bathroom. When he came out, she was talking to someone at the botanical center, saying it was kind of an emergency that the date gets moved a week earlier due to people they cared about having to leave for overseas, "you know, the military." She winked at Jason. After confirming the new date, it was set now for the following Saturday, the fourteenth. Everything was established, and it worked out better for the center with only one other wedding in the morning. Their wedding would be at around three. And the reception room would be cleaned and ready for them to set up.

Jason walked over to the window, looking out, then turned around and watched her in awe of how she was handling the whole business of calling people and rescheduling their wedding. Her next call was to the food vendor, and they were more than happy to move it up. They had way too much going on the weekend of the twenty-first, with it being so close to Christmas. They appreciated this, and told her they'd give her a discount.

And one last call was to the officiant who would perform the ceremony. He was a good friend of Talia's. He was more than happy to show up on that date to perform the ceremony.

"Wow. You just rearranged our whole wedding in, like, forty-five minutes," Jason said and walked over to sit on the bed with her. "You are incredible."

"Well, now it's just family and friends to notify. If no one shows up, except the officiant, and you and me, we'll still say our vows. And even though it's not in Basel, it's still going to be an exceptional and beautiful place. We've waited a lifetime. I love you, Jason Porter, and I'm ready to be your wife," Talia said. "To live happily ever after, if there is such a thing." She put her arms around him. She leaned back on the bed, which had been lowered a bit, feeling tired. Jason placed a hand alongside her face, telling her to rest. It was his turn to make some phone calls. She smiled back at him and closed her eyes. He took hold of her hand and held it while he made some calls. All he could do was look at her and admire her and cherish her.

Jason let her rest until lunchtime and then gently rubbed her arm. He bent over and kissed her on her forehead, then her cheek and then her lips. She opened her eyes and smiled at him. He asked her if she was hungry at all. It took her a moment to think, and then she said she could eat something. They called down and ordered some lunch, something that would get them by until they went home later that afternoon. Jason would be the one to go to the grocery store and pick up some things.

After lunch came, and they ate; now it was just waiting for the clock to move quickly ahead. Jason knew he was ready to get out of there. He called Jim to see if he could bring his Jeep; he had a spare set of keys in his locker, letting him know about what time she was to be discharged. Jim was glad to hear that they'd get to go home. He would be there. It was now Jason who paced. Talia just watched him walk around the room. She told him if he needed to, he could walk down the long hallway and then come back. He looked at her, shaking his head no. The next time he walked out that door, it was going to be with her beside him, and when they were leaving to go home.

☃

Thursday Afternoon – Going Home

As the time got closer for her to be discharged, Talia got dressed back into her street clothes, getting a little help from Jason, and leaving the hospital gown lying on the bed. Dr. Mueller came in, going over a few last-minute things. He said her papers were taken down to the discharge center, and then they could head home. Jim came around the corner with Nadine behind him. Seeing that Talia was dressed, Nadine walked over to her, giving her a gentle hug. She was happy that they could go home. Jim handed Jason his keys, hugging him, as did Nadine. Talia had already commented earlier to Jason regarding Dr. Mueller, to which he agreed.

"Dr. Mueller?" Talia said. "I wanted to thank you for taking care of me, along with the nurses. Jason and I would like to invite you to our wedding next Saturday at the Botanical Garden, if you'd like to come. You're welcome to bring a guest with you. It's at 3:00 p.m."

He stood there a moment, looking at her, then at Jason and Jim and Nadine. He didn't seem to know what to say. "Thank you. I'd like that. I'll check my schedule for sure. I have a girlfriend. May I bring her with me?"

Talia smiled at him. "Yes, please bring her." Before he turned to leave, Talia touched his white coat sleeve and kissed him on the cheek. He looked at her, then back to Jason, gave a little nod, and walked out of the room.

It was going to be cold outside; after all, it was December. When Jason came in with Talia, he had his bunker gear on and hadn't been out since. Good thing for his best friend Jim, who had brought a coat for Jason. Mary Ann walked into the room as they were getting ready to head out. Jason already told her about the wedding getting bumped up. She'd be sure and tell Jeff, Jason's dad, and Grandma Jean. A few of the nurses who attended to Talia came into the room. They were invited to the wedding if they could make it as well, so that they knew; there weren't any paper invitations. One of the young nurses asked Mary Ann if there were any other nice-looking paramedic/firefighters available. Mary Ann looked at her and shrugged, then scooted them out the door.

They headed out the door with Jason's arm around Talia, carrying her overnight bag and blanket from her car. Talia stopped a moment, turning around, heading back into the room. She came back out with her little vase of plastic lilacs and little note sticking out; she wasn't going to forget that.

ભ

Home

Arriving home, Jason grabbed her bag, leaving her blanket in his Jeep, then coming around to open her door and help her out. He gave her a quick kiss. There were some slick spots, and he took her hand, walking slowly with her across the parking lot. After unlocking the door and walking in, they felt the chill. Talia walked over to the thermostat, turning it up, then turned on a lamp. Jason took her bag into the bedroom, then came out, taking off his coat, and then helped Talia take hers off. They sat down on the sofa, so glad to finally be home. Talia grabbed the blanket from behind her and draped it over both of them. She rested her head on Jason's shoulder and closed her eyes. He kissed her forehead, resting his cheek against the top of her head, closing his eyes.

∞

Jason woke up and looked at his watch. It was almost eighty-thirty. He must have been more tired than he thought. But maybe it was because it was quiet without hearing all the other noises or nurses coming in and going out or someone calling for a crash cart. Talia laid down on his lap with a small pillow, facing the coffee table. Her legs somewhat stretched out. "Talia. Hey, sweetie," Jason said. She stirred, trying to sit up, and moaned. Jason helped her up slowly. She'd been lying flat many days. He should have had her go to bed when they got home. She leaned back on the sofa with her eyes still closed. "Talia, why don't you change clothes and go to bed," Jason said softly. She nodded, trying to stand up. Jason stood up and picked her up, then carried her to bed. For now, he left her clothes on her, covering her with a blanket. He wasn't really hungry, and headed to the living room, shutting off the lamp. He laid down next to her, gently pulling her close to him.

The whole next week seemed to be a flurry of getting things done for Saturday, their wedding day. They'd had some snow throughout the week. Talia was still unsure of driving just yet, and of course, no car. She was glad, for the most part, that she could stay home and work. The girls came to her. Jason went in to work at least three days, and then the two of them went for groceries. The girls asked if they were going to take a honeymoon of any kind; they hadn't discussed it.

It was now Friday evening. The room they had reserved for the reception was open, so between Talia and Jason, the two moms, Kurt, Caren, Chloe and Jana, they started preparing the room for Saturday afternoon. Jim and Nadine stopped by to help. Everything that was needed for the conservatory room was set aside so they could quickly put the few wedding decorations up that they wanted to. There were enough chairs for everyone to sit on. Talia had reconfirmed with the food vendor and the cake lady. Everything had come together very nicely.

The *boutonnières* for Jason, Jim and Jéan-Paul, and Talia's bouquet and single roses for Chloe and both moms would be delivered before lunch tomorrow, so someone would have to be there to take them to the spare room where Talia and Chloe would dress; Elizabeth said she would take care of that. It seemed that everything that needed to be done was complete. If something was missing, it was all right. Talia's good friend, Jeff Wright, the officiant, had arrived so they could do a short little rehearsal, so everyone knew where they were to be standing or sitting. After doing a walk-through, they were ready for Saturday to show up. Jim and Jéan-Paul told everyone they had made reservations for dinner in about thirty minutes. It wasn't far away.

Jéan-Paul walked up to Jason and Talia, and told them another guest would be joining them here shortly. Talia looked at him with a smile and said, "Suzanne." Jéan-Paul nodded. She hugged him. Soon, through the main door came the woman Jéan-Paul loves, and adores so much: his wife, Suzanne. He walked over to her, giving her a huge hug, and kissed her. They spoke French back and forth. Then Jéan-Paul brought her over to the group and introduced his beautiful wife. He flew her in, and had a car pick her up and bring her. They would spend several nights together at one of the hotels close by. Her bags were taken to the hotel for her, and now it was time to head over to the restaurant and enjoy the remaining evening.

After the evening was done, Jason and Talia headed home. She wanted to make sure that their clothes were laid out to wear, before heading over to the botanical center. Both of their wedding clothes were in separate bags and hung in the closet by the front door. Jason sat on one of the kitchen high-back chairs, watching her as she went from the bedroom to the bathroom, to the living room and back to the bedroom, finishing up the last few things. It was getting late.

As she walked by him, he reached out to her, pulling her to him. She stood in front of him, and she placed her arms around his neck. He just wanted to look into her beautiful eyes, the ones he would look into when she became his wife and he became her husband. He didn't say a word. She bent near his ear and whispered. She stood up, looking into his eyes with so much love, and he asked again like last time, "Are you sure?" She nodded. He stood up and picked her up, carrying her to the bedroom.

Chapter 45

Saturday Morning – Wedding Day

Morning came, with Talia waking up, looking first at the ceiling. She took a slow, deep breath and turned her head toward Jason. He was leaning his head on his hand, looking at her, looking at her hair, then her cheeks and chin, to her lips and nose, and back to her eyes. He was soaking her in, every curve of her face. He slowly leaned down and kissed her lips, slow, and gentle. She brought her arms up and around his neck, drawing him down to her. She wanted to hold him. He was the love of her life. She moved her head, turning it toward him, and kissed his cheek. She had tears in her eyes when she looked at him.

"Why the tears?" Jason asked softly.

"Because today is the second happiest day of my life, so, tears of happiness. I get to spend my life with you. I love you so much. And you brought so much joy to me," she said.

"What was your first happiest day?" he asked as he kissed her gently.

"The day you showed me that love doesn't hurt, and you filled that empty space to overflowing," Talia said, kissing him back.

"I'm ready for this day to get started. And I'm ready to see where our journey takes us, along with new adventures and hopefully a little one we can share it with," Jason said. "I'm going to go take a shower so that I'm squeaky clean for my bride-to-be." He smiled at her. "Come with me?"

After getting dressed and having some lunch, they put on their coats and gathered their garment bags. Talia had a smaller bag for things she needed to go with her wedding outfit. They wouldn't be taking a honeymoon just yet, but plans were in the making for a beautiful trip back to Switzerland and Germany. It would take a little time to prepare for it. But they knew two young ladies in Basel were ready for them to come back.

Arriving at the botanical center, they found mostly family already working on setting up chairs and putting up decorations. It was looking like a wedding was going to take place. The flowers had arrived, and the food vendor would be there before two-thirty as all the last-minute preparations were being completed. The officiant, Jeff Wright, came through the door. There was about an hour to go. The weather was being decent, which was a plus. The guys headed to their room to change into their suits; Jason didn't want any tuxes.

☙

The moms had changed into their dresses, and now it was time for Talia and Chloe to get changed. Out of the eight designs Talia created, one of the first ones was her wedding gown. It was made of wild tapestry silver brocade, had an A-lined skirt that fell from her waist to the floor, flaring down and around behind her with a chapel-length train, and a white strapless corset made from the same silver brocade with white satin cross ties, and an iridescent organza three-quarter length bolero jacket with tiny little crystal sequins dusted throughout. Talia would also wear the earrings and necklace she bought in Switzerland. Chloe's outfit would match Talia's, a different fabric, but in navy blue. Her corset had small navy satin straps, and her three-quarter length bolero jacket in navy was dusted with blue sequins.

Both Elizabeth and Mary Ann came into the room to see Talia and Chloe. Elizabeth had tears as she looked at her daughter and told her, *"Vous êtes belle"* (You look beautiful).

Talia replied, *"Merci, Maman"* (Thank you, Mom).

Mary Ann picked up the single white rose with a navy ribbon tied around it, giving it to Chloe, and gave Talia her bouquet of white and red roses with white satin ribbons hanging down. She then picked up the single pink roses, giving one to Elizabeth and keeping one for herself. The men already had their flowers pinned on.

Elizabeth asked Talia if she was ready, as it was time to go; Elizabeth would walk her down the aisle. Talia took a slow, deep breath, nodding that she was ready. Mary Ann left so she could be escorted down by her son, Jason, taking her place next to her husband Jeff and Grandma Jean. As they were heading toward the door to leave the room, Kurt stopped and looked at his sister, walking up to her, kissing her on the cheek, and telling her how amazing she looked and how grateful he was that she was so happy. Kurt would go first, then Chloe following him. They headed down the hall as they heard the music. All Talia wanted was music that used the piano and the cello, no words.

As they entered the room, everyone stood and turned toward her and her mom. As the music played, Talia and her mom walked down the aisle toward Jason. He looked at her with such loving eyes and smiled. He could only see her. As they approached Jason, he took a few steps to the edge of the chairs and took Talia's hand, walking with her to their place in front of the officiant. As the music ended, the ceremony began.

☙

Wedding Ceremony of
Talia Elizabeth Rose and Jason Lee Porter

<u>Officiant</u>: "Good afternoon, friends, and family. We've got this little detail of a marriage to take care of before starting the party. We've all been invited here today to share a very important moment in Talia and Jason's lives.

"Their love and understanding for each other have grown and matured, and they have decided to live their lives together as husband and wife. Through an incredible journey, their love has endured its ups and downs, and through the course of encounters, their love grew stronger and deeper. On this path of love and loss, of holding on tight, they've seen how far love will go until it comes home.

"Marriage is perhaps the greatest and most challenging adventure of all human relationships. No ceremony can create your marriage; only you can do that – through love and patience; through dedication and listening; through supporting and believing in each other.

"By learning to make the important things matter, and letting go of the rest. What this ceremony can do is to witness and affirm the choice you make to stand together, despite the occasional urge to run away.

"To make a marriage work, we learn to overlook and forgive the things that may frustrate us — like Talia, speaking Italian simply because she can. Or Jason, thinking now he has to learn Italian and French.

"But marriage isn't all bad; it's having someone to laugh with, and cry with, and to hold onto. Marriage is having a confidant, a partner, and a best friend."

Officiant: "The couple will now say their vows."

Jason, with tears in his eyes: "Here I am, standing in front of you, feeling like that fourteen-year-old boy who fell in love with you at first sight, in a wonderful and magical place far away. We've crossed paths many times in our youth, and all I could think of, each time I saw you, was that I wanted you in my life. And when our paths crossed for the last time, and I saw you standing there, I knew we had come full circle. You brightened my life when it seemed dim and helped me see things in a new way, and I'm so ready to share new adventures with you, and maybe learn Italian. You have filled my heart with so much love and joy. Thank you for loving me the way you do."

Talia, with tears in her eyes: "Here I am, as I stand before you. I was a young nine-year-old girl with a crush on a cute boy, saving it for a rainy day. For a long time, I felt insignificant, like I had standing next to Devils Tower, until you stirred something inside of me with my first kiss. And I began to wonder if you were feeling the same way about me. Little did I know, you had a huge head start in loving me. I learned that whatever it is I wanted for my life, how I wanted to live it and with who I wanted to share it, all I had to do was design it. And there you were; you came to find me, and I'm ready to take this journey with you. I love the way you love me. And yes, I'll teach you Italian. *Ti Amo.*"

Officiant: "This is the point in the ceremony where we usually talk about the wedding bands being a perfect circle, with no beginning and no end. But we all know that these rings do have a beginning. Rock is dug up from the earth. Metal is liquefied in a furnace at a thousand degrees, then molded, cooled, and painstakingly polished. Something beautiful is made from raw elements. Love is like that. It's hot, dirty work. It comes from humble beginnings, made by imperfect beings. It's the process of making something beautiful where there was once nothing at all.

"For thousands of years, lovers have exchanged rings as a token of their vows. The promises which you have spoken today are forever in your minds and hearts, but words are fleeting, and so those who marry wear rings as a visible, tangible symbol of their love and commitment. These rings announce to the world that you have entwined together to become one, and that it is inconceivable that you should ever part."

⌇

Exchange of Rings

⌇

<u>Ring exchange</u>: Jim hands rings over to Officiant.

⌇

<u>Officiant</u>: "Talia, please repeat after me: With this ring (pause), I promise to accept your imperfections (pause), and recognize your beauty."

Talia: "With this ring, I promise to accept your imperfections, and recognize your beauty." She places Jason's wedding band on his finger.

⌇

<u>Officiant</u>: "Jason, please repeat after me: With this ring (pause), I promise to accept your imperfections (pause), and recognize your beauty."

Jason: "With this ring, I promise to accept your imperfections, and recognize your beauty." Jason places Talia's wedding band on her finger.

⌇

<u>Officiant</u>: "Talia and Jason, you have just sealed your relationship by the giving of rings, and you have committed to sharing the rest of your lives with each other.

"The inscriptions you've chosen inside each of your rings hold a special place in your hearts. It represents where you started on this journey of love, and where everlasting love resides."

Talia: "Home at last."

Jason: "Alone is past."

<u>Officiant</u>: "I now pronounce you officially married. You may seal it with a long kiss."

୧

Reception to Follow

୧

Once their wedding ceremony finished, they all headed to the reception room. There were tables lined with navy blue tablecloths and white linen and the usual silverware and glasses.

The food was a variety of meats and roasted vegetables and potatoes. Desserts lined another table. There was wine, juice and water, and a small two-tiered wedding cake with an icing design to match Talia's wedding outfit. After everyone had finished eating, it was time for the first dance. People didn't hear what the proposal dance was, the song they had danced to in Basel on the Rhine River; Jason and Talia wanted to dance to it once again, as it embodied their journey from start to finish. As it played, Jason motioned for others to get up and dance. Jim and Nadine stood up, walking to the floor, as did Jéan-Paul and Suzanne, Kurt and Caren, Chloe and Jana, Mary Ann and Jeff, and anyone else who wanted to dance.

There were many dances that evening. A toast was made by Jim, his best man, and best friend. Before the night finished, Jéan-Paul stood and proposed a toast as well. He ended the first part of his toast, but had a second part. He asked Talia and Jason to stand and face one another. He asked Talia in Italian, *"Ripeti dopo di me"* (repeat after me). Jason looked at Jéan-Paul, who looked at Talia. He asked everyone to raise their glasses.

୧

Jéan-Paul: *"L'amore sembra così."*

Talia looked into Jason's eyes. "Love looks like this."

⚃

Jéan-Paul: *"L'amore si sente così."*

Talia reached for Jason's hand. "Love feels like this."

⚃

Jéan-Paul: *"L'amore dura così."*

Talia kissed Jason. "Love lasts like this."

⚃

Jéan-Paul and Suzanne would stay for a few days in the city, so he could show her around where he worked at the hospital and the fire station. They would then leave the middle of the following week and head home.

Talia and Jason went out to buy a Christmas tree as newlyweds. The one she had was old, and Jason didn't have one at all. While decorating their first tree together, they played Christmas songs and put up lights around the windows to be more festive. Jason was going to go in and work at least three days each for the next two weeks, and then if he worked two days before Christmas, he would have off Christmas Eve until after the first of the year; that worked for him. They entertained their friends, Jim and Nadine, Chloe and Jana, Paul and Ally, and a few others during the holiday.

⚃

Christmas Eve

Jason worked up until Christmas Eve at 4:00 p.m. Talia was squeezed in for her next OB-GYN appointment, also on Christmas Eve, at 3:30 p.m.; Jason wouldn't be able to be at that appointment. Still, he intended to be at all the others, if possible, if the baby were to survive. Talia was barely showing a baby bump. She hoped something would show on the sonogram and that it would be good news. It scared her because now she really wanted this baby to survive and be a part of their new family. After her appointment, her mom took her home and dropped her off. They would all get together later on Christmas Day. After walking into the apartment, she saw Jason sitting on the big overstuffed chair. He had changed clothes and was sitting there looking at the lights on the tree. He got up and helped her take off her coat, hanging it up. He looked at her; she wasn't jumping up and down, and he thought that probably wasn't good. She took his hand and walked over to the Christmas tree, looking at it with all the lights and decorations.

 C୫

Looking into his eyes, Talia asked Jason, "What was your biggest wish for Christmas?"

With his arms around her, looking at her, he tilted his head down. "You know what it was. I wished for a miracle or two for Christmas." She looked at him and smiled the biggest smile she could manage, kissing him.

"The baby moved; it's going to be alright, Dad," Talia said.

"You're not joking, are you?" Jason asked, looking at Talia, and she shook her head no. "I'm going to be a dad, and you're going to be a mom?" Tears rolled down his face as he kissed his beautiful wife.

Miracles do happen, big and small, in their own time.

C୫   ♥   ୨୧

About the Author

Trish Titus is originally from west central Iowa. Her writing continues with her newest book, "A Miracle or Two for Christmas" which was published in December 2019. Having had the opportunity to visit other countries, learn about their cultures, history and people, she felt this would encourage others to travel and be adventurous. And who knows where love will find you.

This romance was inspired because of her travels. She'd like to go back to where this journey began. She's also traveled throughout the U.S. with her family. You can write her at trishtitus.dyd@gmail.com and give her feedback.

Her first book, "DELILAH and Others Like Her" was published in March 2019. It was written because of the loss of her beloved cat Delilah. The love we have for our pets is so valuable. She has given grief-stricken pet owners the opportunity to share their stories and lessons learned. If you'd like to share your story about your beloved pet that passed, you can reach her at tmtpetstories18@gmail.com.

When not writing, she enjoys sewing, traveling, reading, and spending time with her daughter and son-in-law.

www.ingramcontent.com/pod-product-compliance
Lightning Source LLC
Chambersburg PA
CBHW072044190726
48294CB00005B/1404